CITY OF NIGHT

Marina Pacheco

ISBN: 978-1-913672-10-2

Sign up for Marina Pacheco's no-spam newsletter that only goes out when there is a new book or freebie available.

Details can be found at the end of this book.

1

Artema Salonoy, 106th Salonoy of the bluest blue blood Salonoys, eldest daughter of 105 eldest children before her and Lady High Professor of Demonology at the Eternal University of Magic in the Eterna Urbo, jewel of the seven cities of Europe, sat in bed chewing thoughtfully on her toast. Something was amiss, and it robbed her of her appetite. The toast tasted of cardboard.

This was strange as it came fresh from the bakery who spent twenty-four hours lovingly allowing the dough to rise and ferment to produce the perfect combination of chewiness and softness. Chef then toasted it to perfection and slathered it with butter produced by grass-fed cows. Usually it was a perfect accompaniment to her morning cup of hot chocolate, but not today.

She dropped the toast and looked around her room. Her four-poster bed resembled a small island. The posts were the size of tree trunks. Exquisitely embroidered brocade curtains were artfully gathered up with a twisted gold cord ready to be unleashed and swing shut, blocking all light. Not that she did ever close the curtains, but it was a nice optional extra.

She stepped out of bed and slipped her feet into the softest kid leather slippers money could buy.

'Your dressing gown, m'lady,' Giulia said, as she lovingly wrapped her in a heavy silk gown artfully embroidered to resemble a watercolour of a verdant green forest.

'Thank you,' Artema murmured to her maid and drifted towards the French windows.

A footman swung them open before she reached them so that she didn't even have to slow down as she stepped out onto her balcony. It was an equivalent size to her bedroom, dotted about with clumps of potted plants and stretched away to an edge tastefully decorated with marble statues of toga wearing ancient Romans.

The sun shone down from a cloudless blue sky. It was almost always cloudless because of the height of the supraurbo. Artema knelt on the marble seat that ran the length of the balcony and looked over the edge down to the fluffy clouds below. Far, far below them was the azure blue Mediterranean sea. On a clear day you could see the water, although it was an act of imagination to think you could see the white tips of the waves.

The city stretched for kilometres below her, six to be exact. It was divided into three regions, her beloved supraurbo where the sun shone bright and the air was clear. The mezaurbo, a delightful place for nipping off to listen to some jazz in one of their quaint clubs and the suburbo, a dismal place she'd never ventured into nor cared to visit.

Those were the regions she could see. But in depictions of the city they always added a globe floating above filled with angels to represent Heaven and a globe below filled with demons to represent Hell.

It had come as a shock to society when, in the late 21st Century, angels and demons appeared on all the battlefields of earth and proceeded to clobber the living daylights out of each other. They were massive beings with power unseen amongst humanity and their battles shook the heavens, churned the earth and damn near boiled the seas.

The religious took it as a sign of the end of days. The scientists were stunned into silence. What did this mean? Were they suddenly supposed to accept the existence of a heaven and a hell? A supreme God and his arch enemy Satan?

Panic reigned, death cults sprang up like fields of dragon's teeth magiced into life, suicides and murder rocketed. Then, as suddenly as they'd appeared, the combatants vanished.

Nobody knew where they'd come from. Nobody knew where they'd gone. They left nothing, no bodies and no artefacts, just the wholesale destruction from the fighting itself.

What was humanity supposed to do beyond pick itself up, brush itself off, and try to make the best of it? The religious, who'd been rather enjoying their anticipated but brief moment of glory, were stunned. Where was the return of the dead? Where was the rapture?

The scientists regrouped and came up with another hypothesis. They postulated that angels and demons were beings from two different planes. That their planes intersected with earth from time to time, but that science was safe. The way scientists had deducted that things worked was indeed the way they worked. The magic everyone had seen wielded by these angelic and demonic beings was simply a science so advanced it looked like magic to anyone who didn't understand it.

'Close enough,' Artema's ancestor had said at the time.

He should have known, Artema thought. Their family had been demonologists for centuries already by then. In the old days, they had tapped into the realm known as hell and bargained with demons for power. It was a tricky business and looked down upon by the rest of the magical fraternity. They might even have banned it if it wasn't for the tremendous power a demonologist could wield.

The Salonoys had turned demonology from a dubious practice to something that had to be respected but left to the experts. Those experts being the Salonoy family. And so had begun a tradition; the eldest child born to the family became a demonologist. They would then train and hand their power on to their eldest offspring.

Salonoys, especially the eldest, were encouraged to marry young and have as many children as possible as quickly as possible. This was because, well, transacting with infernal beings had a life shortening effect. The 105th Salonoy made it to his 50th birthday. On that day they found his laboratory empty save for a greasy black stain on the wall and a bloody handprint in the middle of the floor.

Artema swore then that she'd be more careful. As she'd just made it to 51, she was pleased with how it was going. How she achieved this feat was to avoid demons as much as possible and stick to the more mundane magic that was taught to the undergraduates of the university.

She'd also broken with tradition by not marrying or producing children. This annoyed both her younger brothers, Marco and Alessandro. Marco especially, as his eldest son, Theodore, now stood to inherit. Marco had no wish for his son to get embroiled in the family business.

Artema's own training had been rigorous and brutal, and she had no wish to inflict it on her nephew. The knowledge was all in her books and in highly encrypted files on the interreto. If they needed it in the future, they could bloody well work it out for themselves. She hoped, though, that they never did.

A burst of song from a nearby thrush drew Artema's eyes to a rambling rose, smothered in fragrant pink blooms, that crept and tumbled its way up the side of the house. The garden and her sunny terrace was a miracle of modern technology. The top of the supraurbo was at the same altitude as the peak of Mount Everest. They should have been knee deep in snow and blasted by icy winds, but for a state-of-the-art force field that gave them their idyllic conditions.

And now, her perfectly pleasant morning in her perfectly organised life was being disrupted by a niggling doubt. She sighed and looked across at the gleaming dome of her laboratory. It had been built two hundred and fifty years ago and was one of the first buildings to go up in the supraurbo. It had been the pride and joy of Salonoy 86, who must, even for that time, have had visions of grandeur.

The laboratory was the size of a large hall. It had a glass dome in its centre that lit the room admirably so that there were very few dark corners. Artema suspected her ancestor may have been afraid of the dark, most probably for very good reason.

The rest of the lab was dwarfed under that dome. It comprised a workaday pentagram laid into the white marble in jet black stone, a couple of storage cupboards and a row of bookshelves magically sealed to prevent theft.

Books were more a status symbol than a necessity these days, although Artema's books were ancient and very dangerous. They were best kept from the prying eyes of students who still thought it was a lark to steal a book and summon a demon. The books had always been locked, but the protections on them were increased when, during her father's time, his favourite student had stolen a book on demon icons.

A thorough search had found neither Benedito Malbone, the student, nor the book. Artema had taken childish pleasure in giving her father an 'I told you so'. She'd never liked Benedito, but she'd regretted her recriminations for what they were, petty jealousy, when her father had died a couple of days later.

The only other items of note in the lab were one comfortable armchair and a long workbench that took up the far wall. Artema wasn't sure what it was supposed to be used for. Most of the components she required for her major spells revolved around large quantities of salt.

Since she could see no useful role for it, Artema had cut out the middle section of the workbench and fitted the computer into it. It was the most sophisticated AI the world had ever known. It was a family heirloom, handed down for generations and upgraded at every opportunity.

At first it had looked like a bank of flashing lights on row upon row of racks. That was centuries ago. Artema's iteration of the family AI was a sleek black cube that merely looked like the bench changed colour in that space. Artema ran her fingers along the top of the bench top, and sensed the change in temperature and texture, from warm smooth wood to cold super slick black computer.

Artema used the machine to study probabilities, the least of which was for gambling. It amused her when people assumed she had demonic insight into how a horse would perform, when she'd just been running the numbers.

Most of her computing power, though, she used for developing and testing predictive models. Others may have put the time the angels and demons appeared on earth into the cupboard of history, but Artema was still trying to work out why they'd come. She wanted to make sure they never came again. Her research revolved around that, although she never spoke of it.

Now she waved the computer to life and a face, much like her own, with sharp angular features, perfectly shaped arched eyebrows and greying dark blonde hair that brushed non-existent shoulders, shimmered into life and floated at head height.

'Yes, master?' the AI said.

The rest of the faculty teased her about having an AI that behaved like an 18th century familiar, but she was rather fond of her family's creation. It was their work that had gone into the creation of her intelligent machine after all and, not that she mentioned this part to anybody, a certain amount of demonic energy. That was there for a reason, but not one she was prepared to explain.

'You've been examining the probability data as I've asked, have you not?' Artema said.

'Yes, master.'

'Have you discovered anything?'

'Several anomalies.'

'Show me,' Artema said as the AI switched to screen mode.

'Dear God, this looks bad,' Artema muttered when she emerged from her analysis three hours later.

With a wave of her hand, she sent an urgent request for the vice-chancellor to come and see her. Then she started going over everything the AI had shown her a second time.

Normando Malto of the Malto blues, not quite as august

as the Salonoys, but blue enough, arrived at the laboratory precisely two minutes later. He was a large man, and his flowing robes made him look like an untethered balloon draped with a sheet. His ambling gait made it look like the balloon was drifting slowly across the room.

'What is it, Artema? I was in the middle of breakfast.'

'Have I ever summoned you before?' Artema said and turned to examine the vice chancellor with her cold grey eyes. She always unnerved him, and she intended to put that to good use now.

'Not that I recall,' Normando said and wiped a bit of egg yolk from the corner of his mouth.

'So you must realise it's important.'

'It's why I left my breakfast only half eaten.'

'And I am really your least troublesome professor in the main, aren't I?' Artema said, although she doubted the vice chancellor would agree.

'Of course you are. Your family funds your department of demonology. A department of one, I might add, with precisely no students.'

'I do my bit with general teaching.'

'You hold an annual lecture called, Demonology, why you should never study it. Nobody else at the university works as hard to keep people out of their department as you do.'

'It's a very effective lecture,' Artema murmured, and she had absolutely no intention of changing the lecture either.

'Pointless.'

'Not at all. It puts all right-minded young magistos completely off the subject. Those who still show an interest, and ask to become my students, are flagged as particularly dangerous. I keep them on my personal watch list and add all their data to my AI. Nobody in their right mind should ever want to be a demonologist.'

'You manage.'

'Only just,' Artema said. Most people never knew what a strain it was to work with demons and were unlikely to be convinced. 'That isn't why I need to see you though.'

'So what is the emergency?' Normando said, dragged the armchair over to face Artema and squeezed his vast bulk within the encircling arms.

'You know my work consists mainly of tracking demon activity on this plane.'

'Yes, I know that. You then fly in and shut down whatever is brewing.'

'Exactly. And it rarely presents any great difficulty. I deal with greedy people who've been offered deals that are too good to be true, or cultists who know precious little about magic. Either that or I'm stopping a student who has decided they know better and attempted to contact a demon.'

'And you do it very effectively. So what's the problem today?'

Artema shook her head and tried to work out how to explain what was bothering her. She decided to keep it simple, at least to start with.

'I am concerned because at the moment I have a background noise of demon activity across the suburbo with a spike right in the centre. It isn't the usual pattern of demon activity. It isn't focused around a single individual.'

'Demon activity without interacting with humans?' Normando said, and he actually looked surprised.

'That's what it looks like.'

Artema assumed, because of her training and experience, she was also more sensitive to demon presence and that explained her own feeling of unease. There was no need to mention that to Normando yet.

'Doesn't the angel-demon accord prevent either group from coming onto our plane without our agency?' Normando said, scratching his thinning white hair.

'That's a common misconception, actually. The demons told us that, but we have no corroboration from the angels.'

'And demons aren't known for their affection for the truth.'

'Exactly. It would be helpful if the angels did speak to us. It would clarify so many things.'

'But angels never turn up, do they?'

'None of the summoning rituals used to draw in demons works to call angels. I suspect their two planes don't connect and they're not related to each other or to us. Either way, since the Great Inter-Plane War, we haven't been able to contact angels.'

'Demons, on the other hand, are all too keen to get in,' Normando said gloomily.

'But never, since the war, have they done it on their own.'

That fact alone was so unusual that it was troubling to Artema.

'Are you sure about this?'

'My analysis has not been wrong so far. But analysis and data collection is pointless without actually going to the source to check.'

'You want to go into the suburbo?' Normando said and his pale blue eyes practically started out of their sockets at the mere thought of anyone going to the suburbo. 'You, a blue blood, want to venture into that cesspit?'

'What choice do I have?'

'But they don't usually mess with the occult. People in

the supraurbo do, much to my annoyance. We've got all sorts of illegal magical activity in the mezaurbo. But I've never heard about anything in the suburbo.'

'Maybe that's only because we never go down there,' Artema said with a shudder.

She really didn't want to venture down into the dark of the suburbo.

'It's far too dangerous,' Normando said, nodding enthusiastic agreement to Artema's shudder.

'More dangerous than working with demons? Or leaving a potential demon incursion unchecked?'

'How would I know?' Normando said and waved his hand vaguely. 'I assume you haven't discussed this with the komitato yet?'

'As you are one of my komitato, you can consider yourselves updated.'

'Not good enough, Artema. The komitato keeps all demonologists on the straight and narrow. Before you do anything you need to send all the members a complete report, including what you intend to do next. If indeed you intend to do anything at all. I suppose it's too much to hope that you will leave it alone?'

'Believe me, Normando, things will get worse if we ignore it.'

'All the same, the suburbo! I'm told there aren't only humans down there. I've heard that some people have mutated so dramatically they could be classified as an entirely different species.'

'Hearsay and superstition,' Artema said and hoped she was right. 'At the very least we should go down and explore the place. The more I think about it, the more foolish it seems that we've never ventured into the suburbo.'

'We leave it to the city government. It's their business to keep control.'

'And it's our duty to maintain magical law and order which we have not done in the suburbo.'

'Because it's dangerous.'

'Unchecked magical use is dangerous. Who knows what they've been getting up to without our supervision.'

'By everything I hear they aren't terribly bright. I doubt they've got the brains to figure it out.'

'That could be the most foolish and dangerous assumption ever made.'

Artema suspected it was this prejudice that had deterred previous magistos from venturing into the suburbo.

'Now steady on, Artema, no need to get nasty,' Normando said holding out his hands in supplication. 'If you are determined, then go, but don't go alone.'

'You want me to take somebody with? Who? A beadle?'

'Well... a couple of beadles would be a good idea. There's none tougher in a brawl, and for raw, battle magic they're definitely the people to call upon. But maybe what you need is a guide. Rather than going in heavy-handed. You might require some subtlety. Maybe blend in with the natives, see what they see.'

'You think I should find a local?'

The vice chancellor's suggestion didn't have instant appeal. How on earth was she supposed to work with someone who was most likely sub-human or, at the very least, grossly undereducated and stupid?

'That's it yes,' Normando said warming to his idea, 'splendid. Find a suburbo person to take you about.'

'And how would I find one of them?'

'Well, good heavens, Artema, how am I supposed to

know that? It's not like we allow those dreadful people into the supraurbo after all.'

'Huh,' Artema said and ran her fingers thoughtfully through her hair. 'But if they were to come here, they'd need a pass.'

'They would.'

'And one assumes that to get from the suburbo to the mezaurbo they'd need a pass too.'

'One assumes so,' Normando said. 'It's really astonishing that I've never considered that. Would the mezaurbo allow suburbo people in?'

'Probably,' Artema said. 'They'll want somebody to do the menial work after all. Somebody who isn't too bright and will do whatever boring jobs the mezas don't want to do.'

'That sounds about right. After all, we get mezas to do our fetching and carrying in the supraurbo.'

'So, it's just a matter of getting their records from the interreto,' Artema murmured and looked meaningfully at her AI. It was a being that understood her superbly. But then, as it was practically a part of her, that wasn't surprising. 'And then get the names and addresses of any likely suburbo people.'

'I believe they're called lowlives,' Normando said, examining his perfectly manicured nails.

'There's a surprisingly large number of them working in the mezaurbo,' Artema said as the AI flicked a stack of virtual files onto the screen like a set of unending mirror images. 'I need some way to reduce that number. I need to concentrate on the... lowlives, was it? That are resident in the area I want to investigate.'

The AI closed its virtual eyes and said, 'Sorting.' A second later it said, 'More than half these people don't have a fixed address.'

'Like I said,' Normando sighed, 'They're savages.'

'Well then, I'll have to use their work addresses in the mezaurbo above the area that correspond with the area in the suburbo.' Artema said. 'I assume they'll try to keep their commute to a minimum.'

'It's worth a try,' Normando said. Then he placed his hands on the armrests of the chair and heaved himself decisively back onto his feet. 'I'll leave you to your search and return to my breakfast, although it will be cold by now.'

'Before you run off,' Artema said and flicked open a virtual file. 'Look at this. I do believe I've found my guide.'

'That's a lowlife?' Normando said.

His surprise was justified. The young man looked like a flawless specimen of humanity, and his pale face projected a calm certainty as it stared out at them.

'Bona sinjoro,' Normando said. 'Any blue blood mother would be happy to have someone like him marry into the family.'

'I doubt it. Aside from coming from the suburbo he had no fixed abode and his name is... Eladio Thirteen. Thirteen? That's an odd surname.'

'Not really, it's for people without known ancestry,' Normando said. 'They're just given any old surname that springs to the registrar's mind.'

'Well, his work address is practically right above the point of origin for my investigation so he'll do.'

'I'll bet he will,' Normando said with a sly smile that Artema ignored. 'Don't enjoy yourself too much.'

Artema sighed, no matter how many times she reminded the vice chancellor that she was gay, he always seemed to forget.

2

His phone alarm woke Eladio with a jerk. Its screen glowed as it buzzed insistently and he groped towards it, patting along the corrugated metal floor. He stabbed the off button with vindictive satisfaction, then yawned widely. Another day, another imp, he thought and pushed himself upright, blinking and smacking his lips. He flicked the screen on so it glowed brightly enough to see what he was doing in the pitch black.

His place was too low for him to stand up, so he scooted along on his behind to the bottom of his mattress. He pulled out a clean pair of underpants from the cardboard box that held his essentials and examined his two sets of black shirts and black trousers. It was Wednesday, so time to get one set washed, and put on the clean clothes. He dressed and then wrapped the dirty clothes into a bundle held together by his shirt. He tucked his money into a slit he'd made on the inside of his hoodie and pulled that on.

Then he put his ear to the door and listened. It sounded like a typical day outside, just the usual hubbub, nothing unexpected or loud. So he carefully opened the door and looked out into the dim surroundings.

They'd stacked containers in rows of five high along both sides of the street. His was in the middle of the stack. It was a pretty good position because the bottom containers were prone to water seepage from the ground. The upper containers had a tendency to leak from above.

They were mini containers, just big enough for a person to lie lengthwise and sit upright in, but not much more than that. Some of his neighbours were sharing with partners and a couple, even with kids. He couldn't imagine how they did it. He slipped down onto the damp path, checked that nobody was too close, and closed the door of his container.

Its corrugated metal sides were painted an azure blue and huge red letters had been sprayed across it when it had been a full-sized shipping container. Only the letters T and S remained and were a useful marker for finding his way back home.

He shut his robust lock with a click. It was probably the most expensive thing he'd ever bought. Then he double checked it was properly closed by tugging on it and looked around again.

It always paid to be careful, especially near home. The street was nearly empty, as most people preferred to hang out in the square beyond. Since he worked an unusual shift pattern, he came and went at different times to most of the labourers. Eladio flicked his hood over his head and made for the square.

'Hey, hey, look who's emerged,' a tall skinny man said as Eladio stepped out into the main road.

'Hello, Benito,' Eladio said. 'How are you today?'

'Still out of work,' the man said and tipped his cap out, the open side facing Eladio. 'I don't suppose you can spare a couple of imps?'

'Sorry,' Eladio said. 'Does anyone ever give you money?'

'Never happened,' the man said with a grin. 'Still, doesn't hurt to ask.'

'I suppose,' Eladio said vaguely. He gave Benito an

apologetic grimace and hurried on to the stall across the road.

'Washing day, is it?' Felicha said as she took Eladio's bundle.

She was a black woman who was so dark she sometimes looked like she'd fade into the shadows all around her, despite the line of light bulbs that hung in a string above the stall.

'It's Wednesday.'

Eladio smiled at Felicha, even though she was unlikely to reciprocate. They'd grown up together, and Felicha seldom smiled even when they were kids.

'So it is,' Felicha said. 'You'll be collecting tomorrow morning, will you?'

'Same as always.'

'Then I don't need to tell you I'll sell your clothes if you're late picking them up.'

'No, you don't need to tell me.'

Felicha had been telling him the same thing for the last four years. Ever since he'd started earning enough to pay someone else to do his washing. He nodded goodbye and walked down the lane to the public baths.

The advantage of having a different shift to everyone else was he didn't have to share the baths with many other people. At this time of day there were just a few parents with their kids, and the temporarily unemployed. Although when they got to being long-term unemployed the money for taking a bath evaporated too.

Eladio took a quick shower. He never liked to leave his stuff in a locker, even if it was robust. He scrambled back into his clothes, brushed his teeth, combed and tied back his hair and headed for the elevators.

Another advantage of his shift was that he was reverse commuting. Most people who went to the mezaurbo worked a day shift. He started at dusk. So he was going up when people were coming down. In the morning, he was going down when everyone was cramming into the elevators to go to work. He passed through the barriers, showed his travel permit to the security guards, and flashed his monthly travel card at the scanner before he made it into the elevator.

It was ancient. The plastic safety wrapping was peeling off all the sharp corners, and it smelled of sweaty people crammed into a small space with inadequate ventilation. There were no seats. Since it was only half full, though, Eladio dropped into a squat, took out his phone and pulled up his study components.

He had saved sufficient money to sit exams, and they were, after years of waiting, in five days' time. Monday wasn't only highlighted in his calendar, it had several red rings drawn around it too. He'd already paid the deposit, and his perfect memory meant he knew everything he needed for the tests themselves. Now he filled his time with supplementary reading around all the subjects. It was a long commute, so he had plenty of time to study.

He was just starting on the literature of ancient English when the elevator came to a shuddering stop and the doors slammed open with a bang. Eladio stepped outside to join another queue at the security booth where their permits to travel were double checked.

Eladio gave the security guard a half smile, as he always did. After so many years of commuting, showing the same man his permit every day, it was odd that the man never acknowledged that he knew him.

Then he was through the main doors of the elevator

terminus and out into the mezaurbo. The sun shone brightly up here. It was still a half hour before dusk, which gave him sufficient time to stroll through the park and breathe in the clean air.

It was said that the supraurbo's air was as fresh as if no pollution had ever existed. But the air of the mezaurbo was good enough. It smelled of almost nothing at all, unlike air in the suburbo. Here, at most, there was a faint chemical whiff from the aerocars that whizzed the wealthiest of the mezaurbo citizens up, down and across its vast structures.

Eladio had never been in an aerocar. There wasn't sufficient room in the cramped quarters of the suburbo for an aero to manoeuvre. It was on his list of things to do, should he ever earn enough. It was an ever-expanding list and included such exotic desires as to eat at a restaurant with waiter service, see a film in an actual cinema and spend the weekend in the mezaurbo. In his more exotic dreams, that weekend stretched to a hotel with its own ensuite bathroom.

He crossed out of the park and to one of the major walkways that interconnected the city. It was busy at this time of day as most people headed for home. But Eladio had no difficulty with the crowds, mainly because he liked to walk along the edge of the hundred metres wide walkway.

Most of the other commuters stuck to the middle. They did it partly because of the strong winds that swept up the buildings, but mainly because of the drop. It was a long way down.

When Eladio looked through the tempered glass safety barrier, he felt as if he was looking into the bowels of the earth itself. Thousand story buildings stretched out below and ended in darkness. The darkness was where the suburbo started.

The suburbo was the oldest part of the city and everything had grown up over it, gradually burying the suburbo in a layer of walkways, access tubes, immense girders supporting the new structures and a succession of ever taller buildings. Interspersed with that were horizontal barriers that prevented people from travelling too far should they fall or leap from the astonishingly tall buildings. Here in the mezaurbo, some light still made it in from above. They also had wider gaps between the buildings that let light in from the sides.

Although, up here, where humanity wasn't packed as tightly together, they said that a person could freeze to death if they stayed on the shady side of the city. There were some places that never received the warming rays of the sun, even in the mezaurbo. That wasn't a problem for the place he worked, Doreen's Coffee Shop. It got the full blast of evening rays, which was one reason Eladio liked it.

He'd taken a calculated risk coming up here looking for work. He'd saved up enough money for a permit to travel and three return tickets on the elevator. So he had three days to get a job, and he'd squeezed in with the position at Doreen's on the last day. He'd therefore accepted it with relief and started his life as a commuter.

The job suited his needs. He got better pay than he'd had before, and he worked a night shift that was so quiet he had a chance to study. On top of that, the shop had a piano.

He'd never tried to play music before, but after watching a couple of the customers play, he thought he'd like to try it. His first attempt had been laughable. He just bashed the keys and wondered how on earth you produced anything that sounded halfway like music. So, despite it not being a subject he was supposed to be studying, he added learning how to play the piano to his daily routine.

'Hello Eladio,' Maeve sang as he stepped into the shop accompanied by the jangle of the bell on the door.

She had an annoying sing song voice that the male customers all seemed to like. Either that or they were attracted to curly-haired blonde women. She wasn't Eladio's type and thankfully, she didn't seem that interested in him either.

'Evening,' Eladio murmured in what was now a familiar ritual.

'There's some leftover cake in the back kitchen,' Anna whispered conspiratorially as Eladio got behind the counter and pulled on his black apron.

Anna was plain, slightly dumpy, and kept her straight brown hair tied back in a ponytail that was so tight Eladio wondered whether it caused her pain. She liked him and always made sure he got some leftover, past its sell-by-date, food.

Eladio had first suspected she did it because she knew he came from the suburbo. But he never mentioned that fact, and it appeared that their boss, Doreen, hadn't told the other staff either. He was grateful for that. You didn't have to spend much time in the mezaurbo to realise that they thought suburbonites were subhuman, ugly and not to be trusted.

Artema breathed in the cool night air as she made her way across the mezaurbo piazza. The space was filled with immense screens advertising the latest films, the newest perfume and the trendiest clothes. Below those giant boards were the lit up signs of food establishments. Each had an apron of space ringed about with potted plants demarcating their territories.

Flocks of sparrows fought over the crumbs that littered the mostly empty tables, making good use of the bright lights to forage well after bedtime. Animals' abilities to adapt to human cities always impressed Artema.

Because of the late hour, there were few people about and the restaurants had started taking in their tables and chairs. Only a few stubborn groups of after work drinkers remained. The bar owners were trying to move them on. The drunken revellers were making it abundantly clear that they wanted just one more drink. It was this rowdy vibrancy that Artema liked about the mezaurbo.

Artema heard the piano before she saw the cafe. It was old and just enough out of tune to be noticeable, but not too jarring. Whoever was playing it started out with scales.

Artema was a scholar of perfection, and apparently so was the pianist. It wasn't just a smooth run up and down of the notes; it was the exact same pressure given to each note and the perfect interval of a millisecond of silence between each one. This was precision in action. Arpeggios followed the scales, executed in the same flawless style.

Artema made herself insignificant with a gesture that was so slight it would hardly be noticed if she was standing under a spotlight. With the spell running, the gesture was all but invisible. She preferred this spell to actual invisibility. It was easier, but she also liked the subtlety of it. She was still visible. People simply didn't notice her now.

It meant she could stand in front of the plate-glass window of the coffee shop and watch the pianist. It turned out to be a young man. The young man she'd come to meet.

She hadn't expected him to be a musician. It was a pleasant surprise. The playing absorbed him. Even without the spell, Artema doubted Eladio Thirteen would have noticed her.

He switched to playing Beethoven's Moonlight Sonata, and Artema felt a twinge of disappointment. It was perfect, an exact replica of the music as written. Every direction followed without deviation.

Artema had heard many versions of this classic. Her mother had been a music teacher, and music had filled the house when she was growing up. It was standard fare for every aspiring pianist, but most of them played with more soul.

She'd been watching for a while before she realised Eladio had no sheet music. He was playing an exact reproduction from memory. That was more impressive.

Still, it was the music of a mathematician, not an artist. Eladio's expression said that too. It was one of concentration, regurgitating back what he'd so painstakingly memorised.

It was a beautiful face, though. If he wanted it, this young man could have all the women of the Eterna Urbo at his feet, and half the men too. His features were regular, if a little too fine for Artema's tastes. Thick dark lashes framed his blue eyes and his hair was so dark as to be almost black. He'd tied it back, probably because of the hygiene rules of the coffee shop. No doubt when he let it hang loose it looked suitably romantic, tumbling to his shoulders.

Artema slipped inside. Her spell dulled the tinkle of the bell so that it went unnoticed. She selected a table that had a view of the pianist's profile and settled down to listen.

She was the only customer, which explained why the

barista wasn't at his post. As she watched, he switched to something Artema hadn't heard before. It was more complex than the Beethoven, but of uneven quality.

It seemed not to please Eladio either, who played with a deep frown etched on his face. It was more interesting to listen to but, curious as it was, it wasn't the reason for her visit and her sense of urgency kicked back in. So as the last notes faded away, Artema dropped her spell and clapped.

'Bravo!'

Eladio jerked, gave Artema a startled look, and leaped to his feet.

'Oh, I beg your pardon, ma'am!' he said and gave a deep bow. 'I didn't notice you come in. What can I get you?' he said as he hurried behind the counter, looking more rattled than expected.

Artema followed him and since she'd had a long day and was about to have an even longer night she said, 'I'd like a bullet coffee, please. Make it with a double shot of espresso.'

'Very good, ma'am,' Eladio said on another quick jerky bow. 'Have in or take away?'

'I'll have it in.'

Artema was particularly sensitive to mood, but anyone could see that this young man was on edge. Her natural curiosity made her wonder if this was Eladio's usual state. It hadn't come across in his ID photo, but then it wouldn't.

She doubted Eladio would normally be so wary of a late night customer. So she suspected it had to do with her work. Sensitive types, and after meeting him, she classed Eladio in that group, could pick up that something wasn't right about her.

Anxious or not, however, he made the coffee with the same precision as he'd played the piano. His work space was also immaculate. He'd laid everything out exactly where needed. No action was superfluous for the production of the coffee. Artema liked that sort of thing.

'Do you want a drop of emulsifier?' Eladio said.

'Emulsifier? Why would I want that?'

'It's made from soy, it's totally natural. It keeps the fats blended into the coffee instead of separating out and floating on top.'

'I like it floating on top. I enjoy sipping the coffee through it. It's like sipping it through a layer of cream.'

'No emulsifier,' Eladio said, and placed a bowl-shaped mug on the counter. It was steaming gently and had a slick of coconut oil and butter floating on top.

'Thank you,' Artema said.

Eladio obviously expected her to go back to her table. Instead, Artema pulled a barstool up to the counter. Now was the delicate moment of sounding this young man out to decide whether she could trust him as a guide. She opened with a neutral question.

'Tell me, is it always this quiet in here?'

'Oh no, this is the quietest time. We're busy till about midnight and then it picks up at dawn with the morning commute.'

'So that's why there's just one of you right now?' Artema said and took a first sip of her coffee. It was better than she'd expected. Mezaurbo coffee seldom measured up to what she got in the supraurbo.

'I cover the night shift,' Eladio said. 'The day shift stays till dusk and comes back at dawn for the morning rush.'

'It sounds like a lonely job.'

Eladio looked disconcerted, as if nobody had ever wondered about his state of mind before.

Then he gave a quick smile and said, 'I don't mind it.'

'I suppose it gives you a chance to play the piano,' Artema said. 'Where did you learn to play? At school?'

'Oh no, they didn't teach music at my school.'

That didn't surprise Artema. It would have been more astonishing to find they taught music in the suburbo. It did, however, make Eladio more intriguing.

'So where did you learn?'

'From the interreto. They have everything on there, including lots of videos of how to play the piano.'

'So you're self-taught? That's impressive.'

Eladio flushed and muttered, 'Thank you, ma'am.'

'And very disciplined. I doubt I'd be bothering with scales and arpeggios if I was teaching myself.'

Artema knew for a fact she wouldn't because she'd avoided exercises when she'd learned to play the piano as a girl. Something now, thankfully, far behind her. She had no aptitude for music.

'Oh no, you have to do the exercises. They help your playing and keep your fingers limber. It's good practice.'

'If you say so.'

Eladio nodded, but it was an uncertain gesture accompanied by a lingering, doubtful glance. Clearly he didn't know what to make of his customer.

The feeling was mutual. Artema had never come across such an accomplished self-taught musician, nor such a disciplined one. She would have been astonished if somebody from the supraurbo had accomplished such a feat on their own, but someone from the suburbo? No, it was absurd.

Artema examined Eladio more closely. He was of average height, and aside from broad shoulders, he had a slight build. He was wearing black trousers and a black shirt. Artema assumed this was the coffee shop uniform as his apron was also black with the name of the shop embroidered along the top in a trailing cursive.

His clothes were clean but threadbare. A section over the right elbow had worn out and carefully patched with another piece of black fabric that had faded to a slightly different, greenish shade.

'How long have you worked here?' Artema asked.

'Three and a half years,' Eladio said with another bob. It might have turned into a proper bow, but he stopped himself.

'Three and a half years. That's a long time. You don't look old enough to have been working so long.'

Eladio gave her an uncertain smile, picked up a mug and started polishing it with his dishcloth. It didn't need it; it was already spotless.

'What did you do before that? Were you at school?'

'No, ma'am.'

'You weren't at school? Why not?'

Artema was genuinely surprised. She expected everyone in the Eterna Urbo to get a full education. It made Eladio's musical ability even more surprising. She was rapidly coming to the conclusion that she should have done more research on the young man. Damn her preconceptions.

'I finished school at grade eight,' Eladio said, blushing so deeply that even in the relatively low light of the coffee shop it was obvious.

'You left after grade eight? Good heavens, why?'

'That's as far as the state will provide free education,' Eladio spoke cautiously, as if worried his words might offend.

'What of your parents, wouldn't they pay?'

Eladio shook his head, looking steadily more uncomfortable.

'I don't have parents.'

'What about grandparents then, or aunts and uncles?'

Eladio shook his head.

'I'm an orphan.'

Artema wondered why her AI hadn't imparted this information to her. It might not be pertinent to her investigation, but it was noteworthy.

'I see... I'm sorry. Didn't the state pay for you then? Surely they should have? I mean, where were you living?'

'In the orphanage, but... you have to leave it when you finish with school.'

'They kick you out?' Artema said and realised her voice had taken on a shrill, astonished tinge.

It wasn't lost on Eladio, who gave a half shrug that barely avoided turning into an embarrassed cringe.

'But what did you do then? You couldn't have been very old... How old were you?'

'I was thirteen.'

'Thirteen? Bona Sinjoro. How did you manage?'

'I got a job.'

'Doing what?' Artema said with a surprised laugh.

She'd been a useless, layabout thirteen-year-old. She couldn't image her younger self being able to find a job or even knowing where to start.

'I was a street sweeper.'

Eladio looked so uncomfortable now that Artema wouldn't have been surprised to actually see his skin crawling. Still, he held her gaze, as if daring her to laugh.

She wouldn't have; there was nothing funny about the

situation. But Eladio's refinement and abilities were at odds with what sounded like a more than usually underprivileged upbringing. Considering they chucked the kids out at thirteen, she couldn't imagine them providing much of an education. This young man had to be very bright indeed to teach himself anything, let alone music.

'How long did you sweep streets for?'

'Three and a half years.'

'That's a long time.'

'Yes.'

Eladio picked up a dishcloth and started polishing the mirror smooth counter.

Artema wondered if he was trying to look busy so that she'd stop interrogating him. She had no choice but to continue though because she needed a guide she could trust.

Searching around for a way to dig up more about his abilities, she said, 'Tell me, in all that time, did you consider getting a genetic test?'

Eladio stopped polishing and blinked in surprise at Artema.

'Why would I do that?'

'Because the genetic test highlights your strengths. If you have particular talents, music for instance, you can get specialised training, bursaries and mentoring. If you come out in the top percentile in certain skills, they'll promote you all the way into the supraurbo.'

Eladio gave a cynical laugh that he smothered in an instant.

Then, answering in a tone of voice that tried hard not to imply she was a lunatic, he said, 'The test costs a lot of money.'

'Does it? I didn't know.' Her reply appeared to surprise

Eladio more than anything else she'd said. Stupid, she thought, she needed to blend in better. 'It's worth it, surely?'

'Only if I had something notable in my genes,' Eladio said, gave the dishcloth a flick and moved to the nearest table to give it a wipe.

'How do you know, if you haven't taken the test?'

'Everyone hopes they have something. But nobody I know who's taken the test has had anything that got them out of their current situation.'

'So what did you spend your money on?'

'I bought a pass for the mezaurbo,' Eladio said, rubbing away at the marble top of the table as if determined to polish it to a shine.

'A pass for the mezaurbo? Isn't that where you're from?' Artema said although she knew full well it wasn't.

'No, ma'am,' Eladio said, straightened up and gave Artema a defiant stare, 'I'm from the suburbo.'

Artema wondered what kind of reaction Eladio usually got from that admission, considering how wary he looked now.

'Are you indeed? So you got a pass for here so you could... why come here?'

'Better pay.'

'And with that better pay, could you not take the genetic test?'

Eladio gave the half shrug Artema had already come to expect and said, 'I have other things I want to spend my money on.'

'A pass to the supraurbo?' Artema said with a grin.

Eladio gave her such a blank look of incomprehension that for a moment Artema wondered whether she'd garbled her words.

Then Eladio said, 'No ma'am. I want to take the exam for matriculation.'

'Even though you never finished school?'

'I've been studying,' Eladio said in a pained tone of voice and moved to the next table to polish it with the same exaggerated care as he took over the last one.

'Using the interreto?'

'Yes, ma'am.'

'And if you don't pass?'

'I will pass.'

'You seem very sure of that.'

'Yes, ma'am.'

It was the first admission Eladio looked absolutely confident about. Artema wondered why, but decided against asking about that yet.

'After the exams?'

'I will find another job.'

'One that pays better, huh?'

'I hope so.'

'What about university?'

Eladio actually smiled at that. 'They'd never let me in.'

'Not even the magical university?'

Eladio's jaw dropped at that suggestion. Then he shook his head.

'I know it exists... I know magic is real, but I've never seen it being done. There is more chance of me getting into heaven than into the magic university.'

'You know, they're not even sure that happens, getting into heaven?' Artema said. 'Either way, you have to die before you can get into heaven.'

'True, but at that moment you have a chance.'

'So you think the magical university is less attainable

than heaven?'

'Do you know of anyone who has ever been there, or even seen it?' Eladio said.

Artema laughed. 'Don't you?'

'They say it is in the supraurbo and you have to be a blue blood or extremely wealthy to get in. So it is well beyond the means of common folk.'

'That is probably true,' Artema said and drained the last of her coffee. She slid the bowl like mug across the counter and said, 'Another one, please.'

'With a double shot?'

'Exactly the same as the last.'

'Are you sure?' Eladio said, making his way back to the counter and tucking the dishcloth into the band of his apron for safekeeping.

'I am about to have a very long day. I'll need it.'

'Yes, ma'am.'

Eladio scooped another serving of coffee out of its foil bag and set the machine to steaming again.

'I used to be a drinker,' Artema said. 'I spent hours propping up bars, talking to the barman. I miss that. I hope you don't mind that I'm doing the same to you. My advantage here is that I'm the only paying customer, so I have you to myself.'

'I don't mind,' Eladio said. 'I only get paid when we have customers in the shop.'

'Is that so? Well, in that case you may as well make me a toasted sandwich as well.'

'Any particular kind?'

'I'm a traditionalist, give me a ham and cheese.'

'Yes, ma'am,' Eladio said and smiled.

So, Artema thought, I'm finally getting the young man to

relax, or at least, to not be so wary of me. This was good because, unusual as Eladio was, Artema had a good feeling about him and usually her feelings were accurate. But she didn't like to rely solely on instinct, so probing was still required.

'Tell me,' Artema said, in her, I'm just a chatty customer voice. 'What is it you like best about working in the mezaurbo?'

'The sunshine,' Eladio said without looking up from the bread he was buttering.

'The sunshine?'

'The sun doesn't get all the way down to the suburbo. I like the dawn and just... seeing the sun. I also like the parks, and the birds. There are no parks in the suburbo.'

'I suppose not, they'd be hard to maintain without sunlight.'

'Yes, ma'am.'

'And what are your favourite subjects? The ones you're studying for your matric?'

'I like maths.'

'Maths? Really? That's unusual.'

'It's a beautiful subject. People think it's difficult, but it isn't, really. It's just... it's another language. One that makes sense of the world. If people could understand that, they'd like it better.'

The accuracy of the description struck Artema. It was one that tallied with all she knew about magic. But most people didn't like maths. This Eladio was getting ever more interesting.

'Maybe it needs different teachers then. What I remember of the maths I studied was that it was dry as a bone. We just crunched our way through numbers and equations by rote.'

'It's like learning grammar. If you do it without a sense of the language you're learning, it feels a bit pointless.'

'I suppose you're right.'

His explanation struck Artema as very considered. She was getting the impression that she was dealing with a very bright boy indeed. Maybe it was possible that a genius might be born in the suburbo. But what were the odds that she would then go in search of this genius to be her guide?

Eladio, oblivious to all her musing, merely placed the toasted sandwich in front of Artema.

'Actually, it's rather fortunate me running into you,' Artema said, deciding that whatever the oddities of the situation it would be better to have Eladio where she could watch him. She had the strange feeling he was somehow connected with her general sense of unease. 'As it happens, I need a guide to take me to the suburbo.'

'A guide? Into the suburbo?'

Eladio couldn't have sounded more astonished if Artema had just asked for a guide into the afterlife.

'I understand it's a place best not ventured into alone.'

'Why would you even want to go down there?'

'I have to find something.'

Eladio blinked at her, apparently trying to make sense of what she was saying. Weirdly, this reassured Artema. She'd have been more worried if he'd just agreed to go along with her without reservations.

'Something?' Eladio asked.

'I'll know it when I see it.'

'The suburbo is vast. Nobody ever gets to know it in its entirety.'

'But I suspect, as you were a street sweeper, you know it

pretty well.'

'Parts of it,' Eladio said warily.

'I will pay you, of course,' Artema said. 'Double per hour of whatever you get paid here.'

'I get the minimum wage.'

'Good heavens, really? That isn't very much. No wonder it's taken you so long to save up your money. And this was still better paid than the street sweeping?'

'Yes, ma'am.'

'That doesn't seem right,' Artema said, and Eladio examined her as if she was fast dismounting her rocker. She realised she'd sounded weird. 'I suppose that's the way the world works.'

Eladio nodded.

'How about I pay you four times your current hourly wage plus expenses? Would that convince you?' Artema asked and reflected that no matter how much it cost her, it was still going to be less than what she was willing to spend.

'What do you mean by expenses?'

'Travel and food.'

'All my travel and food?'

'For as long as you're helping me, yes.'

Eladio nodded thoughtfully, his gaze fixed on Artema as he considered the offer.

'Starting from when?'

'From the moment you walk out of this coffee shop with me.'

'I have to stay till after the morning rush.'

'I don't suppose you can leave earlier?' Artema said, already twitchy about having spent so long sounding Eladio out.

'There's nobody else to look after the shop.'

Artema wondered how serious the demon activity was in the suburbo and whether her current unease was because of that or the excessive amounts of caffeine she'd consumed. She wished she could talk Eladio into leaving immediately, but also appreciated that he was the sort of reliable employee who wouldn't just go off with whoever offered to pay him better.

'Alright, I can wait.'

'You do know it's a two-hour ride down to the suburbo, don't you?' Eladio said, watching her closely, apparently still trying to work out what she was up to.

'Two hours? Really? No, I hadn't realised it would take that long.'

The elevator from the supraurbo was quicker. Since it was approximately the same distance, Artema assumed the elevators were just older but hopefully still safe to ride.

'But you're willing to pay for the time the journey takes?' Eladio said.

Ah, so that was why he'd brought that up.

'I am.'

'And after that?'

'As long as it takes for me to find... my thing.'

'Do you at least know where you need to start looking?'

Artema liked the question; it was practical. It made her feel that her instinct to go with Eladio had been the right one.

'I have a general idea, yes.'

Eladio glanced at his night time customer as he churned out the coffee orders that came with the morning rush, checking she was still there. She was, without a doubt, the strangest woman Eladio had ever met. There was something about her that wasn't quite right, but he couldn't work out what it was.

She was definitely the richest woman he'd ever met. The customers to Doreen's Coffee Shop were mostly city commuters. They wore suits and were groomed and smart, but nothing like the night time caller.

Her nails were perfectly manicured. Her wavy, coiffured hair was styled to perfection. Her clothes were of a quality Eladio had never seen before. For one thing, they were made from natural fibres. He was pretty sure that one of the intricately layered and beautifully embroidered sections was silk; the rest was wool. Wool! He'd never seen anyone wearing wool, a very fine, tight weave at that. It almost looked like satin.

And it wasn't a suit. She was the kind of person who could wear whatever she wanted to work. Which today, happened to be an exquisitely designed jacket in shades of black and grey.

He assumed the woman was trying to be subtle. Or maybe she thought she was dressing down, but it was impossible to miss the quality. She drew attention even here in the mezaurbo, where the rest of the customers were all casting her surreptitious glances that lingered just a little too long.

But that wasn't the strange thing. Maybe it was that she'd spent the entire night at the shop waiting for him. That was distinctly odd for someone claiming a chance encounter.

Her request was also preposterous. Eladio had heard of people who would go down into the suburbo for adventure, or as a peculiar form of tourism. But they'd say that was what they wanted. They wouldn't be so vague about their purpose.

Still, four times his usual hourly wage was a lot of money. For that, he'd take this odd woman wherever she liked... well, not precisely. He'd take her to the safer places and see if he could work out what she was really up to.

At nine o'clock precisely, Artema stood up and gave Eladio an enquiring, raised eyebrow.

'I have to go,' Eladio said to Maeve and Anna.

'But, Eladio, we've still got loads of customers. Please stay and help,' Maeve said in her annoying voice.

'Sorry,' Eladio said, as he pulled off his apron. 'But I have another job today.'

'A day job to go with your night job?' Anna said as she squeezed past with a couple of coffees. 'Don't wear yourself out.'

'I'll be fine,' Eladio said and headed for the door where the woman was waiting.

'Right,' Artema said as they stepped out into the morning sunshine. 'Time for breakfast.'

This surprised Eladio because, although she'd not said it, he got the impression the woman was in a hurry.

'You had a toasted sandwich.'

'That was five hours ago. Besides, I need to top up my coffee. Where do you normally go for breakfast?'

'Er, the suburbo,' Eladio said, uncomfortable to have to admit that. This woman might plan on going down into the suburbo, but he very much doubted she'd be willing to eat there.

'The suburbo? Which, you already informed me, is a two-hour ride away. I don't want to wait that long. Besides, I didn't see you eat or drink anything in the coffee shop, so you must be hungry by now. Why didn't you have anything there?'

'I have to pay for it.'

'By which I assume it's cheaper to eat in the suburbo.'

'Yes, ma'am.'

'I haven't introduced myself yet, have I?' Artema said and held out her hand. 'I'm Artema Salonoy.'

Eladio stared down at the offered hand. Then he hastily reached out and maintained his grip only long enough for a single shake before he let go. He felt like he was squirming and Artema Salonoy was smiling cryptically back at him.

'I'm–'

'Eladio Thirteen, yes, I know,' Artema said. 'You have a name badge.'

'Oh yes.'

Eladio unclipped his badge and slipped it into his pocket. This woman was disrupting his routine. He usually got rid of the name badge at the same time as he ditched the apron.

'So where to for breakfast?' Artema said. 'Shall we attempt one of those... I believe they're called greasy spoons?'

Eladio had always found the name amusing because the establishments in the mezaurbo were all gleamingly clean. It took a suburbo caf to make you realise what a greasy spoon actually looked like, along with a greasy knife, a greasy fork and a greasy plate.

'Is this... is this an expense, ma'am?'

'Yes, indeed. My imperial dolaroy will pay for your breakfast. But let's not go overboard, somewhere decent on the way to the elevators will do me fine.'

'Right,' Eladio said, and considered his usual walk home.

There was a cafe with a view over the major walkway that he guessed was decent enough. It had actual waitresses who wore lace edged aprons. It was astonishing that he was about to eat there. It wasn't quite the grand restaurant with waiter service he'd dreamed of, but it would check off one of his wish list items.

'I know a place,' he said and joined the flow of pedestrians headed to work.

Artema Salonoy strolled along beside him, looking about with the curious interest of a tourist. For a dizzying moment, Eladio wondered if she actually came from the supraurbo. But no, that couldn't be, could it?

Nobody ever met anyone from the supraurbo. Their homes were so beautiful and comfortable that they didn't descend to the lower levels. There was nothing for them in the other parts of the city.

Although this woman did have an air of... Eladio felt like she could get anything she wanted just by raising one beautifully plucked and shaped eyebrow. He doubted the security guards at the elevators would stop her.

She also just expected to get her way, Eladio realised. It was such a powerful expectation that people scurried to obey. Or even anticipate her wishes before she voiced them.

A case in point was the cafe. All three of the waitresses rushed over to ask Artema whether she'd like to sit and then hovered about her, making sure she was comfortable. They ignored Eladio, though, who silently sat down opposite the woman.

Maybe she was even a blue blood? Eladio had to prevent a smile at that thought. No blue blood would walk around the mezaurbo without an entourage. They wouldn't want to go to the suburbo, certainly not on their own. It was all very odd.

Eladio took out his phone and tapped it against the

transmitter at the table to get the menu. Artema took out a sliver of what looked like glass but turned out to be a top of the range phone that projected its screen into the air. Eladio stared at it open-mouthed. It was one of the latest models, probably the latest model.

With a gesture, Artema's screen enlarged to something like an A4 sheet and she perused the menu.

'I like the look of the all day breakfast sandwich. And I'll have a cup of mocha coffee to go with it.'

'Very good, ma'am,' the waitress said as she swept the order to her own phone.

Eladio had no idea what he was supposed to, or even allowed to, have. So, for safety's sake, he said, 'I'll have the same.'

'Two of everything,' the waitress said with a nod and hurried away.

'This is not a bad place,' Artema said, leaned back in her chair and looked around. 'Very quaint.'

Eladio couldn't work out what she meant by quaint. To him it looked smart. It looked like the owner was attempting to be upmarket, even if it was a place for morning commuters and lunch time office workers.

'Yes, ma'am,' he said.

The all day breakfast sandwich was immense. It comprised two eggs, sausages and bacon. It was far bigger than the picture had implied, and Artema tucked in with a gusto that astonished Eladio.

He started off more slowly, but it really was delicious. He'd not eaten much in the mezaurbo. On occasion, he'd used his precious cash for a coffee or sandwich at Doreen's, but mostly he needed to save, so he avoided it. This food was of a quality and quantity he was unaccustomed to.

By the time Artema had finished her breakfast, Eladio was only halfway and struggling. His stomach wasn't accustomed to so much or such rich food. He also didn't want to keep his employer waiting, but it killed him to know the restaurant would throw the food away simply because he didn't finish it.

Nobody ever threw food away in the suburbo. Someone was always willing to pay half price for somebody else's leftovers. Although the portions were smaller down below, and there was rarely anything left. It had appalled Eladio to discover that it was the law in the mezaurbo that you couldn't serve food that had been on one person's plate to another person. It had to be thrown away.

When he could, he'd slip uneaten food into a container to take away with him.

Now he leaned towards Artema and whispered, 'Do you think I can have the rest to go?'

'Take it with you?' Artema said in genuine surprise. 'There's no need. I'll pay for your lunch too.'

'It isn't that,' Eladio said, and felt he was blushing.

'No harm in asking,' Artema said.

It surprised and relieved Eladio that she didn't argue. He was even more surprised when Artema waved the waitress over.

'We'd like to take that with us,' she said and tilted her head at Eladio's plate. 'How much do I owe you?'

'I'll fetch the bill, ma'am,' the waitress said. She took the plate with the half-eaten sandwich and whisked it away without looking in the least offended.

Eladio couldn't help contrast that with how he'd be treated if he'd asked.

The waitress returned with a foil bag that she set down in

front of Eladio without looking at him and waved her phone at Artema.

'Will that be cash, ma'am?'

'Phone,' Artema said, and with a flick of her finger she swiped the payment across.

Eladio waited till the waitress had walked away before he asked, 'Do you have any cash?'

'No, why would I? I have my phone.'

'It would be best not to let anyone in the suburbo see that phone, ma'am. They'll be crawling over each other's dead bodies to wrest it from you. Also, you can only pay with cash in the suburbo. They won't take phone payments.'

'Very well, then I'll draw some cash before we go down. Is there anything else?'

'Well…' Eladio wondered just how far he could go. As he was supposed to be a guide, and his life also depended upon it, he decided it was best to lay it all out. 'Your clothes are way too posh. They'll be taken off you the instant you hit bottom. Also, your hair is too neat.'

'What do you suggest I do about that?' Artema said with a rueful smile.

At least she realised she had to take note, Eladio thought.

'There's a karitato shop around the corner. We can get some old clothes for you there. As for your hair… I suppose you can scruff it up a bit.'

'Then we'll do that. I don't suppose you know where I can pick up an older phone? One that won't ah… cause bloodshed and mayhem if I take it out in the suburbo. I can't be without a phone. It has all my ID and money, after all.'

'I can get you a burner phone,' Eladio said. 'No problem.'

'Fine, then let's repair to the karitato shop. I look forward to blending in with the low-lives.'

Eladio stiffened at that unthinking insult and before he could stop himself he snapped, 'We're suburbonites, ma'am. Not low-lives.'

'I beg your pardon,' Artema said. 'I didn't mean to cause offence.'

Eladio flushed, it was stupid to snap over something like that. But he hated the way people dismissed everyone from the suburbo as if they were worth less than everybody else. Where would they be if the suburbo vanished overnight? He suspected everyone else would be a lot less comfortable.

3

The condition of the elevator to the suburbo appalled Artema. It was nothing like the clean and gleaming elevator from the supraurbo. It gave her a twinge of concern about its safety. It was also lacking in seats. She usually didn't mind standing, but it annoyed her when the choice was taken away and they forced her to stand.

Eladio gave her one of his uncertain looks. The lad clearly couldn't work her out. She was familiar with that expression on many students' faces too, but it was multiplied a hundredfold on Eladio's.

'What is it?' Artema said.

'Ah, I was wondering... do you mind if I take a nap while we travel?'

'Certainly, although how you'll manage that is beyond me.'

'You won't take it out of my hourly rate?'

'I won't.'

Eladio double checked her face, apparently to see whether he believed her. Then he gave a nod of acceptance.

'Thank you.'

He sank to his haunches, wrapped his arms about his knees, rested his head on them and closed his eyes.

It was a posture Artema could never get into; her sinews would not give sufficiently. As she watched, a couple of other people took up the same position. Their feet were flat on the floor, but their bottoms didn't touch it. She supposed it must be more comfortable than standing all the way down. Despite the incredible noise in the elevator, it was a smooth ride, so at least they were unlikely to fall over.

Artema switched back to watching Eladio. He really was a good-looking young man, almost too good looking. The people in the elevator, his fellow suburbonites, weren't half as appealing. A lot of them suffered from skin conditions, looked far too old for what she guessed their age was, and had terrible postures, deformed hands or lumpen bodies. She didn't know which was more alarming, the majority's deformities or Eladio's perfection.

She shifted in her new shoes to get into a more comfortable position. She'd never bought shoes before, not off the shelf. Every pair of shoes she owned were hand made precisely to the measurements of her feet. She'd never had to wear these hideously stiff, clodhopping shoes that felt like putting a box on her feet.

All her new clothes were made from synthetic fibres too and were ill fitting. The cuffs were too long and brushed irritatingly against the back of her hand. The jacket was loose and puffy and stuffed with her new phone. The phone looked like a relic from a bygone age although; she had to admit, not as old as Eladio's. She also had some actual cash tucked into an inner pocket that closed with a zip.

When she'd asked Eladio how much money she should draw and suggested a round hundred, the young man's mouth had dropped open in surprise.

Then he'd said, 'Twenty will be enough.'

Artema compromised and drew thirty, and Eladio looked unimpressed.

It was interesting how much money, and its value, ruled

Eladio's life, Artema thought. It was brought home to her when, upon buying her karitato shop clothes, she'd suggested in an off-hand way that she could donate the clothes she'd arrived in. That appalled Eladio. No, more, shaken him to his core.

Artema realised it wasn't because she was disposing of a thing of beauty. That would be why she'd regret the decision. No, it was because he'd made an estimate of the worth of the clothes and couldn't bear to see anyone just give away something of such high value. Instead, he'd insisted Artema have her clothes and phone couriered to her home.

'For,' he'd said, 'you can probably afford it.'

'I'm touched that you think so, dear fellow,' Artema had said. 'Would it not be cheaper to store it in a locker at the elevator terminus?'

'Cheaper yes, more secure, no.'

So she'd agreed and pretended to have the lot couriered home. She told Eladio to wait outside the courier office. Once she was alone, she'd popped all her goods into a little pocket universe she'd created long ago to hold important items. Best for the lad not to know about that. She had a feeling Eladio might not agree to take her to the suburbo if he discovered she came from the supraurbo, let alone that she was a magisto.

The elevator hit the ground with a solid thump that woke all the slumbering commuters. Eladio unfolded himself and stood up.

'Sleep well?' Artema said.

'Yes, thank you,' Eladio said, yawning widely. 'Do you have your permits ready?'

'I have.'

Artema noted that Eladio had his hand inside his jacket

but wasn't showing his phone with his passes on just yet. It seemed he kept everything hidden till the moment he needed it.

The smell, as the elevator doors opened, nearly overpowered Artema. It was the combined fug of millions of suburbo dwellers living with underperforming ventilation. The second thing she noticed was the humidity.

'It's muggy down here,' she muttered while trying to only take small sips of air. She couldn't bear breathing in whatever caused the stench.

'It's body heat and vapour from all the people,' Eladio said and joined the queue of people who shuffled forward to have their permits checked.

The check was cursory. Artema assumed that was because nobody would willingly descend to these depths. That was the moment when the guard looked at her permit. His eyes nearly bulged out of their sockets and it looked like he was about to salute.

'Don't,' Artema murmured.

'No, ma'am,' the man said.

He was going to tell everyone about her, Artema realised. A supraurbonite who had come all the way down to the suburbo. She waved her hand, casting a discreet forgetting spell. The last thing she needed was for word to get around.

'I have to collect my laundry,' Eladio said when they got through the barrier and crossed a dark space that looked like the dim interior of an office building that had been closed for the night.

'Your laundry?' Artema asked and took a first proper look at the suburbo.

Or tried to. Unlike the other levels of the city where the elevators opened out onto a plaza, here they were standing in a narrow road. Concrete posts the diameter of entire tower blocks stood to either side of them supporting the Eterna Urbo. They had filled every gap between the posts with a patchwork of homes made from whatever material the builders could lay their hands on. With the city looming overhead and the shanty-town all around, it was claustrophobic and dark. Not a single ray of daylight penetrated to these depths. Thank goodness she'd hired a guide, she'd never find her way through the maze otherwise.

'Yes, my laundry' Eladio said, breaking in on Artema's musings, 'and I'm late. Do you mind?'

'Not at all, lead on. It will give me a chance to get my bearings.'

'Thank you,' Eladio said and set off at speed.

Artema looked around for any sign of an automated vehicle to give them a lift and found nothing. There were a few people on ancient bicycles and a couple of rickshaws pulled by skinny, sinewy men. Everyone else was walking, and there were hundreds, no thousands, of them. She supposed there would have to be otherwise it wouldn't be so hot.

Everyone else was dressed in worse clothes than Eladio, Artema realised. Apparently the karitato shop carried better material than anything people could find down here. That was shocking, as were the threadbare clothes in muddy shades that everyone wore.

They were also thin. The thinness that came from lack of food rather than dieting. It left Artema feeling a greater discomfort even than fear of what demons might be up to down here.

The darkness of this lower level was the most disturbing, though. It was midmorning in the supraurbo. At this point she'd be pottering around in her sunny garden watching the bees buzzing about her flowers, but down here it was as black as night.

'So this is it, huh?' Artema murmured. Nobody spoke loudly here either. 'The place they build the rest of the city on. You can't go any further down than this.'

'You can actually,' Eladio said. 'Below us are all the utilities. The sewerage from the entire city lands up under us. They say it takes six hours for shit to travel all the way down from the supraurbo to us.'

'Do they say that indeed?'

'Yeah, not that it comes down piece by piece. They have collection points, and then a whole load is shunted down at the same time.'

'And this fascinates you, does it?'

'I sometimes wonder what the supers think happens to their shit,' Eladio said. 'Turns out, it's just the same as everybody else. It comes down here.'

'I'm sure there's a profound metaphor on rank and privilege somewhere in that fact.'

'Probably,' Eladio said and turned off the road they'd been travelling down into a much narrower street. 'This is Container City. It's where I live.'

'I see.'

Artema stared up at row upon row of metal boxes piled on top of each other on either side of the road. They were makeshift homes without windows. To be fair, there was nothing to look out upon.

Dim lights flickered in front of some doors, but all were firmly shut. She didn't know what she'd expected, but maybe it was more of a peasant idyll where people left their doors open and their children spilled out into the streets. Not this.

Everyone was watchful, and she saw precious few children.

A stench so overpowering it cut through the general fug assailed her nostrils.

'Sankta Madonna, what the hell is that?'

'It's a toilet block,' Eladio said.

'Where? I can't see it. I can smell it, but I can't see it.'

'It's a block away. We're not going past it.'

'Bona Dio, that is revolting.'

Eladio nodded but looked discomforted and Artema regretted making such a fuss. People identified strongly with their homes, no matter how dreadful. She didn't mean to insult the young man or the residents of the suburbo. She'd have to be more careful not to let her disgust show.

The road ended at a dingy square of shanty like shops lacking in windows. Instead, the shop owners used their shutters as makeshift counters. Eladio walked straight across to a stall manned by the most beautiful woman Artema had ever seen. She looked like a Venus carved from ebony.

'You're late,' Felicha snapped.

'I'm sorry. I got another job,' Eladio said. 'Do you still have my clothes?'

'Only because nobody else wanted to buy them.' Felicha reached under her counter and emerged with a small pile of clothes. 'Check it's all there. You won't get a refund later.'

Eladio flicked through what was really a tiny pile and nodded.

'It's all here.'

He reached into his jacket and held out a note that vanished into Felicha's hand like a conjuring trick.

'Who's she?' Felicha said with a nod in Artema's direction.

'I am Artema Salonoy,' she said and held out her hand.

'Don't,' Eladio said and slapped her hand down.

'You're posh, aren't you?' Felicha said, and her eyes narrowed. 'What are you doing with someone like her, Eladio? She'll get you killed.'

'That is certainly not my intention.'

Artema was used to dealing with demons, but sometimes the subtle menace of humans was more disturbing. Or maybe it was just the sheer unfamiliarity of the place and Artema's concerns about what might be going on down here that added a twinge of anxiety to her already niggling sense of doom.

'Maybe you don't mean harm,' Felicha said, looking her over some more, 'But you're so obviously not one of us. Not with your tan and your perfect haircut. You need something to hide that. Here, use this,' she said, and pulled a black knitted beanie down over Artema's head.

'I really don't think—'

'It's better,' Eladio said.

'It's one imp,' Felicha said.

'One imp?' Eladio exploded. 'For an ancient old hat?'

'Supply and demand. She needs that hat.'

'It's fine, I'll pay it.'

Artema reached into her jacket and pulled out her fold of bank notes.

'No!' Eladio squeaked.

He snatched away the wedge of cash and then, like magic, it vanished from his hand and a single dolaro materialised between his index and thumb. The girl snapped this up and disappeared it into Artema knew not where.

'Here,' Eladio said and, standing very close to Artema, he put the money back into her hand and closed her fingers tightly around it. 'Don't let anybody see your money.'

Felicha watched disapprovingly, shook her head and said, 'She is definitely going to get you killed.'

'It will be fine.'

Eladio tucked the clothes under his arm and gave Artema a nod. She followed as he headed across the square towards a narrow path at about the three o'clock point from where they'd come in. He walked with purpose but constantly looked around, checking. Artema suspected that was usual for him.

He also regularly checked up on her. She was grateful for that. It shocked her how very different the suburbo was. In most ways, it was living up to its reputation for degradation. But it didn't feel as wild as she'd been expecting. In fact, a sense of desperation rather than depravity permeated it.

The suburbo was fertile grounds for a demon, and Artema wondered why so few demon incursions came from here. Then again, even demons needed something to work with and these people had next to nothing.

This foray into darkness was going to be tricky. All the same, Artema was distracted by something else. The stunningly beautiful laundromat owner.

'So what is that woman's name?' Artema said as she hurried to get closer to Eladio.

'That's Felicha.'

'She's exquisite.'

'She's an entrepreneur,' Eladio said, and his voice was tinged with respect. 'As soon as she had the money, she set up her own stall. She read that in the mezaurbo and the supraurbo people get their clothes washed for them. She decided it was something people would pay for down here too.'

'It appears she was right. You use her.'

'It's easier than doing it myself. Lots of people use her. One day she plans to set up a shop in the supraurbo.'

'So she's aiming right for the top, is she?'

'She has a plan, and she does her research. She knows everything about the supraurbo.'

'From the interreto?'

'Where else? She's never even been to the mezaurbo.'

'Why not?'

'Because she sank all her money into her business. But she's determined, and she intends to get there so... who knows?'

'You know a lot about her. Could it be you fancy her?' Artema said with a smile.

Eladio gave her a surprised look and shook his head.

'We grew up together.'

'She's also an orphan?'

'Yes.'

'And finished school at thirteen?'

'Same as me. I keep telling her she should study more rather than looking at how the rich live, but she says if you own your own business nobody asks about qualifications.'

'She's probably right.' Artema wondered whether it was significant that the two most beautiful people she'd met in the suburbo were both from the same orphanage. Not only that, but they appeared to be bright and determined. 'What's her surname?'

'Does it matter?'

'Humour me.'

'It's Twelve, Felicha Twelve. She's a month older than me.'

'So they gave you surnames that... what?'

'Just in order of when we arrived. I was the thirteenth to arrive at the orphanage in my year.'

'I see,' Artema said.

Just then an exceptionally tall and very thin man stepped out into the square, nearly blocking their path.

'Here, Benito, I have something for you,' Eladio said, took out the foil-wrapped sandwich and handed it over.

It vanished into the man's jacket as quickly as money did in this place. 'Thank you, Eladio,' he said with a quick bow and vanished into the shadows.

Eladio barely slowed down as he stepped out of the square into a narrow lane lined on either side by more of what Artema could only describe as coffin sized metal containers.

'I thought you intended to eat that sandwich,' Artema said.

Eladio shook his head and said, 'I don't need it. Besides, I don't think Benito has eaten in days.'

'So you just gave him the sandwich? Isn't it worth money to you?'

'It was.'

'So?'

'So now Benito owes me a favour.'

'And what are you going to ask of him?'

'I don't know yet.'

Eladio hoisted himself up a couple of metal rungs welded to the side of the containers. Balancing there, he opened an impressive padlock and put his laundered clothes inside.

'Is that your home?' Artema asked as she took in a thin mattress and a sleeping bag.

'Yes,' Eladio said, slammed the container shut and closed the padlock with a firm click.

So he did have an address, Artema thought. But, looking up at the containers, she supposed it wasn't the type of place recorded on a city map.

'So... where would you like to go?' Eladio said. 'Where is the general area you said you wanted to search for your... thing?'

Artema had been thinking about this as she'd followed Eladio around, and the enormity of her task sank in. This place was vast, dark and worse than a rabbit warren. She'd thought she might start in the geographical location her scans had given her, but in this tightly packed world that would be difficult.

On the other hand, her instincts were good. They usually sent her to the right place, even when she didn't know why. Now she had a feeling there was something to investigate at the orphanage that produced beautiful people in this decaying place.

'I'd like to see where you grew up.'

'The orphanage? Why?'

'Curiosity, I suppose.'

Artema maintained a cool and vaguely interested voice, despite the increasing sense of urgency that was creeping over her. It never did to rush things; it led to mistakes. She also didn't want to spook Eladio. At least he looked less freaked by her now that he was on home ground. Or he had till her last request.

Eladio shifted uncomfortably and said, 'Was it really a coincidence that you found me at Doreen's, or were you actually looking for me?'

'I can see why it might look like I have an interest in you. But until we met, I knew nothing about you.' It was only a slight lie. 'But I wanted to get to this geographical point, and now I need to find my bearings. While I do that, I might as well see your orphanage.'

Eladio looked unconvinced but shrugged and said, 'Okay, it's this way.'

He headed down the path, in the opposite direction from where they'd come. He stopped at an intersection where the same container homes stretched out to the left and right and ahead and looked about.

Artema realised that if Eladio led her deeper in and then sprinted off and abandoned her, she'd have no idea how to get out. It added to the discomfort she felt in this place. As a precaution, she looked around, hoping for some landmarks she could fix in her memory.

Her eyes fell upon a black circular design that had been spray painted at head height onto a container. Her blood froze as she assimilated the letters drawn inside. At first they merely looked like artistically rendered letters. But a closer inspection revealed demon icons worked into the pattern.

She grabbed Eladio's arm and hissed, 'What's this?'

'It's a gang tag,' Eladio said. 'Why? What's the matter with it?'

'It's a gang tag? You mean there's more of them?' Artema gasped, looking back at the complex design. This was terrible news indeed. Possibly what she'd been looking for, if in a surprising guise.

'Sure, they're everywhere,' Eladio said in a far too relaxed tone. 'They mark what belongs to each gang.'

'Do they all look like this? A circle with writing inside?'

'If you can call it writing.'

'But they're all the same?'

'Well, no, each gang has their own tag. How else could

you tell them apart?'

'With the same writing?'

'They're all in a circle, if that's what you mean. But the writing is different for the different tags, and they're different colours too. That's the Black Brotherhood. People say their tag is black, but it looks more like a glowing silver to me.'

'You think it glows?'

Artema's surprise deepened. She made a slight revelation gesture, and there it was. The gang tag went from being a flat black paint to glowing with a silvery light. Demonic magic, for sure.

The thing was... the thing was that nobody should have been able to see the telltale magical energy within the mark with the naked eye. But apparently Eladio did. Not only that, but he treated it like a commonplace.

'You can't see the glow?' Eladio said, but he didn't sound surprised.

'No, it's just black. Do they all glow? All the different gang tags?'

'To me, yes.'

'All of them?'

If every gang here was putting up tags with demon symbols, that was disturbing because all those tags would have magical energy given off by the icons. Not that the energy was the problem. The question was, what were they meant to be powering?

If these things were scattered all around the suburbo, that was a more horrifying problem than even Artema's calculations had revealed so far. She took out her phone, snapped a picture of the tag and labelled it with a geolocator that marked it in three-dimensional space.

'Yes, all of them glow,' Eladio said, looking up and down the lanes as he surreptitiously put his body in front of Artema to hide what she was doing.

He was more anxious that Artema was snapping pictures than about the tag itself.

'When did they start turning up?' Artema asked.

'The tags? They've always been here. At least... for as long as I can remember.'

'And they've always glowed?'

'Sure. So you believe me they glow, do you?'

'I might.'

'Why can't other people see that?'

'Are you sure they can't?'

'Felicha says sometimes they look like they glow to her too, but not always. I thought maybe she was trying to humour me.'

'Can you show me the others?'

'You don't want to go to the orphanage then?'

'Maybe later. Now I want to see more of these tags. Can you show me a tag from another gang?'

'Sure.'

Eladio scratched his head thoughtfully for a second, then turned right. Eladio was a fast walker, but also a wary one. He checked every intersection before crossing it and watched people. He slowed down and dropped back into shadows to let some pass. Or he speeded up to get away from groups, especially men who were acting more rowdy than the average denizen of this deep and shadowy place.

Artema found the soft murmuring of the population disconcerting and said so.

'It would be worse if everyone spoke at the tops of their voices,' Eladio said. 'With all these people living together, the noise would be unbearable.'

'But with that and the darkness, it's very gloomy. You'd think they'd provide better lighting for you down here. I mean, there's excellent energy efficient systems these days that produce a light equivalent to daylight. Why don't you have that? Why do you all seem to provide your own light, which is so dim?'

Eladio shrugged and said, 'The city government doesn't care about us. They leave us to fend for ourselves.'

'But you were a street sweeper, so they must organise some things.'

'It's the gangs who organise all of that.'

That information sent a chill through Artema. It made the gang tags even more ominous. Demons attached themselves to people of power, the gangs were the powerful down here and they were all using demonic icons.

'Are you telling me that the gangs are essentially the suburbo civil service?'

'Civil service?'

Eladio's expression implied that the gangs were anything but civil. Then he shrugged, accepting that a foreigner wouldn't understand how his bit of the city was run.

Artema looked about herself again, seeing everything in a new and more disturbing light. This place was so different to how she'd imagined it physically as well as how they ran it. It was also deeply claustrophobic. They filled every available space with makeshift housing that touched what looked like a very solid ceiling. Now and then, though, they'd pass a staircase that led up into darkness. She saw no stairs leading down.

'I take it we're at the very lowest level of the suburbo.'

'We are.'

'There must be many layers before it turns into the mezaurbo.'

'Yeah, but they're hard to count. Nothing above us turns into a single flat floor. It's full of dead ends and unconnected spaces. It's a maze.'

'Do you know it at all?'

'I know some places, where my friends live. But you never can tell whether the path you're on will lead somewhere or just end at a wall. The thing is, they don't really have streets, so I didn't sweep up there.'

'But the gangs control the space up there too?'

'Sure, everything that's above them. Although all their head-quarters are on this base level.'

'And it's all as densely packed as this, all the way up?'

'Yeah,' Eladio said.

'What about the cultural assets?' Artema asked. 'Do the gangs control them too?' Eladio gave her a blank look, so she said, 'you know, the Colosseum, the Forum Romanum and the Pantheon, among others.'

'Oh that,' Eladio said. 'You can't get at any of those things from down here. You have to take an aerocar to reach them.'

Artema remembered that when she'd visited all the heritage sites as school trips, they'd been shoved into sleek silver aerobuses. It had been quite the adventure making their way down to the ground level of the Eterna Urbo. What she hadn't noticed, what with being boisterous and distracted on the bus, and absorbed by examination of the ruins once they landed, was the lack of an entrance into these historic sites from ground level.

'Have you ever seen any of our heritage?'

'Never,' Eladio said without a trace of interest or regret. Now he came to a stop before a concrete post and pointed up at a gang tag. 'Here, this is from the Green Dragons gang.'

'Ah, I see, yes, it's green,' Artema said.

'It also glows green.'

It did, Artema noted, once she'd cast her own revelation spell on it. Fortunately, she could blend her gestures into the slightly elaborate way she pulled out the phone and took the picture. Then she spent some time inspecting the lettering. It was different to the black tags, but with the same demonic iconography.

All the while Eladio stood scanning the paths that intersected with theirs, making sure nobody came upon them unexpectedly and blocking the view of Artema and what she was doing from any passersby. Not that they appeared interested.

What she was seeing stumped Artema. Her experience of demons up till now was that they found one relatively powerful and super ambitious human to latch onto and provided that person with the means to achieve whatever their goals were. They would expend liberal amounts of their power to help the human reach the pinnacle of success.

But she had never come across something like this: human signs infused with demonic icons that were being used by groups of people. It was entirely out of the demonic character. It was a mystery that had to be solved, but Eladio wasn't going to like her next request.

'Do you think we can meet one of these gang members?'

'A gang member, why do you want to do that?' Eladio said, and he bristled with suspicion.

'I want to ask them about the tags.'

'Why?'

'That is my business, don't you think?'

'Do you have any idea how dangerous the gangs are?'

'Tell me.'

Artema wondered whether some of the danger Eladio feared was because of demonic influence. Usually nobody but the person in contact with the demon knew they were getting the extra support, but given Eladio's mysterious ability, maybe he did.

'The gangs don't just own and run everything in the suburbo, they control the people too. They're the reason everybody has to be so careful. You put one foot out of line and they'll kill you.'

So Eladio's fear had nothing to do with demons, just the human ability to terrify their fellow man.

'I just want to talk to one of them.'

'You can't just talk to one of them, they never go around singly. You'd have to talk to a group.'

'If that's the way it has to be,' Artema said with a shrug that she hoped looked like cool unconcern.

Eladio looked more like she was annoying in her obliviousness and snapped, 'Are you some sort of kung fu master or something?'

That was an unexpected question, and Artema had no idea where it was going.

'A kung fu master?'

'You know, somebody who looks harmless but can fight a hundred men and not get taken down.'

'That sounds like something you'd only see in a film,' Artema said, but supposed her powers as a magisto did make her more relaxed about facing down dangers.

'So why risk your life to speak to a gang?'

'Because it's important.'

'And the reason you're down here?'

'It may be.'

'You don't know for sure?'

'Not yet.'

Eladio shook his head and checked that nobody was close enough to overhear him. Despite nobody being around he still said in a whisper so low Artema had to strain to hear it, 'I know you're paying me a lot of money, but I can't. You'll get us both killed. Gangs don't like people asking questions.'

He looked so frightened that Artema realised he'd reached that point beyond which she couldn't force him. He'd rather walk away from the money than risk his life. So she had to proceed with more caution. She would gather the information she needed from Eladio before she went to the gangs.

Besides, Eladio presented a mystery of his own. He could see magic with the naked eye. Artema had never come across a person who could do that. Both he and the gang tags needed to be investigated. The gang tags had to come first, though, because they were a more obvious connection to demons.

'Alright,' Artema said. 'You're my guide. If you think it's too dangerous, I won't do it. How about you take me to see another gang tag then? How many gangs are there, anyway?'

'Hundreds,' Eladio said. 'Maybe even thousands. There isn't a single neighbourhood in the suburbo that isn't under the control of a gang.'

The scale of the problem horrified Artema. Was it possible that the entire suburbo was under the grip not actually of gangs but demons? If they were, then the entire city was in far more danger than she'd imagined.

Eladio was tired. He'd been showing Artema around for hours now, crisscrossing the suburbo in search of gang tags. It was a very odd thing to be doing. He wished he knew what it was all about. He was convinced that Artema had known nothing of the gangs and their tags till she'd seen that first one, and yet it had set her off on an epic hunt.

It also rattled Artema. Till that moment, she'd been ridiculously calm for a woman entering the suburbo for the first time. She should have been more afraid. The fact that she wasn't was suspicious in itself. Then she'd seen the tag and her nonchalant air became forced. Something about the tags frightened her, and it was contagious.

Then there were her odd gestures. Every time she saw a new tag, she took a picture. But she also did the same peculiar movement with her hand, like a nervous tic. It was a tic that left a barely discernible golden trail in its wake.

She'd done a similar thing to the security guard at the elevator. Not the same gesture, something different, but with the same golden trace. The guard had gone blank faced in that moment.

Eladio was starting to suspect the impossible. He was wondering whether this woman was some kind of magisto. It was preposterous, but he couldn't come up with any other answer for what he was seeing.

It might also explain why she was down here on her own. He contemplated asking and decided against it. Who knew what would happen if he was too curious. This woman had to be either tremendously powerful or impossibly stupid to have come down to the suburbo with only him for a guide. So far he had no evidence that she was stupid.

'If you want to see the next gang tag, we need to go down,' Eladio said as he came to a stop at the top of a flight of stairs. 'That's the Tiber down there,' he said of the black water that flowed below.

'The actual Tiber?' Artema said and looked over the railings. 'Who would have thought I'd ever see that. I had no idea it still flowed.'

'All its tributaries are under the city now. Then it flows out where the city meets the sea,' Eladio said. 'All waste water.'

'I suppose it would have to be. I doubt there's anywhere of its original catchment that isn't covered by buildings.'

'You have to be careful, though. If you hear a siren, it means a flash flood is coming and you must run back up the stairs. That sometimes happens when they have a storm up above and the water comes flowing down to us,' Eladio said as he started down the stairs.

'How does the water get here?'

'Mainly through the drains, but also just dripping down the buildings. It makes the whole place soggy.'

'That would explain the humidity,' Artema said.

'That's just everybody's breath.'

Eladio stopped and pointed at a blue gang tag sprayed onto the post at the bottom of the stairs.

'Whose are these?' Artema said as she reached into her jacket for her phone.

'They call themselves the River Guardians. I see them sometimes patrolling on jet skis, but I've never actually met any of them. Their tags are all up and down the river though.'

'Is that so?' Artema said in a distracted tone and patted the pocket on her other side. She frowned and patted her top pockets. 'Oh damn,' she muttered.

'What's wrong?' Eladio said, although he already had a pretty good idea.

'I think I've been robbed. In fact, I'm sure of it,' Artema said and poked her finger through a cut in her jacket. 'Damn it, the thief took everything, the phone and the money. I need the bloody phone to get out of here. It has my travel permit.'

Considering the dilemma, Eladio thought Artema was pretty calm. He needed to be paid though, so he bent his mind to their journey. He retraced their steps in his memory all the way back to the last tag where Artema still had her phone. She'd taken a photo and just after... just after that...

'Small man, moustache,' he muttered.

'What?' Artema said.

'A small man with a moustache took your phone,' Eladio said, and he started back up the stairs. 'Pickpockets usually work a particular strip, so he's probably still there. But we should hurry.'

'How could you possibly know that he's the one?'

'Because I've reviewed all the people we passed on the way down here, and he's the only one who touched you. He brushed past you more closely than is normal. I should have realised that, but he was very good.'

'Dozens of people passed me on our walk from the last tag. How can you possibly remember what happened with such clarity?'

'I have an excellent memory.'

Eladio got to the top of the stairs and scanned the pedestrians. Most were just about their business and not taking any notice of him. So he set off back into the housing maze and away from the river.

'You have perfect recall, don't you?' Artema said, hurrying after him. 'That explains the piano playing too. You were replicating exactly what you'd already heard.'

'Not exactly,' Eladio said. 'The people on the interreto don't play each note with as much precision.'

'So you learn and adapt. You're quite the prodigy, aren't you?'

'Doesn't do me any good,' Eladio murmured as they rushed down the street.

'What do we do when we catch the man?' Artema said. 'He's hardly likely to confess.'

'Are you any good with your fists?'

'With my fists?'

'The only way you will get your stuff back is if you beat him up.'

'If I beat him up? Me?'

'Well, I'm not going to do it.' Eladio assumed Artema's reluctance stemmed from being a woman. He'd noticed that Mezaurbo women didn't get involved in fights. 'I'm your guide, not a bodyguard.'

'Would you do it if I paid you more?'

'Probably not. I'm not much of a fighter.'

'You're half my age and you grew up here. I have a feeling you'd do much better in a fistfight than I would.'

'Then don't fight him. Wave your hand at him,' Eladio said and snapped his mouth shut.

Idiot, what was he thinking bringing that up. Honestly!

'Wave my what?'

Artema looked intrigued rather than angry, which was a relief to Eladio.

'Your hand,' Eladio said, and wondered how explicit he dared get. 'Do what you did to the security guard at the elevator.'

'Do what I did to the security guard?' Artema said, and now she looked... amused. 'What do you think I did?'

'I don't know, but he was all bug eyed about you till that moment. Do the same thing to this pick pocket and take your things back.'

'Let's find this man first, shall we?'

'There,' Eladio said and slowed down as he approached the spot near the gang tag. 'On the right, in the shadow below that overhead pipe.'

'If I look at him, he'll spot us and run, won't he?'

'Give me a second. I'll go around the back. You just go straight for him. That way if he runs, he'll run into me.'

'Alright, go ahead,' Artema said.

Eladio slipped off down a side street thinking that Artema was indeed one cool cookie and wondered what gave her the confidence. He worked his way around a square till he could see the back of their pick pocket. Artema was heading straight for him and as expected, the man spotted her and turned to run.

'Oh no you don't,' Eladio said and held out his arms to block the path.

'Damn right you don't!'

With a flash of light, a baton appeared in Artema's hand. She flicked her wrist, and it extended to a half metre and she clobbered the pick pocket over the head. The man grunted and fell to the floor.

'That was unexpected,' Eladio said, looking up and down the alley to make sure they were alone.

'Sometimes violence is the best way,' Artema said as she riffled through the man's pockets. She pulled out several tightly rolled wedges of cash and finally a roll that was thicker than any of the others. That turned out to be twenty-nine imps, along with her phone amongst a stash of other phones. 'What do we do with the rest?'

'Leave it,' Eladio said. 'The gang who runs this pickpocket won't be happy he's been mugged, so we'd do well to clear out now.'

'The gang?'

'Yeah, look at his shirt. He's got their tag drawn on it. You can't do that unless you're officially sanctioned.'

'Shouldn't we call the polico?'

'The what?' Eladio said, walking away as briskly as he could.

'The polico, you know, the law.'

'There's no polico down here.'

'No polico? None at all? Not even a station they don't venture out of?'

'There's nothing. I told you, we don't count down here.'

'So the only ones who maintain law and order in the suburbo are the gangs?' Artema said.

At least she was hurrying after Eladio as quickly as she ought.

'I'm afraid so. That is, unless you are a policano?'

'Me?' Artema said and stopped.

'Keep going,' Eladio said over his shoulder and didn't slow down.

'What makes you think I'm a policano?'

'You have a baton. Not that you had it before. Where did it come from?'

'Where do you think?' Artema said and stopped again.

This time Eladio did too. The lane they were in was a quiet one, and they were probably far enough away from the pickpocket too. He gathered his thoughts and his courage, and then he took the plunge.

'I don't know where it came from. But things don't just pop out of thin air in a flash of light.'

'What colour was the light?'

That question threw Eladio, and he realised Artema did this kind of thing all the time. She kept asking unexpected questions.

'It's kind of golden.'

'Ha… so you saw that.'

'Why wouldn't I?'

'Because most people don't.'

Eladio wondered how she knew that.

'So you're not denying you didn't have the baton on you before?'

'It would be pointless, wouldn't it? You know everything I had on me because you watched me dress.'

'So where did it come from?'

'A little pocket universe I use for storing a few key items.'

And there they had it, Eladio thought, blinking at Artema in surprise. She didn't even bother to deny or hide things.

But instead of the million questions that occurred to him in that instant, he simply said, 'A pocket universe? Physics, not magic?'

'One and the same thing really,' Artema said.

'So…' This was beyond all Eladio's expectations and thus difficult to grapple with. 'Are you a magisto?'

Artema shrugged and said, 'If you already suspect it, I suppose it's pointless to deny. Especially as you appear to add things up as you go along.'

'You're really a magisto?'

'As real as we get.'

'From the University of Magic?'

'The one and only.'

'In the supraurbo?'

'I'm afraid so.'

'No way!' Eladio breathed and felt like his eyes might bulge right out. 'There is no way.'

'Why not?'

'You... you lot never leave the supraurbo.'

'I'm afraid that's mostly true. And that may have been a very grave mistake.'

'What are you doing here?'

'That is a rather long conversation and one best not held here.'

Eladio wondered how dangerous it was to know someone from the supraurbo, never mind a magisto. The very idea made him feel dizzy.

'Oh man, if people find out where you're from we'll be in so much trouble.'

'Would it help if I said I have kung fu master type skills to keep us safe?' Artema said, giving Eladio a wry smile.

'I'm not sure.'

'Why not?'

'Because there are millions of people here. Could you keep a million people off your back?'

'That all depends on how I do it.'

Eladio stared at the Artema, trying to understand. She looked like an ordinary woman in ill-fitting clothes with a beanie pulled so low down her face it nearly covered her eyes.

He might have said more, but his phone gave a discreet beep and the screen lit up.

'I have to go to work.'

'The coffee shop?'

'Of course.'

'Can't you postpone?'

'No, Doreen won't have time to arrange cover now.'

Either way, Eladio thought, he needed some time away from Artema so that he could process everything he'd learned and decide what he did next. He couldn't help but feel it was foolishly dangerous to stick with her. His change of heart would amuse Felicha, that was for sure.

'Can't you take a few days off? I don't see how you can be up with me all day and then work all night,' Artema said having to do the occasional skip like run to keep up with Eladio who'd decided getting away was the most sensible option.

'I don't have a choice. I'll take a nap in the elevator.'

'That isn't very sustainable.'

'Well... how long is your job going to last?' Eladio said, adding up the hours he'd already spent with Artema and the amount of money he'd earned. It was a breathtaking sum and gave him pause.

'I have a feeling it will be longer than I expected,' Artema said. 'At this point I don't know how long.'

'I can ask Doreen for a couple of days, I suppose.'

A couple of days would be alright, wouldn't it? Eladio thought. He'd make a tidy sum and have a chance to dig some more information out of Artema who was simultaneously fascinating and terrifying.

'She must owe you some holiday time,' Artema said, still working on convincing him. 'Haven't you got that at least?'

'I suppose so.'

'Have you never taken it?'

'What would I do with time off?' Eladio said and headed towards home. He had to pick up his clean clothes. After that, it was off to the baths. A day spent wandering around the suburbo had left him damp and sweaty. 'Do the expenses you mentioned cover laundry?'

'If you wish, why?'

'Because my clothes get dirtier quicker down here if I'm walking around with you.'

'Fair enough,' Artema said. 'But then I must insist you take time off, so we don't have to interrupt our work.'

'I'll try,' Eladio said.

'Do that and let's hurry. I'm suddenly hungry and could use some food. Not down here, and probably a bed somewhere. I'll take a nap while you work.'

Artema left Eladio at the cafe door after buying them both a dinner of a takeaway sandwich. Then she tumbled into an aerocab and ordered it to get her to the elevator terminal up to the supraurbo. It was annoying, but not surprising, that the elevator from the suburbo didn't continue upwards. Heaven forbid they actually connected.

What did people think would happen? Did they worry the inferior denizens of the suburbo would somehow find their way into the pristine space of the supraurbo? Would that even be such a bad thing?

She laughed at herself for having the thought. One day in the Stygian blackness of the suburbo had already turned her into a radical. Eladio was having a remarkable effect on her.

She wondered whether she was having a similarly formative effect on the young man. What were his prejudices about the supers? They must be pretty extraordinary considering how hard Eladio found it to wrap his head around meeting someone from the supraurbo.

After polishing off her sandwich, Artema dozed in the elevator. It was a long way up, but at least her elevator was brand spanking new and so clean it sparkled. It was covered in a veneer of pearlescent white plastic, and there were sufficient seating to easily accommodate the half-dozen people currently taking a ride.

Even better was that the seats were wide and comfortably upholstered. It easy to lean back and ignore the sideways glances she was getting from the other passengers. Maybe she should have changed back into her supraurbo clothes after all. She'd just felt too tired to do so.

Artema took the elevator right to the university, which was at one of the highest points of the supraurbo. As she stepped out of the security checks for this top terminus and looked up, all she could see above her was the sky, currently coloured in the deeper shades of sunset. She breathed a deep sigh of relief to no longer have buildings looming over her.

'Ma'am... I say ma'am!' an agitated voice said. Artema turned to find the vice chancellor trailing a couple of beadles, making a beeline for her. All of them were in the process of conjuring a spell.

'Hello, Normando,' Artema said and stuck her hands in her pockets. It was impossible, or near it, to cast a spell with your hands in this position. Partly she was signalling that she wasn't a threat and partly she was affecting nonchalance.

'Artema?' Normando said, and his fast waddle slowed to its usual glide. 'Bona Sinjoro, is that really you?'

'It is indeed,' Artema said, and realised that everyone was staring at her. She stood in the great quadrangle of the university that was encircled by classically styled Roman buildings. It was one of the busiest places at the university, as so many lecture halls opened out onto the quad. Several student eateries and bars took up the lower levels, but all the same it looked empty compared to the suburbo. Everyone was also staring at her. All those well fed, well groomed, confident students.

'Ah, it's the beanie, isn't it?' she said and pulled the cap off. 'It is somewhat hideous.'

'Hideous? It looks like you lost a fight with an ancient ball of wool and it half consumed your head.'

'I'll have you know this beanie cost me the princely sum of one imp.'

'What are you talking about?'

'They call the imperial dolaro an imp in the suburbo.'

'So why is a single dolaro a princely sum?'

'Not only a princely sum but daylight robbery,' Artema said, enjoying herself.

'You aren't making any sense,' Normando snapped. 'Were you injured? Did they mug you? You must have suffered a blow to the head.'

'I'm fine, nothing a bit of sleep won't cure at any rate.'

'But why are you dressed like a tramp?'

'Why else? To blend in with the locals, of course. My guide informed me I would cause a riot if I went down to the suburbo dressed in my usual clothes.'

'But you told me you were going to dress down,' Normando said back to looking confused.

'As far down as you see now?'

Artema set off for her house, giving a nod to the two beadles, Riviera and Vulpo, as she passed by them. They'd been listening to the conversation with appreciative grins.

'Well, no. I mean, I thought a tramp had ventured onto our campus,' Normando said.

'No chance of that happening, especially without the necessary paperwork.'

'I suppose you're right.'

'I am right.'

'Always so certain,' the vice chancellor said with a sigh. 'So I assume, as you've returned unharmed, that you got into the suburbo and back out with no difficulty.'

'Thanks to my guide, yes. He has been remarkably useful. I doubt I'd have achieved much without him.'

'Really? He wasn't... dreadfully uncouth.'

'Not at all. He's extremely polite, in fact.'

'Not violent?'

'Quite the opposite,' Artema said, and smothered a twinge of irritation over the vice chancellor's assumptions.

'Some sort of paragon of virtue, huh?'

'No need to get snippy. I found what I suppose travellers to foreign lands often discover. That their preconceptions of the natives are wrong and, surprise, surprise, they're actually more like us than we realised.'

'No, you have suffered a blow to your head.'

'I'm fine,' Artema said and waved her hand to open the laboratory door. 'You'd best come inside because I discovered something to be concerned about.'

'You found something?' Normando said and stopped looking peeved.

Artema had to give him credit for that. He could be infuriatingly self absorbed and obsessed with the reputation of the university. But if something really important happened, he paid proper attention.

Artema pulled out the ancient phone she'd bought for the suburbo and said, 'Good evening AI, I have some new data for you.' She flicked across all the photos she'd taken during the day and said, 'Asses these.'

'Yes, master,' the AI said, which got an impatient tut from the vice chancellor.

Artema smiled at him and waved her hand with the gesture to call her photos up on the big projecting screen. 'Look at this,' she said, and opened up the image of the Black Brotherhood's gang tag.

Normando squinted as he leaned forward. 'What is this? Some sort of... Bona Sinjoro, demon icons!'

'Exactly,' Artema said. 'Now look at this blue tag and this green one and this red one.'

'All different, but all with demon icons.'

'Each of those images represents a different gang in the suburbo,' Artema said. 'So far I have found the tags for the Black Brotherhood, Green Dragons, River Guardians, Red Fists and Yellow Peril.'

'The Yellow Peril? Really?'

'I know, but according to my guide, they are all dangerous and not to be messed with, so the name makes sense. I doubt they know sufficient history to understand where their name came from.'

'I don't understand,' Normando said and conjured a chair which he sank into.

Artema wanted to laugh that he'd taken matters into his own hands when it came to sitting.

Instead, she pulled up the other chair settled opposite the vice chancellor and said, 'It's worse than I've told you so far. All these tags glow with inner power, and there isn't just one tag per gang. They go around like dogs, pissing on every post they pass. They mark everything they own.

'I photographed hundreds of these tags in just a day of walking around. In the whole suburbo there could be thousands if not millions of these magically active tags.'

'This is terrible. How could we not be aware of this happening in our own city? Surely the combined energy of all that magic would have been self evident to us?'

'Apparently not.'

'Why not?'

'That is a good question and one I am working on solving.'

Artema contemplated getting up to get her staff to bring her and Normando some food. She couldn't muster up the energy now that she was seated, so sent a message via her phone while Normando sat opposite her looking increasingly worried.

'You do need more help now. If there are so many demon markings around in the suburbo, you should take a group of beadles with you and—'

'Not yet.' Despite her growing sense of unease, Artema wasn't willing to go in mob handed. 'All I've seen so far is this one indication of demonic activity. I don't know what it means or how these tags are being used. It would be best to proceed with caution and be as inconspicuous as possible.'

'You want to stick with using your guide?'

'He talked me out of going to see the gangs straight away, and I'm beginning to think he's right. We shouldn't be arrogant and just barge in with our own people. We need to work with subtlety and find out what they're up to before they realise we're down there.'

'You like him.'

'I suppose I do. He's different to what I expected.'

'His looks have beguiled you.'

'They so easily could,' Artema murmured, despite the fact that Eladio was a man. 'But no, it isn't that. He's very sensitive, always on the alert and nervous about me.'

'You do give off a... an unsettling air.'

'Too much contact with hell and demons does that to a person. But there's more to Eladio.' Artema wondered whether she should tell Normando about him. Maybe, but first she had to lay some groundwork. 'The people of the suburbo, are not what we think.'

'In what way?'

'We think they're coarse and stupid. But what I discovered... a lot of them are actually afraid.'

'They're scared, what are they scared of?'

'Falling off the cliff,' Artema said, and got a blank stare from the vice chancellor. 'They are extremely poor. Even a single dolaro has value to them. They are all just one step from disaster. I met a man down there who hadn't eaten in days and for all I know has nowhere to live either. They're all one misfortune, one accident away from being where that man is. They live in a place with no light, poor food and no safety net, surrounded by gangs. I have never met a people more cautious than them.'

'It sounds grim.'

Artema nodded agreement and waited because Chico, her butler, had arrived carrying a tray of delicious looking finger food, a jug of lemonade and two elegant carved crystal goblets. He bowed low as if to offer the tray, balanced on one upturned hand, to Artema. But as he did so, the tray sprouted legs, and Chico straightened up and gave Artema an enquiring glance.

She understood and shook her head to signal that she didn't want anything more. The butler bowed and left as silently as he'd arrived.

'It is grim down there,' Artema said as she popped a

beautiful canape that looked like a miniature salad into her mouth. 'It's a lot worse than our caricature of brutish, stupid thugs who get what they deserve.

'It's easier to ignore them under those circumstances. But what I saw... They kicked my guide out of school and the only home he'd ever known at thirteen. He had no family to support him. He had no tradition like ours that stretches back hundreds of years and gives us wealth and status.

'I wonder how many days he went without food before he got his job as a street sweeper. And yet, despite his disadvantages, he saved up money to get a job in the mezaurbo. That must have taken serious discipline. He doesn't see it that way, though. He just thinks he's doing what needs to be done.'

'He sounds like a paragon,' Normando said, temporarily diverted by the food and therefore giving Artema less of his attention as his fingers hovered between a bite sized hamburger and a glossy mini quiche.

'More than you know, because he can see magic.'

There was silence, and Artema watched the vice chancellor. For a while it looked like he hadn't heard or understood.

'He what?' Normando said, pausing midway towards the hamburger.

'He told me the gang tags glow. Something even I can't see with the naked eye. And later, when... well, I pulled my baton out of my pocket universe and he saw it appear in a flash of golden light.'

'Are you sure?'

'He described it unprompted. I think that was what made him realise I'm a magisto. To be fair, he already had his suspicions because he'd spotted some of my gestures.'

'He put it all together himself? You weren't bragging and let something slip?'

'Believe me, I was far too tired, and then worried about the gang tags to be trying to win anyone over. And he's too aware of status to even consider me as a friend, never mind anything more than that. At this point his mind is officially blown just to have met somebody from the supraurbo. Everything else is being processed. I haven't told him I'm a blue blood as well. I think that would make him walk away and I still need him.'

'He'd abandon you if he knew you were a blue blood? Preposterous!' Normando said, popped the hamburger into his mouth and chewed strenuously.

'You think status is important to us, but it seems to be even more so to the suburbonites.' Artema poured herself a lemonade and allowed the tinkling of the ice cubes against the crystal to provide a moment of calming distraction. 'We don't interact with them because we think they're beneath us. They have nothing interesting to say and are, well, thick. But if we wanted to interact with them, we would, and we'd be astonished if anyone told us we couldn't.

'On the other hand, suburbonites seem to believe they are not worthy and that they have no right to speak to us. I suspect they'd be intimidated, even afraid, if we forced them into a social interaction. They are more constrained. Maybe that's why they seem stupid to us, they're holding their tongues lest they offend.'

'Dear, dear, dear,' Normando said, shaking his head while pouring himself a drink. 'Your trip has changed you. Those low-lives have really got to you.'

'So much so that your little jibe calling them low-lives has offended me.' Artema tipped back the last of her lemonade and stood up. 'Now, my dear fellow, I will leave the AI to churn through my new data and I'm going to bed. I've been up for 48 hours and if I'm going to accomplish much tomorrow, I need some sleep.'

4

'I have until Monday night,' Eladio said in reply to Artema's question about whether he'd managed to get time off.

She'd asked the moment he'd stepped out of the shop without even bothering with a greeting. Was that because her own concerns about whatever it was she was after in the suburbo absorbed her?

Eladio had spent the night considering their day of roaming and come to no firm conclusion on what he thought of the matter, which was unusual for him. So now he looked the magisto up and down, struck by how ordinary she looked, which was difficult to square with what he knew.

'Only until Monday night?' Artema said. 'This Monday? Three nights from now?'

'It's all she would give me, and even then she was grumbling about having to find cover, because weekend evenings are the busiest.'

Eladio wondered what the last few commuters that passed by on the piazza, most likely running late, would think of them if they only knew they were ignoring a stranger pair of people than they could ever guess at.

'But you've worked for her for three and a half years without taking time off, haven't you?'

'I have taken one or two days off when I've had things I need to do. I had already booked Sunday night off.'

Eladio wondered whether he should just start walking.

All he did in the end was to move away from the cafe door to allow a rushing commuter access to her urgently needed coffee.

'You'd already taken Sunday off, why's that?' Artema said.

'To take my exams.'

It annoyed Eladio that people didn't remember the things he told them. He always had to remind himself that few had his perfect memory.

Artema looked blank for a moment, then she said, 'The matric exams?'

'Yes,' Eladio said and started moving toward the elevators.

'They're on Monday, aren't they?' Artema said, following along.

'They start at nine am.'

'I don't suppose you could skip them, maybe take them later?'

'Skip them?' Eladio had been afraid he'd get this kind of reaction but this was something he wouldn't budge on. 'I've waited seven years to take these exams. I've saved and studied and worked really hard. I can't wait another year.'

'You'd have to wait a year?'

'They only hold them once a year.'

'I see,' Artema said and stopped to examine him.

Eladio held her gaze. The extra money he was making was beyond all he could imagine, and very welcome, but if it meant postponing his exams, he couldn't do it.

Thankfully, Artema nodded and said, 'Well then, let's pray my work is done before Monday. I hope you won't also need extra time off to study.'

'I've finished my studying,' Eladio said. At least that was

something he didn't have to worry about.

'You've finished? You're a student who, a few days before the exams, is confident enough not to be hitting the books right up to the deadline?'

'I told you I have a perfect memory.' Eladio wondered whether it was wise in the first place to have told Artema that, and secondly to remind her of it. 'I finished studying for the matric two years ago. How long will you still need me, anyway?'

'I'm not sure,' Artema said, giving Eladio a thoughtful look that made him feel distinctly uncomfortable. 'There are a few things I need to explain to you and that's best done up here, away from gang ears. Preferably out of hearing of anyone else, too. Maybe you can take me somewhere noisy for breakfast, a restaurant with music should do the trick.'

'A proper restaurant? Not just a cafe?' Eladio said and considered the route to the elevator. It was pretty much all he knew of the mezaurbo.

'We might as well have a slap up meal before we head into the dark again, and your shift makes this dinner time, doesn't it? I mean, you've finished a long stretch at work and, under normal circumstances, you'd be heading for bed right now.'

'Yes.'

'So let's have dinner. I wouldn't mind a steak.'

'A steak?' Eladio said and wondered how it had happened that he'd landed up with this woman. He'd never had a steak before. Aside from shelling out for a hamburger when he'd first come to the mezaurbo, he'd never had beef. To end up going for a steak, as if it was a commonplace...

'I know somewhere. I'm not sure you'll like it, but Maeve says it does the best steaks in the mezaurbo.'

'Sounds good. Who's Maeve?'

'One of the girls at Doreen's. She's a goth. She says it's a very ancient tradition. Anyway, she often goes out clubbing all night and then arrives for the morning shift. She goes to this place for a meal before coming to work,' Eladio said, and headed towards the restaurant.

He'd mentally filed the information after Maeve had mentioned it. He had no idea why, because he'd never expected to be able to eat there.

The exterior was typical of a mezaurbo restaurant. It had an outside terrace ringed about by a low potted privet hedge. The plate-glass window was painted black with a gigantic ox skeleton with massive horns and the name in a white skeletal font, Breathe Between Bites.

'It certainly looks interesting,' Artema said as she pushed her way in.

The place was half filled with people dressed predominantly in black with interestingly pale faces, black lipstick and smoky black eyes. Rather solemn music blared out from speakers placed above each booth.

Eladio looked enquiringly at Artema, who shrugged and said, 'It will do. It's strangely appropriate, really.'

'Is it?' The staff gave them a surprised look, and Eladio muttered, 'I don't think we're dressed right.'

'I'm not,' Artema said. 'But I reckon you fit right in with your black clothes, pale face and romantic looks.'

Eladio didn't know what to say to that and was glad that Artema just smiled at him. Then she turned to the waiter.

'Table for two, preferably a booth by the window.'

The waiter bowed and headed into the depths of the restaurant and stopped at a table with a spectacular view of the city. Skyscrapers soared upwards into the clouds and disappeared downwards into a network of crosswalks and roads. Aerocars zoomed past so close by that Eladio could see the passenger's faces.

'Order via phone,' the waiter said and wandered away.

In the booth opposite, a couple were sitting side my side making out energetically.

Eladio grinned at Artema who said, 'Their steak better be worth it.'

'Why the window?' Eladio asked.

'Because I want as much daylight as I can get before we go down,' Artema said and gestured with her finger.

'Alright.'

'Don't you find it difficult spending all your time in darkness?'

'I grew up that way, so I guess I don't mind. The first time I saw the sun, I was sixteen.'

'When you came to the mezaurbo?'

'Yes.'

'What did you think?'

'It hurt my eyes.'

'And after that?'

'I like it. It's why I enjoy working at Doreen's.'

'Considering that Doreen sounds like a miser, it's probably the only good thing about working for her.'

'She's just making ends meet,' Eladio said, surprised by Artema's condemnatory tone and his quick defence of his boss. 'It's tough being in the food business.'

'Is that what Doreen tells you?'

'Yes.'

'And you believe her?'

'She doesn't look rich, and she works in the shop every day too.'

'Fair enough,' Artema said with a shrug, then called up the menu. 'I believe I'll have the steak, egg and chips. You can have whatever you want. You don't have to order the same.'

That gave Eladio a dilemma. He didn't know what he wanted, or what his boss would allow. Although, to be fair to Artema, she'd not actually said no to anything yet. He wasn't about to test her now though and went for steak and sweet potato fries. It was slightly cheaper than with the egg. He was curious about sweet potato, too.

'Alright, now,' Artema said and leaned forward. 'I need to explain what I found yesterday and why it's important.'

'The gang tags?'

'Indeed. The thing is Eladio... the thing is, they aren't only gang tags.'

'They aren't?' Eladio said and shifted uncomfortably. He wasn't sure he wanted to know more about gangs and their business, especially when it made Artema look nervous.

'You know about angels and demons, don't you?'

'They came down to earth and fought a titanic battle. Yeah, I read about it in my history studies.'

'The current scientific opinion is that they're beings from two different dimensions. We think they intersect with our dimension. The demon dimension does anyway.'

'Hell?'

'That's what we call it.'

'What about Heaven?'

'We're less sure about that. You see... humans have been able to interact with Hell and its occupants for millennia. The same can't be said for Heaven.'

'It can't?'

'For example, there are demonologists, people who study

and use demons. They have been around since... well, since before the middle ages. But there is no such thing as an angelologist, is there?'

'There isn't?'

'Never has been,' Artema said. 'We theorise the angel dimension is either further away or harder to access or both.'

'But they turned up here.'

This was the strangest conversation Eladio had ever had. The whole angel demon thing was so far removed from his daily existence that he'd barely paid it much attention when he'd learned about it at school. Now Artema was going on about it like it was really important.

'It may have been a case of convergence,' Artema said. 'Much like the stars and planets drift in and out of alignment and are sometimes closer and sometimes further away. We think the same happens with dimensions. We think all three dimensions must have lined up perfectly when we had the Great Inter-Plane War.'

'But Heaven is out of alignment more?'

'That's the theory. Either way, it's Hell we have to worry about.'

'Because demons are less trustworthy than angels?' Eladio said and wanted to laugh to even be giving his opinion.

'Who can tell? Angels appear less interested in us. Then again, they didn't seem particularly worried about human lives when they landed en mass to battle the demons.'

'Oh.'

'What I'm trying to say,' Artema said, 'Is that we deal with demons or rather, we have to work harder to keep demons out of our plane.'

'Do you think they're in the suburbo?' Eladio said, sinking his voice to ensure they weren't heard.

The loved up couple had switched to eating an ice cream sundae, feeding each other with long-handled spoons from the single fancy bowl. They were oblivious to everyone else around them. None of the other tables near them were occupied.

'I don't know for sure, but you see these symbols in the gang tags?' Artema said and pointed to a set of three wavy lines stacked up one above the other and another of a circle with a star in it.

'Yes,' Eladio said. 'They're patterns.'

'They're demon icons. That's what makes the tags glow. The icons power the tags.'

'Power them to do what?'

'That's what I don't know yet.'

'So,' Eladio said, trying to wrap his head around all this fantastical information. 'Are you saying that the gangs are involved with demons?'

'It looks that way.' Artema snapped her phone shut as the waiter arrived carrying two plates, the size of trays, loaded with food. 'I don't know about the quality yet, but this place certainly majors on quantity.'

Eladio had no words for what he was looking at as the waiter put his food down in front of him. This was enough to feed a family in the suburbo. He felt guilty about having it all to himself, then pushed that away. He would have to savour this. It was something he could remember forever, even after this strange job was over.

He didn't even think hearing about demons would spoil it for him. Despite Artema's obvious concern, demons were like mythical beings. Kind of like magistos and people from the supraurbo, he thought with a laugh and looked up at Artema. She was tucking into her steak and didn't notice.

'This is just what we need to get us through the day,' Artema said. 'A good, robust meal. Your friend didn't steer you wrong.'

Eladio nodded, his mouth was too full to say anything. He intended to eat till his sides hurt. This was delicious.

Halfway through the meal, they both started to struggle and Artema said, 'Everything I've told you must be kept strictly secret, you understand?'

'Yes, ma'am.' Eladio couldn't imagine who he'd tell, or them believing him anyway. He certainly didn't want the gangs knowing that he knew anything more than he ought about them. 'So what do you want to do next?'

'Yesterday I was finding out how many gangs are using demon icons. Today I want to focus on the Black Brotherhood. I need to find every one of their tags.'

'What will you do with that?'

With the multitude of tags around the suburbo, there was no way Artema would get around all of them within the next three days. Eladio also worried that the Black Brotherhood would take note if they were only looking at their tags.

'I will record their geolocation to feed into my AI and–' Artema stopped because Eladio had dropped his knife.

'You have an AI?' Eladio said, stunned by the revelation.

He ducked down and scrabbled on the floor for his knife and to gain some time to recompose himself to look as calm as Artema.

'Yes, I do.'

'An actual AI?'

'My boy, I've been talking to you about demons and

you're more stunned that I have an AI?'

'Do you know how much they cost?' Eladio asked, even though he didn't have the faintest idea himself.

He guessed it was in the millions, though.

'A lot, I imagine. But we've had this AI in my family for generations. Ever since the first AIs were developed.'

'So it's an old model?'

'Top of the range, actually. We give it an upgrade every time one comes out. It started off as a set of circuits and flashing lights way back in the twenty-first century. Nowadays it's got a rather fetching holo-projection of a face, so it speaks to us.'

Eladio was lost for words and just blinked at Artema. How rich was this woman?

'The AI will analyse the tags positions' and hopefully give us an idea of what the tags are being used for,' Artema said. 'Because at the moment all the demon icons seem to do is power each tag, and that doesn't make sense.'

'Is that what you were looking for all along?'

'I am assuming so. I gather data all the time to track demon activity around the globe. It surprised me when I got a probability spike in the suburbo.'

'A probability spike?'

'Demons, like people, act in certain, predictable ways. I keep track of activity on earth by inputting all the data of events, social media reports, news, weather patterns, parties, pretty much everything that's happening. Certain patterns within the usual hum of human life are not natural to us. They're caused by demon interference.'

'Patterns like what?' Eladio said, and despite his determination to eat himself to death, he found himself distracted by Artema's unsettling information.

'Like a politician who comes from nowhere and makes it to be a leader. Or a film star who has too many lucky breaks. Or a person who is suddenly more ostentations and throwing more parties than they used to.'

'Because they've made a deal with the devil?' Eladio said and felt stupid asking the question.

Who made deals with the devil?

'Let's just say it's often facilitated by a demon's intervention. They'll vanish opponents, or trick them into doing something stupid. They'll beguile influential people who can smooth the path of their protegé, or boost their natural talents. Usually it's one demon working with one person. They set them up for success at whatever the person wants, fame, fortune, power, the stuff you would expect.'

'Why do they do that? Why help humans if they don't like them? Are they doing this so they can get the person's soul?'

'Probably not. We have no evidence of souls in people. Current thinking is that the demons are manipulating people for the fun of building someone up. Mainly, I suspect, for the sheer bloody enjoyment of the fall. Nobody who is helped to succeed by a demon gets to enjoy their triumph for very long.'

'So they aren't working on world domination?'

'For them, it's probably entertainment. We can find no evidence of them building a network of human allies that they work with. I doubt they could contain their disgust for us long enough to build anything particularly lasting.'

'That all just sounds insane,' Eladio said. Worse than that, it was actually putting him off his meal. 'How would you even land up being helped by a demon? I mean, does anyone actually call them up?'

'Not usually. People in their hour of need or distress are

more likely to call upon god or heaven. Very few people actually call upon demons. Even now that we know they exist. Those people who've done deals with devils, that I've been able to speak to, almost all reported that the demon appeared out of nowhere and made them an offer.'

'Do you think they've done the same thing to the gangs?' Eladio asked, even though he was certain he didn't want to hear the answer.

'That's what I have to find out.'

'But you think whatever is going on is big.'

'I'm afraid it could be huge, especially if one or more demons have got their claws into every single gang in the suburbo.'

'How come you didn't spot it sooner?' Eladio asked and felt a familiar surge of anger.

Through disaster, fire, plague and famine, the rest of the city behaved as if the suburbo didn't exist.

'Because we ignore the suburbo, I'm sorry to say,' Artema said, confirming what Eladio already knew. 'There are fewer movers and shakers and less data generated by the poor. The result being that it wasn't being noted by my AI.'

'So... you use statistics, not magic to track down demons?'

'Pretty much, yes.'

'And then? What do you do when you find a demon?'

'I destroy it.'

'Using magic?'

'Mainly using very advanced physics.'

'Is there no such thing as magic?'

'It's a fine line, my boy. My little joke is we use statistics to find demons and physics to deal with them. It upsets my students, who like to think magic is an art. But I liked your analogy of mathematics as a language. Physics, especially the advanced physics I use, it's... magical in its sophistication.'

'But we've had magic far longer than we've understood advanced physics, haven't we?' Eladio said, trying to wrap his head around all this new information.

'For some reason our ancestors could conjure advanced physical effects with certain gestures that became codified and called magic. As science progressed, we discovered that the two fields were converging. More and more we could use physics and physiology to describe what we do. Science hasn't caught up completely, however. Some magic is still unexplained. We dedicate entire university departments to eradicating the gap, but we have some way to go.'

'I see,' Eladio murmured, but he didn't and that wasn't usual for him.

He would have to trawl the interreto for more information about magic to see if he could understand it better. That nearly made him laugh. Never in his life had he thought magic was interesting or useful, let alone something he wanted to investigate.

'I assume we're going to collect your laundry?' Artema said once they'd cleared the security checks in the elevator terminal of the suburbo. She was trying for a light, unconcerned tone of voice that definitely didn't give away how depressed she felt to be back down in the dark, whispering depths of the suburbo. She also definitely didn't want Eladio picking up on her increasing concern about the gang tags and her fear that time was running out.

'If we don't, Felicha will sell my clothes.'

'Would she really do that?' Artema said. 'It seems like a counterproductive business strategy.'

'It gets people to pick their clothes up on time,' Eladio said as they threaded their way through the mass of people heading towards the elevator.

Artema assumed they were all day labourers if their dress and the state of their hands was anything to go by. It seemed very few of them did the genteel work that Eladio had found. It marked him, yet again, as different to his fellows.

'Considering how Felicha looks, I doubt getting people to turn up for their laundry would be hard.' Artema's words caused Eladio to stop and give her a thoughtful look that prompted her to say, 'What is it now?'

'Nothing,' Eladio said with a shrug and went back to walking, weaving past the people.

'Don't give me that. I may only have met you yesterday, but I have already realised that you work things out pretty quickly. What do you think you know?'

'Do you fancy Felicha?'

A laugh was surprised out of Artema and she said, 'What made you think that?'

'You look at women more.'

'So you went straight for me being gay, did you? Not the way I'm dressed and groomed, not my mannerisms, just that I look at women more.'

'If I was wrong, I apologise.'

'There's no need to apologise, you are right. Not that it should embarrass me. Unless I'm misreading the values of suburbonites again.'

'No, it doesn't bother us,' Eladio said. 'As long as it doesn't cost us money, people can do what they like.'

'I am relieved to hear that.'

Artema was struck, once again, with how important money was down here. It was important anywhere, sure. Her peers in the supraurbo also obsessed about money. But it wasn't a life or death matter for them, much as they might think it.

Eladio turned into the narrower lane Artema recognised from the day before and then into the square with Felicha's laundry. That was possibly too grand a name for it. The stall looked like she'd built it from whatever pieces of salvaged metal and wood she'd been able to scavenge. She stood like some proud Amazon at her counter as she watched them cross the square.

'So one day wasn't risky enough for you, huh?' she said to Eladio, pointedly ignoring Artema.

'I'll be fine,' Eladio said, and looked expectantly at Artema.

She realised it was because she had to pay and tried to hand over the money as surreptitiously as a local. Felicha tutted and snatched away the wedge of cash Artema pulled out of her pocket. Felicha stuffed it into her own and held out a slightly smaller wedge of money that Artema hurriedly pocketed. She assumed, although she couldn't see how, that Felicha had given her the right amount of change.

'Are you sure she's alright?' Felicha said. Eladio smiled at her, and she shook her head. 'It's too risky. You always take too many risks. You think your gift will protect you, but one day you'll come short.'

'If I do, you'll have to save me,' Eladio said and his smile widened.

'What rubbish.' Felicha reached under her counter for Eladio's bundle of clothes and said, 'Go, I don't need troublemakers here.'

'Thanks, Felicha,' Eladio said, scooped up his clothes and headed away.

'What did she mean by your gift?' Artema said, adding the strange conversation to the list she'd started making on Eladio.

'What do you think?'

'You are getting comfortable with me, aren't you?' Artema said and noted that it turned Eladio's danger radar on. It looked like he was about to apologise, so Artema headed him off. 'I assume it's your picture perfect memory.'

'The memory is only one part. Any recording device can spew back everything it's seen without having to understand it. I can make connections and assumptions. I can figure things out. That's my real gift.'

'You certainly figured me out faster than anyone I've ever met. I have a couple of acquaintances who've known me for years and still don't know what I am,' Artema said. 'Does Felicha have a special power too?'

'Why do you ask?' Eladio said, turning wide innocent eyes on Artema.

'How else could she rescue you?'

'She's strong, and very tough.'

'By which I assume strong and tough are different things,' Artema said, curious as to why Eladio relaxed enough to give her this information.

'If you hit her, it doesn't hurt. And if you try to stab her, it's very hard to get through her skin.'

'Literally tough,' Artema murmured. 'Well, well.'

'She's needed it.'

'Why?'

'Because, like you said, she's beautiful and down here... a

girl without family...'

'Men go for her?'

'All the time. No matter how strong or tough you are, sometimes you get overwhelmed.'

'Which is why she's cultivated her no nonsense demeanour.'

'That and she destroyed every man who ever got the better of her. Not immediately, but men know, they would have to kill her after they had their way with her, because she will come for them. Some place and time when they're alone and then...' Eladio shook his head.

'Bonan doloron,' Artema murmured while wondering whether Eladio might have helped on some of the revenge getting. 'It really is the law of the jungle down here.'

'It's the only way she can keep herself safe,' Eladio said and nodded a hello as he passed Benito.

'Are we not giving him the food?' Artema said of the huge stash of steak and chips Eladio had tucked under his jacket.

'No, it's too much food for just one person. Besides, then he'd owe a massive debt, and he'd never be able to repay me.'

'So what do you want to do with today's doggy bag?'

Eladio stopped beside his container and examined Artema in his weighing up way.

'I thought we might take it to the orphanage.'

'Where you grew up?'

'It will do the kids good to get some protein.'

'Unless there's only a few of them, they'll get little more than a mouthful each.'

'It's better than nothing.' Eladio climbed up to the container, opened it, deposited his clean clothes and shut the place up again. 'Besides, you want to see all the Black

Brotherhood's tags and they've got an especially big one sprayed on the orphanage wall.'

'A big one? Really? I assumed they were all the same size,' Artema said, and her alarm, which she'd been suppressing, gripped her with renewed intensity.

'They have bigger ones on the important buildings they own.'

'And the orphanage is important?'

'The gangs like to brag about the help they provide. It makes the people grateful.'

Eladio set off down the container maze and a path Artema thought they'd not used before, but she couldn't swear to that.

'Where else do they put the larger tags?'

'Their headquarters, the moneylenders, the fire brigades, on the schools and on the... Well they call them hospitals but you really don't want to get treated there.'

'So you do actually have doctors?'

Artema hadn't considered the question before, but she found it hard to believe that the suburbo had the means to train their own doctors and she couldn't see professionals actually choosing to come down from the other levels to work in this hell hole.

'We have a few. Some believe they need to come down here and help.'

'You have no home-grown doctors?' Artema asked for form's sake.

'We barely have an education down here, and the universities mostly won't let suburbonites in. Even if they could scrape together the money needed. So no, we don't have any doctors of our own.'

'That's just crazy.'

'It is how it is,' Eladio said and stepped into another square.

Compared to the others, it was relatively well lit. The base of one building above, that covered the suburbo, was higher than in other places and sloped at an angle so it looked like a pitched roof. Tucked in under the lower end of this space was a long three story building. It had rows of perfectly square windows staring blindly out of the concrete block facade.

Kids spilled out of the door and entertained themselves in the space in the building's front. They were playing games or gathered in knots, chatting. They were dressed in similar clothes to the other residents of the suburbo and were as thin. Artema didn't know why, but she'd expected to see worse.

Painted over the front door was a gang tag about two metres in diameter.

'Does it glow?' Artema asked as she slipped out her phone and took a picture.

'Yeah, brighter than all the others,' Eladio said.

'Not surprising when it has such large demon icons.'

'Does the size make a difference?'

'I'm afraid it does.'

Eladio nodded and went back to examining the building. Then he took a deep breath to fortify himself and said, 'Come on, I'll show you the inside.'

'They'll let you in?'

'They will if I tell them I have a donation,' Eladio said. 'Can that magic of yours do...'

'Do what?'

'If we give the staff the food, even if we say it's for the children, they'll eat it themselves. Is there anything you can do to force them to give it to the children?'

'I believe there is,' Artema said. 'I'll make sure the kids get it.'

'Good.'

Eladio smiled and nodded hello to the children who'd stopped playing to watch as they went past. Then he stepped into the lobby of the orphanage.

Unlike the rest of the building that overflowed with children, this space had no kids. It was nothing but a grey square. The concrete blocks they built it from were neither plastered nor painted, which gave the space a gloomy air.

A fat woman sat at a reception desk, absorbed by something on her phone. She was the first fat person Artema had seen in the suburbo.

'Hello, Maria,' Eladio said.

She looked up and squinted at the two of them. Then recognition dawned.

'Eladio! As I live and breathe, what brings one of The Thirteen back here?'

'I have a donation,' Eladio said and held out his large foil wrapped bag. 'Food for the children,' he added and glanced back at Artema.

She held out her hand as if to shake the receptionist's. As she got close, she cast a suggestibility spell with the twirl of her finger and said, 'The food is only for the children. Misfortune will follow you if anyone else eats it.'

'Of course,' Maria said as she rose to shake hands.

Artema took her hand in a firm grip and drew a triangle on her skin with her thumb. She felt the spell take hold as the receptionist shuddered and let go of her hand.

'For the children, you understand?'

'For the children,' Maria muttered as she took the parcel

from Eladio. Then her face lost its momentary slackness, and she smiled brightly. 'They'll be thrilled to have it.'

'Good,' Eladio said, nodded and started backing out.

'Wait, Eladio,' Maria said. 'Tell me how you've been? You look like you've prospered.'

'I'm fine,' Eladio said stiffly.

Artema wondered what a child would look like if they hadn't prospered because Eladio was thin, pale and dressed in karitato clothes. He had prospered for this place, Artema realised. But in ways that the orphanage staff wouldn't know, and Eladio would not tell.

'You have a job then?' Maria said and stood up.

'Yes,' Eladio said and took a step back.

He didn't like her, Artema realised. Furthermore, this had not been a happy place for Eladio. So it was time for her to come to the rescue.

'We have to go,' she said with a bright smile to the receptionist as she took hold of Eladio's elbow. 'Make sure the children get the food.'

She pulled the young man out through the door and once they got back onto the street, Eladio gave a great sigh of relief.

'You didn't like the place,' Artema said as a statement of fact.

'No,' Eladio said, taking in the children playing all around them and ignoring the adults. 'But I don't think it was any worse than growing up in a family down here. I've seen families and they also struggle to feed their children. They keep them in line with beatings too. So I think it's the suburbo, not really the orphanage.'

'I suppose so. Although in the mezaurbo and the supraurbo it is definitely worse to be brought up in an institution.'

Eladio nodded and said, 'That's done. Now I'll take you around all the tags. I think the easiest way to do this is go to the edge of Brotherhood territory, work our way all around it and then spiral inwards.'

'That sounds reasonable,' Artema said. 'While we walk, you can tell me what the receptionist meant when she called you one of The Thirteen.'

'It's nothing.'

'Young man, never lie to me. I am very good at sniffing out lies. Nobody speaks with such emphasis as the receptionist did, if it's nothing. I mean, I could practically hear her capitalising the words. So it means something.'

5

Eladio sighed in a way that suggested Artema was pushing at boundaries he didn't want to cross.

Nevertheless, as Artema had now come to expect, he said, 'Come on then, I'll explain as we walk.'

He headed into a dark underpass that Artema really didn't like the look of. It was gloomier than the rest of the area, covered in graffiti and so poorly lit as to be almost pitch black. Eladio didn't seem worried by it as he strolled off. Although stroll wasn't the right word. He had a way of walking that looked like a stroll but was brisk.

They emerged from the underpass into another maze like section of container homes. If it wasn't for the fact that she was sure they hadn't doubled back on themselves, Artema might have assumed they were in the area Eladio lived.

'They really are fond of their containers,' she muttered.

'The Brotherhood has a connection with a shipping company. They have a monopoly on container homes.'

'Is this a good thing?'

'The more people you control, the more tax you get.'

'You pay them?'

'Coming and going,' Eladio said. 'I pay them rent and for protection and if I go to the hospital or call out the firefighters, and you don't even want to consider the moneylenders. You borrow from them and you might as well end your life.'

Artema looked around to check they were alone and wasn't sure if she preferred these empty dark lanes between containers or the busier murmur filled major routes.

'I've been meaning to ask you. How should I pay you?'

Eladio double checked they were indeed alone before he leaned closer to Artema and whispered, 'I have a bank account.'

'In the mezaurbo?'

'You can't get paid up there without one. Apparently that would be illegal. So now I also pay taxes on my earnings,' Eladio said, and carried on walking.

'Then I can do a phone transfer?'

'Best way, really.'

'Do you like having a bank account?'

'It's a safer way to keep my savings. Before that I hid half in my jacket and half in my house, which was risky.'

'I imagine so,' Artema said, realising that Eladio had diverted her from her original question. 'Now, enough of the digression, tell me about the Thirteen.'

'There isn't a lot to tell,' Eladio said and stopped at a street corner to point at an icon. He waited till Artema had taken a picture and then carried on down the lane. 'Each year the kids in the orphanage get assigned a theme for their surnames. One year it might be flowers, another famous people, or animals. There's a Milo Lion from the year below me, I always quite liked his name. For our year, they must have been feeling lazy because they just gave us numbers for our surnames. They started with Seraf One, Then Dimita Two, and so on. I was the last to arrive at the orphanage that year and I was Thirteen.'

So, an explanation but not really, Artema realised. Eladio appeared willing to impart information, but he'd not actually given her anything she couldn't easily find out another way.

'That explains the names, but nothing else. You and Felicha have... gifts, were the rest of the thirteen the same?'

'We were all different to the others,' Eladio said, but more hesitantly so Artema knew they'd got to the information he didn't want to reveal. 'We were healthy, none of us got sick even when the rest of the orphans always seemed to come down with one virus or another. And we were... we were better looking.'

'Interesting,' Artema said, noting that Eladio was still skirting around the more specific gifts. 'So aside from being perfect specimens of humanity, each of the Thirteen have a gift that's unique to them, not so? Can you tell me what they are?'

Eladio gave her a look that nearly passed for exasperation.

'Twelve now,' Eladio said. 'Josepa Six died during the great famine.'

'The great famine?' Artema said.

'Yeah, you know, twelve years ago, the famine that ravaged the Eterna Urbo and killed thousands?'

This came as terrible and incredible news to Artema.

'I have never heard of a famine in the Eterna Urbo, certainly not one that killed thousands.'

'Nobody had food,' Eladio said, turning to her in amazement. 'Over a dozen kids starved to death at the orphanage. We all thought we would die too, but only Josepa did amongst the Thirteen.'

'No, I'm sorry,' Artema said, shocked by the discovery. 'We never had a famine.'

'We were told the entire city was starving.'

Eladio looked hurt, but not angry and not really

surprised. If Artema had just discovered that a disaster she'd believed to be city wide was restricted to the suburbo, she'd be enraged. Apparently Eladio expected nothing less.

'I'm sorry,' she murmured.

Eladio looked like the apology was far too little too late, especially coming from somebody who'd never known about it. Perhaps to distract himself, or escape a terrible memory, he said.

'As for the gifts, yes, we each have different ones. Seraf is a natural leader. Dimita is extremely charming and can get you to tell her things you wouldn't normally divulge. Luca is enormous. He was taller than the staff by the time he turned twelve and he's very strong, but thick.'

'Astonishing.'

This was all very interesting, but Artema's intuition now told her she was drifting away from whatever was niggling at her. So the Thirteen were a mystery, but not the one she had to solve right now.

'What about this Seraf you mentioned?' Artema asked because demons tended to go after humans with leadership potential, so if they were going to target anyone it would be him.

'Seraf...' Eladio said and his face twisted in disgust tinged with pain, 'the last time I saw him was five years ago. He was lying in the corner of a rat-infested drug den, thin as... he looked like a skeleton.'

'A drug den? What were you doing there?'

'Looking for Seraf. I tried to get him to leave, but he didn't want to.'

'So, do you think he's dead?'

'He didn't die. A while later he became the number two of the Black Brotherhood.'

'From nearly dead drug addict to gang leader?' Artema said, and an alarm jangled in her mind. That was a perfect match for somebody being aided by a demon.

'Yeah, it was quite the transformation,' Eladio said, conveying that it wasn't a surprise to him.

Artema wondered why.

'You must have been friends if you tried to help him.'

'We were more like family. When we were growing up, the other kids didn't like us because we were different. So we stuck together and vowed we'd always look out for each other.

'But life outside the orphanage was... It was harder to keep in touch. And after Seraf joined the gang... I mean, he was the oldest and always deciding what we should do. So when the suburbo turned him into a gang member... some of the Thirteen joined him. Luca especially. He's Seraf's faithful hound. Wherever he goes, Luca follows. The rest, like me and Felicha, didn't want that. It kind of destroyed our group.'

'I see. This still doesn't explain why the receptionist spoke of the Thirteen with such awe.'

'We didn't understand it either. Aside from being different, we were still orphans. But the staff always treated us like something special. That's probably also why the other kids didn't like us.'

'So you have no idea? Even with your deductive reasoning abilities and all the time you spent there?'

Eladio shook his head with a wry smile and said, 'I don't think the staff knew anything about us either. From what I have worked out we were sent to them one by one, with instructions to look after us. But they kept the staff in the dark just like everybody else.'

'Who would have that kind of clout?'

'Down here? Who do you think?'

'The gangs.'

'I can't imagine it was anyone else.'

'No, I suppose not. It is intriguing, though.'

'Do you think so?'

'Don't you?'

Artema was certain now there was something odd about Eladio and his fellow Thirteens. She just couldn't work out what it was and whether it had any connection to the gang tags or her feelings of unease. Seraf One seemed a likely connection, though, and someone she needed to meet.

'Nothing came of our so-called specialness,' Eladio said. 'Nobody swooped in to save us when they chucked us out. Nobody has intervened in our lives since. The strangest thing that's happened to me so far is meeting you.'

Artema held up her hands and said, 'Don't jump to conclusions. I knew nothing about you till yesterday.'

'Fair enough,' Eladio said, and stepped out into a lane that also looked like a border.

On the one side was a container maze, on the other a weird shanty town made mainly, and surprisingly, from salvaged wood. Tall, rickety constructions snaked their way up the sides of the massive pylons that supported the mezaurbo above.

'A different gang?' Artema said.

'The Purples,' Eladio said.

'Just the Purples, no Purple Dragon or Purple Hand or purple anything else?'

'They're a female gang.'

Eladio pointed at a purple tag sprayed onto a wooden post rammed into the... Artema looked down at her feet.

She'd not considered what they were walking on before. It seemed to be a mixture of rubble and damp clay.

'A female gang? Led by women?' Artema said and found she rather liked the idea.

'Mainly women. And they really don't take any shit. You're taking your life in your hands if you go in there without permission. Well, I would be. You'd probably be okay.'

'So we can't go in there,' Artema said and took a photo of the purple tag. 'After all, I need my guide.'

'It would be dangerous. Even if they said yes, they'd want a good reason.'

'I see,' Artema said, and noting a Brotherhood tag directly opposite the Purple's she took a picture of that too.

She turned around to find Eladio taking a very close look at the purple tag.

'Some of these patterns are repeated in all the tags,' he said, and pointed at a triangle with a dot in the middle of it. 'And this is also the shape you traced on Maria's hand when you shook it.'

'You noticed that, did you?'

'It glowed where you drew it and then it sank into her skin.' Eladio said. 'Does that mean you use demon magic too?'

'As little as possible and never for something as unimportant as that. The triangle is just another gesture for a human spell, albeit similar to the demon icon. I assume you also saw my hand gesture before I touched her?'

'It's the same gesture you use on the elevator inspector.'

'I temporarily deprived their brains of some key nutrients while boosting a couple of hormones that make a person suggestible. That works well, but for a limited time.

So I used a second spell to scare the orphanage woman. That one releases a wave of adrenaline that induces fear. It's a nebulous, undefined sensation of dread. Combined with the suggestion spell, it's rather potent for getting people to do what you want them to do.'

'So you never use demon icons?'

'Do you think you've worked something out about me?' Artema said with a slight smile she hoped hid her alarm at how easily Eladio figured things out. She'd never had any intention of letting a guide know she was a magisto in the first place, and she wasn't keen for him to learn more.

'I'm wondering whether you're a demonologist.'

And there she had it. He'd put another block together. If she was to keep his trust she was going to have to be honest though because Eladio could probably sniff out a lie.

'I am the only demonologist of the Eterna Urbo.'

'Really, the only one?'

'You're supposed to be more surprised by my revelation,' Artema said, not bothering, this time, to hide her exasperation. 'There are very few of us. I am the only one here. There are maybe a half dozen more in the other mega cities of the planet.'

'But you're a lecturer, so you must teach your students about this stuff.'

'How did you work out I'm a lecturer?'

'I looked you up.'

Artema wanted to laugh at the prosaicness of the answer when she'd been so ready to ascribe it to something deeper.

'Last night?'

'Yeah. You're listed as a lecturer for the University of Magic. Although they didn't say what you teach,' Eladio said and headed on down the path, keeping the wooden shanty town of the Purples to his right.

'There's a reason for that. I have no students.' It was best to keep moving as they spoke. After all, she had a lot of icons to locate.

'But… how can you be a lecturer if you give no lectures?'

'I have tenure,' Artema said with a grin, knowing full well that Eladio wouldn't understand.

'What does that mean?'

'It means my job is guaranteed for life. It's a peculiarity of the academic system. I have seen people who have worked hard their entire life, just stop and go into a soporific stupor when they finally make tenure.'

'You mean… the job is yours no matter what? You don't even have to do any actual work?'

'Exactly,' Artema said, beaming at him as they stopped before another pair of gang tags and she took their pictures.

'No work at all?'

'Some tenured professors even give up the pretence of doing work. You never see them at their desks or lecture halls again.'

'But not you.'

'What makes you think that?'

'You're down here,' Eladio said, waving his hand to encompass the darkness and the mass of containers, 'and this isn't fun.'

'No, it isn't, you're right.'

'So why don't you have any students?'

'Because demons are damned dangerous and nobody should be studying them. I give a very good lecture once a year on why that is so. You should come to the next one.'

'Me?'

'You're dangerously bright and far too talented to be

bumping into this stuff uninformed. And heaven forbid you actually try it.'

'Would that be bad?'

He spoke in such a way that Artema realised he was already considering it.

'Very. In fact, I don't think I'll wait till my lecture. I'll have to give you an abridged version now.'

'Why abridged?'

'Because I don't have all my visual aids handy. And believe me, some of those are very persuasive.'

Eladio shrugged and said, 'Go ahead. It's not like they'd let me into the supraurbo or your university, anyway.'

That drew Artema up short and she said, 'Why do you think that?'

'Because nobody from the suburbo has ever been allowed into the supraurbo.'

'Do you have any evidence of that? I mean, it isn't like you have the city statistics available to you, is it?'

'Well, I do actually,' Eladio said and had the grace to look embarrassed.

'Don't tell me you're a technical wiz too.'

'No, but I'm good at following information. I looked up the city statistics. They're all on the interreto. I was trying to convince Felicha that she had no hope of getting into the supraurbo, and I was right. There are no records of one of us ever getting up there.'

'There's always a first time,' Artema said.

Eladio felt like he'd woken up in a strange alternative world. Everything looked familiar and yet, he was walking around with a woman who spoke of demons as if they were a commonplace. Well, no, not exactly commonplace, but real and here.

They were following the border between the Brotherhood and the Purples, taking photos of things that had been background noise to him. Yet now they had a new and sinister meaning, and he wasn't so sure he wanted to know more. It also looked like Artema would not give him a choice.

'Demons,' Artema said, and the deep breath she took made it look like she was gearing up for a long speech, 'as I've already mentioned, come from another plane. It would be best if you discard any preconceptions you may have from any previous religious instruction.'

'That will be easy,' Eladio said. 'I never got any religious instruction.'

'Best to ignore what society thinks of demons too.'

'That they're evil and cunning and best avoided?' Eladio said in his most innocent tone that he knew wouldn't fool Artema for a second.

Artema tutted and said, 'Not that, of course. They are evil and cunning and, as I've already made plain, they are to be avoided.'

'Okay.'

'No, not dismissive like that. A little knowledge is a dangerous thing.'

'But you just told me not to get involved with them. Now you're saying a little knowledge is dangerous and you want to give me more?'

Eladio was pushing Artema, partly playing and partly wondering whether he really wanted to know more. His sensible side, that often took on Felicha's exasperated tone of voice, was urging him not to add to his already unhealthy amount of knowledge.

'I want you to understand why demons are dangerous,' Artema said. 'A child told that a knife or a plug hole or fire is dangerous will still not be able to resist the allure. They will inevitably try out a knife, stick their fingers in a plug hole or light a fire. We, as a species, seem incapable of learning just through words. We usually have to experience the pain from doing something to learn our lessons. Thankfully, as we grow older, we will, occasionally and not frequently enough, take the wise council of somebody more experienced.'

'I understand,' Eladio said and stopped at another gang tag. Along this path the Purples had made sure their tags were opposite the Brotherhood's at every point.

Artema took a photo of both. Then she slipped the phone back into her jacket.

'Demons are more complex than most people realise. We caricature them exactly as you did, as evil, tricky and dangerous. Most of our experience bears that out. But the religious frame that we have used over the centuries, has not been helpful.

'Since the Great Inter-Plane War, however, we have been applying a more anthropological approach. We have been trying to understand demons and their values without imposing our own preconceptions on them.'

'How could you do that?' Eladio pulled up everything he'd ever heard of anthropology from his memory. It wasn't much, but seemed to involve researchers moving in with primitive tribes to study them. 'You can't go to Hell to study them, can you?'

'Not for very long, at any rate.'

Eladio stopped dead and stared at Artema.

'You can go to Hell?'

'It has been done, but it is extremely difficult.'

'Have you done it?'

'Once.'

The change in Artema's expression on that one word shocked Eladio. Haunted was an understatement.

But he couldn't stop himself from asking, 'What was it like?'

'Hell,' Artema said dryly. 'Like being in the middle of a volcano where I stepped out. Although other researchers have landed up on something like an ice plane. So we know there is a wide variation there. Also, because of the research, I went in fully kitted out in the proper survival gear. The thing is... the thing is, it isn't the extreme physical conditions that are hard to bear. It's... the air of malevolence.'

'Malevolence?'

'You know how sometimes you'll walk into a shop or a pub and know, without a word being said, that you are not welcome there?'

'Yeah,' Eladio said and glanced into the Purples' territory. A woman was standing in the lane that intersected with theirs, watching them. 'I know that feeling well. You get out as quickly as possible too.'

'Try to imagine that magnified a thousandfold. Try to imagine arriving in a place where you know you'll be turned inside out. Your sentience will be kept intact and the demons will use your body as a plaything for as long as they can keep you alive.'

'That's what the religious say about Hell too.'

'They say your soul will spend an eternity burning in Hell. It's slightly different. There were no souls in the Hell I visited, or people. We don't last long without the right equipment. Even with it, you just know you need to get out.

And that's without even seeing a demon.'

'They're ugly?'

'Not in the sense that you might imagine where their corruption shows and their skin is diseased and they've got horns and hoofs. They manifest themselves to look very much like humans.'

'They manifest themselves?'

'We aren't convinced that in their own plane they look at all human. We suspect they either change to blend in here or... or the plane changes them. It is possible that when I appeared in the hell dimension, I may have looked more demon like.'

'Did they see you?'

'I specifically chose an area that appeared to be uninhabited. Researchers who go into inhabited areas are seldom seen again.'

'Oh.'

'Quite,' Artema said, and stopped to take another photo of a pair of tags. 'The reason we think humanity has represented demons as corrupted is probably not because of how we see them with our eyes, but what we feel when they appear.'

'It's bad?'

'It makes you feel physically ill. Although it is something they can control. If they're in the mood, they can pull that feeling of impending doom right in. Which they would have to do when trying to make a deal with a person. If they're annoyed though, they don't bother shielding humans from their true presence.'

'How would you know that?'

'Because, on occasion, I have summoned them.'

Artema called up a video on her phone and handed it to

Eladio. To his surprise, it showed a picture of a pentagram. It was something he'd seen in hundreds of films. He'd just assumed, as with everything else Artema was telling him, that they'd got that wrong.

A being was standing in the centre of the pentagram. A considerably younger looking Artema was standing on the outside of the diagram.

'There's no sound,' Eladio said, and hoped Artema wouldn't put the sound on.

Just seeing the image was unsettling enough. The... well, he looked like a person, standing in the middle of the pentagram, but he felt dangerous. Even at his small scale on the phone screen, he looked evil. Eladio wanted to look away. He wanted to turn the damn phone off and hand it back as quickly as he could and then to wash his hands over and over again.

'Do you see?' Artema asked and took the phone from Eladio's unresisting fingers.

He wiped his hands up and down his trousers and said, 'He's horrible.'

'Exactly, and that's just a recording. I've deliberately removed the sound, although a transcript is available of our conversation.'

'Why do that?'

'Because demons have a hypnotic quality to their voices that remains even in the recording. They can make you so suggestible you'd happily go home and disembowel your family. Even if they don't give you those instructions.'

'They turn you evil just with their voices?'

'They can.'

'That must make them hard to study.'

'And what gives them a reputation for cunning and

manipulation. We aren't convinced they're cleverer than humans. They just have a way of tapping into our primitive animal brains and making us do terrible things.

'Their words don't seem to match what people subsequently do, so we feel they have tricked us. In a way, they have but not how it would happen if it was one human trying to manipulate another. The problem with demons, you see, is that they aren't human. This means we have no framework to build upon.

'Here on earth, every living thing evolved from the same ancestor. So even with animals, we have a common base to start from. This means we can understand animals even if they can't speak.

'We recognise when an animal is calm, or stressed. We can tell if it's trying to get you to do something for them. We can see from the intensity of a gaze when they're hunting. We can interpret their intent.

'We have none of that with demons. It makes it challenging to understand them, and yet we must understand them if we are to defeat them.'

'Are you trying to defeat them?'

'All the demonologists of Earth are trying to defeat them. Although, these days I mostly just keep on top of local problems.'

'Why?'

'They keep turning up on our plane and we don't know why. But it has never been to our benefit whenever they show up. We're not sure if they just find us amusing, or if they have a darker purpose. But we do what we can to stop them.'

'So that's why you're down here all on your own trying to figure things out?'

'Correct.'

'These demons can't be so tough if a handful of demonologists can keep them in check.'

Artema stopped and scowled at him, 'Are you taking the piss?'

'No,' Eladio said. 'It just seems you're not serious enough about shutting down the demons. If you wanted to make sure that they never come onto our plane again, you'd have an army of demonologists working on the problem. You wouldn't have just one person per city.'

'Ah yes, the army of demonologists argument. I haven't heard that one in a while.'

'I don't see why you think it's funny.'

Eladio was used to people laughing at him, but they were usually stupid, uneducated people laughing when Eladio knew he was right. Artema was clever and powerful, and right now she was the one laughing. He didn't like it.

'It's just, it's an old idea and one that surfaces now and then,' Artema said. 'The first record we have of the formation of an army trained to fight demons was in this very city. Pope Simplicius I in 470 AD declared war on hell itself and raised an army of... Well, they were probably very fanatical individuals, but poorly trained.

'Most didn't survive their first encounter with the demons they raised to fight. They should have called them up one by one. But in their arrogance, they just opened a portal to hell and let the buggers flow right in. Although it isn't recorded that way in the history books, the demon incursion led to the demise of the Western Roman Empire.'

'How many demons are there?' Eladio asked, astonished to hear of this alternative history.

He double checked his surroundings, thankful that

Artema had adopted the murmur come whisper of suburbanites to impart this information. At least it kept it from the occasional passerby who didn't even give them a curious glance.

'Considering we have billions of people on our plane, it's probable that demons have the same,' Artema said.

'So what are the other records of demon fighting armies?' Eladio couldn't resist asking, even though he doubted he'd like the answer.

'Popes thereafter were more careful about how they went about fighting demons, but not necessarily the people they chose to do it. They concentrated on fighters rather than cerebral types. Boniface the VIII in 1295 had over a thousand men trained for his demon army. They did only call up one demon at a time to dispatch them. They were busy for the remaining eight years of the pope's reign.'

'What went wrong?' Eladio asked, certain now that something had gone wrong.

'Do you think demons would sit around passively while a bevy of humans called them up one by one to kill them?'

'I don't suppose they would, no,' Eladio said and glanced back into Purple territory. He had a feeling they were being followed, but he couldn't be certain yet. So he just upped their pace.

'The demons were subtle in their counterattack,' Artema said as she hurried to catch up with Eladio. 'They infiltrated the ranks of the demon killers and turned them against each other. Although the official records don't show it, they landed up killing each other more often than they killed demons. Finally, the survivors killed the pope which, again, was covered up.'

'Okay, I can see that a traditional army won't work. But

still only a handful of demonologists to protect the entire planet?'

'It's about finding people with the right temperament. Then training them so rigorously that whatever a demon might use as leverage is hammered out of them.'

'Is that what happened to you?'

'Remember when I told you I used to drink? Well, I still don't know if that was my way of trying to cope with what I was learning or some subtle demon corruption. But that, along with a lot of other things, had to be fought and overcome. And that was one of my easier challenges.'

'Then what?'

'Then you are watched for the rest of your life by a group of colleagues, called the komitato. They are tasked with making sure you don't get corrupted. In this day and age, I am also monitored by my AI. It gets a thorough annual maintenance from people unrelated to me. All this just to ensure I can't tamper with its base programming. Even with these protections, few demonologists live very long lives. We are either killed by a demon or our colleagues finish us off when we slip from the safe path.'

'How do they do that?'

Eladio wondered how dangerous a demonologist who had gone off the rails could be and eyed Artema up with more concern than he had till now.

Artema stopped and gave Eladio an unnerving grin as she checked their surroundings and waited for a couple to pass by. They looked ridiculously mundane to Eladio at when he was getting a load full of the most outrageous information.

'I have a beacon implanted in my head.'

'Why have you got a beacon?' Eladio asked, astonished

that anyone would voluntarily do something like that. 'Isn't that a violation of your human rights?'

'I did it voluntarily. Every demonologist has one.'

'Why?'

'In case we end up being seduced by a demon, ditch any outside technology like a phone, and go on a rampage.'

'But if you know you have a beacon and you're being controlled by a demon, couldn't you just get rid of the tracker? Surely you've got magic that will enable you to do that.'

'It's implanted physically, and by magic, in the brain. Any attempt to remove it would make my head explode, literally.'

'Sancta Maria Patrino de Dio,' Eladio gasped, staring at Artema in horror. How she could look amused by what she was saying was beyond him. It brought home to him more forcibly than all the rest what a dangerous job Artema had. 'That sounds shit.'

'Shit enough to no longer tempt you to dabble?'

'I suppose.'

'Not good enough, Eladio,' Artema said. 'What do you still wonder about?'

'How easy those icons are to use. I mean, if I drew that pentagram, the one from your video, would a demon appear?'

'Bona Dio... could you do that? After only seeing a 90 second clip?'

'Yes,' Eladio said, and wondered if he should tell Artema this. 'I just close my eyes and call up the image, and then I can look around it and dissect all the parts. Even things I didn't notice the first time. I can see everything there was to see. It might take a while, but it's all here,' he said and tapped his temple.

'I shouldn't have shown you that clip then.'

'Is it that dangerous?'

'It is, partly because it's that easy. The demon icons power spells like... like the most efficient battery you've ever come across. They are temptingly easy to use. But each time you use them... it's a poor analogy, but each time you use them they take a little piece of your soul with them.'

'And finally?' Eladio said, realising that he was so absorbed in the conversation that he hadn't noticed they'd come to a stop again.

'Finally, you end up a greasy smear on the wall as your colleagues blow you away. And that's only if you're lucky.'

'Because the demons will get you otherwise?'

'Exactly.'

'What do they do with humans if they don't want our souls?'

'We aren't entirely sure.'

'After all this time?'

'We know they use humans and once the humans have achieved whatever it was the demons wanted for them, they drag them bodily into hell. They are probably dead within minutes, an hour at the most. We assume at that point the demons just eat them.'

'Demon food?'

'Possibly. We have recorded sightings of demons eating humans, but we don't think they're after us just as a source of protein. I personally think they get some entertainment from manipulating people.'

'Entertainment?'

'Call it a sophisticated form of reality show.'

'They're playing with us?' Eladio said, and it outraged

him.

It angered him more even than when he considered the injustice of the city and the callousness of the supraurbonites.

'That's my theory,' Artema said.

'What do you do about it?'

'I monitor demon activity and swoop in and shut it down wherever I find it.'

'That will be quite a job down here.'

Eladio waved his hand to encompass the suburbo and noted that the woman he'd seen earlier in Purples' territory was back, leaning against a wall deep in shadows. So they were being followed.

'I mean, the suburbo is vast, and if all the gangs have these kinds of tags, there must be millions of them. This... demon incursion could be massive.'

'That is what I am afraid of.'

'So... we can't go along this slowly. You need to get more people involved. If it's just you and me walking around taking photos of tags, it will take years.'

'Do you have a suggestion?'

'Yeah,' Eladio said, rather pleased with himself. It was a cracking idea as long as he could get Artema to agree with it. 'Use social media.'

'To do what?'

'Turn the hunt for gang tags into a game and get people to upload their images, with the geotag, to your AI.'

'Turn it into a game? Eladio, have you been listening to a word I've said? This is extremely dangerous work.'

'And you're probably running out of time. But if you offer prizes for people who upload tags, you'll have people scrambling over themselves to get them. They'll upload hundreds of tags each. And you'll be able to get tags from places you and I can't get into,' Eladio said and flicked his thumb toward the Purples' territory.

'But the gangs will be alerted, and most probably the demons too.'

'They probably already know,' Eladio said, keeping to himself that they were being followed. 'There are surveillance cameras all over the suburbo. It won't be long till they know two people are going around photographing their tags. In fact, that pickpocket might not have been as innocent as he appeared. The gangs might have ordered him to get your ID so they can look into you. At least with my way we'll get a lot more information before we need to run and hide.'

'Running and hiding is the exact opposite of what we must do if we're going to shut this thing down.'

'We?'

'You're in it up to your neck already, Eladio.'

'I thought you didn't want me messing with demons,' Eladio said irritated, for the first time, with Artema for having dragged him into what looked to be a very messy situation.

Artema didn't want anyone to be pulled into her world, but she had a bad feeling that was what she'd done to Eladio. 'I should send you home right now.'

'You can't. Even if you are a powerful magisto, you can't get out of this place without me.'

'So you want to stay?'

Eladio shrugged. 'This is the best-paid job I've ever had.'

Artema nodded and walked on, looking out for the next

gang tag. The path, like the suburbo, was unplanned and meandered left and right so it was hard to get her bearings. All along the route, especially in the Purples' territory, they'd strung rows of light bulbs that gave off a faint orange light.

They were apparently low energy bulbs, but she couldn't work out why they produced such little light. In this darkness it was also hard to believe that it was only afternoon. Except, despite her huge breakfast come dinner, her stomach was rumbling. It was probably because of all the walking. She wasn't used to being on her feet all day either.

As she was thinking this, the smell of grilled meat wafted across to them. 'Maybe we should have some lunch. I could use a sit down.'

Eladio grinned at her and said, 'You won't want to eat what you're smelling.'

'Why on earth not? It just smells of meat.'

'Rat,' Eladio said as they rounded a corner.

The space opened out onto something that looked like a market at a crossroad. Three roads met and around them were dotted a couple of stalls. There was an actual shop like building with a glass frontage, the first Artema had seen in the suburbo. But what drew the eye was a man with a food cart. Spatchcocked rats with a wooden skewer thrust through them hung from a bar over the grill, and several more of the grotesquely flattened creatures were being grilled over coals.

'You have got to be joking.'

The creatures transfixed Artema's horrified gaze. As she watched, a couple of women arrived to buy a grilled rat and then slipped off back to Purple territory.

'Why not?' Eladio said with a shrug. 'There are plenty of

the buggers around eating all our stuff. It's only fair that we eat them too.'

'So you've eaten rat?'

'Yeah, quite often,' Eladio said and looked embarrassed to admit it.

'I suppose you'll say it tastes like chicken.'

'No. It tastes like rat. Nothing like chicken at all.'

'Mmm,' The sight of the benighted creatures had robbed Artema of her appetite. 'I don't think I can bring myself to eat that.'

'It's okay, the general store will have stuff you recognise,' Eladio said and headed for the shop with the glass front.

In amongst all the graffiti that covered the edges of the building and spilled onto the outer bits of the glass window, Artema could just make out a sign that read, simply, Super Market.

Eladio paused at the door and put a meaningful finger on a purple tag sprayed at shoulder height on the doorpost.

'So the shop belongs to the Purples?' Artema said.

'Probably just protected by them,' Eladio said and stepped inside.

A bell tinkled, and the few customers paused and looked at him before resuming their shopping. Artema sneaked a photo of the tag and went inside, generating her own tinkle.

Eladio took a shopping basket and said, 'I may as well buy soap, I'm running low. What do you want to eat?'

The range of tin cans and paper wrapped goods in the store profoundly depressed Artema. The designs on the packaging were minimal. She assumed she was looking at the cheapest of the cheap goods the corporations produced and bothered to ship down to the suburbo. There were tinned sausages, a range of tinned vegetables, a lot of tomato-based products, biscuits and crisps.

Artema never went shopping, she had staff who did that, but she doubted any shop in the supraurbo was this grim. She followed Eladio, who picked up a bar of soap and a packet of biscuits. He then headed to the back of the store and an ancient refrigerator that wheezed as it pumped out cool air.

'How about some fruit?' Eladio said. 'That you can eat, and there's milk here too.'

'Take whatever you fancy, my boy,' Artema said. 'I find this place too depressing to contemplate.'

Eladio looked around, perhaps seeing the shop as an outsider might, and murmured, 'It's a pretty good store, actually.'

'No doubt it is,' Artema said. 'Now let's go.'

Eladio took four apples, a pack of biscuits and half a litre of milk. He gave Artema an uncertain look and said, 'Chocolate?'

'Go ahead,' Artema said, and was surprised by the smile that got from Eladio.

He grabbed a couple of chocolate bars at the checkout to add to his basket. The checkout was a raised counter placed, Artema assumed, so that the shop owner could see her entire store over the customer's heads.

Eladio cleared his throat suggestively and Artema said, 'Ah yes, the money.'

'I'll pay you back for the soap and biscuits,' Eladio said.

'There's no need,' Artema said as she watched Eladio vanish all his shopping into the pockets of his jacket.

The jacket was a multipurpose device down here in the suburbo, she realised as she followed Eladio back outside.

'Here,' Eladio said, and gave Artema a couple of grubby

dolaroy.

'I said there was no need.'

'I will not be in your debt,' Eladio said and held the money out.

'Fine,' Artema said, because she could tell Eladio would be unhappy if she didn't take the cash.

It would be futile to point out that a couple of dolaroy meant nothing to her. She followed Eladio to a low wall where she sat with a sigh of relief and accepted an apple.

'I assume this is an apple and nothing more.'

'It is just an apple,' Eladio said back to grinning. 'You have my word.'

'Thank goodness,' Artema said and took a big bite as her gaze drifted over to the rat seller. Thankfully, the fumes from his cart were drifting away from them. 'Where does the store's fresh produce come from, anyway?'

'The same place as the rest of the city's produce,' Eladio said. 'From the farms outside and the edge farms.'

'Ah yes, the edge farms.'

Artema had seen pictures of them when she was at school. No doubt she'd seen the occasional documentary about them as well. They were vast agricultural holdings that sprawled up the sides of the city. They were lush vertical farms that situated themselves as close to their customers as possible and primarily relied upon hydroponics. Because of that, the produce tended to be less tasty than that grown in actual soil.

One bite into her beautiful looking apple made her suspect it was edge farm produce. It was peculiarly tasteless. Not that you'd guess it from the way Eladio was tucking in. He eased the half litre of milk from a pocket and held it out to Artema.

'Have a drink, it's good and cold.'

'Straight from the carton?'

'Yeah.'

'I doubt that's hygienic.'

'It won't kill you.'

Artema was thirsty and supposed it was best to get her sip in first before Eladio. She didn't like the idea of sharing the same container with someone else. She supposed suburbonites were less picky because they had less choice.

Eladio broke his packet of biscuits open in the middle and, much to Artema's surprise, held the packet out to her.

'Will I be in your debt if I eat these?'

'Only a very little. Don't worry, I offer them in friendship.'

'Is that so? Despite who and what I am?'

Eladio shrugged and said, 'We all have our disadvantages.'

'I am struck by the wisdom of your words.'

Watching Eladio, Artema gathered that you were supposed to eat the biscuits with the apple. As the biscuit was sweet and slightly spiced with cinnamon, it pleased her to discover it improved the fruit no end.

'It's like apple pie,' Eladio said from a full mouth. 'One of my favourites.'

'What I don't understand is why so much of the produce in that shop is dry goods, and so little fresh.'

'Nobody's got a fridge.'

'Ah... of course. Stupid of me not to realise that,' Artema said and took another bite of her apple.

Eladio took the two chocolate bars he'd bought out of his pocket. He handed one to Artema and then with great ceremony eased open the paper wrapper of his own bar. He broke a strip of chocolate off, wrapped the remaining bar and vanished it into his pocket. Then he took a bite. He closed his eyes with a sigh as he chewed, savouring every mouthful.

Artema finished her apple and biscuit and tore open the chocolate. She had no particular attraction to chocolate, unlike Eladio, but was curious to try it. It had been the only chocolate bar in the shop. They had wrapped it in brown paper with the word Choc stamped in red across it.

She was disappointed; it was dry and crumbling and not very tasty, although the cocoa flavour was present. It was cheap chocolate of a sort she would never want to eat. She considered giving the rest of the bar to Eladio, but suspected that wouldn't go down well. So she wrapped it and put it back in her pocket and turned to contemplating Eladio.

She had an uncomfortable feeling that the young man was too good to be true. He was handsome, polite, intelligent and helpful. He was everything, in fact, that would make him appeal to Artema.

She had no illusions about herself, well, only as many as most people did about themselves. Eladio was a rather perfect match for what she needed. Too perfect. If the demons wanted to lure her in, this young man was the ideal pawn for that.

A niggling doubt had been bugging her all day, and after Eladio suggested using social media to speed up their work, it turned into a greater alarm. Which was why she'd not made anything more of the suggestion and changed the subject. To give Eladio his due, he'd not pushed it cither.

The problem was, it was a good idea. It could also be a trap. Maybe the demons needed mass action to trigger the icons they'd spread across the suburbo.

Would she be helping them if she got more people involved? Or would it help them if she carried on as she was, slowly scratching the surface of what these tags meant and where they were placed. This was the kind of dilemma working with demons always caused.

Artema needed to consult somebody else. She needed to get her thoughts straight before she proceeded and make sure she wasn't being paranoid. She'd also need more information on Eladio, not only for herself, but for her supervisors.

'Eladio, I want to ask you to do something for me.'

'Sure, what is it?'

'I want you to take the genetic test.'

'Why?' Eladio said, back to being wary. 'You know it costs 500 imps, don't you? And I don't have that.'

'I will pay. I'd also like Felicha to take the test.'

'Because we're both from the Thirteen?'

'There is something in that, something odd.'

'Sure, but not something to do with you.'

And Eladio looked... Artema was trying to put her finger on it. He looked upset, confused, worried and trying to hide all of it.

'It may sound odd, but in a situation like we've got here, something so huge, I need to investigate thoroughly. I need to follow every lead and any hunch that occurs to me. I have learned, to my cost occasionally, that nothing is too trivial to be investigated. The Thirteen... my instinct has been buzzing, telling me I should look.'

'It won't tell you anything. All of us suburbonites have been down here for generations. Nothing new has been added, so you'll find nothing but inferior suburbonite genes. It's a waste of your money.'

'How can you be so sure?'

'Because nobody who does the test down here ever gets a result that gets them out of here. They aren't even dreaming big. Nobody seriously believes they'll find blue blood in their veins. But they hope they might have something that will get them into the mezaurbo. And that doesn't happen either.

'It's why I haven't bothered. It's more sensible to buy an annual permit to work in the mezaurbo than it is to take the test. Nobody has ever even been able to claim mezaurbo status and live up there based on what they find in the genetic test.'

'You fear, in fact, that the test will dash any hope you might have of moving out of here?'

Eladio shrugged, which confirmed Artema's theory. The young man didn't want the door closed on that potential dream. He also seemed certain that his test would give him no advantage.

'Let me put it to you this way,' Artema said. 'I'm willing to pay for you and Felicha. You'll never get a better deal; so what do you have to lose?'

'This is crazy,' Eladio said, shaking his head.

'Will you do it?'

Eladio's gaze flicked around the small crossroad of shops and the people about their daily lives. It surprised Artema that he was so reluctant when he was being offered such a good deal.

'We'd be doing this because it's something you want, right?' Eladio said. 'There will be no obligation from us to you after you've spent so much money?'

'The only obligation is that I want to see the results of the test.'

'I'll speak to Felicha.'

'Good, then I'll transfer the funds to your phone. It would be good if you did the test as soon as possible.'

6

Eladio watched Artema till she vanished into the elevator terminus hall. It had been another strange day, and he was dead on his feet. Two days of working night shifts and then accompanying the woman about during the day, with only snatches of sleep in between, was taking its toll.

He would have liked nothing better than to crawl into bed right now and rather looked forward to the chance to sleep at night and to sleep in. Artema had said she'd probably only get back for late morning tomorrow. But he had something to do first.

Artema had gone off looking preoccupied. In fact, she'd been preoccupied for most of the day and a lot of her concern seemed to focus on Eladio. What was the mystery? After all, they'd only known each other for two days.

But the fact that a magisto was troubled about him was worrying to Eladio too. It was also a new and unaccustomed feeling. Usually he was just ignored.

Except for girls, they gawked and giggled and occasionally flirted. That he didn't mind. He wouldn't even mind if Artema was like that, flirting. But she looked so severe, and that was... sinister.

He shook his head as he strolled down the street, barely paying any attention to the people streaming about him, many of them on their way home after a hard day of work. Maybe Artema wouldn't be half so sinister if it wasn't for the talk of demons. Demons!

Why would they be interested in the suburbo, anyway? Surely they were more likely to hit upon the high fliers of the supraurbo. But apparently not.

It would serve the rest right if there was a revolution growing. Especially if nobody knew about it because it was in the forgotten lands of the suburbo, Eladio thought with some satisfaction. The only problem was they'd probably end up being worse off after the dust settled too.

There was no point in mulling it over, and now he had to gather his courage and talk to Felicha. Her shop frontage was closed, so he went around the back and knocked. At least she had a proper door. Her spy hole darkened for a second.

'What is it?' Felicha said and pulled the door open.

Eladio held out an apple and said, 'Can't I just come by and say hello?'

'You're giving me an apple?' Felicha said, but stood aside to let him in. 'This when you gave Benito half of a huge sandwich and the orphanage steak and chips?'

'How do you even know that?' Eladio said as he walked into the back of the shop.

One wall was lined with washing machines, all churning away, the dirty water sloshing against their glass windows. The opposite wall was lined with humming tumble driers. At the back of the room was Felicha's bed, an actual bed with actual legs. Eladio was always rather impressed by that. In the middle of the room, was a table and piles of clothes in the process of being folded.

'As you're here you can help,' Felicha said and tossed a bundle of clothes to Eladio. 'Fold those.'

'Alright.'

Eladio leaned back on the stool by the table and began folding. It brought back memories of the orphanage this, sitting in the laundry, surrounded by the smell of soap, folding clothes. Only it was comfortable here with Felicha, and it had seldom been comfortable at the orphanage.

'Have you sent that crazy woman packing yet?' Felicha said.

'Do you know how much she's paying me?'

'I doubt it would be enough,' Felicha said.

'It's 28 imps an hour, plus expenses.'

Despite trying not to, Felicha looked impressed.

'What are expenses?'

'Food and travel,' Eladio said.

'She's buying you food and all you bring me is an apple?'

'Have some biscuits with it,' Eladio said with a grin and pulled what remained of his biscuits from his pocket.

'What is she? Why is she down here? People want to know.'

'Have you been telling them about her?'

'Only when others have brought her up. They say she's been taking lots of photographs.'

They, Eladio realised, were all Felicha's customers. The same they, no doubt, that had told her about the food. 'Yeah, she's been taking photos.'

'What of?'

'This and that.'

Eladio was relieved that people hadn't worked out they were looking at gang tags. It was only a matter of time before they did realise it, though.

'Do you know why?'

'A bit.'

'Are you going to tell me?'

'Eventually. Just not today.'

'Why not? Is she up to no good? Are they going to develop the suburbo and chuck us all out?'

'Is that what people think?'

'They think she has something to do with city administration. Why else would she be down here and why else, even if they don't know it, would she be paying you so much?'

'Felicha... she's a magisto,' Eladio said and waited for the inevitable disbelief.

'A what?'

'You know, someone who does magic.'

'Don't be ridiculous.'

'I've seen her do things... things that shouldn't be possible.'

For the first time since Eladio had ever known her, Felicha was speechless and just stared at him. He gave her a wry smile.

'She's interested in us... the Thirteen.'

'She's down here because of us?'

'I'm not sure. She says not, but I took her to the orphanage and Maria mentioned the Thirteen and... she didn't show it straight away but it made her curious.'

'All the more reason to stay away from her,' Felicha said.

'The thing is, she's so interested she's offered to pay for us to do the genetic test.'

'Us?'

'You and me. Her only condition is that she wants to see the test results.'

For the second time in her life, Felicha was speechless.

But after a moment of surprised blinking she said, 'She'll pay for the test? When?'

'Now. She's already given me the money. She said we should do it tonight so we can see the results in the morning.'

'And you said that was okay?'

'I thought you wanted to do the test?'

'I do. You never did.'

'I've told you before; it won't change anything. But she asked, and I know how much you want this.'

'And what do you want in return for arranging such a deal?'

'Whatever you'll give me,' Eladio said with a shrug and a smile and was annoyed when somebody thumped on the door before Felicha could reply.

'Honestly, people should leave me alone once my shop closes,' Felicha muttered and put her eye to her spy hole. 'Sankta Madonna!' she hissed and opened the door.

A man so broad that he blocked all light and so tall that you couldn't see his head stood outside.

'Luca!' Eladio said, and his stomach clenched with fright.

'Hi, Eladio,' Luca said. He ducked, eased himself inside and gazed around.

His hair was trimmed so short as to make him look bald, and he'd put on weight since Eladio had last seen him. Now he had such a thick neck it bulged over his collar. Eladio waited, like Felicha, for Luca to continue. It always took him a while to gear up for speech.

To both their surprise he turned to Eladio and said, 'Seraf wants to see you.'

'Me?' Eladio said, and his alarm grew.

'You and the woman you've been going around with.'

'I told you she was trouble,' Felicha hissed.

'She isn't here right now,' Eladio said.

'Where is she?' Luca asked.

'She went… up for the night,' Eladio said and pointed at the ceiling.

Luca's face was blank for a moment and then slowly a frown developed.

'Up where?' he said in his deep bass voice.

'The mezaurbo.'

It was a guess. Eladio had no idea whether or not Artema was going all the way home. Either way, the less he said about the woman, the better. And thinking was never Luca's strong suit, so there was no point in adding complexity to the situation.

'When will she be back?' Luca asked.

'Tomorrow, late.'

Eladio had to buy time and not build any expectations.

'Well, you tell her, she has to see Seraf.'

'I will.'

'Okay then,' Luca said, but didn't move.

Eladio had the impression that usually at this point of any message Luca had to deliver, he added a menace. But he was struggling to do this with what was, to all intents and purposes, his family.

'You be sure to go,' he muttered.

He cleared his throat noisily, spat on the floor and eased himself back out through the door.

Felicha slammed it shut, bolted it, and hurried to her sink for a cloth.

'That bloody animal spitting in my house!'

'Wait,' Eladio said. 'Don't clean it up.'

'What do you mean, don't clean it up?'

'You can get DNA from spit, can't you?'

'Yes, so?'

'Do you have a container that will preserve it? I think Artema might want it checked too.'

'If you want to scrape up his disgusting spit, you do it.' Felicha dug out a small glass jar and handed it over. 'He's always done that. No matter how much we tried to stop him.'

'You girls tried. At least you didn't have to share a room with him. He used to pee in the corner at night because he was too scared to go downstairs to the toilet in the dark.'

'What an animal,' Felicha said, shaking her head.

'So now,' Eladio said once he'd done scraping up the spit and screwed the lid closed. 'Do you want to take the genetic test?'

'That's all you can ask me when you've just been summoned by Seraf?'

'I can do nothing about that till tomorrow. But I can do the genetic test tonight,' Eladio said, determined to maintain an unconcerned air.

It wasn't easy, especially when Felicha was so worried for him.

'You,' Felicha said, shaking her head. 'You've always taken way too many risks.'

Artema was so tired that she was tempted to sit on the floor of the elevator from the suburbo. She felt she hadn't quite sunk to that level yet, so resisted and stood all the way. As a result, when she finally got there, she settled with a relieved sigh into the plush seats of the elevator up to the supraurbo. She also had a rather pleasant nap for the rest of the way.

She was disappointed to find that it was dark when she finally emerged from the elevator. She didn't know how

Eladio coped with the minimum of light that he got. Or even how people like Felicha managed. To never have seen daylight in her entire life was shocking.

'Welcome back, ma'am,' Chico said, and held the door open.

The contrast with Eladio's home struck Artema forcibly. Her house was bigger than the entire orphanage the young man had grown up in. Hell, just her door was bigger than Eladio's current home.

And the whole house was built in an ancient Roman style that matched the university. It had tall sandy coloured ornamented columns and a porch that would have been damned as wasteful down below. Not to mention that she had servants, and she paid those servants more than Eladio was currently earning. She felt bad when she considered that.

Maybe she should pay him more... would that be a good thing? She wasn't sure it would please Eladio. He had a sense of fairness. Artema suspected that he already felt like he was getting too much out of the bargain, including the genetic test. Not that he'd wanted that.

Should she be worried that he wasn't keen? Artema wondered as she passed through her hallway, tastefully decorated with original paintings, into the main hall that was dominated by a double staircase with a left and right branch that curved away from each other in an elegant arc to make a very attractive circular feature. I could probably fit an entire neighbourhood in here, Artema thought, and then dismissed the idea. It wasn't her fault she'd inherited all this, and there was no need to feel guilty about it either.

'Welcome back ma'am,' Chico said as he hurried to catch up with Artema. 'You have guests waiting.'

'Guests? At this time of night?' Artema said, wishing she could just go to bed.

Guests now could never be for a good reason.

'It's the vice chancellor, Doctor Leopold, and a virtual lady, ma'am. I provided refreshments for them while they were waiting. They said it was important they see you this evening.'

'A virtual guest?'

'She didn't give her name.'

'No? Well, never mind,' Artema said with a shrewd idea of who it was. 'It was sensible to put them in the dining room. It's the vice chancellor's favourite room.'

'Yes, ma'am,' Chico said.

Artema knew it was the training, but she always admired the way Chico could keep his face entirely impassive while conveying that he'd enjoyed that slight jibe at the vice chancellor's expense.

Two footmen stood at the double doors to the dining room and swung them open on a bow as Artema sailed through. By the time she turned to smile brightly at her three guests, the doors were already silently and unobtrusively closed behind her.

The contrast to the suburbo continued to strike her. This was the house she'd grown up in. Usually she hardly noticed it. But now the walls and ceilings that were painted with rural scenes and the three preposterously large chandeliers that hung along the length of her long dining table looked outrageous.

'Vice chancellor, Doctor,' Artema said on a bow.

Then she turned to a well-built woman wearing loose and informal clothing. She had a broad face sprinkled with freckles and blonde hair turning to grey.

'Lady Ophelia,' Artema said and took the proffered hand. It coruscated with a golden glow, but the sensation of a living hand was conveyed remarkably well by the technology. 'How is London?'

'Doing just fine, thank you, Artema,' Lady Ophelia said in her clipped British accent.

'I assume you have been keeping up to date with my research?'

'I know as much as you have shared with Normando, which is scarcely enough. Really, Artema,' Lady Ophelia said, 'you, of all people, know the dangers. Why are you being so lax about keeping the komitato informed?'

'I agree,' Doctor Leopold said.

He was a medical doctor as well as the professor of healing medicine at the university. He was another lover of food, but his girth paled into insignificance compared to the vice chancellor.

'You should have kept us more fully informed. There's no use in only speaking to Normando.'

'I humbly beg forgiveness. Would it help if I said I was about to call you this evening?'

'What's the problem?' Normando asked.

He settled back into his chair and examined his plate heaving with roasted meats, a range of delicately sculpted vegetables and some forms in jelly that Artema couldn't recognise. Apparently her chef had pushed the boat out for the vice chancellor.

Artema sat down at the head of the table so that she had the vice chancellor and the doctor to her left and Lady Ophelia to her right.

'The problem,' Artema said as she helped herself to a jelly, 'is my guide.'

'So he's stiffed you? I thought he might,' Normando said with satisfaction.

'Not at all, Normando. Really, you shouldn't jump to conclusions. He's been a... a perfect gentleman. And I mean that in the traditional sense.'

'So what's the problem?'

'I fear he's too perfect, a plant put in my path by the demon or demons I am chasing.'

'Do you have anything other than your suspicions over perfection?' Lady Ophelia said.

'His origin is a mystery. He and the twelve other orphans he grew up with are apparently ideal specimens of humanity, each with a special gift. Eladio, for example, has perfect recall and is astonishingly quick to put things together. But nobody, including Eladio, knows why that is.'

'Has he had the genetic test?'

'Not yet, but I have given him money for him to take it.'

'So we'll have some answers by the morning,' Normando said.

Artema, who had braced herself for an explosion on how she was wasting her money from Normando, gave a reflective laugh. Why would Normando explode? 500 imperiay dolaroy was nothing to him.

'Tell us the rest,' Lady Ophelia said. 'Leave nothing out.'

'I will, just as soon as I've sent the latest results from my search to my AI,' Artema said, and send the information from her phone with the swipe of her finger. 'At least it can crunch the data while we speak.'

Then, because it was also useful to her, Artema recounted everything that she'd seen and done with Eladio over the last two days.

'Curious indeed,' Lady Ophelia said when Artema

finished. 'Eladio Thirteen does seem to be the ideal guide. It is also suspiciously convenient that you came upon him when you did. I can scarcely imagine a better person. You could have been floundering around down there for days without spotting the gang tags.'

'Well, I would have spotted the gang tags, I saw the first one without his help. It was the fact that he could see it glowing that surprised me.'

'That is very unusual, certainly. I don't recall hearing or reading of anyone with that ability before this. Have you, doctor?'

'Never,' Doctor Leopold said. 'It is highly suspicious.'

'There is an alternate possibility,' Normando said. 'It could be argued that it is extremely inconvenient for the demons that Artema came across this Eladio.'

'Why's that?' Artema said and skewered a vegetable doing an excellent impression of a rose and popped it into her mouth.

It was delicious, with a subtlety you just couldn't get from food in the lower levels.

'Think how inconvenient it would be, if a demon was trying to be subtle, to suddenly have all his secret work exposed by this young man.'

'It would only be an inconvenience if he was still trying to hide his activity,' Ophelia said. 'What if he's ready for the final play and he needs some external agent to give his project its last push?'

'Exactly,' Artema said. 'I mean, maybe that social media game would be an excellent way for me to maximise data collection. On the other hand, everyone noticing and uploading thousands of demon icons might be a trigger for something worse.'

'We can't do nothing,' Normando said. 'Now that we know about the damned tags, we have to act. And it's typical bloody demon psychology that we've got this dilemma.'

'For all we know, the demons aren't aware that we're onto them at all,' Ophelia said. 'It could just be our own paranoia.'

'With good reason,' Artema said.

'I am not questioning that, but we do need clarity over Eladio Thirteen. I can see only one solution.'

'I was afraid you'd say that.'

'You need to remove all doubt before you can proceed. The provo de doloro is our most effective way of doing that.'

'Oh, I say, no!' Normando said. 'It's positively medieval. There's got to be a better way.'

'I wish I could agree vice chancellor,' Artema said. 'I've been subjected to the test myself and it nearly killed me.'

'It also cleared you,' Ophelia said. 'And if it hadn't, we wouldn't be sitting here today speaking of the future.'

'I can be on hand to make sure the young man makes it through in one piece,' Doctor Leopold said.

'Unless, of course, he is in league with a demon,' the vice chancellor said meaningfully.

'Indeed,' Lady Ophelia said. 'But we will have to wait for our answers about him. In the meantime, we have these tags to worry about. What more can you tell us about them, Artema?'

'All I can say before full analysis from my AI is that every gang tag has exactly the same demon icons.'

'Which suggests they're for something specific,' Lady Ophelia said. 'If they were just being used as ornaments, you might expect each gang to choose a different set of icons.'

'Why on earth would anyone use demon icons as

ornaments?' Normando snapped. 'That's nonsensical.'

'Not at all. Demon iconography is very simple and as we all know has worked its way into many human graphics. Most famously and disastrously into the cards used for ESP.'

'Till we, at least our demonologist forebears, stepped in and stopped them,' Artema said.

'Even so, the symbols they use are simple, common shapes like triangles and wavy lines that crop up again and again in human art and design.'

'But seldom infused with magic. All these tags glow,' the doctor said.

Artema felt too tired for this conversation but it was important so she pushed on and said, 'It needs a certain level of skill to activate the demon icons. But once a person acquires that skill, the demon no longer has to be around to ensure they take.'

'It's what makes them so dangerous. Remember, some humans have a natural ability and when they draw anything like a demon icon, they can unwittingly activate it.'

'Something else must be going on here, though,' Artema said. 'There is no way a single individual is going around painting the gang tags. It would take too long and I doubt the gangs would tolerate strangers on their turf even if they were painting tags for them.'

'Something else that needs to be discovered then,' Normando said. 'Which icons specifically are being used?'

'Some pretty common ones,' Artema said. 'There's the icon for mind control, the one for inducing fear, a couple that revolve around communication, powering a message across a distance, that sort of thing. It's hard to say what they all add up to.

'With demon icons, context is everything. There are

thousands of icons and how they are used together is the important point. Not what each of them represents individually.'

'So you have no idea what their aim is?'

'Not yet. You sometimes need to see the end result before you can understand the icons and of course, at that point it's often too late.'

'Is it possible it's being used to control the people within each gang's territory?' Doctor Leopold said. 'Mind control and communication with a dose of fear seem to indicate that.'

'It's one possibility,' Artema said. 'The thing is, mass control of a population isn't really in character with the usual demon activity. They usually focus on a single individual.'

'Indeed,' Lady Ophelia said. 'But it does sound like a very human preoccupation.'

Artema hadn't really considered that. Usually demon activity ultimately was to benefit the demon. She couldn't see why they would want to control the denizens of the suburbo. Then she remembered her conversation with Eladio about the demon killing army. Maybe the demons were preparing something similar for themselves. That thought so alarmed her she realised sleep was going to be elusive after all.

7

A message from Artema that she was on her way down finally got Eladio out of bed. He'd stayed at Felicha's. Despite her company, gene tests and magistos, gangs and demons jostled through his dreams and made for an uncomfortable night. Felicha had clambered over him to get up far too early in the morning and he'd stayed, lying with his eyes closed, hoping for some rest.

Maybe it was just that his body was no longer used to sleeping at night. No, that was a small part. It was the tumult Artema had introduced to his boring life that had him so shook up.

That and wondering about the genetic test. It surprised Eladio it meant so much to him when his sensible side kept telling him it would come to nothing. Still, there was that feeling you got when you bought a lottery ticket that maybe, just maybe, you'd be the one. You'd win the genetic lottery. You'd have blue blood and be whisked up to the supraurbo and a life of degenerate luxury.

Maybe not degenerate. It had stunned him to learn about tenure and to discover no envy for the idea. He wanted a more interesting job and a life that meant something. Sitting around doing nothing but watch the money roll in wasn't as appealing as he'd imagined it might be.

No time to consider that now, he thought, as he threw off the covers and stood up. The other advantage of Felicha's place was that she had her own supply of running water and therefore her own shower and toilet. Now that was a luxury.

If he'd not spent all his money on his pass to the mezaurbo, maybe he would have such a luxury now too. As it was that, and his upcoming exams, had eaten all of his cash. But hopefully, in the long run, he could get a place of his own with an indoor bathroom.

In his more extravagant fantasies, that place was in the mezaurbo and his home would have a window to let in the sunlight. He tried not to dwell on that too often. Very few people from the suburbo achieved permanent resident status in the mezaurbo. He had to be realistic. But if the genetic test...

He shook his head. He had to get a move on and there were bigger problems to be faced today. Fantasies about the future would have to wait.

After a quick shower, Eladio scrambled into his clothes, waved his thanks to Felicha, who was busy with a customer, and headed out to meet Artema. She was earlier than he'd expected, and he wondered why.

His phone gave a discreet ping as he stood waiting at the elevators and his stomach clenched with fright. He'd set an alert only for important messages, and he'd marked the gene test results as important. His hands were actually shaking as he pulled out his phone and jabbed at the mail app.

There it was, the official result. He took a deep breath and opened the message. It was a long document, and he scanned it rapidly.

There was nothing, and the crushing disappointment that wrapped around his heart was almost more than he could bear. Eladio read it more carefully now, praying that his quick search had missed something, trying not to let his disappointment show. He didn't want the people streaming past him to know he'd been dealt a blow, but it was worse even than he'd expected. He felt physically ill.

'Eladio, are you alright?' Artema said.

Eladio looked up with a start, surprised that Artema could sneak up on him.

'My results,' he said, and practically threw the phone at Artema.

Damn this woman, if she hadn't wanted the gene test this would never have happened. He'd never have known how completely average, no, subnormal, he was.

'This can't be right,' Artema murmured as she ran her finger down the test results.

'I told you, nobody down here has any worthwhile genes.'

Eladio found it difficult to look at Artema and half turned away, trying to hide his disappointment.

'No,' Artema said. 'These results should have flagged up your perfect memory, it's genetic. It should be listed here under special genetic traits and yet that entire section just says, none.'

Eladio shrugged, what did this magisto expect? He was about to say so when his phone rang.

The ring tone was the one he'd assigned to Felicha, so he snatched the phone away from Artema and said, 'Yes?'

'Did you get it?' Felicha said.

'Yeah.'

'Mine's wrong.'

'Why? Because it didn't tell you, you're special?' Eladio said and regretted how bitter he sounded.

'No, stupid. It says my mother was black.'

'Oh,' Eladio said.

'Do you have that woman with you?'

'She's here.'

'Ask her about it.'

'Why would she know anything?'

Eladio was painfully aware that Artema had overheard the whole conversation and wasn't even pretending not to listen in.

'Just ask her. I'll send you my results too,' Felicha said and hung up.

'Felicha thinks her results are wrong?' Artema said.

Eladio was so angry with Artema that he could barely bring himself to speak to her. It was irrational he knew; the results weren't Artema's fault.

'Yeah,' he muttered. He opened Felicha's results and held it out for Artema to see. 'The orphanage records said that Felicha's mother was white.'

'Really? But she's so dark.'

Eladio shrugged. 'I'm just telling you what the records said.'

'They let you see your records?'

'No. We sneaked into the office one night and accessed the records.'

'Why?'

'Felicha wanted to find her parents. She was convinced they'd take her back.'

'But she was an orphan.'

'Not everybody who lands up at an orphanage is actually an orphan. Unwanted kids are dumped there too.'

'So you discovered her mother was white.'

'Yeah, that was a surprise.'

'How did you discover that?'

'It's on the birth certificate. Mother's age, ethnicity and place of birth.'

'That's a surprise.'

'None more so than to Felicha's father. He was also on the birth certificate, which isn't so common for orphanage kids. He was listed as white too.'

'Surely that can't be right.'

'That's what we thought, so we went to find him.'

'How old were you at the time?'

'Eight.'

'And you were wandering the suburbo looking for parents?'

'Felicha was having a really tough time. She thought anything would be better than the orphanage.'

'Did you find him, the father?'

'He was still living at the address he'd shared with Felicha's mother. But he wanted nothing to do with Felicha. He said she obviously wasn't his, that his mother must have slept around. She died shortly after the birth so we couldn't ask her about it and there was nothing more we could do except go back to the orphanage.'

'I see. That is curious indeed.'

Eladio shrugged and decided he had to pull himself together. There was no point in dwelling on something he couldn't change. Artema was watching him with her usual thoughtful expression too, and he didn't want to show how upset he was. He pulled out the glass jar with Luca's spit in it and handed it to Artema.

'That's from Luca Ten. I thought you might want to have that analysed as well. Only now... there doesn't seem to be any point.'

'On the contrary, there's something suspicious about these results,' Artema said. 'I do believe we need a second test done and clearly the laboratory down here isn't the place to do it.'

'Where then?'

'Up.'

'That will be even more expensive.'

'It will be worth it. I don't like mysteries, and this is one we can solve fairly easily.'

Eladio felt a spark of hope again and cursed himself to be so easily pulled into this damned rollercoaster of dreams.

'We have another problem, actually.'

It had to be faced as well, and while the crushing disappointment of the genetic test had distracted Eladio, the other matter was bigger and more urgent.

'What other problem?' Artema asked.

Eladio checked all the passersby, he'd been so upset about his results he'd become oblivious to them. But thinking about the gangs reminded him of his surroundings and the need to be careful.

'Seraf wants to see us.'

'Seraf? Seraf One?'

'Yeah. He sent Luca around last night with a message.'

'So they have noticed us.'

'They don't know what we're doing yet. At least I don't think so.'

'Considering we don't know what we're doing, that's hardly surprising.'

Eladio wished he could smile at Artema's flippant words, but he wasn't in the mood for it. Going to see Seraf would not make it better.

'Seraf's dangerous and untrustworthy, we can't tell him anything.'

'No, we really can't,' Artema said far more seriously. 'Once you get me to his... where are we going?'

'The Black Brotherhood headquarters.'

'Fine, well, once we get there you'd better let me do all the talking.'

Eladio shrugged acceptance but said, 'It would be best not to say anything at all.'

'Somehow I don't think that would work,' Artema said with an infuriatingly calm grin. 'So you lead the way. We might as well get this over with.'

It hadn't taken Artema long to realise that most of what Eladio did was about self improvement. She also knew the young man was pragmatic and tried to control his own expectations. It surprised her, therefore, that Eladio was so upset about the gene tests, even though he was trying to hide it.

Now, as he guided the two of them through the dark daytime streets of the suburbo, he was less inclined to speak than usual. This suited Artema, who did a quick sidestep to avoid getting mowed down by a burley man coming the other way, and contemplated what happened next.

It was inconvenient that the gangs had spotted them, but not altogether terrible. It meant she was finally going to meet one of them. That would give her a chance to gauge how deeply in league with the demons the gangs were.

The senior people in particular would be the ones the demons used. So meeting the second in command would be useful. To see how Eladio interacted with them would also be interesting.

'We're nearly there,' Eladio said as he slowed his breakneck speed. 'Don't say anything to anyone here and try... try not to look funny at anyone.'

'How does one do that?' Artema asked as she examined a substantial corrugated metal gate that completely closed off the lane, bottom, sides and top.

In front of this impressive gate, which had a huge gang tag spray painted across it, were a dozen gang members. Five women and seven men, mostly young, with shaggy hair, sallow skin and stubble on the men. What set them apart from other suburbonites was that they looked well fed.

They were all wearing black leather jackets proudly sporting their tag, demon icons and all, emblazoned on the front and even bigger on the back. Aside from the ostentatious demonic display on their clothes, Artema could detect no other taint on the people. If anything, they seemed oblivious to the significance of the tags.

'Don't look them in the eye,' Eladio said and held his empty hands out in front of himself, much like a man saying don't shoot. 'I had a message from Luca Ten that Seraf One wants to see us.'

'And what's your name?' The hairiest and ugliest man Artema had seen in the suburbo said.

'I am Eladio Thirteen and this is Artema...' he petered out and looked enquiringly at Artema.

'Smith,' Artema said. 'My name is Artema Smith.'

Eladio looked incredulous, but the gang members accepted the name. With a nod, an electric whine started up, and the gates creaked open. Lights spilled out onto the two of them and Artema blinked at this sudden and unexpected brightness. Apparently the gangs had sufficient money for full spectrum daylight bulbs. The courtyard that resolved itself from the glare was filled with gang members mostly lounging about.

'This way,' the ugly gang member said with a tilt of his

head as he led them across the courtyard.

The buildings surrounding them were made from the same shipping containers as Eladio's little home, but here they were full sized and they had cut windows into them. At the lower level, they'd even added glass sliding doors, and they painted the interiors a dazzling white. On the upper levels, the containers were all linked by an outer walkway come balcony. Gang tags the size of a mural were painted on the back wall of each room.

Artema was about to point that out to Eladio, but stopped when she turned to look at the young man. His gaze was darting about this way and that, and he looked on edge. Artema decided not to distract him. After all, Eladio could understand this scene of the gang headquarters better than she could. The only difference between this and a corporate HQ, as far as she could see, was the clothing and general untidiness of the gang member's.

'Up here,' ugly said and stopped at a set of stairs that zigzagged up the outside of the containers, linking each balcony. 'You go right to the top. Luca is outside Seraf's door.'

'Thanks,' Eladio muttered and started climbing.

'Remember,' Artema murmured. 'Leave the talking to me.'

'Just don't piss him off,' Eladio said.

The top floor was the fifth floor, and Artema wasn't used to such a long climb. She was huffing and puffing by the time they got there and annoyed that Eladio looked like all he'd done was go for a stroll on the flat and level. She was also shocked by the size of Luca Ten, who eyed them both with what Artema could only describe as menace.

'Is he in?' Eladio said and flicked his thumb in at the

door.

It took a while for Luca to process the question, then he nodded and stepped aside.

'Eladio,' a warm voice said as he and Artema entered the office to find three men standing behind a desk.

The middle one was without a doubt the most handsome man Artema had ever seen. He stood half a head taller than everyone else, was wearing a tight fitting white t-shirt, had blond hair that fell in waves to his shoulders and fascinating blue eyes. They positively glowed in contrast against his tanned golden skin. He was the only tanned man Artema had seen so far in the suburbo.

'Hello, Seraf,' Eladio said with no pretence at the pleasure Seraf was showing. 'This is Artema.'

'Artema Smith?' Seraf said and flashed a dazzling smile that revealed perfect white teeth.

'You have surveillance?'

Artema resisted holding out her hand in greeting as no hand had been offered.

'We see and hear everything. Please, take a seat,' Seraf said and sat down. The two men flanking him remained standing.

Artema had the distinct impression of sitting down in front of a shark.

She mirrored Seraf's smile and said, 'I am honoured to meet you.'

'You may not think it but, yes, you are. And what, may I ask, are you doing in the suburbo?'

'I am a professor of anthropology from Central University. I'm down here studying gang culture.'

'Are you indeed?'

Seraf flipped on a computer screen that showed up

bright despite the light of the room. This room had a window, another rarity in the suburbo, and the computer was obviously state-of-the art.

'Professor Artema Smith, was it?' Seraf said and typed it in.

'Well, no,' Artema said. 'It's actually Artema Donu. I was trying to get around incognito.'

'Donu?' Seraf said, and typed that in. A CV scrolled down the screen that included an unflattering picture of a younger looking Artema.

'Well, well, so you are studying us, are you?' Seraf said. 'Is that why you spent all of yesterday tracing the outline of our territory?'

'I'm afraid so,' Artema said and tried for her best impersonation of a harmless academic. 'I didn't mean to cause offence, sorry if I did.'

'What I don't understand,' Seraf said and sat back in his chair, his gaze fixed on Artema, 'is why you didn't come and ask our permission first.'

'Ah, well, I find I get a more honest impression of what's going on if I can work ah, undetected, as it were. People change their behaviour once they know they're being observed.'

'Do they indeed?' Seraf murmured. 'Well, that's all very interesting, Professor, but your investigation must stop.'

'Oh... that is disappointing. I mean, there is so much more to be learned. Your gang tags alone are worthy of their own thesis,' Artema said, dropping in the tags to see what kind of reaction she'd get.

Seraf was either supremely in control of his emotions or unaware of their significance because he just sighed.

'My boss doesn't like people poking their noses into our

business, no matter how irrelevant they may be.'

'Maybe I could speak to him?' Artema said.

That made Eladio's face twitch. It was the first sign of emotion he'd shown. Artema knew full well she was walking a dangerous line, but she needed information too.

'No, Professor Donu, you cannot speak to him,' Seraf said.

His voice told Artema he'd go no further, so she smiled and stood up. 'Then I suppose my research is at an end. I apologise for causing you any discomfort.'

'Discomfort?' Seraf said, and his eyes gleamed in amusement. 'Eladio, where did you find this woman? You really should avoid picking up strays.'

'Yes, Seraf,' Eladio said as he stood up.

Artema was struck by the thought that Eladio was wary of Seraf, but not cowed by him. Which was surprising considering how scared he'd been of the gang members and this man was their number two boss. In fact, if anything, Eladio seemed angry.

'Off you go then,' Seraf murmured. 'Oh, and, Eladio?'

'Yes?'

'We are now even.'

Eladio's eyebrow flickered upwards, then he gave a slight nod. 'I understand,' he said and walked out.

He said nothing till they'd cleared the gang compound and walked a dozen more blocks in what Artema suspected was the direction of the elevator.

'Are you sending me home, Eladio?'

'It isn't safe down here for you anymore.'

'Really, it didn't seem to me like we were threatened?'

Eladio shook his head, then lowered his voice and said, 'I didn't tell you the full story of what happened when I found

Seraf in the drug den. I didn't leave him behind. I carried him to my home, put him in my bed and fed him for a fortnight. Then one day I came home, and he was gone, along with the savings I'd stashed in the container. I haven't spoken to him since.'

'So he owes you,' Artema said. 'And now he's just told you he's paid off his debt.'

'Exactly.'

'It hardly seems like an equal exchange.'

Eladio shook his head.

'He was telling me, in a way that his goons wouldn't pick up, that if he hadn't intervened you and I would both be dead already.'

'He's saying he saved our lives?'

'I'm guessing his boss ordered him to kill us.'

'That is serious.'

'Yeah,' Eladio said. 'Which is why you have to go home now.'

'You should come with me.'

'I'll be fine down here if you leave. There's no need for me to go.'

'Whatever is happening down here won't go away just because I've left, Eladio. I have to keep investigating and for that I still need you.'

'It's too dangerous. You should just go home.'

'If this is serious, and I fear it is, then hundreds, even thousands of people could die. I can't ignore that just because a gang threatened me. I'll double what I'm paying you if you'll keep working with me.'

'This isn't about money,' Eladio snapped. 'It's too dangerous. You can go back to your life and be safe. I have to stay down here with all of them.'

'We can't speak about this properly down here,' Artema said. 'For all we know, we are being surveilled as we speak. Come up to the mezaurbo with me at least, so we can thrash this out.'

'I can't go anywhere with you. Not now.'

'Alright. How about I go up and you follow later, as if you're just going to work tonight? I can meet you at the elevator terminus.'

Eladio shook his head but muttered, 'At Doreen's,' and hurried away into the crowd.

Well, at least she'd got that concession. Artema felt better about Eladio, too. She didn't want to abandon the young man, and she was pleased that he'd been so willing to break it off. A demon's agent would have tried harder to stay with her.

Eladio hardly noticed the people as he pushed past them, walking away, just away. He didn't have a plan at first. He'd had such a shit day that all he wanted was to put it behind him. But he couldn't. Something was definitely up, and if Artema was right, they were all in danger. If Artema was anything she said she was, really.

That surname and her job from the information Seraf had pulled up were not the same as the surname Artema had first told him, and it wasn't the job he'd guessed at and Artema had admitted to. Nor did it explain why Artema was listed at two universities, the University of Magic and Central University.

Why was that? Who was she lying to? Was it Seraf or him? Eladio wondered. He needed to find out the truth, and he wasn't convinced he'd get it from Artema. The woman was slippery.

Although… Eladio had evidence. The tags obsessed Artema, and she'd done things that no mere anthropology professor could do. So maybe he was the one being told the truth. It was best Seraf didn't know that.

Seraf, who looked… different and not in a good way. He could puzzle that one around and around in his head all day to no benefit. He needed to talk to somebody about it, somebody who could help.

Felicha was good in that she listened, even if she wasn't sympathetic. But Three… Three would have answers, Eladio thought. He must have been subconsciously considering her already because he was halfway to her place. Before he got there, though, he had to get some supplies.

After a brief detour to a shop, he made for the river. It was a route he hadn't taken Artema yet. He went down a blackened, slippery set of stairs to the river's edge. A tingle between his shoulders reflected his hyper alert state. He was ready to run at even a hint of an alarm.

He made his way along the empty path that traced the edge of the river. It looked quiet today, slipping past with hardly a ripple. A light shone dimly at a door that sat discreetly under one of the many bridges that crisscrossed the river. A couple of women stood at the door, one with a child on her hip. Eladio resigned himself to a long wait because the women at the door were just the tail end of what had to be a long queue.

As he got to the women, he looked through the door and up a set of stairs that were green with algae. Women lined the steps all the way to a solid circular metal door that had an impressive locking mechanism. The door, Eladio knew, had been designed to keep water out and was essential for whenever the river flooded. It was a strange place to live, but then again, Three was a strange woman.

Eladio wished he didn't have to wait, but this was how Three made her living. Since she helped people, he couldn't complain. It was odd that he was the only man, though. He wondered why men didn't come and see Three. She could be as helpful to them as she was to the women.

The door above opened with a metallic shriek, and a woman stepped out. Instead of letting the next one in, she whispered something urgent to her and then the next one and the next. They all turned and made their way out, clinging to the railing so as not to slip on the stairs as they went.

'You are Eladio, aren't you?' the women who'd emerged from Three's room said.

'Yes?'

'Mistress Three said you were to go in, and to hurry, the water is rising.'

'Okay,' Eladio said and waited only long enough for the rest of the women to clear the stairwell before he grabbed onto the railings.

Going hand over hand to be as quick as possible, he ran up the stairs. He didn't fancy getting caught in this enclosed space when the river burst its banks.

'Seal the door,' a voice said out of the darkness as Eladio arrived.

He pulled the door shut with a bang and spun the locking mechanism all the way till it wouldn't turn any more. He felt the door suck into its seal and gave it a final pull. It was solid and secure.

Three sat cross-legged on a rug near the entrance to her home. Around her, a dozen artificial candles cast a flickering circle of light that left the rest of the room in darkness. She had a black scarf tied around her eyes, which she undid as Eladio settled opposite her.

She blinked vaguely at him and smiled. Her face had that peculiar blue tint of a woman of Asian extraction who got no sunlight. To enhance the effect, she'd painted a series of mysterious blue patterns down the side of her face.

Eladio checked them to see whether any were demon icons. None were. At least, none matched the ones he'd already seen.

'Eladio, my dear, it has been a while,' Three said in her gentle voice.

'I brought you some stuff.'

'Show me.'

'Soap,' Eladio said as he placed it on the floor in front of Three.

She reached forward and felt the bar with her fingertips. 'Scented, how lovely.'

'Rose scent, the one you like,' Eladio said. 'Also chocolate, biscuits, a couple of apples and a scented candle.'

'A scented candle?'

'It's filled with a fragrance and it comes out in regular puffs.'

'How delightful,' Three said, and then paused to listen.

There was a distant hum, and the room vibrated. The hum grew to a roar, the sound of a mighty train barrelling through a tunnel, only it was longer and more sustained. The vibration turned into such a hard shaking that the candles tipped over and rolled across the floor.

The water banged against the door, and Eladio watched it nervously. There was no escape from this place now. If the door gave, they would drown.

'Now would I allow that to happen?' Three mouthed over the noise.

The shaking persisted but the noise suddenly dropped off and Three said, 'We're under water now. It will be quiet for the rest of the day.'

'I'm stuck here for the day?'

'Don't worry, you'll be in time for your meeting this evening.'

Despite knowing what Three was capable of, she still surprised him. 'You know about that?'

'I have seen it.'

'I wasn't even sure that I would go.'

'You will go. Your memory is your strength, your curiosity is your weakness. Even if your sensible side told you to stay, you would still end up going. Aside from that, you have a helpful streak that will also drive you to go.'

'I have a strength and a weakness?'

'We all do.'

'Really? Well, your second sight is your strength,' Eladio said, 'but what is your weakness?'

'My terrible eyesight. I can see the future but not what is right before my nose.'

'What about Felicha?'

'Her strength and toughness you know about, but she is more fragile than she shows. That is her weakness. It isn't one I would divulge to anybody else, but I trust you with this knowledge.'

'And Seraf?'

'Ah Seraf, who abused your helpful nature. He is a natural leader. Men want to do what he directs. His weakness is that he needs to be needed. Part of the reason he left you the way he did was because he couldn't stand to be so reliant upon another. In his mind, he is always the hero. He is always the one doing the rescuing.'

'And now?'

'Be more specific, Eladio. Don't try to test me too.'

'He looked different to when I saw him last,' Eladio said, desperate to know the reason even while he found it difficult to believe it was possible. 'He was... he looked like he was breaking out of his skin. All across his body and face were cracks and golden light shone through the cracks.'

'It sounds beautiful.'

'It wasn't.'

'Why not?'

'Because it felt like he was changing, metamorphosing into something... something dangerous.'

'And if it can happen to him, it can happen to the rest of us, huh?'

As usual, Three had got to the nub of the issue. The Thirteen were united in more ways than merely being orphans all born in the same year.

'We are different, Three.'

'And you have been waiting to discover why your whole life.'

'I'd begun to think I was mistaken. To think there was nothing but coincidence about all of us. Then everything started to happen at once: Artema, Seraf, demons, what does it all mean?'

'You will find out in time.'

'Why won't you just tell me?'

'Because I don't know yet. You know my foresight isn't very long range. I see two, three days at the most. So far I see nothing that would provide an explanation.'

'But?'

'But they worry you. You might not have my premonitions, but you have a brain that's always calculating, always collecting data. You put it all together in ways that allow you to draw conclusions from things the rest of us might never connect. If you are worried, that is sufficient.'

Eladio felt it was far from sufficient and that, as usual, Three was withholding information. But then, all of them had learned the hard way that sometimes a misinterpreted future acted upon could cause more harm that the thing they were trying to avoid.

'What of Artema? I don't even know if half of what she's told me is true. I'm not even sure she's given me her real name.'

'She is dangerous, far more than you realise, but I can't see that she is a danger to you. Not directly, anyway. In fact, her feelings towards you are quite benign.'

'Only quite benign?' Eladio said with a laugh.

'Wait and see.'

8

Artema sat nursing her second coffee in Doreen's, watching the steam rise. Despite herself, she looked up every time someone came through the door. So far none of them had been Eladio. She hoped the young man would come and that he hadn't talked himself out of it, or worse, been ambushed by the Black Brotherhood.

She could always track Eladio down again. After all, she knew where he worked. She also had sufficient information on his bank account that her AI would only take seconds to track it down. If she wanted to be very mean, she could force Eladio to come to her by blocking his access to his money. But she didn't want that. She needed a volunteer, someone willing to help.

Artema sighed as she examined the other faces in the cafe. They were well fed, well-dressed people stopping by on their way home for a last cup of coffee. She'd dressed to blend in with this crowd and was thankful she didn't have to wear suburbo clothes today.

The cafe crowd was a cheerful bunch. They were unaware of the turmoil brewing below their feet. This was the danger of their stratified society. They were living over a hell, and they didn't care.

They all knew there was a suburbo. Some of them might even have met a couple of the residents. But the conditions the people lived in didn't bother them. How could it be okay for them to have people living in their city who slept in a metal box only slightly bigger than a coffin? She was ashamed that till she'd been down there herself, she'd neither known about that nor bothered to find out.

She'd never even questioned why people from the suburbo weren't allowed into the supraurbo. It wasn't a hard and fast rule, but when she'd applied for Eladio, it caused a bureaucratic ruckus and an instant refusal. She'd pushed them for a reason and none was forthcoming, which made it clear it was prejudice, pure and simple.

The door tinkled, and Artema looked up with little hope and was surprised to see Eladio. He hesitated in the doorway, apparently uncertain he should come in, so Artema stood up. Eladio gave her a wry smile and started to head over. He was watched all the way by a plump woman behind the counter that Artema guessed was the eponymous Doreen.

So Artema intercepted Eladio, put a firm hand on his shoulder and turned him around.

'Come on, we need to talk, just not here,' she said and pushed him back outside.

'What are you doing?' Eladio said, looking back at the cafe.

'You booked today off, didn't you? So why spend time in your place of work when you don't have to?' Artema said and flagged down an aerocab. 'In you get,' she said and shoved a bewildered-looking Eladio inside.

'An aerocab?' Eladio said as he looked about wide eyed. 'An actual aerocab?'

'Certainly, and that's just the start of the journey if you're still willing.'

Artema engaged the cabin's privacy settings so that the

glass window between them and the driver came down and reinforced it with her own magical protections.

'Where are we going?' Eladio said.

But he wasn't really paying Artema any attention. He scooted over to the window and peered outside, twisting to see the drop to the suburbo.

'Up,' Artema said, and waited.

Eladio was so transfixed by the view that it took a few seconds. Then he spun around and gasped, 'Up? All the way up?' and pointed into the sky.

'All the way.'

'I can't,' Eladio said. 'I don't have the permit that will let me in. I'd have to work for a hundred years to get enough money and even then they still wouldn't let me in.'

'Yes, they will,' Artema said as she opened her pocket universe.

It looked much like a small black hole, and Eladio's eyes widened even more as he watched Artema scrabble about inside.

'Ah, here we go,' she said and handed Eladio a phone. 'This is the latest in supraurbo tec. It has your permit on it. To get in all you have to do, as I had to do in the other direction, is blend in.'

She reached into her pocket universe again and handed Eladio a black, heavily tailored and embroidered jacket and a pair of black trousers. 'Put that on. With that and the phone, you'll not have any difficulties.'

'Why?' Eladio said without making a move toward the clothes. 'What do I need to go up for?'

'Because we need to plan and I feel safer on my home turf. And... there is a test. A test I need you to take that can't be administered anywhere else.'

'A genetic test?'

'Not that, although we'll do that up there too. That way we can guarantee honest results.'

'I have another sample for you to test,' Eladio said and handed over a bottle.

'Another?'

'From Three, she's also one of the Thirteen. I thought you might want it.'

'Three? She goes by her surname?'

'They called her Madonna, and she really didn't like that.'

'Could I be so indelicate as to enquire what her special ability is?'

'She can see the future.'

He spoke with such absolute certainty that it surprised Artema. If Three was a fraud, she'd expect Eladio to spot that.

'How?'

'I don't know. She just sees things. Not far into the future mind, but that can be a real help sometimes.'

'You're sure of this?' Artema asked, astonished that anyone could see into the future.

That wasn't even something a magisto could do. To hear that somebody living in the suburbo had such an ability was astonishing. That she was one of the Thirteen added yet another layer to the mystery surrounding the orphans.

'We tested Three all the time when we were kids,' Eladio said. 'She also knew I would see you this evening, and I hadn't even told her about you.'

'She could have heard from the gang.'

Artema wasn't quite ready to accept future sight from any human. After all, there were mentalists who could fool people with their so-called abilities too.

'No. I still wasn't sure I was coming when I saw her. And I didn't tell her your name, but she knew it. She does that all the time. She told us Felicha's father's name before we went off to find him and warned us he'd be angry and beat us up.'

'Was she right?'

'Yeah, although we were more on our guard than we might have been otherwise and ran when he started hitting us.'

'Do you see anything when she looks to the future?'

'She doesn't make any gestures like you, if that's what you're asking,' Eladio said. 'She just sees it.'

'Fascinating. I've never heard of somebody with the natural ability to see the future.'

'So you have spells that can do it?'

'There is one spell. It opens a temporal wormhole. It's ridiculously dangerous and the act of looking can change the future so its use is heavily proscribed.'

'It doesn't really work for you,' Eladio said, translating this with his straightforward mind.

'Not really, no.'

Eladio nodded, apparently satisfied with her reply.

'Are you really Artema Salonoy?'

'Ah yes, I couldn't explain before. I have a cover for when I'm out and about. It's awkward enough telling people I'm a magisto, let alone a demonologist when I get asked that normally innocuous question of what a person does. I came up with Artema Donu to make things easier.'

'Isn't it excessive to have a fake CV?'

'My boy, I even have a couple of fake papers published under that name. Sometimes it pays to have that extra background. Now,' Artema said as they were getting near the elevator, 'are you going to get dressed and come with me?'

Eladio gave a slight, self-reflective laugh and said, 'Three says my weakness is my curiosity. Even when I doubt the wisdom of something I still do it.'

'Then you'd best get dressed,' Artema said and fished her suit out of the pocket universe too.

They were so well dressed that the inspectors saluted as they walked into the elevator terminus, which practically caused Eladio's eyes to bulge from their sockets. His hand still trembled as he held the new phone up for the man to inspect his pass, though.

'Thank you, sir,' the man said and snapped off another salute.

Then they stepped into the elevator and Eladio spun around to walk straight out again. Artema grabbed him and guided him firmly to one of the plush red velvet seats. Unfortunately, they weren't alone in the elevator. There was an overdressed woman with her two daughters sitting opposite him. The girls obviously found Eladio attractive because they stared and smiled at him.

He looked alarmed and pushed further back into his seat to get away from them.

'Surely you're used to girls hitting on you?' Artema said in an undertone.

'Yeah,' Eladio hissed 'But not girls like them.'

'Would it help if I give them the wrong impression and kissed you?'

'What?'

Artema laughed. 'Sorry, my little joke. I wouldn't do that.'

'Not funny,' Eladio said, and his eyes darted about the elevator.

Artema wondered whether she'd looked as

uncomfortable when she was heading to the suburbo for the first time. She didn't think so. Then again, she was a more jaded person. She might have only recently visited the suburbo, but she'd travelled the world and had the comfort of her status. She had to keep reminding herself how much of an advantage that gave her over Eladio.

'It's quite a long ride,' Artema said in the same undertone so the other passengers wouldn't overhear her. 'So you can fill me in a little more on the Black Brotherhood and their leader.'

'What about their leader?' Eladio said warily.

'Don't worry, I've checked on the security feed for the elevator and it doesn't have sound.'

'Alright,' Eladio said and glanced up at the corners of the elevator, no doubt trying to spot the cameras, but they weren't visible. 'What do you want to know?'

'His name for a start. My AI tried to look into him last night and could find nothing on him. It got something about Seraf and some other senior gang members, but nothing about the big boss.'

'He's not one of the most outgoing gang leaders,' Eladio said.

'Meaning?'

'I've seen other gang leaders and know more about them than I do about Rushabarbo.'

'So his name is Rushabarbo. Does he have a red beard?'

Eladio shrugged in a vaguely dismissive way.

'You live in their territory,' Artema said. 'Surely you'd know what the head of that gang looks like?'

'It isn't like I want to know though.'

At least Eladio looked puzzled that he didn't know what Rushabarbo looked like, but Artema thought this was worth probing. 'Tell me, do you know the name and appearance of the leader of the Purples?'

'Sure, that's Bellecannon.'

'How about the River Guardians?'

'I don't know anyone from that gang, nobody does.'

'Okay, how about the Yellow Threat?'

'Tommy Lee, and before you ask the leader of the Red Fist is Mauro and the Green Dragons is Isca, I know what Tommy Lee looks like and Mauro but not Isca.'

'Do you see the point I'm making?'

'Yeah,' Eladio said, winced and massaged his forehead with his fingertips.

'It's not that upsetting.'

'It's giving me a headache.'

'Ah, maybe that isn't because of what I'm talking about but the altitude. Did you suffer from altitude sickness when you first went up to the mezaurbo?'

'No.'

'Well, the supraurbo is considerably higher, so it may be because of that. Don't worry, you're not the first traveller to suffer from it. For that reason the elevator terminus has vending machines with ventilators, you'll feel fine with those.'

'Okay.'

'In the meantime, try to think about the leader of the Brotherhood. Do you think you've ever seen him?'

Eladio closed his eyes and Artema hoped it was because he was searching his vast and impressive memory for the man and not just that his headache was getting worse.

After a moment he opened them again and said, 'I've got nothing.'

'That is very odd. If a gang survives by showing off their

great works and making sure the population knows who they should thank, you'd think, at the very least, this gang leader would turn up at key events.'

'Events like what?'

'Like the opening of a hospital or some such thing.'

Eladio gave him a slight smile and said, 'Like the mayor of the city turning up to every school opening in the mezaurbo with a big fat gold chain around his neck?'

'So you've seen that, have you?'

'We get the news in the suburbo too.'

'I'm sure you do. But apparently what you don't get is any great show from the leader of the Black Brotherhood.'

'No.'

'That is very odd.'

'Yeah, I suppose so.'

'Perhaps it's something you can look into,' Artema said as the elevator glided to a halt. Artema jumped to her feet and said, 'Come on,' to Eladio, who looked disinclined to stand up.

'Are you sure they'll let me in?' he whispered.

'You'll be fine,' Artema said as they followed the woman and her daughters to the checkpoint.

It took only seconds before they were through and walking across the spectacular elevator terminal. The ceiling was high clear glass and built like a multifaceted crystal. The late evening sun sparkled on its many surfaces, turning them golden. Eladio looked stunned but also had his mouth open and was panting hard.

'Here,' Artema said.

She led Eladio to a booth and punched a red button. A metallic tube popped out of the dispenser. Artema opened it, pulled out the respirator and gave it to Eladio.

'Push that into your nostrils and then breathe normally. It's an oxygen dispenser. It will provide extra oxygen while you need it and gradually ease off as your body gets accustomed to this rarified air.'

'Thank you,' Eladio said, and now his lungs were pumping like bellows.

'It works best if you close your mouth and breathe through your nose.'

'Alright,' Eladio said and took a deep breath through his nose and the newly inserted respirators.

'Come on, I'll show you the campus. This elevator drops us off on the western campus and we need to get across it to reach my house.'

Eladio nodded and followed Artema out of the terminus, then stopped.

'Sky!' he gasped, looking up.

'Ah yes. What do you think?'

'Don't know,' Eladio muttered, but didn't move.

He looked just short of terrified, Artema realised. It disappointed her because she'd hoped it would enchant Eladio. She hadn't factored in his lack of experience. If she was being fair, she wasn't sure how she would react to all this openness if she'd lived with buildings over her head all her life too.

'Shall I call us an aerocab?'

Eladio looked like he dearly wanted to say yes.

But he shook his head and said, 'I'll walk.'

Eladio had a splitting headache. It had come on while he was still in the elevator, and he'd just put it down to nerves till Artema had suggested otherwise. It was a very unaccustomed experience. The only times before his head had ached was when Luca had hit him. On top of that, as the elevator had got higher, it had grown harder to breathe.

Now he was sucking air frantically through his nose and still felt like he wasn't getting enough. The filter wasn't doing the job. It wasn't just the people he'd feared would look down on him, the whole damn supraurbo was making sure he couldn't stay. All the same, he didn't want to show he was struggling and followed Artema out into a vast square.

There was nothing above him. Even in the mezaurbo there were buildings towering up on all sides and cross walks and plazas. You only caught glimpses of sky through the crisscross of man-made structures and the flashes from aerocar windows. Not like this. If he raised his eyes just a little, there was nothing but a deep blue emptiness streaked with violet and a few clouds lit up in orange colours. Thank goodness it was late sunset and it would be dark soon. He'd be able to cope better in the dark.

In the meantime, he kept his eyes fixed on the ground and just concentrated on breathing as he walked along behind Artema.

'Evening, Professor,' a couple of students said as they walked by and eyed Eladio up and down as they passed.

'Evening,' Artema said.

Eladio looked back and noticed them giving him a second look too. So he did look different. He feared as much, despite the clothes. The jacket was thicker than he'd expected and lined with a warm fabric he didn't recognise. He supposed it was because it was colder up here. A lot colder than the suburbo, and the air he was dragging in through his nostrils felt like ice water with no scent at all.

Nausea welled up from his stomach and he felt

unbearably dizzy.

He stumbled and would have fallen but Artema grabbed him as he tripped and said, 'Here, you better sit down.'

Eladio was so breathless he couldn't reply, and more collapsed than sat on the long stone block Artema led him to. But as he sat, his eyes went up and he gasped.

'The moon!'

'Yes, indeed,' Artema said and leaned down to examine his face.

'I thought there was only one of them.'

'How many can you see?' Artema said, and she came even closer.

'None with your face in the way.'

'Alright, how many fingers am I holding up?' Artema said.

'Huh?'

'How many fingers, Eladio?'

She sounded so severe that Eladio concentrated and looked at the fingers.

'You need to hold them still. How can I count them if you keep moving them around?'

'Alright,' Artema said. 'This is serious. I'm getting us a cab and calling the doctor.'

'I'm fine,' Eladio said and tried to get to his feet, but another wave of dizziness overwhelmed him and he dropped back onto the seat. 'There's magic everywhere,' he muttered, 'everything's golden.'

'Well, it is the university of magic,' Artema said.

She waved to get the cab's attention, hauled Eladio forcibly to his feet and shoved him into the cab.

'It isn't far,' she said to the driver. 'But I need to get there quickly.'

'Righto, ma'am,' the driver said and skimmed across the quadrangle and down a wide avenue that had no other vehicles.

Students scattered at their approach, and Eladio wondered why. 'He won't hit them, he's too high,' he muttered.

'Actually, cabs aren't allowed on campus,' Artema said. 'I told the authorities I have an emergency though.'

Eladio nodded and wondered what the emergency was. He was finding it tremendously difficult to think. At the moment, just staying upright was challenge enough. The cab stopped, and Artema ran around to open the door and haul Eladio out.

'I thought we were going to your house,' Eladio muttered. 'Is this a hospital?'

'No, this is my house,' Artema said. 'I've called a doctor he'll be here shortly and then you'll feel a lot better.'

The building was enormous, four stories high with gigantic windows on every floor and carved stone ornaments, not to mention the sweep of stairs up to a porch supported by impressive columns and a double door that was two stories high. Eladio laughed. It was uncontrollable, hysterical laughter.

'This is your house?' he gasped, hiccuping air as he tried to get himself under control. This was worse than being drunk.

The doors swung open, and a man dressed in black trimmed with silver ran down the stairs, followed by two other men dressed nearly the same but with purple waistcoats. The purple waistcoated men grabbed Eladio from each side, lifted him off his feet and hurried him into the house.

'No, it's alright,' he muttered. 'I can walk.'

They ignored him and put him down gently on a bench in what Eladio assumed was the entrance hall, although it was massive. The ceiling was so high he couldn't see it in the darkness. Fringed lamps ringed the space and cast a subtle downward glow.

Another cab pulled up at the front door, signalled by a flash of light as its beams momentarily passed the door and a man jumped out.

'I'm here, where's the patient?'

'This way,' Artema said and held her arms out wide to guide the man in. 'He's from the suburbo and hasn't been much higher than the lower levels of the mezaurbo. I should have realised the altitude would be a problem, but I just didn't think of it.'

'The suburbo, huh?' the doctor said and sat down next to Eladio. 'Can I have more light, please?'

The lights flicked to full brightness. It was so bright it hurt Eladio's eyes as he blinked at the doctor.

'Let's get you more air first,' the man said and clamped a mask onto Eladio's face.

Eladio took a deep breath and for the first time since getting to the supraurbo felt like he wasn't choking.

'Thank you,' he muttered through the mask.

'I'm guessing you've got a tremendous headache and are feeling nauseous too?'

'Yes.'

'And dizzy?'

'Yes.'

'Well, we can treat all of that.' The doctor took a metallic cylinder from his case and pressed it against Eladio's neck. 'It's my high altitude cocktail. I give it to all my visitors,' he said as a puff of air blasted Eladio's skin. 'Better?'

It was so sudden it took Eladio by surprise.

'Yes,' he said. 'I feel fine.'

'You feel better,' the doctor said, 'compared to how you were before. But you will have to take it easy for the next couple of days till your body acclimatises. You can also take the mask off now. I've boosted your red blood cells, but keep these nasal ventilators,' he said as he handed Eladio another metallic tube. 'You'll probably need them for the first day. And don't worry if you can't sleep much this evening. It's another symptom of altitude sickness. It will also pass.'

'Thanks, Doc,' Artema said. 'I appreciate the speed with which you got here.'

'Not at all. Is this the young man you wanted me to do the genetic test on?'

'He is.'

'Shall I take a sample now?'

'Eladio?' Artema said.

'Yeah, fine,' Eladio said, just relieved at this point that he no longer felt the urgent need to hurl.

The doctor held yet another implement to his wrist. He took a small skin sample and said, 'I'll come back with the results in the morning.'

Eladio nodded and watched as Artema saw the doctor out. Then he took another look around the room. It was difficult to wrap his head around the size of the space. He'd never been in a place with such a high ceiling before, nor anywhere with so much wooden panelling. The closest he'd come to anything this grand was the public library in the mezaurbo, and that was half the size.

He also felt acutely uncomfortable to be watched by the three servants who'd remained in the entrance hall. They looked neutral, but he wondered what they really thought.

Artema turned back from seeing the doctor out and gave him a bright smile, 'All better?'

'Yes, thank you,' Eladio said and stood up.

He still felt shaky and a little high. He wasn't sure if that was the altitude sickness or the drugs used to treat it, but he felt odd.

'Right, well, let's grab a bite to eat. No doubt you're starving by now,' Artema said and headed into the house.

Eladio hurried after her and tried not to show how stunned he was at the size of the place. The stairwell was as big as stairs in the outdoor public spaces in the mezaurbo. Nobody would waste this much space in the suburbo. And the dining room looked like something transported from a home back in the 1800s. The only reason Eladio knew that was from the interreto and a history module he'd taken for his exams. Everything was painted with pictures. Actual pictures painted on the walls.

He'd seen nothing like it before and only realised he'd stopped and was staring when Artema said, 'Eladio, would you like to take a seat?'

'Are you sure about this?' Eladio said, glancing at the servants who stood ready to draw out a chair for him.

'Of course. Please, sit down.'

Eladio made cautiously for the table. Artema was sitting at the head and they had laid a place for him to Artema's left. This placed him with his back to the row of windows that looked outside but facing the door into the room. At least, this way he'd see any danger as it entered. Although he wondered what on earth, he'd do if somebody tried to attack him in this fancy house.

It surprised him to have his chair pushed in as he sat, which nearly took his feet out from under him. He sat with a bump and then gazed at the table in dismay. There were three plates stacked one on top of the other before him. To the left were three knives and to the right three forks, and in front of them were three crystal glasses arranged in descending size order.

'Is this normal?' he whispered.

'The setting?' Artema said. 'It is. You start with the utensils on the outside and work your way in.'

It was probably meant as helpful advice, but it mystified Eladio. He didn't have much chance to think about it when another bevy of servants came in. They were wearing white gloves and served something Eladio assumed was soup. It was a swirl of three different colours and had flowers and a foam horse's head decoration on top. Fortunately, they also placed a bread roll, using a pair of silver tongs, on the plate to his left. He recognised bread, at least.

Artema didn't go for the food first. There was an upright roll of cloth to the side of her plate, which she shook out and laid on her lap. Eladio had seen nothing like it. The closest, and what he guessed it was, were the little paper napkins the cafe in the mezaurbo gave you. Although most people wrapped that around the food they'd bought. They didn't put it on their laps. He decided that it was best to copy Artema and shook the cloth out and placed it on his own lap.

He watched as Artema took the soup spoon and dipped it into the soup, tilting it to allow the liquid to flow in. No big scoops here, Eladio thought, and did the same. Despite the beauty of the dish, it tasted bland and he couldn't work out what it was supposed to be. Probably something he'd never come across before, he decided.

He wondered what the next dish would be like. He didn't feel hungry, but guessed he'd disappointed Artema in his reaction to the supraurbo. For reasons he hadn't figured out yet, he didn't want to disappoint her.

A plate filled with peculiar looking flowers replaced the empty soup bowls.

They were so odd he couldn't stop himself from blurting out, 'What is this?'

'Ah, the very latest in supraurbo haute cuisine,' Artema said. 'It's something they're calling floroy. It's a subtle combination of vegetables and protein, usually meat but sometimes egg or cheese, sculpted to look like a flower. This brown one, for example, looks like it's finely sliced mushroom and probably crab, and the dusting of red on top is smoked paprika. Try it,' Artema said and popped the creation into her mouth. 'You're supposed to eat it in one, not cut it up.'

'Can I take a picture of it first?' Eladio said. 'Felicha will never believe me about this without evidence.'

'Go ahead,' Artema said. 'Does she know you're up here?'

'I didn't tell her.'

'Probably sensible.'

'Yeah, the last thing she needs is the gangs knocking on her door,' Eladio said.

He took out his phone and snapped a couple of pictures.

'You're still using the old phone?'

'It saves me having to transfer anything back to it when I go.'

'The new one's too flashy for the suburbo, huh?' Artema said.

'Far too flashy,' Eladio said, and too great of a gift to just be handed over.

All the stuff Artema was giving him made Eladio nervous. He kept waiting to see what she would ask of him in return. For now, he'd just concentrate on the food.

And the room. This dining room, with the servants standing ready to jump at any request and the fancy crockery and cutlery, was really grand. It was far grander than any restaurant he could have visited in the mezaurbo.

It blew his mind that he was up here at all. It had such an absurd quality to it that it didn't feel real. And he was drinking too much. It was a nervous gesture to reach for his glass. It took him a while to realise that every time he took a sip, a servant would step up discreetly and top the glass up again. He should have taken the opportunity to get thoroughly sloshed, but he was too much on edge to enjoy doing that.

Instead, he popped the brownish grey floroy into his mouth and experienced a popping sensation as juices oozed between his teeth. It was peculiar, but not unpleasant. He'd never eaten crab before so wasn't expecting the fishy flavour, but overall, a success. He examined the plate again and selected a green flower with alternating yellow petals.

'Probably asparagus,' Artema murmured. 'With omelette.'

Eladio chewed thoughtfully. This flower was crunchier, and he didn't care for the flavour of asparagus, he decided. Then he examined the plate again.

It was filled with things he'd never eaten before, and suddenly that was appealing. It was a chance to try something so different to his usual life that he'd be a fool to let the opportunity slip away. So he selected a white flower with, he thought, beef interlayers and popped that into his mouth.

Artema left him to it, which was also a relief in that he didn't have to come up with anything to say. Now he could focus on the food. His memory would be an advantage too, as he could relive this moment over and over again.

While he ate, he also looked about the room, taking in everything. It had a sideboard filled with silver platters and crystal jugs, and side tables decorated with fresh flowers. The windows were draped in velvet curtains, cutting the chill from outside. He tried not to think about the outside too much. It was more terrifying than he'd expected to have nothing but clear sky above him.

'Now dessert,' Artema said. 'You're going to like this.'

'Am I?' Eladio said as a slice of something brown, decorated with a pattern of cream and dusted with fine sugar, was laid before him. 'It smells of chocolate.'

'I told chef you like chocolate,' Artema said. 'So tuck in.'

This was a whole other level of chocolate, Eladio realised, as he took a first cautious mouthful. The rich flavour of the chocolate was only slightly sweetened and velvety soft, so it melted in his mouth.

'Well?'

'It's delicious,' Eladio said. This he could eat all day.

'I thought you'd like it,' Artema said and paused as they heard footsteps approaching and the dining room doors swung open. 'Theodore?' Artema said.

Eladio blinked at the young man who'd just walked in. He looked remarkably similar to Artema. He was slightly shorter and squatter, but a relative without a doubt.

'Hello, Aunt,' Theodore said as his gaze swept the room. 'I heard you had an unusual visitor.'

'Did you indeed?'

'Doctor Leopold dropped in for dinner and told us all about him.' Theodore turned to look pointedly at Eladio. 'I heard he's from the suburbo.'

'Ah yes, allow me to introduce you. Eladio Thirteen, this is my nephew Theodore Salonoy.'

'A low-life?' Theodore said, turning back to his aunt. 'You brought a low-life into your house?'

'He's a suburbonite, Theodore. There's no need to use derogatory language.'

'Are you crazy? We don't allow those people up here. Why did you bring him up? Doctor Leopold told us he had altitude sickness, a sure sign that he's not fit to be here.'

'People can adapt,' Artema said. 'And I'll thank you not to be rude to my guest.'

'Your guest, Aunt?' Theodore shouted. 'As your heir, I protest. You do some odd things. We all know why that's important, but this? This is beyond all that's reasonable.'

'My boy, you won't be my heir for long if you keep spouting such rubbish,' Artema snapped. 'I can make other arrangements, you know.'

'I'd like to see you try.'

'Don't tempt me. Now take yourself off before you really anger me and tell your father that he can come over himself next time if he has any objections.'

'My father and I agree on this matter.'

'More's the pity,' Artema said.

Eladio wondered whether he looked like a fool watching the two argue over him. Artema's position was the one he didn't expect. This Theodore Salonoy was what he'd expected all supraurbonites to be like.

'So you really won't reconsider?'

'The longer you remain and badger me, the more

determined I am to keep Eladio here.'

'You'll regret this,' Theodore said, but apparently took his aunt's threats seriously, because he left as abruptly as he'd arrived.

'I'm sorry about that, Eladio,' Artema said. 'He'll come around.'

Eladio barely noticed the apology because a new and horrible realisation had hit him.

'You're a blue blood.'

'I'm afraid so.'

'This was a mistake,' Eladio said as panic gripped him. 'I have to go.'

He pushed back his chair so fast it clattered to the floor and Eladio ran for the door. He had to get away from this place. It was crazy and dangerous, and he wasn't wanted. He ran through the house past astonished servants, his feet pounding on the soft carpets, to the entrance hall.

He reached for the door when a voice like thunder said, 'Eladio, stop!'

A gold band of light wrapped itself around him and no matter how hard he tried, he couldn't move.

'I'm sorry,' Artema said as she arrived, panting. 'I couldn't stop you any other way.'

'Let me go,' Eladio said, and the dizziness returned. 'Please!'

'How exactly were you planning on getting back? I doubt you remember the way to the elevator and you don't have the funds for the fare.'

'I can tell them I'm from the suburbo. They'll deport me faster than I can say the words.'

'Huh,' Artema said and came around so she could see Eladio's face. 'I'm sorry to say you're probably right. But will you please at least sit down and let me explain? If after that I can't convince you I will get you an aerocab back to the elevator and I'll give you the money for your journey. Please, will you at least do that?'

At this point, Eladio just needed to sit down. Maybe the doctor's drugs were wearing off. Or maybe it was too soon to try something like running, so he nodded. It would give him a rest and at least a way out of the place too.

'Alright.'

'Thank you,' Artema said and settled on the dark wooden bench in the entrance hall.

This suited Eladio, who didn't want to go back into the house.

'So you are a blue blood as well? I should have realised it with this fancy house and the university and everything.'

'I am a blue blood,' Artema said. 'The 106th Salonoy of the house of Salonoy.'

'What do you want with me?' Eladio whispered.

He was so scared he could hardly speak.

'Nothing more than I've already told you. Listen, Eladio, what do you think a blue blood is?'

'I don't know... somebody not to be messed with. I shouldn't be here. I shouldn't be speaking to you.'

'My dear fellow, I am no different to you.'

'Yes you are, you're... you have a lineage.'

'So do you. Or do you think you just sprang from the soil? You had a father who had a father who had a father ad infinitum. The only difference between me and you is that my family got lucky a long, long time ago. In our case, being demonologists brought fame and fortune. So we started recording our offspring, and now I have books and books filled with names of relatives stretching back over a thousand years. But before that, who knows. My people were like yours, progenitors stretching back to the beginning of time.'

'No. You can do magic.'

'An ancient art that science is rapidly catching up with. In fact, science is explaining a lot of what we used to call magic and harnessing that too.'

'Not the demon part, it isn't.'

'I already told you I'm the only demonologist in the city. The others, the students at this university, are mostly wealthy dilettantes studying a subject that is so esoteric and irrelevant that it's left as the domain of the wealthy. The rest of the world concentrates on more practical matters like science. That has a far more straightforward and easier path to what we do.'

'You just stopped me at the door. I couldn't move.'

'Have you not heard of force fields? I blocked you with a force field. Entirely explicable by a physicist.'

'Physics isn't magic.'

'Magic isn't magic. I've already told you that. It's the way we tapped into the natural laws of the universe before we understood them. Do you know that in the early middle ages they accused Pope Sylvester II of being in league with the devil because he could do mental arithmetic at what they deemed to be a supernaturally fast rate? It wasn't magic. He'd just discovered arabic numerals and was using them for his calculations. But to people observing his work, it was so fast it looked like magic.'

'That can't be true.'

'It's a documented fact. You can look it up. I am just a person like you. What's more, I'm a person who needs your help if we're ever to untangle the mystery of the gang tags.'

'You can't go back.'

Eladio was feeling nauseous, confused and very much out of his depth. He didn't want to have this conversation with Artema. He didn't want to be here at all, but he had no choice. What he did know was that the suburbo was no longer a place Artema could venture into.

'Maybe I can't go now,' Artema said. 'But maybe, at some point, I won't have a choice. In the meantime, I need you to be my eyes and ears.'

'I can't do that from up here.'

'And I won't keep you here. I brought you here for a very important reason.'

'The test you mentioned.'

'Exactly.'

'Why does it have to be done here?'

'It's a complex thing and best explained tomorrow. First you need some rest and a chance to regain your balance. It's difficult entering another culture. I'm afraid we'll always have idiots like my nephew behaving badly. But you have to admit that in that way our two urbos are similar. You wouldn't dare tell people where I was from in the suburbo either, would you?'

'No.'

'It's foolish. We should all get along, but I'm afraid it's also human nature. Now, what do you say, will you stay?'

'If you want me to.'

Eladio had neither the physical strength not mental ability to reason against Artema this evening.

9

Artema wasn't convinced that Eladio would stay. Because of that, she was up earlier than usual to check. Sleep had been elusive for the last few days anyway, she thought, as she strolled down the wood-panelled corridors of her house. What with the unknown demon threat, a couple of long nights and the turmoil of discovering the suburbo, she was more shaken than normal. At least, more shaken than she'd been in the last couple of decades.

The demons had gone so quiet that she'd seriously believed they no longer represented a danger. That looked supremely foolish now. She'd been living the easy life and thinking about not replacing her post as demonologist in the Eterna Urbo.

She hadn't bothered to train her nephew. She'd hidden all her knowledge away in files that only the AI had access to. Was she wrong to do that?

She wasn't convinced Theodore was the right person for the job, anyway. He was too temperamental, subject to swings of emotion that were perfect for a demon to manipulate. Artema considered her other nieces and nephews. All nice enough kids, but not really demonologist material. She didn't want to subject them to it, anyway. It was a miserable life, dangerous and short.

Was it right that she was considering stripping the Salonoys of a role they'd held for thousands of years? At least she wouldn't have much argument from her brother. If he'd wanted Theodore to be a demonologist, he'd have pushed for it much earlier.

No, he'd been just as happy to let sleeping dogs lie. But now Artema was questioning her earlier decision. The thing was, if not amongst her own family, then where would she find a successor?

Artema stopped at the door to the guest room and gave it a gentle tap. There was no answer, so she eased it open. It was dark inside because the curtains were closed.

What was more surprising was that the curtains around the four-poster bed were also drawn. Was that Eladio making the bed more like his home? Did he prefer to sleep in a small tight space rather than this big open room?

Was he even in the bed? Artema wondered and was glad of the thick pile of the carpet that made it possible for her to sneak across the floor unheard. She eased the curtain open, her heart in her mouth lest Eladio had fled.

He was there, fast asleep, propped up on a pile of pillows. He was wearing the white silk pyjamas Artema's staff had found for him, with a book clasped loosely in his hands. To either side of him were more stacks of books.

Artema leaned back, searching the room for a bookcase and discovered there was one against the far wall. It had been so long since she'd been to the guest room that she'd quite forgotten. An entire shelf now stood empty, transferred to the bed.

For the life of her, Artema couldn't remember what the books were about. No doubt something so uninteresting they didn't deserve a place in the library.

'Huh hmm,' Artema said, clearing her throat noisily.

Eladio gave a start and his eyes blinked open.

'What time is it?'

'Seven,' Artema said, 'or thereabouts. Did you sleep alright?'

Eladio stretched and looked about vaguely.

'Not really.'

'Well, the doctor did say the altitude sickness would make it difficult to sleep. I assume that's why you were reading.'

'Yeah. I've never read a book before. I mean, not a paper one.'

'They are a rarity these days. Was it interesting?'

'It's about philosophy. I didn't know such a subject existed. It was very interesting.'

'Really?' Artema said surprised that anyone would be interested in philosophy, especially someone with Eladio's life experience.

'Did you know about philosophy?' Eladio asked.

'It's an integral part of a classical education. So yes, it was drilled into me, from present day all the way back to the ancient Greeks.'

'There are so many different ideas, and so much infighting about it.'

'They are an argumentative lot, the philosophers,' Artema said. 'Now tell me, did the footman show you the bathroom?'

'He did,' Eladio said. 'I took a picture for Felicha too.'

'Not for yourself?'

'I don't need pictures. I'll remember it exactly.'

'How exactly?'

'Everything,' Eladio said. 'If you like, I can tell you the titles and authors of all the books left on the bookshelf.'

'That exact, huh?'

'Yeah, for all time.'

'What a peculiar gift,' Artema murmured. 'Do you also feel better today? Not so breathless?'

'I feel fine. I even took out the respirator,' Eladio said, and climbed out of bed.

He looked heart stirringly handsome with the white silk clinging seductively to his body and his black hair hanging loose.

'My staff will show you to the dining room for breakfast. Come over when you're ready. And make full use of all the facilities the house provides,' Artema said, nodded and strolled away.

Overall, it relieved her that Eladio had stayed. He was a curious young man. There weren't many students who would voluntarily wade through a pile of philosophy texts. She remembered a sense of frustration at being forced to learn philosophy when she was younger.

She wondered how much Eladio had taken in. She had a feeling that one of the two piles of books on the bed made up a read pile. If that was the case, it meant Eladio had worked his way not just through one book but half a dozen in one night. Artema herself would have needed at least a week to read and digest one.

She'd have to check how much understanding Eladio got from what looked like extraordinarily fast reading. Honestly, the young man was wasted in the suburbo, and as a barista. She had to get him doing something else.

Artema settled at the dining room table and examined the breakfast laid out before her. With her new perspective from the suburbo, it looked wasteful. There was a tray full of bacon and another with smoked salmon, more toast than she and Eladio could consume, and a mountain of scrambled eggs. All delicious she knew, and she dug out a pat of delicious yellow butter to smear on her toast and topped it with egg. She took a leisurely sip of coffee and decided she'd check on the news.

Artema had only just started reading from her pop-up screen when Eladio arrived dressed in a highly embroidered, figure hugging black jacket that stopped just below the knees.

'Well, well, you scrub up nicely,' Artema said.

'This is a different jacket to yesterday,' Eladio said, 'and it stinks of flowers.'

'Fabric softener,' Artema murmured. 'I can't help feeling the suburbo would benefit from more perfume.'

'Maybe, but Felicha said they wouldn't pay the extra to have it done. Anyway, it makes me smell like a girl.'

'Some people find that appealing,' Artema said with real feeling. 'Now sit and have some breakfast. You didn't need to rush by the way, you had time to dry your hair.'

'I did, with the towel.'

'Didn't you notice the hairdryer?'

'The what?'

'Never mind. I'll show you this evening.'

'No,' Eladio said. 'I have to go home this evening.'

'Go home this evening? Why?'

'I have my exams tomorrow, remember? I need to get some proper sleep before that. And it takes too long to travel all the way down to do it in the morning. The exam starts at nine am.'

'Your matric?' Artema said vaguely recalling more than one conversation on the subject, although that felt like it was decades ago.

'Yes,' Eladio said, and his eyes widened as he took in all

the food laid out on the table.

'Can't it wait? We are in the middle of something rather important.'

'No,' Eladio said, shaking his head emphatically. He sniffed the salmon suspiciously, then took some bacon instead. 'I told you. I've been saving up for seven years for this. I will not wait another year.'

Artema sighed. 'Could we arrange for you to do the test up here?'

'Here? In the supraurbo? Why? What do you need me for that means I can't go home? I have to go back to work on Monday night too, remember?'

'This is very inconvenient,' Artema snapped. 'I understand you have a life to live, but that might not be the case if all hell blows up.'

'Those gang tags have been around my whole life. For all you know, nothing will happen with them for another twenty years.'

'I think we'll know before then. My probability calculations spiked. It wouldn't do that if the threat wasn't imminent,' Artema said and wished she could convey her creeping sense of doom to Eladio. It was what spurred her on.

'But I'm no use to you up here,' Eladio said. 'I know nothing about this place. What can I possibly do?'

At this critical moment Chico cleared his throat discreetly and said, 'Doctor Leopold is back, ma'am.'

'Ah, show him in, show him in,' Artema said and stood to greet the doctor.

'I apologise for the earliness of my arrival,' Dr Leopold said. 'But my results from the genetic test are so fascinating I couldn't wait to share them.'

'Not at all, Doctor, come in. And help yourself to some breakfast,' Artema said. She was well aware that the doctor was rather good at timing his visits to mealtimes, as his portly figure proclaimed.

'So these are the initial results,' Doctor Leopold said as he flicked them across to Artema's phone.

'If they're Eladio's you should let him see them first.'

'Of course,' the doctor said, but looked surprised.

It annoyed Artema that people treated Eladio like an afterthought. It was as if he wasn't a whole person. Eladio, on the other hand, did not show his feeling on the matter. It was probably for the best.

'These are completely different from the results I got yesterday,' Eladio said as he scanned the document.

'Well, as to that,' Doctor Leopold said, 'I found it odd too, so I did a little investigating. I discovered that the lab in the suburbo isn't actually doing tests. They've got about a dozen results per racial type all worked up. They just hand out the most appropriate one for the person's age and race as submitted in their application form.'

'They're not doing the tests at all?'

'Well...' the doctor said, giving Eladio a cautious look. 'Nobody wants suburbonites coming to their levels and the best way to keep them out is to fail you all on the genetic test.'

'The bastards!'

The doctor shrugged uncomfortably and said, 'There's more though.'

'About the tests?'

'About your test, at least all three samples you gave me.'

Eladio looked back down at his results and said, 'This says nothing about my memory either.'

'Exactly!' Doctor Leopold said, and he was practically vibrating with excitement. 'Artema was adamant that you have an exceptional memory, but it didn't show up in the results. In addition, the big, muscular man described to me comes out as average and strength from his genetic test.'

'What about the clairvoyant?' Artema said.

'That one is trickier. We don't know what the genetic markers are for clairvoyants, so I don't know if they showed up.'

'I don't understand,' Eladio said.

'Neither did I. As an aside, your results do put you in the upper quartile for intelligence. With that score you have all you need to get out of the suburbo,' the doctor said, beaming at Eladio. 'Only I don't like a mystery. So I did a sequence by sequence check on all the genes. I thought at first that there's something wrong with the test, so I did a manual check. I got nothing.'

'That can't be right,' Artema said, and her unease grew with this additional information.

'Exactly what I thought. So I widened my search. I won't bore you with the details, let's just say I've been up all night doing this. Finally, when I could find nothing at the subatomic level, I zoomed out and kept going until the whole cell was visible to me. Blow me down if I didn't spot this,' the doctor said and flicked an image of a cell up onto Artema's screen.

'It glows,' Eladio said.

'What glows?' Artema said.

'That little dot on the side.'

'Does it?' Doctor Leopold said and leaned closer to the screen.

Artema cast a revelation spell and murmured, 'Well, I'll

be! It does glow.'

'That's impossible,' the doctor said. 'We don't have magic in our bodies. Aside from that, it wasn't the glowing I discovered. I didn't even think to check for magic.'

'You're a magisto too?' Eladio said.

'I'm the university doctor, of course I'm a magisto. But, damn it all, that wasn't the point of my story.'

'So what is your point?' Artema asked.

'That… that glowing dot is supposed to be the cell's mitochondria.'

'So?'

'It isn't a mitochondrion. It took me a while to notice, but the structure is completely different. Our mitochondria are ovoid, cell-like structures. That thing is more like a multi-sided crystal. I've never seen anything like it in my life.'

'Is that bad?' Eladio asked.

'Bad? It's unheard of. The mitochondrion is the engine of the cell. It provides the energy necessary for life to happen. You three, and possibly all the Thirteen, don't have it. You have this bizarre little structure instead. Which, to add insult to injury, glows! I don't know what to make of it.'

'It is very unusual,' Artema said, which she felt rated as the understatement of the century. 'Yet another mystery from the suburbo to grapple with.'

'I have started trying to solve it. I got all the records of the Thirteen from the city administration and another curious fact appeared.'

'Which was?'

'All the mothers of the Thirteen died from anaphylactic shock. It either killed them during childbirth or a couple of days later.'

'They had an extreme allergic reaction?' Artema said. 'To

what?'

'I'm hazarding a guess it was to their babies.'

'How could they be allergic to their own children?' Eladio said.

'It isn't uncommon the other way around. Some mothers react against the male foetus they're carrying. It can lead to the death of the child, or birth defects at the least. So I suppose it's possible that this happened in reverse. During the birth, some babies' blood must have got into the mothers and killed them. I suspect it's down to that glowing dot.'

'Why?'

'Because it's alien to us. I want to see if the mothers had it. I'm willing to bet they didn't, but I am waiting for tissue samples so I can check.'

'Tissue samples?'

'They're collected when a death is unexplained. The year you were born, Eladio, there were sixteen deaths of post-partum women from anaphylactic shock.'

'Sixteen?' Artema said.

'Two died along with their children at the birth. The other child made it to the orphanage but died a few days later.'

'Is it possible,' Artema said. 'That there are other mothers who survived? And that there are more children with this... magical mitochondria than we know about?'

'I'll look into it,' Doctor Leopold said. 'In the meantime, my best guess is that it's that magical mitochondria that gives the Thirteen their special abilities.'

'It certainly makes them unique.'

Artema wondered whether Eladio had another link to the gang tags and demons from this discovery. It was now more imperative than ever that she found out all she could about the young man.

'Does this explain why Seraf looks different now?' Eladio murmured, his gaze fixed on the image of the cell.

'What do you mean?' Artema asked.

'Seraf has changed. When we went to see him he looked... he looked like a person who was outgrowing his skin and golden light shone from where he was bursting out.'

'Bona Sinjoro, you didn't tell me about that before,' Artema said, and her anxiety kicked up a notch.

'I couldn't in the suburbo, it was too risky. And then I forgot.'

'You forgot your friend was metamorphosing before your eyes?'

'I don't know what's happening to him. You don't know what it is either. But now, I wonder if the same thing will happen to all of us. I mean, he is the oldest but not by much.'

Eladio stared and stared at the golden blob in his cell. It was like a magnet that he couldn't pull away from. His entire life he'd wondered why they were all different, and here he had an answer. At least, there was something physically different at the cellular level, but no explanation of how it was possible.

It brought up more questions than it answered. Why did they have this thing? Who had done it to them? What did it mean for his future?

'How is this possible?' he muttered.

'It shouldn't be possible,' Doctor Leopold said. 'Not at all. I don't just mean physically, I mean ethically. No ethics board on the planet would allow such a drastic experiment to go ahead. Whoever did this committed a crime. Which may be why they did it in the suburbo. You can get away with murder in the suburbo. I am aware of all sorts of shady medical experiments done on low-lives that nobody would tolerate anywhere else. But this? This goes beyond even those boundaries.'

'So how will you find these unethical people, Doctor?' Artema said.

'That rather depends upon Eladio and the Thirteen. Before I can raise this with the Medical Council, I need their permission to go ahead. It is their medical data after all.'

'Will you also expose the genetic testing company in the suburbo?' Eladio said.

'Expose them?'

'They're taking people's hard earned imps and lying to them.'

'Ah, yes, that isn't really my—'

'You uncovered a fraud. Why won't you do anything about it? People who could have got out, haven't because of those bastards.'

'Yes, yes, I see your point. I'll report them to the authorities too.'

'They think because we're poor, we're stupid,' Eladio snapped. 'But we aren't. We're just trapped, and people abuse that situation for their own gain. We should make them pay everybody back and redo their tests for free.'

'I say,' Doctor Leopold said, 'let's not be hasty.'

'I'm not being hasty. This happens to my people all the time. We should rise against it.'

Eladio was so angry he had to force himself not to shout, not to spin out of control. So he bottled up his rage and pursed his lips shut.

'One thing at a time,' Artema said. 'Doctor, I suggest you report the genetics lab to the polico. They can take that one further. Rest assured, Eladio, I will make sure they do something about it. Then, Doctor, you need to concentrate on what this magical mitochondria does because if it is changing people that needs to be dealt with as a matter of urgency. Do you agree, Eladio?'

'I suppose so,' he muttered.

'The ethics and finding out who's behind this must be secondary. We need to know if this presents a risk to anyone's life.'

'And what of the other matter?' Doctor Leopold said.

'The demon incursion must remain my top priority. I leave the medicine to you,' Artema said. 'And for that I need to explain the provo de doloro to Eladio.'

Eladio's finely honed sense of danger pricked up at that. He didn't like anything that included mention of pain.

'Is that the test you want me to take?'

'It is.'

'And the name for it... the test of pain, is that accurate?'

'I'm afraid so.'

Eladio scanned Artema's face to understand, but she was difficult to read at the best of times. Now she was being particularly inscrutable.

'Why?'

'Why take the test, or why is it painful?'

'Why do you want me to undertake a trial by pain? That sounds... it sounds medieval.'

'You're not wrong there. The test was first developed during the middle ages. We've honed it ever since, but what we haven't been able to remove, try as we might, is the pain element. It appears to be necessary.'

'So why must I take it?'

'Because you're too perfect. You were in the right place just when I needed you. You have been exceptionally helpful and you've suggested things I can do to speed up my research which, on the face of it, looks like an excellent notion.'

'The game for collecting gang tags? I thought you didn't like the idea.'

'It would speed up my work, but it might also serve as a trigger for whatever the tags were placed there for.'

It outraged Eladio that they accused him of – What was he being accused of exactly?

'Do you think I'm in league with a demon?' he said and surged to his feet. 'Listen, I only went along with you because of the money. Now suddenly I'm being accused of things and being made to take tests. No, I don't need this. I have my exams tomorrow and I will not miss them. You can take back your fancy clothes and all your damned tests. I'm going home, and don't you try to stop me,' he said and stalked to the door expecting Artema to fling a spell at him.

It was only once he was out that another thought occurred to him. He couldn't stop himself from turning back and shouting through the closing doors, 'Maybe it would be a good thing to trigger whatever's lurking in the suburbo. At least then you'd know what you were facing.'

Then he ran, although it was probably pointless. This house belonged to Artema. She had an army of servants she could use to stop him, probably an entire arsenal of weaponry in the house and her magic that had stopped him dead before.

He needed another way out. The front door was too obvious. The only problem was that he didn't know the rest of the house. Then again, he didn't need to. Every room had windows.

He opened a door in the corridor he'd been running down to find himself in something that looked like a sitting room. If a sitting room had over a dozen sofas. He supposed it all had to do with scale.

Normal people had rooms that could fit a single suite. This room was so large a single suite would look stupid in it. Normal people in the mezaurbo, Eladio thought. People in the suburbo were lucky if they could squeeze a comfortable chair into their living quarters. People like Felicha.

The room had a row of windows, so Eladio ran across and examined the first one. It looked to have quite a basic locking mechanism. He twisted it and pushed the window open. There was a drop to the road outside, but it was manageable.

He checked the street. It was made from in the same light coloured stone as the buildings all around and looked more like a pavement than a road. There were no aerocars nor, at this moment, any pedestrians.

People were headed his way from inside the house, though. He could hear running, so he swung himself out of the window. He slid down the side of the wall, hanging onto the window ledge with his fingers and, when he was at full extension, let go and dropped to the ground.

He looked around again. Two people, young enough to be students, had just turned the corner and stopped, watching him in surprise. So he ran in the opposite direction and ducked down the first side road he came to.

He couldn't spot any security cameras, but that meant nothing. Cameras were so small and discreet these days that they could be anywhere. To make sure he was far enough away, he ran to the end of the road and stopped as it opened out into a vast quadrangle.

The buildings all around only reached to a height of about five stories. Above that was a clear blue sky. Eladio froze, unable to step into the space in front of him as dizziness rolled over him. He staggered backwards into the wall behind and stood propped up against it, gulping in air.

'Pull yourself together,' he muttered as he kept his gaze fixed on the ground.

It's just sky, he told himself. It can't harm you. Still, it took all his courage to look back up and he made sure he could feel the reassuringly solid stone against his back.

It was pure blue. There wasn't even a cloud to blemish this empty perfection. It felt like it went up forever.

'Are you alright?' a woman said and touched his arm.

It made Eladio jump. He hadn't heard her approach.

'I'm fine,' he muttered.

'Only you look very pale and shaky. I can go with you to the infirmary if you like?'

She was really pretty. She had long blonde hair that fluttered gently in the cool breeze, blue, blue eyes and skin tanned to a honey gold. Any other day, Eladio would gladly have gone anywhere with her.

'I need to get to the elevator. Can you tell me where it is?'

'Sure, it's just at the other end of the quad. You see that crystal like structure?' she said pointing one slender arm with a perfect wrist.

'Yes, thank you.'

'Are you sure you're alright?'

Eladio tried for a reassuring smile and muttered, 'Altitude sickness.'

'Oh... you're not from here?'

For a second Eladio contemplated telling her he was from the suburbo, but he didn't want to scare her.

Instead he muttered, 'I'm from the mezaurbo.'

'I see,' she said, her friendly warmth becoming more distant. 'Well, once you're back down at your level, you'll feel much better,' she said, gave him a nod and hurried away.

Would he feel better at his own level? He had his doubts. But he felt deeply uncomfortable at this one. It left him ashamed of himself as he kept his hand against the reassuring solidity of the wall and walked as quickly as possible to the elevator.

It would put a considerable dent in his bank balance to get a ride out of here. He wondered whether he could flog the fancy phone Artema had given him to recoup the costs. It was theft to do so. Then again, the woman had taken his clothes and stuck them in a pocket universe so he couldn't get at them. Which meant he'd have to spend some money replacing them.

Eladio shook his head. He'd worry about the ethics of everything once he was safely away and could think straight. He was too tired right now to do anything rational. Besides, his mind was buzzing with so much information that he wasn't sure he could sleep. The one thing he wished he could do was tell Felicha all about this place. He took a deep breath and stepped into the elevator terminus.

'Aren't you going to go after him?' Doctor Leopold said as Eladio ran for the door.

'Not this time.'

Artema wished she could reassure Eladio, but stopping him a second time would just leave the young man feeling trapped. She had to let him go if she was going to build up trust again later.

'Why not?'

'Call it a test. If he was in league with a demon, he'd want to stay.'

'Not if he had to take the provo de doloro, he wouldn't. If he's in league with a demon, he knows full well the test will reveal it. The demon will know that too and keep him from your path. I suspect you won't see him again. If a demon still wants to see what you're up to, he'll send you somebody new.'

'I suppose that's also true,' Artema said, aware that this was a possibility. Try as she might, though, she couldn't see Eladio as a demon's pawn. He didn't fit the typical profile. 'I wonder though, doctor, whether the provo de doloro would be safe to use on a young man who has a magical structure built into every one of his cells.'

'Ah! Good point. I hadn't considered that. It rather blew me away when he pointed out that it was magical. I mean, just being able to see magic... Can they all do it?'

'According to Eladio, his friend Felicha Twelve can see magic intermittently only.'

'Which is more than we can do.'

'Indeed. I wonder about the others. Especially Seraf One. When he looks in the mirror, do you think he can see what Eladio sees?'

'That is an intriguing question.'

'He seemed very calm for a man who is changing so drastically. I'm not sure I'd behave as if nothing was happening with such a change.'

'But what can you do about it from up here?'

'I think Eladio may be right, I have been proceeding with

caution. Now may be the time to lob a grenade in and see what happens.'

'Meaning?'

Artema heaved a great sigh and said, 'I may need to summon one of those bastards. I have an old family retainer. I need to get him to tell me what's going on.'

'You want to call up a demon?'

'There are a few who are bound to my house. They don't like it, but so far they haven't been able to break the bond. I will call upon one of them.'

'That seems rather extreme. You should consult the komitato on this.'

'The komitato can be told, but I will go ahead, regardless.'

'Then we must sit in.'

'That's far too dangerous. Only a Salonoy can be present. I believe I'll get Theodore to attend.'

'Your nephew? With no training?'

'He's a qualified magisto who is studying for his doctorate. He is suitable. Call it a test if you will.'

'I thought you'd decided to end your demonologist line.'

'Much to the komitato's dismay,' Artema said. 'Lady Ophelia has been haranguing me to find a replacement.'

'It looks like she was right.'

'I'm afraid so. Now I really must get on with this. I'll call Theodore first,' Artema said, and messaged her nephew.

'What if he's busy?'

'Really, you're asking that under our circumstances? Besides, I know Theodore. He has plenty of flexibility.'

'You think he's lazy.'

'He has a lot of advantages. We are so wealthy as a family he doesn't really have to work. He's taken up magic because it's the family trade and he grew up in a household where magical use is a commonplace. Both his mother and father are magistos from long lineages of the same. He is so familiar with magic he had to put very little effort into his studies. I fear it has bred a certain complacency.'

'And the last thing you want is a complacent demonologist.'

'Precisely. Although he's been sheltered from that too. I wonder how easy he thinks it is. I also wonder what he has been doing on the side.'

Doctor Leopold shrugged and said, 'Thankfully, that isn't my problem. I have a far more intriguing question to look into myself. I'll leave you with your mystery and go solve mine.'

Artema waved him away and considered her half eaten breakfast. She'd lost her appetite. She glanced over at Eladio's plate, which was also still half full. Artema wished the young man had at least been able to finish his breakfast before taking off.

She also wondered whether he'd use his own money on the elevator or get himself deported. Knowing Eladio, she suspected he'd pay. So she flicked to her bank app and transferred the fare. She didn't want him to be out of pocket.

'You wanted to see me, aunt?' Theodore said as he strolled into the room. Considering the argument they'd had the night before, he looked remarkably relaxed.

'I did.'

'Where's the low-life?'

'He's gone home,' Artema said. 'And I would prefer if you referred to Eladio either by his name or as a suburbonite.'

'You sent him home?'

'He chose to leave.'

'It's probably for the best.'

'Not really, but that's a conversation for another day. I need calm for what I'm going to do next and that won't be possible if we have another argument.'

'What do you want to do? It isn't like you to summon me so suddenly.'

'I intend to call up a demon,' Artema said, watching her nephew closely.

It relieved her that this pronouncement shocked the young man.

'A demon? Really? Today?'

'Now.' Artema wiped her mouth with her serviette and stood up. 'It might be a good idea if you watched.'

'Me?'

'Yes, come on.'

Artema stepped out through the French windows of the dining room onto the balcony that led to the lab.

'But you've never wanted me to have anything to do with demons before,' Theodore said, hurrying after her. 'Whenever I've raised the subject, you've shut me down. Why the sudden change of heart?'

'Because strange things are happening in the suburbo that need to be investigated. So far I've avoided getting a demon involved because I didn't want to tip my hand, but now it's time.'

'Why me then? I'm not prepared.'

'Nobody is truly prepared for an encounter with a demon, Theodore. But I have a feeling you've looked into the subject.'

'You have an AI who will have told you that.'

'Most likely. What exactly have you experimented with?' Artema asked as she stepped into the lab and made for the cupboard that held her salt stores.

'I've used a few of the icons to power certain compatible spells.'

'What do you mean by compatible?'

'I added the stop icon to a spell that will stop any moving object from a runner to a bullet. I added a forget icon to a forgetting spell, that sort of thing.'

'Why?'

'To add power to the spell. It also makes it easier.'

'Oh yes, very much easier.' Artema dragged a sack of salt across the floor to the edge of her inlaid pentagram and said, 'In fact, you hardly need bother casting the spell at all.'

'But if you do, it doubles the power of the spell.'

Artema sighed and stood up to examine her nephew. 'Did you not listen to a single word I said in my lecture on why demonology is so dangerous? You, of all people, who have lost relatives to demons, have been experimenting with icons.'

'It's in our family's blood.'

'No, Theodore, it expressly isn't in our blood. It isn't in our blood for the very good reason that we know better. Although it is now in your blood. You have contaminated yourself with demon icons. You have also spread the taint to any of your colleagues who have been engaged in this folly with you. Who else have you involved?'

'Just my tutor group. Serena and Professor Bianchi.'

'So your girlfriend and your supervisor. Are you sure there was nobody else?'

'We knew the risks. We kept it away from the juniors.'

'You had no bloody idea of the risks. Now, because of your dabbling, all three of you will have to take the provo de doloro.'

'Isn't that a bit extreme?'

'It's you getting off lightly. Depending on the test outcomes, that is.'

'Auntie!'

'Don't you auntie me. But now is probably a good time for you to see what demons are all about. It might explain better than I can why they are not to be messed with. I will summon a family familiar.

'He's bound to the house of Salonoy and has been for over a thousand years. He doesn't like us. This is partly because of his prolonged link with us, but mainly because he's a demon, and therefore doesn't like humans.

'You are to sit quietly to one side and neither move nor speak a single word during my interaction with him. Is that clear?'

'Yes, Aunt.'

'Good, then I will begin,' Artema said and waited till her nephew had sat down.

He looked like a rebellious teenager, which didn't bode well. But at least he was doing as he was told for now.

Artema poured the salt in a ring around the outer edge of the pentagram. Once she'd sealed the whole thing with salt, she took her position at the northern point of the pentagram. She paused, slowed down and cleared her mind of all but the need to speak to the demon.

Then she waved her hands in the form that called up a demon and said, 'Haurel, servant to the house of Salonoy, I summon you. Come before your master, Artema.'

She forced herself to maintain a meditative like calm as she watched the centre of the pentagram. That simple summoning was usually all that was needed to summon a demon, but they didn't always turn up on the first attempt.

She counted slowly to ten. Just like knocking at a door, you didn't want to look too impatient. Still nothing.

She was about to recite the incantation again when a thin wisp of red air rose from the middle of the floor, followed by a powerful whiff of sulphur. Her stomach did a sick somersault. The red smoke grew denser and with the sound of an elastic sheet being snapped, a man stood in the middle of the pentagram.

He had his back to Artema. The light dimmed as if a storm was on its way and a hot wind blew across the lab, scattering granules of salt, but not sufficient to break the circle. Haurel turned around slowly, and Artema fought her intense nausea to see the creature again. She'd hoped this day would never come.

He was taller than Artema. Demons made sure they were just that bit more impressive than the surrounding humans. He was dressed in a white suit that was the height of fashion in the supraurbo. It was heavily embroidered and layered. His hair and beard were also trimmed to perfection and in the latest style.

'Well, well,' Haurel murmured once he was face on to Artema. 'If it isn't Artema Salonoy, 106th Salonoy, and, if I'm not very much mistaken, number 107 quivering in the corner.'

'Hello, Haurel,' Artema said, pleased that her voice sounded level and calm and in no way reflected how her heart was hammering in her chest.

'You've got old.'

'It's what happens to humans.'

'Not to Salonoys. Although to give 105 his due, he didn't look so bad when I finally got him. You've aged less well.'

'You took my father?'

'Who else?' Haurel said, and grinned in a way that no human could. His smile grew wider than a human mouth could physically accomplish. 'It is the only thing that makes my bondage to you bearable that one day I will consume you.'

'Not today,' Artema said, although it was hard to continue the conversation.

She'd had her suspicions over who'd taken her father, but she couldn't dwell on that now. It was a deliberate distraction by the demon, and she had to push past it.

'I demand to know what the demons are up to in the suburbo of the Eterna Urbo.'

'What we are doing? Foolish little woman, we aren't doing anything.'

'Then why is the suburbo filled with demon icons like this?'

Artema held up an image of one of the demon icons for inspection. To her surprise, Haurel blinked, leaned closer and then raised an eyebrow.

'Nothing to do with us.'

'These things crisscross the suburbo and you claim not to know about it? Pull the other one, Haurel.'

'This circle is unfamiliar to me,' Haurel said and swept one perfectly manicured hand around the edge of the gang tag. 'If this is a demon at work, he hasn't told the rest of us.'

'That's usual. You lot are worse gossips than humans. Why would a demon keep this level of infiltration a secret?'

'Maybe to keep it from you,' Haurel said with his same uncanny grin.

'You need to discover who is behind this.'

Artema was confident that the demon would. Curiosity would drive him to it, even if the Salonoys didn't have a hold on him.

'Why would I betray the work of one of my own?'

'Because I command you to find the demon behind this. As a Salonoy I make this your mission for my house.'

'Give it a rest, Salonoy. I'm stuck with you as much as you are with me. But I want a bargain. You get your information and you release me from this bondage. A thousand years is more than enough.'

'You will gain your freedom when your kind gives up on Earth and goes away. Until then you are bound to us and I won't make any deal that involves your freedom. I have asked politely though and that should be sufficient.'

'Politely? Does a slave become less of a slave just because the master says please?'

'If that slave is set on the destruction of my family and my world and admits to killing my father, does he deserve better treatment?'

'I will do as I please.'

'And I will recall you for my information. Don't disappoint me,' Artema said. 'Now, before you go, I have another question for you. Are you aware of a group of children who have been modified to have magic built into their cells?'

Haurel took a surprised suck of air.

'What kind of magic?' he snapped and any pretence at amusement evaporated.

It surprised Artema, who'd never seen the demon look rattled. She called up the image of Eladio's cell and held it up for Haurel to see.

The demon let out a string of what Artema assumed were demon expletives. She'd never heard such a foul sound come from any creature, and his face contorted to such a shape that it barely looked human.

'Take that away,' he shrieked.

Artema shut the image down and said, 'What is it?'

'Nothing to do with me and, if you're wise, nothing to do with you either.'

'If I'm wise, the last thing I'd do is take advice from a demon.'

'That... that thing has nothing to do with us or anyone on my plane. You think we're dangerous, you have no fucking idea,' Haurel said and vanished with a puff of red smoke and a snapping sound.

Theodore leapt to his feet, ran for the door and threw up. Artema managed to keep herself under control long enough to sit down in the chair and looked down at her hands clasped in her lap. They were shaking.

'Is it always like that?' Theodore said from where he was propping himself up against the wall.

'That one wasn't so bad. He was holding back today,' Artema said. 'I've had it a lot worse.'

'He didn't tell you much, did he?'

'They never do. You usually get more information from what they don't say and their reaction to things than from their words.'

'Well, whatever was in that cell you showed him looked like it was literally making his head unravel.'

'Yes, it was odd,' Artema said and focused on clearing her mind and calming down.

Speaking to a demon was like going on the most dangerous rollercoaster ride on the planet, and it took a while to come down from the adrenaline surge.

'What was it anyway?' Theodore asked.

'Something that needs to remain between me and Doctor

Leopold for the moment.'

'Was it anything to do with the low– the suburbonite you had hanging around?'

'I don't know,' Artema said.

But she was wondering, more than ever, how it was she'd landed up with one of the Thirteen. The population of the suburbo alone numbered nearly a billion. To have met one of thirteen from that mass defied her sense of probability. What was puzzling was that Eladio's changed cell didn't seem to have anything to do with demons. Either that or they were better actors than she'd assumed.

Eladio was so tired when he finally got back to the suburbo that all he wanted was to go home and sleep. His second thought was to run to Felicha and tell her everything and show her his photos. He did neither.

Instead, the thought that had formed in his mind on his very long journey back into the bowels of the city turned his feet in an entirely different direction. Artema might or might not continue looking into the mystery of the Thirteen's cells, but he couldn't let it lie. Especially not if it would cause a change in them.

To test that theory, he needed to see Dimita Two. She was only a couple of weeks younger than Seraf. If everyone would undergo the same change, it should logically show up in her next. If nothing else, he had to see whether she also looked like she was bursting from her skin.

It was risky going to see her though because her special ability was charm. She was so wonderful to be with that you wanted to stay and you wanted to please her by telling her everything. If she'd turned her mind to it, she could have been the perfect spy.

Instead, when she was still too young, she'd been chucked out to fend for herself. He remembered the rest of the Thirteen clustered around a window, watching her take the lonely walk away from the orphanage. They'd seen it with countless orphans before. They'd watched Seraf go and now it was Dimita and one by one it would be the rest of them.

Dimita had turned to prostitution to survive and done well by it. In a few short years, she'd graduated to being a madam. Now, seven years later, she owned a thriving brothel on the edge of Purple territory. The Purples provided protection while being at the edge allowed the punters in without fear of being torn limb from limb by the gang.

Eladio made his way to the wooden frontage of the brothel and stood for a moment admiring the exterior. It was custom made and carved with suggestive figurines. A large purple gang tag glowed over the top of the door and men strolled in and out. A half-dressed woman stood at the door sucking on a vape stick, watching the people go by.

Eladio had never been into a brothel before and wasn't sure what he should do. But it was probably easier than arriving at Artema's house, he thought with a shudder and walked in.

'Hello, Hon, what can we do for you?' another scantily clad woman said.

He smiled mechanically at her as he took in the red-painted interior filled with comfortable chairs on which a couple of women lounged and a few men sat waiting. One had a woman on his lap and was fondling her breast. That made Eladio blush, and he hastily looked away.

'I need to see Dimita Two.'

'She doesn't see clients any more, Hon. You must pick someone else.'

'No, I don't... I'm not a client. I'm a friend and I just need to speak to her.'

'She's very busy.'

'Tell her Eladio Thirteen needs to see her. She can decide then if she'll come down.'

'Thirteen huh?' the woman said. 'I'll call and ask.'

As her attitude had changed, Eladio wondered whether Dimita had a standing order about anyone with a number for a surname. He was about to find out because the curtains that closed off the corridor at the top of the stairs flicked back and Dimita smiled down at him. She crooked her finger for him to come up and vanished back behind the curtain.

He nodded thanks to the woman and hurried up after Dimita. She had walked to the end of the corridor and was now standing at an open door.

'Come on in,' she said in a warm welcoming voice. 'I can't wait to hear absolutely everything you've been up to.'

And that was precisely what he was afraid of, because suddenly Eladio wanted to tell her everything.

'Hello, Dimita,' he said.

It relieved him that Dimita looked her normal self. Her skin wasn't cracking with light shining through. Her long dark blonde hair was artfully coiled up in a bun, and her clothes were surprisingly modest.

He stepped into what looked like her private apartment and closed the door. The room was small but tastefully furnished with a large double bed. It was something he'd never seen in the suburbo. The room also had a round table with a couple of comfortable sofas drawn up to it and a window looking down into the street. He assumed the other door in the room led to a bathroom. Yesterday this room would have impressed him tremendously. Today it looked a little dowdy.

'What have you been up to, my dear?' Dimita patted the sofa invitingly before sitting down on the one opposite with the table between them. 'I heard you were running around with a professor.'

'How can you possibly know that?'

'Seraf is a regular of this establishment and I invited him up for tea last night.'

'Seraf is a regular?'

'My dear, we all have needs, even Seraf.'

'He's got an entire gang full of women to pick from. I'm surprised he'd want to pay for something he could get for free.'

'Ah, but he doesn't pay.'

'He doesn't?'

'I like to keep on the good side of the gangs so a little freebie to the number two of the Black Brotherhood is an investment.'

'What about the number one?'

'You know, I've never met him.'

'Oh,' Eladio said and looked around frantically, trying to think of another question. It was the only way he had of not answering one of Dimita's questions. 'Have you seen any of the others?'

'I speak to Three occasionally. She can be so very helpful for an up-and-coming businesswoman. Felicha does the laundry for my house, so I see her regularly. Seraf and Luca come around as I've said. Betto and Piero are also regulars and Francesca worked here for a while, but she didn't like it much. Nanni seems to have vanished, unless you've seen her lately.'

'The last time I saw her she was heading to the edge
lands to become a farmer.'

'That's a shame. I liked her. I suppose with her abilities
with plants it was the logical place to go. As for the others,
they are around but don't come by to visit. Much like you.'

'Sorry.'

'Don't be. You've built a life for yourself. I hear you got a
permit to the mezaurbo.'

'I work in a coffee shop.'

'Good for you. I went up to visit once, but it was too
bright and I felt... out of place and ashamed of where I came
from. What do people make of you?'

'I don't tell them I'm from the suburbo and people don't
really notice shop workers.'

'What about the other employees?'

'They're nice enough. They think I'm local, but that I
don't go out much.'

'It isn't right, is it?' Dimita said in her wonderful voice
that oozed sympathy. 'People should accept us for who we
are. You and I have just as much value as anybody else up
there.'

'Yes,' Eladio said, and only just cut off what he was about
to blurt out about the genetic test.

Then he thought, no, I need to find out what's going on
and Dimita can help. She smiled at him in such a warm way
he just wanted to wrap his arms around her and cry.

Maybe she realised that because she said, 'I could use a
cup of tea. How about you?'

'Yes, thank you,' Eladio said.

With that, she flicked an order across from her phone.
Seconds later a young woman arrived bearing a tray with a

teapot and a couple of cups. She was dressed in black and white like a maid.

'Thank you,' Dimita murmured and waited till the woman left before she poured out the tea.

'Now tell me,' she said as she handed over the cup, 'What has brought you here?'

'I saw something strange,' Eladio said, being careful to not actually touch Dimita's hand. He could resist her questions with difficulty when she spoke, but if she touched him he'd just start babbling like a fool.

'In the suburbo seeing something strange hardly counts as news, my dear.'

'Something glowing.'

'You've seen stuff glowing before, all the gang tags. What was different about this one?'

'It was Seraf,' Eladio said, struggling to come up with a description that would explain what he'd seen.

'Seraf is glowing?'

'Not exactly. He looks like he's bursting from his skin and where this... new Seraf is emerging, that glows.'

'Good heavens, that sounds like a bug not a human being.'

'I know. But you believe me, don't you?' Eladio said and finally took a sip of his tea.

'Eladio, my dear, you have always had more curiosity than the rest of us. You've always wondered about why we were different while the rest of us were just struggling to survive. So I suppose I'm not surprised that you've seen this odd thing about Seraf and jumped to certain conclusions. That is what you do, after all.'

'Do you think I'm wrong?'

'Of course not, darling. I'm sure you see this thing. Is

that why you came to see me? To discover whether I am also bursting forth.'

'Yes,' Eladio said, glad that Dimita had worked it out for herself. 'Sorry.'

'Why be sorry?' Dimita said with a laugh. 'I'm glad you're checking up on us. Am I glowing?'

'No.'

'I'm not sure if that's a relief or not.'

'Has Seraf changed at all?'

'Only when he joined the gang. He was somewhat lost before that. The gang gave him direction, and he regained his followers. It's a very sad thing to see a leader without a flock.'

'He hasn't changed since? Maybe acted strangely?'

'He's behaving less strangely than you are, my dear.'

'Oh, sorry.'

'Seraf tells me you and Felicha took the genetic test.'

'Yes, but it was wrong,' Eladio said, trying to keep his answers short. A mistake would be to begin explaining. The next thing he'd know, with Dimita, was that he'd told her everything.

'Are you sure?'

'They thought Felicha's parents were black.'

'Do you know, I always wondered about Felicha. I'm not sure her birth certificate is right.'

'I think it is. I think we're stranger than even we realise. I–' he stopped, damn, but it was hard not to tell Dimita everything.

Only it was too soon to talk about what their cells looked like. He wished he could get them all tested by Artema. Unfortunately, that bridge was well and truly burned, so there was no point in bringing it up.

'Would you like me to talk to Seraf about this?' Dimita said.

'Would you? We don't have a good relationship any more.'

'What would you like me to ask him?'

'I don't know, really. I mean, he didn't look like he was in pain or anything when I saw him. Just find out if he's feeling strange.'

'Should I tell him he's glowing?'

'I guess. I'm not sure he can do anything about it though.'

'If this is going to affect the rest of us, then we'd better learn more about it, I suppose,' Dimita said. 'I hope it doesn't. Maybe it's something specific to Seraf only, like all the rest of us and our gifts.'

10

Eladio looked around the empty coffee shop. It was late and the last few customers had collected their drinks and left a couple of hours ago. The next big rush would be when the pubs and clubs closed, but for now he had a decent two or three hours where he could do his own thing.

It was weird to be back. It felt as though nothing had changed and yet he'd never had five stranger, more eventful days in his life culminating in his exams earlier that day. It was flat now, back to the daily grind.

At least he had the piano again. That was what he looked forward to the most in his job. So he opened it up, gave his fingers a stretch and then ran them up and down the keys on a scale. He was tempted to launch into his latest creation that he'd been composing in his head, but discipline was everything. So, despite his urge to skip it, he did them all. Then he played a quick and easy waltz, and finally he could play his piece.

It was mathematically perfect, and he was looking forward to hearing how it sounded. The rhythm worked well as his left hand kept a perfect constant beat, but the melody was just plain odd. Music was supposed to be a sister to maths, but if it was, he was doing something wrong.

'Not bad,' a voice said from behind that made him jump.

He slammed the piano shut, shot to his feet and spun around.

'Artema!'

She was sitting at the same table she'd occupied when they'd first met, and she held her hands up to show they were empty.

'Relax. I come in peace.'

'What are you doing here?' Eladio said as he hurried to put the counter between them.

'I wanted to make sure you got home okay.'

'I did, thank you for the fare,' Eladio said and checked to see whether Artema was going to get up. It didn't look like she was, so he said, 'Wait there. I have something for you.'

He ducked into the back room, riffled through his locker and came back with the clothes and the phone Artema had given him.

'Here.'

'My dear young man, what do you want me to do with this?'

'It's your stuff. I'm giving it back.'

'I don't want it.'

'Well, I want my clothes.'

Eladio felt sick confronting this woman, knowing how powerful she was. A blue blood could do anything, including getting anyone they wanted thrown in prison.

'Ah yes, I'm sorry. I should have given them to you,' Artema said, and with a flash of golden light she pulled Eladio's folded clothes out of her pocket universe. 'Here you go. But you may as well keep the rest.'

'I can't, it's worth too much. That phone alone is worth over a thousand imps.'

'You looked it up, did you?'

Eladio had, but he just shrugged at the question.

'I should have known you would,' Artema said. 'Do you

realise that I neither know nor care how much that phone costs? It's immaterial to me. Furthermore, if you don't take it and the clothes, I will take them around the corner to the karitato shop and donate it to them.'

'You didn't know?' Eladio was shocked. How could Artema not know? Was she so rich? 'What am I supposed to do with such things?'

'Whatever you want. You're resourceful. I'm sure you'll come up with something. You might like to wear the clothes and come and visit me someday. You do have a pass to the supraurbo that is valid for a year, after all.'

'I have no reason to visit you and I won't take any of your tests either.'

'That is probably for the best. Doctor Leopold was of the opinion that it might be too dangerous because of your unusual cells.'

That threw Eladio. Artema always turned the tables on him with something unexpected.

'He's... he's still looking into it?'

'He's remarkably energetic when he's roused. And actually, he's pretty enraged that such an unethical experiment was conducted. As he's from an extremely high ranking blue blood family, even more august than my own, he has put the fear of god into the entire medical establishment. They are all scrambling to find out who it was that messed with the Thirteen. Although, at this point, he is keeping you lot anonymous. But he has already received the cell samples from all your mothers.'

'He's really still looking?'

Eladio felt overwhelmed. He'd just assumed they'd be dropped as unimportant. To have caused this much upheaval was surprising.

'Do you think you could get me a coffee, dear fellow?' Artema said with a slight wry smile.

'Of course. I'm sorry, I should have asked,' Eladio said, relieved to have something to do. 'What kind of coffee?'

'You'd best make it a bullet coffee, go heavy on the coconut oil.' Artema strolled over and settled herself on one of the high stools at the counter. 'Make yourself something on me too.'

'No, thank you,' Eladio said and avoided looking at Artema.

'How did your exams go?' Artema said in her same tranquil voice.

It was fine for her, Eladio thought; she had the upper hand.

'I passed.'

'I knew you would. What grade did you get?'

'Ninety-nine percent.'

'Really? Only ninety-nine? Why's that?'

'One of their questions was wrong.'

'I don't see why you should pay for that.'

'I don't mind,' Eladio said. 'All I needed was a pass.'

'So what will you do now?'

'Update my CV and find a better-paying job.'

'Do you have anything in mind?'

Eladio finished making the coffee and slid it across the counter to Artema. He couldn't understand why she was interested.

'I'm hoping I can get a job as a store manager.'

'You don't want to study further?'

'I can't afford it.'

'Maybe not immediately, but who knows? Your genetic test put your intelligence in the top quarter that makes you eligible to live anywhere in the city, even the supraurbo.'

'I couldn't breathe in the supraurbo.'

'You adjusted, and remarkable quickly at that. All I'm saying is it seems a waste of talent to only aim for shop manager.'

Artema was exasperating, Eladio thought. She had no idea how difficult it had been to simply get to this point. To finally have a well-paying job in his sights and maybe even a move to the mezaurbo. Anything beyond that was... it still had to be figured out. One step at a time.

'It's what I can do next.'

'I suppose so. Tell me, Eladio, what year was Plato born?'

'What?' Eladio said.

As usual, Artema was throwing him with an out of context question.

'Humour me.'

Eladio thought back to his reading and said, 'Somewhere around 428BC they aren't entirely sure.'

'Why is he famous?'

'For setting the foundations of philosophy and he created the first institute of higher learning, taking people beyond the basics. Men, at least.'

'And what particularly was his contribution to philosophy?'

'Lots, they consider him the father of western political philosophy, religion and spirituality. He brought method and rigour to the whole enterprise of philosophy.'

'Good, and when did you learn all of that?'

'You know when, on Saturday night,' Eladio snapped, frustrated by the digression.

'When you were suffering from altitude sickness.'

'Yes, so?'

'My dear fellow, it took me years to understand philosophy and I doubt even now I could give you such a succinct description of Plato's influence.'

'So you think I should go to university. I get that. But I've already told you, I can't.'

'Well, I hope you don't give up on the idea entirely. You'd thrive at a university.'

University was so far out of what he'd hoped to achieve with his life that Eladio hadn't bothered looking into it before. He therefore didn't know whether it would suit him.

'Fine,' he muttered.

'Good. Now, you might want to look at this,' Artema said and held her phone out so that Eladio could see the screen.

Eladio felt his stomach twist as a figure appeared in what moments before was an empty pentagram.

'You're showing me that demon again?'

'I am,' Artema said and pressed the pause button. 'It's important that you see this.'

'Why? You told me to stay away from them.'

'Watch, it will become clear.'

'I don't want to.'

It felt like evil was coiling off the phone. The last thing Eladio wanted was to watch what was on it.

All the same, he was curious, so he steeled himself and said, 'Okay, play it.'

It was strange how such a small image could have such a strong effect. Artema was right, it was worse if you could hear the demon. He wished it was only the sight because the sound was like a hundred fingernails being dragged down a slate. It reverberated through his body and made him feel like he might tear himself apart just to get away. But what the demon had to say was just as shocking.

He'd killed Artema's father? Eladio looked up at Artema when the demon said that, but she was just holding the phone passively, like it didn't matter. Only that couldn't be true. And the revelations continued till the end, when the demon vanished.

Eladio looked up at Artema and said, 'Was that demon scared?'

'I've never seen a demon who was, so I'm not sure,' Artema said. 'But that is what it looked like to me.'

'And... you are aware of only three planes, aren't you, Heaven, Hell and Earth?'

'That's right.'

'Any others?'

'Not that we know of.'

'Are demons afraid of anything on Earth?'

'If they are, I've never seen it.'

'So if this change in our cells isn't from Hell and possibly isn't from Earth, that leaves only one option, doesn't it?'

'That's the way I'm leaning, yes.'

'What does Doctor Leopold think?'

'I haven't spoken to him about it yet. I want him to be sure it isn't a human agent before I send him down this path.'

'That's a bit unfair.'

'It won't hurt big Pharma to be put under the spotlight. Also, I don't want to contaminate the doctor's thinking. It will ensure we aren't being led astray. Although...'

'Although what?'

'That little magical structure of yours glowed white.'

'And?'

'Human magic only glows yellow or gold, depending on your point of view.'

'So it's not human magic?'

'That's not to say a human agent didn't do the inserting. Just that they got the magic from somewhere else.'

'Like where?'

'That is still to be determined.'

'This just brings up more questions than answers.'

'True, but more questions than you had available to ask before, not so?' Artema said.

'Well, well, look who we have here,' Seraf said as he stepped into the cafe. 'I should have known you wouldn't leave well enough alone, Eladio.'

'Seraf!' Eladio said, stunned that he'd shown up here and more that he was glowing even brighter with even more cracks in his skin.

'Even after I told you she was dangerous, you continued to see her,' Seraf said and flicked a thumb at Artema.

Artema looked relaxed. Then again, Eladio thought, she's used to speaking with demons.

'I think we should tell him,' Artema said, giving Eladio a level stare.

'You can't trust him.'

'All the same.'

'I don't know.'

'You said I was being too subtle. This would shake things up.'

'I didn't say that.'

'Close enough. And I wanted to speak to the gangs, remember?'

'Hey!' Seraf snapped. 'Stop behaving like I'm not here. And I'll thank you, Eladio, not to go around telling people I'm changing into a bug.'

'I said nothing about a bug,' Eladio said, and the

irritation Seraf always caused him bubbled up again. 'That's what Dimita said. And I doubt she told anyone other than you.'

'Well, it's one tale you'd better not spread.'

'I never spread tales.'

'Don't you?'

'If I did, the whole suburbo would know you're a thief,' Eladio spat, unable to contain his rage.

'You little shit,' Seraf said and leaned over the counter to grab him. 'Is this the gratitude I get after I've just saved your life?'

Eladio ducked and said, 'But why did you do that, out of friendship or guilt?'

'You bastard,' Seraf roared and rushed around to Eladio.

He sidestepped and moved a little closer to the door. If Seraf snapped, he wanted to be able to make a quick getaway.

'Because of you, I had to work for three more years before I could take my exams.'

'I offered you a way out. I said you could join the gang. I told you I'd give you a good position.'

'I don't want to join a gang. I don't want to spend my days intimidating our people and squeezing them for every imp they earn.'

'Oh, the high and mighty Eladio, aren't you so noble?' Seraf said cricking his head like a man preparing to attack. 'Did you give Dimita a speech over her corrupt ways as well?'

'I didn't tell you or her how to live your life. I'm just telling you it's not the way I want to live mine.'

'What a noble little street sweeper you are.'

'He is actually,' Artema said calmly. 'Now why don't you sit down and Eladio can make you a drink. I would recommend the bullet coffee but you might just be a little too over stimulated by that.'

'Who the hell do you think you are?' Seraf said, glaring at Artema. 'You're just some jumped up professor from a mediocre university. You better watch yourself or I'll flatten you.'

'I doubt that,' Artema said and waved her hand at Seraf.

Eladio wondered what she'd just done. It was the same gesture she'd used on the gang tags, and it didn't seem to affect Seraf.

'Would you like a drink?' Eladio said.

'On me,' Artema said. 'It's the least I can do.'

Seraf looked angrily from Artema to Eladio, then clambered onto a chair. 'I'll have a black coffee.'

'Okay,' Eladio said and kept his eye on Seraf while he made the coffee.

'Are you really a professor of anthropology?' Seraf said.

'I'm the Lady High Professor of Demonology at the Eternal University of Magic,' Artema said and took a leisurely sip of her coffee.

Eladio hadn't heard her full title before, and even he was surprised by it. Seraf looked so astonished he was in danger of toppling off his chair.

'And Eladio is right about you,' Artema said and continued gazing up at the ceiling as if she didn't have a hulking gang member directly opposite her. 'You do look like your skin is splitting and you are glowing like a miniature sun underneath.'

'That's impossible.'

'I might have said so too a couple of days ago. Which just goes to show, it doesn't matter how old a person gets, there are always things to surprise them.'

Now this is a turn up for the books, Artema thought as she worked on maintaining her cool despite the fact that her spell had just revealed the most astonishing sight she'd ever seen on Earth. Seraf didn't look to her like a man who was bursting from his skin as Eladio had described. He looked more like a smouldering coal that might burst into flame at any moment.

Would it help if they kept him calm? Was his physical state linked to his emotional state, or were the two unconnected?

'Might I ask if it hurts?'

'Hurts?' Seraf snapped. 'I feel nothing and I see nothing because there is nothing to see. Do you think I haven't checked in the mirror?'

'I dare say you have, but if whatever is happening to you comes from magic, you won't be able to see it. The only one I have ever met who can see magic in action is Eladio. Even we magistos have to use a spell to reveal when magic is present.'

'Did you just cast a spell on me then?' Seraf snapped.

'Not on you. I cast a reveal spell. It shows up all magic use.'

'So this cracking thing is magical?'

'It must be.'

'What's it doing?'

'That is the big question, isn't it? I have no idea.'

'That makes you as useful as an actual anthropology lecturer then,' Seraf said with a sardonic smile as he leaned back in his chair.

He was growing more comfortable in his surroundings,

and Artema decided to use this moment to get what she wanted.

'Fascinating as your condition is, it wasn't the reason I was down in the suburbo.'

'It wasn't? Then why the devil were you running around down below? What is your fascination with gangs if you aren't an anthropologist?'

'Your gang tags intrigued me.'

'These things?' Seraf said and grabbed the collar of his jacket to twist the tag up to examine it. 'Why?'

'Do you know where they come from?' Artema said. She was aware that Eladio, standing silently at the bar, had stiffened in anticipation of what he might say.

'I think our boss designed the first one.'

'Your boss, the mysterious Rushabarbo?'

'Huh?'

'I hear people don't know what he looks like, which is unusual, don't you think?'

'Not really.'

'Why not?'

'Because the boss doesn't like people seeing him.'

'But you've met him?'

'Of course. He picked me to be his spokesman.'

'So why is he so camera shy? Is he hideous or scarred?'

'I'm not going tell you,' Seraf said with a dismissive laugh.

'Are you sure you've met him?'

Artema was certain she could goad Seraf into revealing everything he knew. He was a showing off kind of man who always wanted to look like he knew more than anyone else.

'Of course I've met him.'

'But you seem to know so little about him. Why would

any boss not want his face known? Doesn't he gain respect from being out and about and recognised?'

'How should I know that?'

'Really?' Artema said, giving Seraf an incredulous smile. 'You're a leader yourself. I'll bet everybody in Container City knows who you are when you walk down the street, and yet your boss goes about incognito?'

'He told me to be the face of the organisation.'

'When?'

'When he recruited me, okay? He found me and he took me to the gang HQ and told me I could be useful.'

'Doesn't that sound odd to you?' Artema said, and realised that Seraf didn't actually care. No doubt it suited him to have a low profile boss.

'I don't know why he wants to be in the shadows,' Seraf said, his voice tinged with annoyance. 'He does his own thing and mostly leaves me to do mine.'

'As long as you keep what he looks like a secret. I have to say, I've never heard of anything like that before. It makes me wonder why he's hiding.'

A look of cunning spread across Seraf's face and Artema guessed he'd just realised that if his boss was actually hiding, it might be beneficial for him.

'Okay, okay, if it will get you off my back,' Seraf said and looked around the cafe, checking for cameras. 'His name is Rushabarbo because he's got a massive red beard. Aside from that, he isn't particularly memorable. Okay?'

Then he paused and looked around again, as if expecting something to happen.

Artema wondered whether Rushabarbo had cultivated his beard as an extra layer of camouflage. It sounded like it was extraordinary enough to draw people's eyes to it and make them not notice the rest. It was rather an extreme measure to go to and also out of character for anyone using a demon to rise to power.

She needed more to confirm Rushabarbo's role.

'So your boss designed the tag?'

'That's what he told me,' Seraf said back to lounging on his stool as if he was completely in charge. 'I wasn't sure I believed him.'

'Why not?'

'I don't know,' Seraf said with a shrug. 'It's the way he spoke.'

'Why were you talking about the tags?'

'Because one of the boys got sloppy. Rushabarbo is obsessed with all the tags being perfect, and this boy wasn't doing it right. He nearly had him killed. I only just talked him out of that. So I asked what the big deal was. I thought for a moment he'd kill me too. Then he said I had to mind my own business. But he looked shifty.'

Rushabarbo's extreme annoyance with sloppy work made Artema certain she had found the person who actually knew about demon icons. Seraf was too relaxed about them to be in the know.

'Does Rushabarbo have specific places he wants the tags to go?'

'Not really. We have big ones on all the buildings we own. We have little ones at any key point, more to mark our territory than anything else. We also have to wash off and replace any tags that fade or get damaged. It's a pain in the ass keeping up with that. And it falls to muggins here to oversee all of it.'

'Do you know when the first tags went up?'

'No idea. They've been around as long as I can

remember. You'd have to ask mister miracle memory over there,' Seraf said, flicking his thumb over his shoulder in Eladio's direction, 'if you really want to know when they started appearing.'

'Eladio says they've been there for as long as he can remember too.'

'Oh well, there you go then. Mind you, Rushabarbo is old. He's as old as you or maybe older, so who knows when he started putting up tags.'

'Do you think you could find out for me?'

'Why the hell should I?'

'You might need some help with your particular ah… problem.'

'Since you've seen nothing like it, I doubt you can help. Besides, it isn't bothering me.'

'Not yet, but one day I might be the only one who can help.'

'Then I'll wait for that day.'

'Why did you come here this evening?' Eladio said as he pushed Seraf's coffee over to him.

It annoyed Artema to have her questioning interrupted, but she supposed it was fair for Eladio to ask.

'I wanted to ask about the bug thing. Dimita told me this morning, and it took a lot of discipline for me to wait till now to track you down.'

'You could have called him,' Artema said.

'I can't,' Seraf said with a sardonically arched eyebrow. 'Eladio's blocked my number. Besides, Rushabarbo monitors phone traffic just like he monitors surveillance cameras, so it wasn't worth the risk.'

'You could have asked me in the suburbo,' Eladio said. 'Why did you come all the way up here?'

'Because you're still under threat of capture. I'm–'

'Capture?' Eladio said. 'I thought you were warning me he wanted me dead.'

'Rushabarbo wants her dead,' Seraf said, pointing at Artema. 'Real bad. He just wants you to be taken to him.'

'Why?'

'How the hell should I know?'

'You are his number two.'

'He tells me nothing,' Seraf snapped. 'He just wants me to take you in. He wanted me to make a proper effort about it too. No leaving you to wander about till I bump into you. Which was why I couldn't bloody well talk to you at home.'

'Your boss still wants me? Even though I took Artema out of the suburbo?'

'He said to get you no matter what. So no, you're not safe just because you're no longer going around with this woman,' Seraf said, looking pointedly at Artema.

'But they left me alone after I left your HQ?'

'For now, because I'm not pushing it. But eventually we'll be expected to deal with you. Sooner if Rushabarbo hears I'm soft peddling on his instructions.'

'You would capture me just for walking around with her?' Eladio said, pointing at Artema.

'Look, as long as we don't see you in the suburbo you should be fine.'

'But that's where I live!'

'Move,' Seraf said with a shrug. 'It's what you've always wanted, isn't it? You just couldn't wait to get out.'

'I didn't want to be banished!' Eladio said.

It was the closest Artema had ever heard him coming to a shout. She decided it was time to get back into this conversation before it escalated.

'Why, may I ask, do the two of us running around looking at gang tags warrant such a strong response?'

'I have no idea, and if you knew Rushabarbo, you'd know it isn't a question I can ask him either. He expects obedience without question.'

'It seems an extreme reaction for such a minor infraction.'

'He's like that sometimes.'

'Maybe I should speak to him, explain–'

Seraf burst out laughing.

'You really have no clue, do you? Rushabarbo isn't the kind of man who will stop and listen. If you try to go back down to speak to him, I will pick you up on our surveillance. Then I'll send a group of men out to kill you before you even reach our HQ. If you got as far as the boss, he'd shoot you without hesitation. You wouldn't even have time to say hi. Never mind ask why he wants you dead.'

'Alright, speaking to him is pointless. What about the tags, though? Can you tell me anything else about them?'

'I just thought we were marking our territory.'

'So there's no particular pattern to the tags?'

'Not that I know of. But I'll tell you what, if the tags have meaning to Rushabarbo and you've been going around cataloging them, that will be your reason.'

'Doesn't that strike you as odd?'

Seraf shrugged again and said, 'None of my business. My only concern right now is keeping Rushabarbo happy and keeping my position as number two. The longer I stand around here talking to you, the greater the risk. So I'll be going.'

He stuck his hand into a jar of biscotti, helped himself to a bunch, grinned at Eladio and strolled out.

'Bastard,' Eladio said, and made a note on a piece of paper of the number of biscotti taken.

Then he hurried to the window and watched Seraf sauntering away down the broad walkway.

'He isn't much like you,' Artema said, joining him to gaze through the large plate-glass window.

'Seraf is all about Seraf. He always has been. I just didn't realise it as a child. We all looked up to him then, and that's the way he likes it. He's very nice to you as long as you're his follower.'

'Mmm, I know a couple of people like that too.'

Eladio nodded and said, 'Has your AI not found a pattern in the tag placements?'

'Nothing. The problem is there are so many of them it would be possible to create any number of patterns from them. I may have to go with your game idea. I was thinking of setting the reward at one dolaro per tag.'

'One imp? That's way too much. By the time they've collected ten, they've got enough for a slap up meal and they'll stop. If you want proper data, you need to make it one imp per hundred tags. That will make them work for it.'

'A hundred huh?' Artema said and thought Eladio was a pretty good businessman. Or maybe just a tight one. At the moment, also a distracted one.

'You have to create a hunger for people to want to do it.' Eladio tilted his head, his eyes still fixed on Seraf. 'Do you see that?'

'See what?' Artema said and turned from Eladio to look out at the walkway.

'Those two men talking to Seraf, they're also Black Brotherhood.'

'Was he lying? Do you think he means to get us after all?'

'I don't know. Looks like they're arguing.'

'More than arguing,' Artema shouted as one man drew a knife. There was a glint of steel and he plunged the knife into Seraf's back.

A flash of searing white light blinded them, followed by an explosion that blew out the windows, lifted Artema off her feet and threw her across the cafe.

Alarms blaring at high pitch brought Eladio round. He coughed, breathing in smoke and dust as he did. His head throbbed in time to the siren. Everything else felt numb. Adrenaline, he reckoned, give it time, and it would hurt. He looked about for Artema and spotted a dusty grey figure slumped against the back wall.

He pushed himself onto his feet, covered his mouth with his apron and staggered over.

'Artema!' he shouted, even though it hurt his head even more. He took a firm hold of the woman's shoulder and gave it a squeeze. 'Artema, are you alright?'

He got no response, so rolled her over and pushed his fingers against Artema's neck. 'Come on, woman, you face off against demons, you can't die like this,' Eladio said and gave Artema a shake.

She groaned and her eyes fluttered open.

'What the devil just happened?'

'I think Seraf exploded,' Eladio said. 'Is that even possible?'

'Sankta Madonna,' Artema said and staggered to her feet. 'Not possible, surely not.'

'We need to get help,' Eladio said as he followed Artema outside.

'I think they already know about this,' Artema said and waved a hand at the scene of devastation.

The great walkway was shattered, as were the facades of all the buildings that surrounded it up to about seven stories above them. It was dark too, as most of the lights had blown out or were buzzing on and off. Bodies, body parts, masonry and twisted metal lay scattered in a circular pattern away from the hole in the walkway where Seraf had stood. Further away an aerocab lay on its side, its glowing advert flickering with an intermittent short. A few dusty and bloodied people had started to emerge from the shops.

'Come on, we have to check,' Artema said and made her way across the field of debris towards the hole.

'No, it's too dangerous,' Eladio said and tried to pull her back. 'The walkway could collapse.'

'Let go of me. I have to check. Besides, they've designed the city with explosions in mind.'

'Maybe, but there's no point in risking it.'

'I have to know, and so do you. Seraf was your friend.'

Artema pulled her arm out of Eladio's grip and limped on.

'Do you want to get us both killed?' Eladio said and wished the ringing in his ears would stop.

He felt sick now, sick about what had happened to Seraf and scared.

'Look,' Artema said and pointed at a blackened and twisted hunk.

Eladio realised with a nauseous surge that it was the remains of somebody's chest. Somebody who was wearing a jacket emblazoned with the Black Brotherhood's tag.

'Seraf?' Eladio said, but he suspected not.

'I think he went down there,' Artema said as she reached

the lip of the hole. Iron girders the size of tree trunks had curved downwards with the force of the blast that had punched an aerocar sized hole through the concrete.

Eladio shuffled cautiously up to the lip of the blast and prayed that none of it crumbled as he put his weight on it. He peered over the edge and down and down into darkness.

'It goes all the way down. Whatever it was, it punched its way through level after level.'

'Exactly, and we need to find out what it was.' Artema grabbed Eladio's arm in a vice like grip, shouted, 'Don't let go!' and launched herself into the hole.

'No!' Eladio shouted as Artema pulled him over the edge and plummeted down.

The world was a blur. He couldn't make out empty space from solid building. Wind whistled in his ears, as did his terrified scream.

'You will be alright,' Artema shouted.

'Artema!' Eladio shrieked. 'Artema, you bitch, what have you done?'

'The fastest and best way to find out what has happened to Seraf is to follow his trail,' Artema's said, her voice whipped away by the rushing air.

'You're fucking crazy! Stop it, stop it now!' Eladio screamed.

He doubted Artema could do anything, but he was desperate.

'We don't have time. We have to find Seraf. At the very least you should be worried about what's happened to him.'

'I've got bigger problems just now,' Eladio wailed.

'Just relax your body and breathe,' Artema said. 'I've got everything under control.'

As she spoke the air changed about them, the night got

blacker and sound suddenly cut off.

'We're falling through solid concrete. We're falling through a solid tunnel,' Eladio shouted.

He was panic-stricken and hanging onto Artema's arm for all he was worth. There was a spark of golden light that whipped off and away above them as they plummeted downwards, and suddenly their descent was lit.

'I don't want to see this,' Eladio cried as they emerged from the tunnel.

He guessed they'd hit maximum velocity as floor after floor of the city flashed past his eyes. No matter how much he relaxed his body, there would be nothing but a bloody splatter when they hit bottom.

The buffeting wind banging against his ears eased off as a golden pillow of light took their weight and they sailed past the next floor, more floating than plummeting now.

'Is that better?' Artema said.

'Sankta fucking shit, have you lost your bloody mind?' Eladio screamed.

'I'm sorry, but we didn't have time to discuss it.'

Eladio wanted nothing more than to pummel Artema to death while bursting into tears. Then he realised something. 'Stop, stop we can't go any further down!'

'Eladio, I've already explained there's–'

'No, no, that's the sewerage stores below us. Unless you can breathe methane we can't drop into that.'

'Ah, right.'

With a gesture that left a trail of twinkling gold dust, Artema nudged them sideways and they dropped gently to the ground. Eladio ran a couple of metres from the edge of the hole, dropped to his knees and hugged the path. His whole body was shaking. His heart was hammering, and he felt so light-headed he thought he might pass out.

Sirens were blaring around him, and red lights were flashing. It was the escaped gas alert that every suburbanite dreaded hearing. He pushed himself to his feet and looked about for Artema, who was standing too close to the hole.

'You idiot, get away. Methane rises and if a cloud of it envelops you, you'll be out for the count,' he shouted.

At least Artema backed off sharpish just as a group of men kitted in hazard suits ran into the space.

'What the devil do you think you're doing here? Didn't you hear the siren?' one man said. 'You two clear out!'

The suit muffled his voice, but what alarmed Eladio were the double oxygen tanks strapped to their backs. He took Artema's arm in a firm grip and pulled her, running, or rather staggering away to put as much distance between them and the emergency team as possible.

'Did you see that?' Artema said as Eladio dragged her into a quiet alleyway. 'Something dropped all the way through every structure in the city and kept on going even through the sewerage works.'

'Do you see something else?' Eladio snapped. 'We're in the suburbo. Everyone has cleared out because of the gas leak. No not leak, fucking gas disaster and we're back in Black Brotherhood territory. So stop talking and run!'

A click, more felt than heard, reverberated through the suburbo and everything went black and silent.

'Shit!' Eladio muttered.

'What's just happened?' Artema said.

It was so dark Eladio couldn't even see her, so he tightened his grip on her arm and said, 'They've just shut off the power.'

'Why?'

'So that nothing can ignite the methane. But we're in big trouble now because the fans have also gone down so the oxygen levels will plummet and the methane's spreading too. The only reason we're not dead already is that bloody great hole. The methane's probably boiling up through there, especially now the fans are down.'

'That team,' Artema's voice said from the blackness. 'Will they be able to fix the hole?'

'I don't know. It's a big hole,' Eladio said, but he had his doubts. 'It's not like they can use welding equipment and they will have to be damn careful not to let off even a single spark or we'll all be blown to smithereens. Now come on, we can't stay here.' He reached for his phone and realised something horrible. 'I don't have my jacket!'

'Why do you need it?' Artema said.

'My phone was in there. We could have used it for a torch, but it's still in my damn locker.'

'I can give us light,' Artema said, and with a sprinkling of golden stars the surrounding space lit with a gentle glow.

Artema didn't look worried enough, Eladio decided, as her face resolved from the gloom.

'There's no point in covering your mouth, it won't help. Helium displaces oxygen. No oxygen and you're done,' he said and snapped his fingers.

'Then we must help the emergency team.'

'By doing what?'

Eladio wished he could drag Artema away, but she was holding her ground.

'I don't know yet, but something. If we run we just end up like everyone else, don't we? Stuck in the dark, running out of air.'

'What can you do?'

'I think,' Artema said and turned back the way they'd come, 'I can enhance the chimney effect and funnel the methane up. If we can get it to the mezaurbo it will at least have somewhere to disperse, won't it?'

'Yeah, but they won't know it's coming and there were open flames when we jumped.'

'Then you must call them and warn them. Either way, they need to know because if this tank explodes it will do more than just damage the suburbo, won't it?'

Artema slapped her phone into Eladio's hand and took off at a run.

'Me call them? Why not you? They'll listen to you,' Eladio said as he ran after Artema.

'I have to do something about the methane.'

Artema said slowed as they reached the edge of what remained of the buildings that had shattered when whatever it was had crashed through the city.

Artema ducked down behind a torn edge of what had once been a container and said, 'Call my AI. It's listed in my contacts. Tell it everything and it will direct the emergency services. Now, no more questions; I have to concentrate.'

Eladio peered over the edge of the metal barrier at the men who were standing by the hole. Their torches lit everything in an eerie blue glow. They looked aimless, as if they didn't know where to start.

Eladio felt dizzy, probably from lack of air. He had to act quickly. He turned around, slid his back down the metal and flicked Artema's phone open. It was probably new and modern enough that it wouldn't create a spark as it clicked on.

A perfect air screen glowed before him. Everything was crystal clear. He went straight for the address book and looked up AI. It felt like a stupid thing to do, but it was actually listed, just like a person.

Beside him, Artema waved her arms in the biggest gestures Eladio had seen from her. A trail of gold dust flowed from her fingertips, snaked along the ground to the hole, twisted around it and then upwards in a spiral. Eladio prayed the guys in the enviro suits wouldn't spot them as he tapped the connect button on the phone. Then again, the emergency services had bigger problems to worry about.

'Yes, Master?' a holographic face said appearing in the air.

'Sancta shit!' Eladio said. 'Are you really an AI?'

'I am. Where is the master?'

'Busy,' Eladio said and tilted the phone so the face could see. 'Listen, you must warn the authorities that a big funnel of methane is on its way up to the mezaurbo,' Eladio said, and explained as fully as possible.

'It will be done,' the AI said and clicked off.

Eladio kept low and turned around again to peer over the top of their cover. The gold dust was a tube now, spinning like a whirlwind around the hole. The men in their protective gear seemed oblivious to it as they gingerly manhandled the remains of a large container and started edging it over the gap.

'I think they're trying to cover it.'

'Mmm,' Artema grunted.

Sweat was beading on her brow and running in dusty rivulets down her face. Her eyes were fixed on the centre of her golden whirlwind, her hands making a turning gesture that echoed the shape of the swirling golden dust.

Eladio wondered how long she could keep this up because her hands were shaking. Blood also stained the edge of her sleeve. She was injured.

Eladio wondered whether she knew that, then looked down to see if he was hurt too. Everything was starting to ache, but he couldn't see any signs of bleeding. That was at least something. Since breathing was still the hardest thing to do, he could ignore the rest. He was tempted to cover his mouth then shook his head; it was pointless, just a useless instinct.

A bright spotlight flashed down onto them from above. The sound of a siren followed it, and an emergency vehicle appeared in the space above them, well three city floors above them, Eladio estimated. That spotlight was damned bright. Coming down from the hovering vehicle were several rappelling emergency services specialists.

'Thank God,' Eladio said. 'Some professionals to help.'

'I'd say they're much needed,' Artema muttered, but maintained her swirling tube of magic. 'Our men on the ground look a bit lost.'

'Those gang members are okay for the minor emergencies, but not for something like this,' Eladio said. 'Now we should get out of the way.'

'Just a few more minutes. I've created an air vortex and the crafts above will have accounted for that. I will have to ease off slowly, but hopefully the general motion of the air will continue upwards.'

Eladio watched as about twenty men came to land on their small strip. They were all dressed in protective gear with oxygen supplies. It was only him and Artema who were unprotected. Considering how light-headed he felt, they were in danger of not getting out.

'We have to go now,' he said and pulled Artema away.

Artema kept her hold on the spell for as long as she could as Eladio dragged her backwards away from the hole. It was dazzlingly lit by the spotlights the new people had brought in. Thankfully, everything looked a lot more organised now, not like a group of desperate men trying to jerry rig a covering.

'I hope they turn the power on soon,' she wheezed. 'I'm struggling to breathe.'

'Me too,' Eladio said.

He kept up the same dogged pace though, using Artema's phone to light the way.

'Are we going to the elevators?'

'It will be mayhem at the elevators. Everyone with a pass will be fighting to be let out and without power the elevators won't be running, anyway.'

'What about stairs?'

Eladio stopped and grinned at her. It was a shaky, wild-eyed grin.

'Stairs? You want to try the stairs? They're dark. It will be crowded because everyone else will try to get out that way and it's about two kilometres of climbing. That's assuming the mezaurbo even opens the stair doors. You might reach halfway and just get stuck.'

Eladio's words prompted a vague memory of a disaster that Artema had read about. Thousands crushed or suffocated to death because they'd crammed into the stairwells trying to escape and the mezaurbo hadn't open their gates. At least that was a disaster she did recall, unlike the famine.

'Where to then?'

'You're bleeding,' Eladio said. 'So we should go back to mine. I have a few medical supplies that will hopefully work on you.'

'Can we risk it?'

'The Black Brotherhood is far too busy trying to keep control to be out looking for me tonight.'

'I hope you're right.'

'Yeah,' Eladio said.

'So you know where we are?'

'Not yet, but I will soon.'

'At least we know we're in the right gang's territory,' Artema muttered. It was hardly a benefit, but she was trying to see the positive.

She was also trying to ignore the dark and the silence. People had either fled or were hunkered down in their homes praying they got through this. She and Eladio were walking through a maze lit only by the glow of her phone. Structures loomed briefly out of the dark and vanished a few metres after they passed. If she wasn't feeling so damned dizzy, she'd be more freaked out and claustrophobic than she was in this suffocating black hole.

'What do you think happened to Seraf?' Eladio said.

'I don't know,' Artema said. 'I've been going through everything I know of magical explosions and there isn't a single spell I can think of that could punch a hole through kilometres of city.'

'But he was right in the centre of the blast, so it's most likely he was just obliterated, isn't it?'

'I suppose so, but the hole is strange. It goes straight down. Most explosions radiate outwards in a ball, they don't plummet in one direction vaporising everything in their path.'

'Like something falling.'

'Exactly, and the only thing I can think of is a glowing

Seraf.'

'He seems like the only option, but he's just a man. How could he have exploded?'

'I'll answer that when I can work out why he was cracking out of his skin.'

Eladio nodded and said, 'Even if he did explode, how could he have survived?'

'If he was still in one piece and landed in the sewerage surrounded by methane, then he might not have.'

'That is also true.'

Artema was glad that Eladio was worrying away at the problem. It helped distract her from the pain. Besides, it was one almighty big question of what was going on that made everything else she'd seen so far in the suburbo pale into insignificance. If it was demon inspired, it was all the more terrifying.

'Here,' Eladio said, and turned into yet another lane of the container maze. 'I've found it.'

Artema hurried down the path after Eladio and then stopped because Eladio was standing stock still, looking up at his place open mouthed.

'What's the matter?'

'They've kicked me out,' Eladio said, shining the phone up to his container.

Someone had sheared the lock open, and the door hung at an angle. Across the front was polico tape that said, keep out.

'Those bastards broke my lock and have taken my stuff. It's all gone. My home, my money, my pass, my place of work. Seraf blew up–' Eladio's voice cracked and his hands dropped helplessly to his side. 'Kristo, Artema.'

He shook his head, dropped to his haunches, covered his

face with trembling hands, and his shoulders shook in silent tears.

'Hey, hey, it's okay,' Artema said and reached down to give him a reassuring squeeze. 'We'll find a—'

'Sancta Madonna, there he is!' a voice cried from the end of the alleyway. There was a band of about five gang members. They were all holding torches in one hand and bats in the other. 'I didn't think he'd come back, but look at that. The boss was right.'

'Run,' Eladio said, and took off away from the gang.

Artema found hidden depths of reserves and ran after him. Being chased by a gang had remarkable restorative value, but she doubted she could out run five fit young men.

She followed Eladio around a bend and nearly ran into him. Directly in front of them was another group of gang members.

'There's no way out,' Eladio said through gritted teeth. 'So if you've got something we can use, now's a good time.'

'Ok, stay still. No matter what happens, don't move or speak,' Artema said and cast an invisibility spell. Immediately afterwards she cast a levitate spell and the two of them drifted upwards. The two groups of gang members let out a howl and ran towards them. Then they stopped and stared at each other.

'Where'd they go?' one of them said.

'They can't just vanish,' another said, and they all looked around.

Artema kept going up till they reached the top of the container homes and then carefully manoeuvred them onto the roof. It was important they didn't make a sound as they landed, so she brought them down as gently as she could.

Eladio blinked at her, his eyes wide with surprise in his

pale face. Then he ducked down and wriggled along the roof to the edge of the containers and peered down at the gang members. Artema had never had to do this much magic in her life. She'd certainly never had to do it after getting caught up in a bomb blast. Still, she gathered what remained of her strength and crawled along the roof to see what the gang was up to.

They looked confused. A couple were banging on the doors of the lower containers, trying to see if their quarry had somehow slipped inside. A couple more headed down the alley, flashing their torches this way and that, to see whether they'd somehow slipped past. The rest were arguing over whose fault it was that they'd lost a couple of people who, only seconds before, were trapped.

Artema wanted nothing more than to close her eyes and rest. Everything ached, especially her arm. But it was far too dangerous to do that now. Instead, she checked out the roof. She had to find the best route for getting away once the gang cleared out.

'The boss will not be happy,' one of the men said.

'That's why we got to keep looking. In the meantime, someone call it in. Get more men sent down here. They can't have got far.'

Artema glanced across at Eladio to see what he thought. His gaze was fixed on the gang, watching and waiting. He looked like a coiled spring ready to run the moment he had to.

Artema felt terrible about dragging him into this whole sorry mess. Eladio had worked so hard to build himself up. Now, in the space of a few short days, he'd lost everything. His brief meltdown left Artema feeling guilty because, assuming they got out of this hellhole, she could go home.

Nothing had changed for her. She still had a house, all her money, her job and as much protection as she needed to keep the gangs off her back.

All the same, she had no wish to be a wanted woman just because some jumped up gang boss had taken against her. In fact, it was highly suspicious that Rushabarbo was using so many resources to get at the two of them.

It was especially odd now when his energy should have been focused on the disaster. A disaster he might be to blame for if he'd sent his men up to kill Seraf. Why attack Seraf anyway? That made little sense.

They needed to find out, and for that she needed Eladio. She wasn't sure how the young man might take her next suggestion. If their places were reversed, she'd happily have told herself to go to hell.

'We need to get out of here,' Artema whispered into Eladio's ear.

'How?' Eladio mouthed and tilted his head at the gang members below.

'If you know a back way out of here, I'll make sure we aren't seen,' Artema whispered.

Eladio looked back into the blackness, thinking. Then he nodded and started crawling away down to the darker end of the containers. Thankfully, it was away from the alley with the gang members still walking up and down it. Artema had to give him this, he got on with it. When she was in her twenties, she'd have been throwing a stop.

Eladio reached the far end of the containers where they were in pitch blackness and whispered, 'There's a ladder down from here.'

'Good, let's take it,' Artema said just as a torch beam pierced the darkness.

A couple of gang members came around the corner, giving all the containers a cursory glance.

'Keep still, we're okay,' she muttered and cast her insignificance spell. It would work well here in the dark. The spell would ensure they'd just fade to nothing.

One of the gang said, 'Let's look up here. Don't know how they could have got here, but we've looked everywhere else.'

The other guy grunted acceptance and said, 'You go up. I'll stay down here.'

'Damn,' Artema muttered, but put her hand out to make Eladio stay.

The two of them waited, stock still, as the gang member climbed up the ladder. He got high enough to shine his torch into the gap between the container roofs and the concrete above. The light briefly illuminated them.

'There's nothing up here,' he shouted.

'I didn't think there would be,' his mate replied.

'Yeah, well, at least I can say we looked,' the man said and climbed back down.

Artema and Eladio waited until the sound of the men faded away.

Then Eladio whispered into Artema's ear, 'What did you do?'

'It's an insignificance spell. People see you but don't take any notice of you.'

'And before?'

'Let me guess, it looked like I turned to gold, didn't it?'

'Yeah.'

'That was an invisibility spell. Great for the naked eye and even electronic surveillance, but useless if you reveal the magic.'

'Because it covers the whole body?'

'Exactly. In physics terms we turn into human shaped, perfect reflectors of our surroundings. That's why it works so well in dark places like this. Now I really think we should get going, don't you?'

'Okay.' Eladio headed for the ladder and clambered down without making a sound.

Artema followed close behind. Her arm really hurt now, and it took more effort than she wanted to show to swing herself over the edge and down the ladder.

11

Eladio saw the spray of gold that came from Artema and showed magic, but it was incredible to him that the Brotherhood soldier didn't see them. It was especially unbelievable when the torch flicked over them, and they still weren't seen.

There was only one safe place he could think of now, and that was Three's. If anyone knew what was going on, it would be her and they really needed to know what was going on. So he headed towards the river.

Artema followed along behind without a word, which was unusual for her. It was also odd that she wasn't taking charge as she had before. This worried Eladio even more.

They were both tired; the air was hard to breathe, and the darkness was disconcerting. He was used to the dark. But his dark had trailing lights hung at regular intervals and glowing phones or the odd shop window and lit sign. This total blackness that was also devoid of the hum of conversation and the deep dull drone of the fans was horrible.

He'd grown up with tales of suburbo disasters. He'd heard of times when the fans had gone down or fire had swept through parts of the lower levels. Thousands had choked, burned or suffocated then, but he'd never experienced more than the occasional power outage.

Nothing had gone on for this long, he thought, as they

hurried down pitch black paths. Thank God for his perfect memory, or he doubted he could have worked out where to go. He prayed the darkness wouldn't last longer.

That thought brought him back to how this had all started. How Seraf had exploded and… He kept seeing the same thing in his mind's eye. That knife sinking into Seraf's back and then the blinding white flash.

But there was something inside that flash. There was something he couldn't quite see, something else that happened. Something else must have happened.

'Eladio,' Artema said, and her voice was faint and further back than he expected.

Eladio swung around and could hardly make Artema out. She was leaning against the rickety outline of a shop, now shrouded in darkness.

He hurried back and said, 'Are you okay?'

'I just need a breather,' Artema said. 'I'm not used to all this running around.'

'You look like hell.'

'Thank you, my boy. That makes me feel so much better. Might I ask where we're going? You look like a man with a plan.'

'Do you have something you want to do?'

'This is your home turf; you know how to get around here. I'll follow your lead. I'm just curious.'

'I'm taking us to see Three. She'll know what's happening.'

'Now and in the future, huh?'

'Yeah,' Eladio said. 'Although it's more of a risk going to see her now. If the river floods, we'll have no warning that it's coming.'

'At this point, that's the least of our worries.'

'Probably,' Eladio said. 'Do you need a hand?'

'I can manage. Besides, if you're as bruised and battered as I am, the last thing you want is to drag me around. Let's just take it a little slower, huh?'

'Can't you use magic to fix yourself?'

'I wish I could, but magic is hard work. It takes energy to produce an effect just as the laws of physics demand. I would have to draw energy from my body to put energy back into it for the healing. How well do you think that would work?'

'It doesn't sound like it would work at all.'

'Especially not after I've been blowing through my energy budget, as I have over the last couple of hours. What I really need is a slap up breakfast, which I doubt will be forthcoming.'

'No,' Eladio said and started on a much slower walk to the river. 'I'm afraid not.'

'In which case, I'll struggle on.'

Artema pushed herself away from the wall she was leaning against and limped on. Eladio didn't like the look of that. So far, Artema had been the one that had kept them alive. Of course, she was also the one who'd plunged them down the bloody hole and into this mess. Eladio was trying not to blame her for that.

He had a bad feeling that whether he'd been dragged into this by Artema or not, something would still have happened to Seraf. If it happened to him, it might happen to the rest of them. He didn't want to end up as a fireball crashing through the city. He had to do whatever he could to prevent that.

Artema might have wanted to come down to the suburbo looking into something else, but their paths had crossed.

He'd learned more about himself in the process. More than he could ever have done on his own. So maybe he also had cause to be grateful to the woman. He wasn't willing to go that far yet.

'We're nearly there,' Eladio said, turning to Artema. 'You can actually hear the river today.'

'Shows you how quiet it is down here,' Artema muttered.

Eladio leaned over the wall that separated them from the river and gazed down into blackness. It was so dark that he couldn't see the water.

'Eladio, pssst, Eladio?' a voice came out of the gloom.

'Now what?' Eladio said, and adrenaline surged through him again.

'It's me,' the voice whispered, 'Benito.'

'Benito? Where are you?' Eladio said, trying to track down the source of the voice.

'Back here,' Benito whispered, and his face was briefly lit by the glow of his phone, that he flicked on and off again.

'What are you doing here?' Eladio said as he hurried over.

Benito was tucked away in a narrow alcove and all but invisible with the phone turned off.

'I have a message for you from Three.'

'You do?'

'They took her, Eladio. The Black Brotherhood took her and all her stuff away.'

'They did? But... why did she let them do that? She'd have known they were coming. Why did she hang about?'

Benito shrugged.

'She told me to wait here for you. She said you have to find Seraf.'

'Did she tell you where I could find him?'

'Somewhere dark,' Benito said, and gave a helpless shrug.

'When did she tell you this?'

'Yesterday morning. I was minding my business, and suddenly there she was, right beside me. She said I owed you and I could pay you back by giving you this message.'

'Did she say anything else?'

'She said to hurry.'

'Hell!' Eladio said, and he felt lost. 'I have to warn Felicha.'

'It's too late for her. The Brotherhood took her, too. They cleaned out her shop at the same time.'

'What about Dimita?'

'Who?' Benito said.

'Never mind,' Eladio said. 'Thank you, your debt is repaid in full.'

'Good luck. Oh yeah, don't go into Three's place; it's been booby-trapped.'

'Did she tell you that?'

'Nah, I saw them doing that with my own eyes,' Benito said, and slipped off into the darkness.

Eladio's world was crumbling around him, and for the second time he felt overwhelmed. He thought he'd already lost everything, but now this.

'He's rounding everyone up, Artema.' He turned to the magisto, who was watching him in her inscrutable way. 'Why is Rushabarbo doing that?'

'I don't know. This whole thing is very odd. Nothing like my usual interaction with demons.'

Eladio sighed, leaned his back against the wall and used it to slide to the ground. It was all very well Three saying he had to hurry; he was exhausted. He also needed to think.

'It seems Seraf did make it out alive.'

Artema eased herself down to join him and said, 'Are Three's predictions that trustworthy?'

'Yeah', Eladio said and realised, despite his feeling toward Seraf, he was relieved that he'd made it. 'If she's telling us to find him, then he's definitely alive.'

'Then we should try to find him,' Artema said, and eased her bloody sleeve up to take a look.

'Do you think Rushabarbo is behind everything?' Eladio asked as he directed the phone's light onto Artema's arm to reveal a nasty gash that went from her elbow to her wrist.

'It's looking that way. A gang boss fits the profile of a demon target, but the icons all over the place are weird. Most demons don't share their knowledge of icons with humans. I've never seen them in the homes and properties of those working with a demon.' Artema grimaced at the sight of the wound. 'No wonder it's so bloody painful.'

'It's shallow, though. It doesn't look like it sliced anything vital open,' Eladio said. 'I can tear up some of your jacket and wrap it around the arm for the moment to help stop the bleeding.'

'Go ahead,' Artema said and eased her jacket off. At home she would throw it away. It was beyond saving, shredded and heavy with dust. 'Make sure you give it a good shake. That dust won't do my wound any good.'

'I'll take the lining.' Eladio said as he ripped it out.

'Do you know how to find Seraf?' Artema said as Eladio tore the lining into strips.

'Not really. I mean... it's sounding more likely that Seraf was the one who punched through all the layers of the city. But where he ended up...'

Eladio gave a helpless shrug.

'Somewhere dark,' Artema said with a grin.

For a second, Eladio wanted to slap her for being flippant. Then he laughed.

'Yeah, real helpful.'

'Maybe it is. I mean, Three lives down here. She knows it's always dark, but she told you to look somewhere dark. I assume that must mean it's darker than usual.'

'Right now the whole suburbo is pitch black. Maybe all she saw was this.'

'You know her and her predictions, I don't. Do you think she was only talking about this blackout?'

'I don't know,' Eladio said. 'And the problem is I cut myself off from Seraf so I don't know where he's most likely to go. Although, since the gang tried to kill him, he would probably avoid any of his old gang hideouts.'

'Which probably means he'll revert to places he knew as a kid.'

'Maybe,' Eladio said. 'I know somebody we can ask. At the very least, I want to swing past her place and see whether she's okay.'

'Is she a Thirteen?'

'Yeah, Dimita. She was the closest to Seraf. If anyone knows where he's gone to ground, it will be her. Unless he's stuck in a deep dark hole somewhere near the centre of the earth.'

'If he is, I doubt Three would tell you to find him,' Artema said.

There was a click, and the lights went on all around them. A second later, a deep bass hum started up.

'The power's back,' Eladio said with an overwhelming sense of relief. 'At least we'll be able to breathe more easily in a few minutes.'

'I suspect having the lights back will also make us easier to spot,' Artema said as she hauled herself to her feet. It took more of an effort than she wanted to show Eladio.

'Yeah, we should probably change our clothes, but I don't think we have time for that. Let's keep going,' he said and headed for the stairs down to the river.

'Why down? I thought you didn't want to risk drowning.'

'The thing is, despite the blackout and the methane, the Black Brotherhood are hunting us. Even when they should be keeping order amongst the evacuating people. So it's safer to go into another gang's territory where they don't control access to the cameras, and the River Guardians are the closest.'

'Alright.' Artema gripped the slick wet railing tightly as they made their way down the stairs. 'Remember though, that the River Guardians are also using the demon icons so for all we know the gangs have come to an agreement.'

'If they have, we're in such deep trouble, that flooding will hardly matter.'

Eladio reached the bottom of the stairs and looked left and right. He turned right and started making his way along a wide lower walkway.

Artema had a feeling it was centuries ago. At one point, it must have been a pleasant riverside promenade with steps that led down to it at regular intervals. She guessed the only reason such an empty space hadn't been built over was that the river would wash away any new rickety structures that the locals might put up.

They walked under a bridge that had the old lights encased in thick glass set into the stonework of the bridge.

Surprisingly, they were still working and lit the space with a dull yellow glow. She was about to point this out to Eladio, but stopped because the young man had tilted his head and looked to be listening intently.

'What is it?'

'Somebody's coming,' Eladio said, and picked up his pace.

'Somebody's coming from where?'

'Downstream,' Eladio said and flicked his thumb over his shoulder as he broke into a run.

Adrenaline should have surged through Artema, fear did, but it was impossible to keep up with Eladio. Even when she heard a high pitched mechanical whine from behind, it just gave her a jolt as she staggered along as fast as she could. Moments later, four people on vehicles that resembled aerobikes came surging past, jets of water spurting from what looked like exhausts.

A wave swept across the path and knocked Artema off her feet. She landed face first in the icy cold black water. The water rolled back, dragging her with it, and she scrabbled frantically for a fingerhold.

The water bikes shot ahead for a distance as Artema pulled herself onto her knees. They swung around in an arc that left a fluorescent trail in the water and sped past again. They came so close to the bank that another wave drenched Artema and knocked her over again.

She kicked out, pushing against the ground to pull herself further inland. Her head broke the surface, and she coughed up ice cold bitter tasting water. Her world was reduced to just clinging on for dear life.

Eladio crashed through the spray. He grabbed Artema's arm and the side of her trousers, swung her up into a fireman's lift over his shoulders and surged through the water. The bikes turned again, heading straight for them.

'Drop me,' Artema said. 'I think the water's rising.'

'Shut up,' Eladio gasped.

He ran for the stairs just ahead of them that led back to the upper level. Eladio hauled the two of them up the stairs with what felt like superhuman effort to Artema, who was just desperately hanging on. Water surged after them, rising as quickly as they did. It washed around Eladio's thighs as he clambered out of it and up to the street level. He staggered a couple of steps and dropped to his hands and knees, coughing and gasping for breath.

'Sankta Madonna, that river rose fast,' Artema said as she rolled off Eladio's back.

She lay on her side watching the water flowing past, white, churned up and roaring. The bikers swung around in a great arc and sped off upstream.

'Were they trying to warn us, do you think?'

'I don't know,' Eladio said through gasps for air. He rolled onto his back and stared up into the darkness.

'Eladio... if that kind of thing happens again. You should just leave me.'

'You would have drowned.'

'Better one of us than both. Somebody has to find Seraf, and that's unlikely to be me.'

'But you have magic. You got us away from the Black Brotherhood when I wouldn't have been able to.'

'I'm too damn tired to use magic.'

'Then use the demon icons. You said they're like batteries.'

'It's far too dangerous.'

'You'd rather die than use them?' Eladio said and sat up

to examine Artema.

'I don't think it's come to that. But I do have one resource we should use.'

'What's that?'

'Do you still have my phone?'

'Yeah,' Eladio said and handed it over.

Artema wondered why she'd left it with the young man. Maybe because she trusted him. It was an interesting thought. Time to explore it later, though. She dialled the vice chancellor and was relieved when he answered on the first ring.

'Artema, what the devil is going on?' Normando said as his face appeared on the screen. 'All hell has broken loose in the mezaurbo.'

'What do you mean by all hell, Normando?'

'I mean a bloody great explosion where you were last seen. There's a hole all the way to the bottom of the city. The news is full of it. The only reason there weren't thousands of casualties was because of how late it was in the evening. Even so, the casualty count is creeping up to the hundred mark. What happened?'

'That's what we're still trying to find out. I don't suppose they made any mention of the methane leak in the suburbo?'

'Was there one?'

'The hole you mentioned went straight through a giant sewerage tank down here. You'd have thought that would be worth a mention on the news,' Artema said, and noted Eladio's cynically raised eyebrow at her comment. 'Never mind, it's been worse down here than you can imagine. Eladio and I are being hunted by the Black Brotherhood, so we could use some reinforcements.'

'I'll send the beadles straight away,' Normando said.

'Thank you, use my beacon, not my phone to find me.'

'Will do,' Normando said. 'Be careful, Artema.'

'I'm trying,' Artema said, and hung up to discover that Eladio was grinning at her. 'What?'

'You're being careful?'

'You weren't listening properly, I said I was trying,' Artema said and handed the phone back to Eladio. 'You hang onto that just in case.'

'Because you have a beacon?'

'Partly. At least this way we can find you via the phone too if needs be.'

Eladio nodded and pushed himself back onto his feet.

'Come on, we can't stay here.'

'Right,' Artema said and accepted Eladio's hand as she forced herself to stand up. 'Listen, Eladio, I was being serious when I said next time you leave me behind. Somebody has to get out of this alive.'

'You have help coming, so it should be okay. What's a beadle, anyway?' Eladio said as he looked around, getting his bearings.

'They're university security. They keep the students safe and make sure they behave themselves. They're all magistos, and their speciality is battle magic.'

'What's battle magic?' Eladio said as he pulled off his soaked apron and wrung it out. A stream of water splashed onto the ground as Eladio squeezed it hard. Once it was as dry as he could get it, he used it to towel down his face and hair.

'Anything that either strikes, protects or confines.'

Artema considered wringing out her jacket but couldn't muster up the energy to take it off. She gratefully accepted the apron Eladio held out to her though, and wiped the water from her face, then tried to squeeze out her hair.

Eladio waited while she did that, then he set off again, leaving squelchy wet footprints along the path. She struggled even to keep up. Her clothes that clung to her like chilly slime weighed her down.

'Mostly beadles try to prevent violence from occurring,' Artema said, because talking would pull her mind back to focussing on their key problem. 'Their priority is to stop a confrontation. That's where the force field comes in. They can cut people off or trap them in one place. If that fails, they have a range of blast spells. But my personal favourite is displacement. That is especially useful when you want to take a weapon off somebody and put it in your own hand, or just out of use.'

'Like into a pocket universe.'

'Exactly. I have a baton in my pocket universe. I got it from a beadle, incidentally. They have a whole range of weapons they stash away,' Artema said, and stopped as a gang tag caught her eye. 'We're in Purple territory?'

'Yeah, so best to keep our voices down.'

'Another attempt to avoid the brotherhood?'

'That and Dimita has her place on the border of Purple territory. Hopefully that means she's still okay and hasn't been rounded up.'

Eladio's senses were on high alert. He listened for every sound, scanned every street before they crossed it, even sniffed the air, just in case. He and Artema reeked of river water, so that was pointless. All the same, he had to be careful.

When he'd first seen his home broken into and

everything taken, he'd thought it was because of Artema. Now he wasn't so sure. Three was also gone along with all her things and Felicha was... Shit, he shouldn't have thought of Felicha. He'd been trying not to think of her and not to worry about her.

She could look after herself. He nearly laughed as he thought about the fight she must have put up and heaven help them when they tried to take all her stuff. Although, Seraf would have known that and if he'd been involved–

Another thought struck Eladio. What if the gang had come for Seraf too? What if the two that had confronted him weren't there because of him and Artema? What if they hadn't even realised they were there? They'd just gone for Seraf. If that was true, it put a whole different light on the matter.

He was about to mention it to Artema when the pungent smell of wood smoke accosted his nostril.

'Fire!' he gasped.

'What?' Artema muttered.

'There's a fire nearby,' Eladio said. 'Fire down here is terrible, and we're near Dimita's place!'

'Bona Dio, can this day get any worse?' Artema muttered.

Eladio ran ahead, Artema could catch up. Right now he had to know if it was Dimita's. He rounded a corner and ploughed into a thick column of smoke billowing down the lane. He pulled his damp shirt over his face and, eyes smarting, he blinked and tried to work out what was burning. There was a dull orange glow directly ahead, with more smoke gushing out like water. He couldn't see anyone, but that wouldn't last. Residents and the gang's firefighters would be here soon. That meant the fire hadn't been raging long.

He walked closer till he could make out flames. It was as he'd feared. The fancy carved wooden facade of the brothel was aflame. The suggestive figures were glowing and writhing in one final ecstasy. It looked like the Brotherhood had taken Dimita as well. It was bloody stupid to set the place on fire, but it would keep the Purples busy and distracted. Fire was a nightmare here, especially with all their wooden buildings.

A siren went off nearby, and those citizens who'd not evacuated during the blackout burst from their homes. It would be chaos soon and there was no point in hanging about. Eladio turned back to find Artema and froze.

Artema stood at the end of the lane flanked by four tough looking Purples. The ones on either side of her had a very firm grip on each of her shoulders.

'Run, Eladio!' she shouted.

'Artema.'

'Bloody well do as I tell you!' Artema yelled as a couple more Purples ploughed through the smoke at full tilt towards Eladio.

He turned and ran down the lane that passed Dimita's front door and into the denser smoke. The women were closing on him and questing fingertips brushed his collar. He put every bit of energy he had for a spurt to carry him past the flames that scorched his side as he went. His shin connected hard with something and he flew through the air, hit the ground, slid along, scrambled onwards, broke out of the smoke on the other end and staggered on.

Eladio was a hundred metres further along when he realised he wasn't being followed any more. He glanced backward through a grey haze with a dull orange in the centre. People were running towards it. Everyone who passed him was carrying buckets of water. It seemed the Purples thought the fire was more important than he was.

He staggered to a wall, leaned his hands on it, bent over double and coughed and coughed till he felt he would retch up his lungs. His eyes smarted with tears, and he was shaking. Now that he had time to notice it, he realised his shin bloody hurt too. This was, without a doubt, the worst day of his life.

And now he didn't even have Artema. Annoying as the woman was, misery loved company. Sharing the awfulness of the day was easier than having to bear it alone.

He prayed Artema would be alright and that the beadles would find her. At least the professor had somebody to help her. Now he had to do the rest. Three had told him to find Seraf.

He had no clue where to start. He'd pinned his hopes on advice from Dimita. Now that was a bust.

So where did he go? He wondered whether Three had seen him finding Seraf. Maybe all she knew was that Seraf needed to be found, but not what happened next.

If she didn't know what happened next, it meant that at the time she'd seen the vision, Eladio hadn't found him. That meant he wouldn't find him at least today and – What day was it, anyway? Eladio thought and pulled out Artema's phone to check.

It was Tuesday. What did that matter? Not a jot. Nothing mattered except finding Seraf and getting the two of them away from the Black Brotherhood and Rushabarbo.

On the other hand, he had a phone. If he needed to, he could call for help. He could call the AI again and – and? He had no idea.

He snapped the phone shut and shoved it into his trouser

pocket. It was excellent tech. It had survived a drenching, which he doubted his phone would have done.

Eladio shook his head and forced himself to focus. He tried to think about Seraf and where he might be. Nowhere near the Brotherhood, which meant...

Maybe he'd gone back to the drug den. Would he do that? It was a dark, depressing place, the emphasis being on dark. Drug addicts didn't bother spending money on lighting.

That would do. While he walked, he could think of other places to search. He ducked down a row of container homes, keeping to the shadows as much as possible. He kept his head down to make it harder to pick his face up on camera. It was a shame he couldn't trade the phone for a jacket with a hood, but the phone was a lifeline and one he needed to hang onto.

The drug den was on the edge of Yellow Peril territory in one of those rare no man's lands that no gang wanted to claim. It was right beside a public toilet, so the stench coming from it was dire at the best of times. After a couple of hours without fans, the place stank even more. Or maybe it was a particularly badly maintained facility.

Either way, Eladio couldn't prevent his lip from curling with disgust as he made his way past it. He pushed aside the random debris that littered the ground, stuff so crap that nobody else wanted it. A man lay comatose under a torn strip of cardboard. His back was against the toilet wall and one foot was in a stream of human waste that had leaked through the open door.

He was too thin to be Seraf, so Eladio kept going. He checked each of the people he came across. It didn't look like anyone here had cleared out during the blackout. Listless figures sat or lay all about him. Eladio was heading for the building where he'd found Seraf the last time.

It was an ancient place. It looked like it must have been here before the rest of the city went up, although these days only the frame remained. They had filled some holes in with bits of cardboard, or ancient plastic. It was a dangerous place to go into, not least because of the rotting floorboards.

A young girl lay propped up against the wall in a daze with a drug dispenser in her loosely curled fingers. Eladio stepped over her and looked about. The floor was covered with bodies. Most were in some form of blissed out state. Others maybe just sleeping. One old man with dishevelled hair was lying on his side, watching Eladio. He looked like someone working out how much Eladio was worth.

None of them were Seraf, so Eladio made his cautious way upstairs to the next level. It was the same, filled with people. A small group was sitting in the middle of the floor around a fire they'd made from scraps of paper. Considering the floor was wood, it was a bloody stupid thing to do. Then again, junkies didn't really think about danger.

He got as close as he dared and said, 'Have you seen anybody new here?'

'New like what?' a man with heavily scabbed over lips asked.

'Like he arrived late yesterday, or maybe today. Tall and blond.'

'Tall and blond?' the man said with a grin that revealed rotting teeth. 'If he's good looking, he'll be out pimping himself for a score. No need to come here till you got nothing left to sell.'

'That's right, dearie,' the old woman next to the man said. 'What you want to do is go to his home. He'll be there.'

'He can't go home.'

'Maybe he can, maybe he can't. People go back to their roots when they're most in trouble,' the woman said in a singsong voice. 'Best for you to do that, too. You look far too nice to be hanging around here.'

'Yeah, thanks,' Eladio said and backed off. It was better not to engage. It got you noticed, and these were desperate people. On top of that, he had a phone worth so much in his pocket it would keep the entire building's occupants in drugs for a month.

He hurried up the next set of stairs and made his way along the edge of the wall. It was the most secure bit of floor and the way his day was going; it paid to be careful. He stopped at the corner where he'd found Seraf before. A couple of women occupied it. One was folded over the top of the other and both were out cold.

He backed out and headed down the stairs. This was a bust and best left as quickly as possible. The old man who'd eyed him when he came in was now whispering to another man in the corner. They both watched him as he came down. It was definitely time to get the hell out of here.

Artema watched Eladio take off into the smoke and prayed he'd get away. The Purples had pounced on her so suddenly that she'd had no chance to run. Not that she thought she could. She was at the limit of what she could do. She barely had the energy to shout at Eladio. Only rage at him for disobeying gave her voice any volume at all.

Now she concentrated on staying on her feet. She let the women either side of her hold her up as people ran past to tackle the fire. They were lugging water in a variety of containers as they came. It looked like chaos and worse, terrifying because the people looked scared. In this enclosed space, and a district built almost entirely from wood, that made sense.

'Who's that?' a woman's voice said from behind them.

Artema was swung around by her captors, who all stiffened to attention. She was a tall woman and built like a bodybuilder. Unlike the other inhabitants of the suburbo, she wore a tight fitting vest and no jacket. It showed her admirably toned body off to perfection. Artema guessed she was Bellecannon, the leader of the Purples.

'She's one of the people Rushabarbo is after, boss,' her guard said.

'One of them?'

'The other one took off. The girls have gone after him.'

'Did you start this fire?' the boss said, glaring at Artema. She felt a moment of panic at the rage she saw.

'No,' Artema said. 'It was already going when we got here.'

'That's probably true, boss,' her guard said. 'We caught her going towards the fire. If they'd started it, they'd be running away.'

'Then who started the fire?' Bellecannon said, looking at her gang members.

'If I may,' Artema said, 'I suspect Rushabarbo was responsible.'

'Nobody asked you,' Bellecannon snapped. 'Did the girls get out?'

'We don't know yet. We can't find Dimita.'

'Because Rushabarbo will have taken her,' Artema persisted.

Short of killing her, they couldn't do much worse to her

than she'd already suffered, so it was worth the risk.

'Then we'll trade you for her,' Bellecannon said.

'You don't understand, he won't do that. He's rounding them all up. He's taken Madonna Three and Felicha Twelve, he even went for Seraf One and–'

'He attacked Seraf?' Bellecannon snapped.

'Yes, and he's after Eladio as well. I think he wants them all.'

'All who?'

'The Thirteen.'

'The who?' Bellecannon shook her head. 'Don't tell me now. I have a fire to deal with. You lot take her back to base. Make sure she can't get snatched and guard her with your life.'

'Yes, boss,' the women said.

They were about to leave when two more of them appeared from the smoke.

'He got away, boss,' the two new girls said.

'Ok, don't worry about that now, just help guard our prisoner.'

'I really don't think you need six women just to guard me,' Artema said. 'Surely the fire is more urgent.'

'Not to keep you from running,' Bellecannon snapped. 'To keep Rushabarbo from getting his hands on you before I work out what the hell is going on.'

'Oh, fair enough,' Artema said, but it was to Bellecannon's back as she ran for the fire.

The people around had finally formed a bucket line. They were sending their containers along it in an orderly row. Just then another couple of gang members ran in with a hose. Hopefully that meant they would contain the fire, especially since they led Artema into the heart of the collection of wooden buildings.

Artema had to say this for the residents of the Purple's territory, they didn't waste time gawping, gossiping or panicking. They'd moved in to quell the fire. True, their lives depended on it, but she'd seen plenty of cases where people fell apart in desperate circumstances.

They moved deeper into the twilight of Purple territory. Artema had to keep reminding herself that it was day, and she was in a modern city. Even though wooden structures loomed all around her. They closed off the pathways overhead so that buildings from one side of the street practically met one or two stories above her. It was just like in medieval towns. Even the strings of yellow lights dangling along the edge of the buildings did nothing to dispel that impression.

She guessed she was right in the middle of Purple territory when they arrived at a stockade built entirely from wood. They'd painted a massive Purple's gang tag across the gate. One of the gigantic concrete posts that held up the city formed the back wall and towered up above them and vanished into the next level of the city. The HQ, Artema assumed.

It was barely occupied as they stepped inside. Presumably most of the gang were tackling the fire. They took Artema across what amounted to a square inside the fortress and pushed her into a corridor. The place looked like a dungeon. It had a row of doors to either side, each with bars on them. Ah well, it wasn't like she was an honoured guest. At least each little cell had a bed.

'In you go,' one of her guards said and pushed her in.

'Could I make one small request,' Artema said. 'Might I have some water, please; my throat is raw.'

The woman appeared to ignore her and Artema sighed. Then she sank gratefully onto the narrow wooden bed. It was more like a bench, but at least it had a thin mattress.

A few moments later, the woman reappeared and handed her a blanket. 'Here, you might need that. You should at least get out of your wet clothes.'

'Oh, thank you,' Artema said.

The guard had a point, not that she'd noticed, beyond the discomfort. It was so much hotter and more humid in the suburbo she'd all but forgotten she was sopping.

'How did you get so wet?'

'We nearly got caught by the River Guardians.'

'The River Guardians failed to catch you?' the women said, frankly disbelieving. 'Ma'am, if they wanted you, you'd be caught. Since you're still alive, they were probably helping you.'

'Do you think so?'

'It would be a first, but nobody knows what those bastards are thinking anyway,' the woman said.

She stood aside as one of the other guards arrived with a bread roll and a steaming mug of something Artema guessed was soup. She sniffed at it. If she used her imagination, it was possibly chicken soup. It had such an unnatural yellow colour that she wasn't convinced. All the same, it was food and something she desperately needed.

'Thank you,' she gasped. This was far more than she'd expected.

'Here,' the woman said.

She pulled a bottle of water out of her jacket pocket and handed it over.

'Even better,' Artema said. 'Thank you once again.'

The woman shook her head as she left and was followed

by the more chatty woman. They locked her in, but then took up position outside her door. It should have outraged Artema to be locked up. Instead, she was relieved. She felt safer in here than out there. They had also given her food and a place to rest where Rushabarbo might not get her.

Since she was parched, she unscrewed the bottle and took a deep and satisfying swig of water. Then she drank the soup. Today she'd ignore all the hideous chemicals it was probably made from. She even dunked the roll in it to make both of them more edible. It was criminal how poor the food was down here. Once she'd eaten everything, she wrapped herself in the blanket, curled up on the bed and passed out.

12

Eladio was stumped. He squatted down in the darkest corner he could find and tried to work out his next move. He had no idea where to look for Seraf. He had even less of a clue who he could ask. Luca popped into his mind as a possibility but was dismissed. First, because Luca might have been rounded up too. Second, because even if he wasn't, Luca wasn't bright enough to tell Eladio where Seraf might hide.

Luca had always hero worshipped Seraf, so it was no surprise he'd become his chief enforcer when Seraf joined the gang. Would he be angry if he discovered the gang had tried to kill his hero? Maybe. But would he do anything about it?

Eladio remembered Luca's epic rampages in the orphanage when he was upset. He'd go on a destruction spree, but not with any real purpose other than to smash everything before him. He'd keep going till he wore himself out. Then he'd curl into a ball and fall fast asleep.

It didn't matter where that was either. Once it had been on the stair landing. They'd all had to clamber over him to get up and down because he was too big and heavy to move and they couldn't wake him. Funny to remember that now.

It gave him an idea, though. Luca had just collapsed anywhere after his rages. When the rest of them were hurt or upset, they'd hide. Their favourite place was the basement, which matched Threes description of a dark place. It was a long shot, but as he didn't have any other ideas, it was worth a try.

He would have to hurry because people were sorting themselves out from the blackout and soon it would be harder to pass unnoticed. As it was, Eladio stuck to the narrower, darker lanes in the least well maintained sections, hoping the surveillance was as poorly maintained here as the streets were.

So far the gang, despite the effort they were putting into catching him and Artema, hadn't found him again. Damn, he'd been trying not to think of Artema. Now an image of her, surrounded by a group of Purples, yelling at him to run popped into his head.

He shouldn't have run. He was wasting his time pretending he could find Seraf. But it was too late now, and there was no way he could get Artema away. He'd have to let the woman make her own escape. After all, she had skills few other humans possessed.

Eladio stopped at the edge of the orphanage square. He kept to the shadows of the lane he was in and examined it. It looked normal. There were no extra people here. There were no obvious signs of gang members either, but also no sign of the kids.

Usually there'd be a horde of them playing out front. If they'd been evacuated... He nearly laughed at that. Who would have bothered to evacuate the kids? The staff would have cleared out at the first sign of trouble. They'd not have given a second thought to the kids. Maybe the kids followed them or just took the opportunity to run away.

Eladio contemplated going straight to the front door, but that was just plain stupid. There were cameras pointed at all the entrances of the place. It was how the staff kept the kids in line.

The staff were also all brotherhood gang members, so they'd be on the lookout for him. They all knew what he looked like too. That meant the front entrance was out.

The only way in was the secret entrance, known only to the kids. They used it because it wasn't covered by a camera. It was the way they all sneaked in and out. It was the route he and Felicha had used when they'd slipped off to find her father.

It was at the lowest end of this space, where the ceiling of the next level of the city practically touched the roof of the orphanage. It was dark and cramped and also the alleyway where they chucked all the rubbish, so it usually stank. All good reasons for the staff to avoid it.

Eladio worked his way through the alleyways to the side of the building. He checked that he couldn't see anyone and dashed across the small space that separated him from the orphanage. He ducked behind the dumpster and felt along the damp ground till his fingers touched wood. That was the trapdoor for the basement below.

He ran his fingers along the wood to the latch. There was a technique to getting it to open from the outside, and it pleased him to see it still worked. The question now was, would he still fit through the gap? The last time he'd used this trapdoor, he'd been twelve.

He exhaled to make himself as thin as possible and wriggled head first through the gap. Just inside was a metal bar that you had to catch onto. If you missed it, you'd crash headfirst into the basement.

It was an easier reach now that he was taller. But he really had to pull on the bar to get the rest of himself through the gap and his clothes caught and pulled and he felt his shirt rip. Still, with not too much effort, he was in. Whether Seraf could pull off a similar feat was debatable; he had far more bulk.

Eladio waited for his eyes to adjust. He breathed in the damp musty air and took a first look around. The basement was filled with the same crap it had always held.

Cardboard boxes were piled up along one wall holding children's clothing. He remembered digging through these boxes as a kid, trying to find something halfway decent to wear. Shelves on the other side of the wall held a collection of plastic cutlery and crockery, a shelf of blankets and the bottom shelf had ancient and holey shoes. Against the adjoining wall was a pile of lumpy mattresses, unwashed and used by hundreds of kids over the years.

A faint scratching noise drew his attention. This place didn't have rats, they would be caught and eaten. So what made that noise?

He pushed aside a box and scanned the gap between the mattresses. Something pale and curved shifted in the gloom. It took a while for him to realise it was a naked man curled up on the floor.

'Seraf?' he whispered and dropped down beside the man. 'Mia Dio, is that you?'

The man turned his head away, but this close Eladio was certain it was him. He had a nasty gash over his shoulder blade, but at least he no longer had the glowing cracks. He looked perfectly ordinary.

'You're injured.'

Seraf slowly opened one eye and murmured, 'Oh, it's you. I should have known.'

'How did you get here?'

Eladio reached for one of the nearby cardboard boxes and rummaged through the clothes for something to fit Seraf.

'I have no fucking idea,' Seraf said, and he closed his eyes.

'Well, you need to see a doctor. Your shoulder looks bad.'

'Why don't you just leave me alone?'

'I can't because we're both wanted men. Your boss–'

'My boss? My boss?' Seraf hissed. 'He told me to detain you. Then, when I let you go, he decided to kill me instead. How's that for a boss? Say what you will about me, Eladio, but I was never such a shit to anyone. Was I?'

'He's rounded everyone else up too.'

Eladio discarded a t-shirt that was far too small and went back to sorting through the clothes.

'Everyone who?'

'The Thirteen, the whole lot. Do you think he intends to kill them?'

Eladio hoped not, but Rushabarbo was an unknown quantity and he didn't have enough information to make a guess at his intentions.

'I don't know,' Seraf said and wrapped his arms even tighter around himself. 'I wouldn't have guessed he'd go for me. I thought it was because I was trying to build my own power base.'

'You were planning to overthrow him?'

'What do you think?'

The sarcastic note that often tinged Seraf's voice was back, if fainter than usual.

'Mmm, well that still doesn't explain the rest.'

There was a smash, and the basement door swung open. It hit the wall with a bang and six Brotherhood gang members stepped inside. They were followed by Luca, who squeezed himself through the frame.

'Eladio, come with us,' he said in the manner of someone reciting words he'd been taught. 'We have you surrounded.'

'So I see,' Eladio said. 'Are you here for Seraf too?'

'Seraf?' Luca had the panicked expression on his face of somebody who didn't understand what he'd just heard. 'Seraf's dead.'

'No, he's right here.' Eladio pointed at Seraf, who stayed in his curled up ball and didn't even open his eyes. 'Who told you he was dead?'

'Rushabarbo said you blew him up.'

'Me?'

'He said you were a terrorist. He said you killed Seraf and then tried to blow up the sewerage works,' Luca said and looked to be working up into a rage.

'Well, he lied.'

Eladio spoke as calmly as he could. It sometimes worked to keep Luca from going into a rage. He also stepped back because the other gang members were fanning out, preparing to rush him. He bumped into the back wall. He had nowhere to run. What puzzled him was why Three thought this was a good place to be.

Luca looked steadily more confused as he stepped forward and squinted into the gloom.

'Seraf, is that really you?'

'Leave me alone,' Seraf said and finally turned to face everybody.

He also started to glow. It was so faint Eladio thought it was his imagination for a moment till the glow grew stronger.

'Seraf, calm yourself.'

'Shut up,' Seraf snapped, and he turned from a dull orange to a bright yellow.

'Seraf, what must I do?' Luca said.

'Stay back,' Eladio said.

'I can help'

Luca took another step forward as the rest of the men closed in.

'Rushabarbo will want them both,' one man said.

'Well, you can tell him to fuck off!' Seraf shouted and he exploded.

The room went white and the last thing Eladio felt was being hoisted off the floor by the shock wave.

The pungent smell of smoke cut through Artema's exhausting dreams. Then a surge of adrenaline had her sitting up before she even opened her eyes. She blinked, trying to clear her vision. Bellecannon was watching her, her head tilted to one side. She'd come straight from the fire and her muscular arms were streaked with ash.

'Who are you?' Bellecannon said.

'I'm Artema Salonoy.'

There was no point in lying. That never worked well when you were trying to win an ally.

'Is that supposed to mean something to me?'

'I suppose not,' Artema said. 'I'm a magisto from the Eternal University of Magic.'

'Is that so?' Bellecannon was less impressed than Artema had hoped by her confession. Which was confirmed when she said with a sneer, 'Next you'll tell me you're a blue blood as well.'

'As it happens, I am.'

'Then I should get a good ransom for you.'

'Really, that's the way you want to do this?' Artema asked, trying to keep her calm. She had become too used to Eladio, who was honourable and would never have considered ransoming anyone. She'd been stupid to think a gang leader would be the same.

'What else should I do?' Bellecannon said. 'The fire caused a bloody mess. It will need a lot of money to fix it and just at this moment you fall into my lap.'

'Aren't you the least bit curious to know what I'm doing down here in the first place? Or even why Rushabarbo wants me dead?'

Artema was willing to spend both magical energy and money to win Bellecannon over, but first she needed to find out what made her opponent tick.

'Were you causing trouble in his territory?' Bellecannon asked.

'No more than in yours. All I was interested in were the gang tags. Does that sound threatening to you?'

'You were looking at gang tags? Everybody's tags?'

At least Artema now had the gang leader's attention. She was clearly wondering why the tags had any relevance to their current conversation.

'Yes, all of them. I was wondering why they all looked so similar. And now I'm also wondering why Rushabarbo was so sensitive about what I was doing that he ordered my execution.'

Bellecannon turned and snapped her fingers at one of the guards. The woman vanished and reappeared moments later with a chair. Bellecannon settled cross-legged on it and eyed Artema up and down.

'Alright, I'll bite. I've wondered about the tags myself.'

'You have? But… didn't you put them up?'

'Yeah, we did. At least my predecessor did, and I've kept it up.'

'Why?'

'It's part of an agreement.'

'What agreement?'

'Hey, you're supposed to be giving me information, not the other way around.'

'Consider this give and take. You tell me what you know about the tags and I'll tell you what I think is going on.' Bellecannon looked underwhelmed by the offer so Artema said, 'How much ransom would you ask for?'

'What?'

'However much it is, I'm willing to pay that for your information. But then you can't hold back. I need to hear everything.'

'Then I should squeeze you for even more,' Bellecannon said, and her eyes glowed with the thought of her potential riches.

'I don't only have money,' Artema said, deciding it was time for shock and awe. She made a circling gesture followed by a push. The force welled up inside her and shot out of her hand as a powerful percussive force that blew the cell door off its hinges. It flew across the corridor, slammed into the opposite wall and broke into dozens of shards.

'Sankta fiksa pikita!' Bellecannon shouted as she surged to her feet, took a step towards the door, then swung round, staring at Artema in horror. 'What was that?'

'I told you I was a magisto.'

'Bellecannon, are you alright?' the guards outside said as they clustered about the shattered door, keeping their distance from the suddenly more intimidating prisoner.

'I'm fine,' Bellecannon said and waved her people away.

They moved back down the corridor, but still within hailing distance if necessary.

'So what you're saying, is that you can leave at anytime,' Bellecannon said, looking Artema up and down with more respect.

'In about a hundred different ways,' Artema said.

'So why did you let us capture you in the first place?'

'Because I need information and I thought this would be the best way to get it.'

It wasn't a complete lie. At the moment of her capture, Artema was so exhausted she couldn't have cast a spell if her life depended upon it, but she'd also realised her capture was an opportunity. At the very least, it had provided her with a safe place to recharge her batteries.

'Alright,' Bellecannon said, returning to the chair she'd knocked over. She set it back on its feet and sat back down, watching Artema with a new wary glint in her eye. 'What do you want to know?'

'Tell me everything you know about the tags, and when they started to go up.'

Bellecannon took a deep breath, gathered her thoughts and said, 'About twenty-five years ago the suburbo was in chaos. Gang warfare was rife. We fought over everything. Territories changed hands all the time, and deaths were an everyday occurrence.

'Then Rushabarbo appeared on the scene. He took over the Brotherhood and immediately started trying to make peace with all the other gangs. From what I hear, he was persuasive. When words didn't work, he got more brutal on his opponents than anyone down here had ever seen.

'Anyway, part of any peace agreement signed with

Rushabarbo includes a clause to put up the tags, as designed by him. At first we thought it was stupid. But it defines our boundaries and our most important properties and they've become... You could say sacrosanct. I wouldn't dream of trying to take territory that had another gang's tags on it now.'

'So it was Rushabarbo who designed the tags and insisted you all put them up?' Artema said.

This sounded more like demon interference working through a single human. Although the scope of the ambition seemed vast.

'Yeah, it was all him.'

Artema shifted her position so she could get a better view of Bellecannon. At the moment she was more shadow than light and Artema wanted to see her facial expressions.

'Did he say anything about where the tags should go?'

'On the most important buildings and anywhere else we fancied. He didn't much care. The only rule was that there had to be a gang tag every twenty-five metres along the border of each gang's territory.'

'And you've all stuck to that?'

'Rushabarbo makes certain that we do.'

'Doesn't that strike you as odd?'

'We all have our kinks.'

'That's true. What I also find curious though, is how little I have been able to find out about Rushabarbo.'

'He is a mystery,' Bellecannon said with a shrug that reflected her disinterest. Her attention was clearly all focused on her gang and her territory. 'But information, like everything else down here, comes at a price.'

'I've already said I'm willing to pay. How about I fund the rebuild of the house that burned down? Would that get me the information I want?'

'The complete rebuild?'

'I'll even throw in some extra funds for some decent lighting down here.'

Bellecannon frowned and examined Artema even more closely.

'This is about more than just the tags, isn't it?'

'Ah yes,' Artema said, realising she'd offered too much for her information. Like Eladio, Bellecannon knew the value of what she had. Artema kicked herself for having been so careless. 'The tags are a very physical marker of something far more serious that I have yet to understand. Which is why I need to know more about Rushabarbo.'

'More serious how?'

Artema sighed, obviously this woman would not give up her information without a fair exchange. 'The tags all hold the same demon icons.'

'What?'

'You know about demons, right?'

'Of course, everyone knows about them. What's that got to do with the tags?'

'Some symbols in the tags are demonic.'

'Demonic,' Bellecannon said with a snort of amused disbelief, 'what do they do?'

'That's what I'm trying to work out. The symbols themselves appear to be based around control. They are intended to keep people within boundaries, keep them calm and keep them obedient.'

'Are you serious? You're actually taking about demons?' Bellecannon snapped. 'Why should I believe you?'

'Because I'm a demonologist.'

Artema wished she didn't have to reveal this. It usually

involved a lot more explaining.

'Mmm,' Bellecannon said, looking her up and down dubiously. 'I've heard a rumour, and that's all it is, mind you, that Rushabarbo has a demon as a captive.'

'That's impossible.'

'That's what I've heard. Take it or leave it. I don't care.'

'Aside from the demon,' Artema said, dismissing the idea because it was too improbable, 'What can you tell me about him?'

'He's a big man, foreign, old.'

'Foreign?'

'Not from around here. My guess was that he's the same as you, from the supraurbo.'

'Foreign, you mean from the same city as you?'

'Sister, if you think the suburbo and the supraurbo are the same city you're stupider than you look.'

'Well... I suppose I can see your point.'

'Damn right. Aside from that, like I said, Rushabarbo appeared down here about twenty-five years ago. I'm not sure exactly when, but that was when he took the Brotherhood over. He isn't a very hands on boss. He usually recruits a number two who does all the work and represents the gang at our regular meetings.'

'He doesn't come to meetings?'

'Hardly ever. He showed up when I became gang boss and looked me up and down like I was a piece of trash. Then he said, "you'll do", like he had a say in the matter, and fucked off. Since then I've seen him maybe twice more.'

'What happened at those meetings?'

'One was for a new leader of the River Guardians, the other was a dispute over the border between us and the Yellow Perils. He insisted the current borders couldn't be changed, no matter how much we wanted it. The Yellows and us were in agreement over the move, but Rushabarbo was having none of it.'

'I see,' Artema said. So the borders had significance. Maybe that was more important than the tags placed inside the territories. That was useful information. 'Anything else? Is he close to anyone?'

'I have no idea. He lives by the colosseum in just about the biggest house you'll find in the suburbo and keeps it locked up tight. Hardly anyone goes in and out.'

'So you watch him?'

'I watch everyone.'

'He doesn't even let his number two in?'

'As far as I know, he only let Seraf One in once. He was there for about twenty minutes and then he was out again.'

'When was that?'

'Mmm, let me think... last Thursday I believe.'

'Thursday?' Artema said, and her stomach gave a frightened squeeze. That was the day she'd first come to the suburbo. 'Really, this last Thursday?'

'Yeah.'

'And that was the first time he'd let anyone in?'

'That I know of, yeah. What's the big deal about that?'

'I don't know yet, but it feels relevant,' Artema said. 'As does Rushabarbo's insistence on unmovable borders. Do you have a map of all the borders?'

'Sure, but it will cost you.'

'My dear lady, I will willingly pay the market rate. Might I trouble you to mark Rushabarbo's house on the map too?'

'Sure,' Bellecannon said, and was about to say more when a gang member tapped on the cell wall.

'Excuse me, ma'am,' she said. 'There's these two weird

looking characters at the gate. They want to speak to one Artema Salonoy. They were adamant she was here. I guessed they meant this woman,' she said with a jerk of the head in Artema's direction.

'What do they look like?' Bellecannon asked.

'One man, one woman. They're both tall, built like fighters, wearing fancy hats and long, blue coats and carrying enormous, golden clubs. The only reason no one has mugged them yet is probably that people are so surprised when they walk past they're gone before the muggers pull themselves together. They also said that if we don't let them in, they'll blow the gates down and take their woman by force. Although they'd prefer not to,' she said with a wide grin.

'Could they do that?' Bellecannon said, turning to Artema.

'Oh yes, with very little effort. And those gold clubs are called maces. They're a very ancient weapon. We've imbued them with magic so powerful it will take your head off if you even think about wresting them away from my university's beadles.'

'They're your enforcers, are they?'

'The toughest in the business. There is a tale of a single beadle holding off an entire contingent of a hundred armed polico's with just his mace when they came after one of our students.'

'You'd best let them in,' Bellecannon said to her gang member. Then she turned back to Artema. 'Will you still pay for the repairs as you promised?'

'I am a woman of my word, I will do what I said.'

'Okay then,' Bellecannon said and paused to listen.

It sounded like a small army was arriving as the two

beadles marched down the corridor in lockstep. They came to a halt at the cell door, removed their bowler hats and gave a quick bow.

'Professor Salonoy, we are happy to find you well,' the man said.

'Thank you, Vulpo, it's good to see you and Riviera.'

'Do you have any orders for us, ma'am?' Riviera said.

Her voice was unusually deep for a woman.

'We need to locate the young man I'm working with. He'll need help. At this point it's all about—'

A thump shook the room, followed seconds later by a distant rumble that sounded like thunder. Artema and Bellecannon exchanged a look.

'Do you think that was a bomb?' Artema said.

'If it is, it's the second one in as many days,' Bellecannon said and ran out of the cell.

'With me,' Artema said to the beadles as she followed Bellecannon. She had a bad feeling this had to do with Eladio.

He was wet, Eladio realised, and consciousness came rushing back in. He sat up with a gasp, floundering in water that sounded like it was pouring in from somewhere above him. The floor was slick under his hands.

He felt for Artema's phone and heaved a sigh of relief when he could flick it on. Not that it helped work out what he was seeing in the pale glow from the phone. A haze of grey dust filled the air with a jumble of stuff that had been shredded. Bits of mattress floated around him and the floor was littered with concrete blocks.

'Seraf?' Eladio felt too battered and bruised to breathe

deeply enough to shout. 'Don't tell me you've made another hole.'

He angled the phone to face more or less where he guessed Seraf had been. A pool of water filled the space. Floating on the surface was a pale figure. Water gushed from a ruptured pipe in the gaping hole above them. Above that the ceiling of the next floor looked intact, so apparently this was a more limited blast than his first.

Eladio slid his foot forward, feeling for the floor, and found it dropped away. How was he going to get to Seraf? And how long did he have?

The man was floating face down with his golden hair drifting about his head like a halo. How ridiculous to think of that now, Eladio thought as he shuffled cautiously forward. The water from the pipe was a real gusher and yet it had only just started to overflow, so the hole was probably deep.

Eladio swung around as a grunting sound came from behind him. Luca sat up and pushed a couple of concrete breeze blocks off.

'Luca, thank goodness. Come here, I need your help to get at Seraf.'

'Seraf?' Luca looked vaguely around the room.

His slow brain was apparently trying to work out where he was.

'Yes quickly,' Eladio said, 'Or else he'll drown.'

'Help Seraf.'

Luca surged to his feet, kicked debris out of his way and sloshed into the water, sending a splash washing over Eladio. He'd been through so much hell that it hardly felt like it mattered. He watched Luca sink into the water till only his head was visible.

He pushed onwards like a dog swimming, till he reached Seraf. He grabbed his arm and dragged the body back until he reached the edge of the pool. There he scrabbled at the edge, trying to get out.

'Throw him to me.'

It worried Eladio that Luca hadn't bothered to turn Seraf over.

Luca hoisted Seraf into his arms, flipped him up so he was holding him much like a basketball, and heaved him at Eladio. He tried to catch the hurtling body, but Seraf slammed into him with such force that they both went down.

Eladio pushed Seraf's heavy body off him and bashed his back, shouting, 'Seraf, Seraf, can you hear me?'

It didn't look like Seraf was breathing. Eladio hoped he'd read something, anything on what to do with drowned people. He searched his memory and came up with nothing.

'Damn it, Seraf, breathe!' he shouted, rolled him over and pummelled his chest.

Seraf coughed up water, rolled onto his side and took several gasping breaths.

'Thank god,' Eladio said.

Then he turned to check on Luca. He was still trying to get out of the water by walking straight up the side of the hole. He'd get halfway and slide back, then try again. If they left him to his own devices, he'd probably keep making the same attempt over and over again.

Eladio wondered whether he should leave him and just try to get himself and Seraf out, then dismissed the idea. Seraf looked like he needed help to walk, if he could get up at all. He was still hacking and wheezing.

Eladio doubted he had the strength to carry Seraf. He was bigger and heavier than him. So Seraf would be a challenge, especially now when Eladio's body felt like a steamroller had flattened it.

He waved the torch around, trying to find something that might help get Luca out. Maybe there was a length of rope or a pipe. Instead, the light illuminated a human arm hanging from a shattered rafter.

'Ah,' he cried and retched. Shit, he'd forgotten about the rest of the gang.

He reluctantly shone the torch around the room again. It was still hard to see through the dust that filled the space, but it looked like everyone else had been shredded. There were body parts scattered all over. They were hard to distinguish from the clothes that had also been blown about the room.

They weren't just dead; they were in pieces. So how come he and Luca were okay? Sore, but in one piece. There could be only one explanation, and that was their shared, altered cells.

Something to think about later, because the water in the pool was now spilling over at speed. They needed to get out of here. He spotted a section of shelving that had been blown half off the now fractured wall and pulled at it. It came away with a chunk of the wall, and the building shuddered. Best to get the hell out of here.

Eladio held the plank out to Luca and said, 'Here, grab onto this.'

Luca practically pulled him into the water as he grabbed the plank.

'Wait, I need to find something to brace myself against,' Eladio shouted as he looked about. The best he could do was the now crumpled central column that stood in the middle of the room, presumably holding up the ceiling. He put his feet to either side of the post and said, 'Okay, now.'

Luca hauled himself up, hand over hand. It felt like he'd pull Eladio's arms off. At the very least, he would drag the plank out of his hands. He was a heavy bastard and struggling to get up the last few steps of the pool.

'Here,' Seraf said as he crawled to the water's edge. He lay flat on his stomach, grabbed Luca's trousers and steadied him as he waded up the last few paces.

'Ahh,' Luca shouted as he scrambled out of the pool. 'Who did that?'

'I think it was me,' Seraf said as he lay his face on the floor and water lapped around his mouth.

'Boss, are you okay?' Luca said, leaning down.

'Do I look okay?'

Luca scratched his stubbly head and said, 'No, boss.'

'Help me up.'

'Yes, boss,' Luca said and lifted Seraf into his arms as effortlessly as if he was carrying a child. Seraf closed his eyes with a relieved sigh.

'Here, wrap him in this,' Eladio said and threw a blanket over Seraf. He wondered whether he was still conscious. 'And let's get out of here. That explosion will have gang members on their way.'

'Right,' Luca said, and surged towards the door out of the basement.

Eladio worried it might crumple as Luca pushed his way through because the lintel had a nasty crack. Fortunately, it held and Eladio hurried through after the big man.

It was slow going up the stairs behind Luca, but possibly a safer place to be. 'How did you know I was here, Luca?'

'Rushabarbo told us to wait here, and at your house and at Felicha's.'

'Just to get me?'

'He's got everybody else.'

'Except you huh, Luca?'

'What?' Luca said and stopped.

'Keep going, we have to get Seraf away from here,' Eladio said. It was better to appeal to Luca on behalf of Seraf. He'd do anything for him, whereas he'd hand Eladio over to Rushabarbo without a thought. 'Where did they take the others?'

'To a secret place.'

Luca reached the top of the stairs and headed for the front door. Eladio wondered about the wisdom of that, and then shrugged it away. Everybody would have heard the explosion. For now, it was best just to get out.

'We have to take Seraf to Rushabarbo,' Luca said as they stepped out into the square in front of the orphanage.

It was hazy with dust out here too, and the building was sagging at one end. It wouldn't take much for it to collapse. It was just as well the kids weren't around, Eladio thought. If they'd laid an ambush, maybe that was why the children and staff had been removed.

'We have to keep Seraf away from Rushabarbo,' Eladio said. 'We should head for Purple territory.'

'They're all women. Women don't like me,' Luca rumbled. 'We have to go to Rushabarbo. His orders were for me to take you there.'

'And I'm telling you, he'll hurt Seraf if we go there.'

'He's got doctors. They're seeing to everyone, they'll–'

'Doctors?' Eladio said. 'What do you mean, doctors?'

Luca gave him a big grin, hugely amused to know more than Eladio.

'Men in white coats with stethoscopes, of course.'

'But why?'

'I don't know. But they are seeing to everyone.'

'Who are they seeing to?'

'Dimita and Three and Beto and–'

'You mean the Thirteen?'

'Not all of them.'

'Are the doctors looking at anybody other than the Thirteen?'

'Huh?'

'Alright, name them all.'

Eladio was too tired to explain in a way Luca would understand. Even if it meant he'd start at the beginning again. He always did if you tried to cut him short.

'Dimita and Three and Betto and Piero and Franchesca and Felicha.'

'Only six,' Eladio said, but that was bad enough.

'So they can see to Seraf as well.'

'I doubt it.' Eladio gave Seraf's arm a squeeze. He didn't respond. It looked like he was out cold. 'We have to get Seraf to safety and I give you my word, Luca, he won't be safe with Rushabarbo.'

'Rushabarbo gave me an order,' Luca said, and turned toward the Black Brotherhood's HQ.

Eladio swore. It was always a job to shift Luca when his mind was made up.

'Look,' he said as he hurried after the big man, 'Did Seraf trust Rushabarbo?'

'Rushabarbo is the boss.'

'Yes, but did Seraf tell him everything?'

'No,' Luca said and stopped.

'So you see. It would be better to wait till Seraf wakes up. Then we can ask him what he wants to do. Can we at least do that?'

'Wait where?'

'How about at Dimita's place?'

'With all the pretty girls?'

'Yeah,' Eladio said.

There'd be time to explain that it had burned down when they got there. At least for now, it got them to the edge of Purple territory. It probably wasn't much safer, but it was better than being on Brotherhood turf. At that point, he could think about what he did about Artema. He nearly laughed at that; what could he do?

'Okay, we'll go to the pretty ladies,' Luca said and changed direction, heading for the brothel.

Eladio's phone went off. At least Artema's did, and Eladio scrambled for it. He prayed it was Artema, but it was more likely the university trying to find Artema.

'Hello?' he said.

'Eladio?' Artema said, peering out at him. 'Thank god! My boy, are you alright? We heard an explosion.'

'Yeah, I'm okay and I've got Seraf, and Luca,' Eladio said and angled the phone so that Artema could see. 'The Brotherhood will be after us, though. They'll have heard the explosion too. We're heading to the brothel.'

'The brothel? It would be better if you made for Purple HQ.'

'No,' Eladio said. 'Luca and I are taking Seraf to the brothel,' he hoped Artema would understand.

Apparently she did because she said, 'Hang in there. I'm coming and I'm bringing reinforcements.'

13

The brothel was a charred, blackened mess, but for the moment there was nobody tidying things up or even on the streets. Eladio wondered why till he checked the phone and discovered it was night. That also explained his exhaustion. He sank to the ground with a groan. At least he had a moment to rest.

'They burned it down,' Luca said, looking around. 'There are no girls here.'

'No, it looks like they've all run away.'

Eladio put his head between his knees. It was a struggle to keep his eyes open, never mind work on persuading Luca.

'We can't stay here,' Luca said.

Eladio sighed and looked up again.

'Luca, I just need a rest and so does Seraf. Look at him.'

Luca looked down at the man in his arms.

'He's not strong. He thinks he is, but he isn't.'

It was a surprisingly profound comment from Luca, Eladio thought. Then again, he was probably being literal.

'No, he isn't as strong as you. Tell me, Luca, aren't you sore?'

'Sore?'

'Don't your muscles ache? I mean, you were caught in a bomb blast.'

'I'm fine,' Luca said. 'Why did Seraf use a bomb?'

'I don't think he can help himself.'

'That's stupid. He didn't need to let off the bomb.'

Eladio contemplated telling Luca that as far as he could work out Seraf was the bomb, then he dismissed the idea. Luca would never get it, and he was too tired to find a simple way to explain.

'He was trapped. He thought it was all he had left. He doesn't want to go back to Rushabarbo. Do you see?'

'No,' Luca said, but sat down on a beam that had fallen across the front of the brothel, still cradling Seraf in his arms. A second later he surged back to his feet. 'There's someone coming.'

Artema rounded the corner, flanked by the two most extraordinary people Eladio had ever seen, and that was including Artema's footmen.

'It's okay, they're friends,' Eladio said and patted Luca reassuringly on the arm as he forced himself to his feet.

'Are you alright?' Artema asked.

'Only just. Are these your beadles?'

'Riviera and Vulpo.'

'At your service,' the two beadles said.

'You remember Luca,' Eladio said, waving in Luca's direction.

The big man loomed behind him, scowling at the newcomers.

'And Seraf?' Artema asked.

'He's out cold. I think he needs medical assistance.'

'What happened?'

Eladio looked around and said, 'We shouldn't stay here. It's too dangerous. Have you pissed off the Purples or is it safe to go into their territory?'

'We left with their blessing. They even offered to come along and help, but I thought it best to keep them out of this for now.'

'Okay, well, let's go then.'

'We need to head to the Colosseum,' Artema said.

Eladio didn't want to stop now that he'd got himself moving, so he just turned as he walked and asked, 'Why there?'

'Because that's where Rushabarbo lives.'

'It is,' Luca said from behind them. 'And he has doctors.'

'Yes, Luca,' Eladio said. He turned to Artema and asked, 'Did the Purples tell you that?'

'Among other things. I'll fill you in as we walk. And have this,' Artema said and handed Eladio a chocolate bar.

It was funny how little things could make such a difference. The sight of the chocolate bar cheered him up. Eladio tore the packet open and bit off a sizeable chunk just as the phone rang.

'Here, it's probably for you,' he said and handed it to Artema.

'Yes?' Artema said, and Doctor Leopold's face appeared.

'Bona Dio, Artema, you look like hell.'

'Thanks, that's improved my morale. What can I do for you, Doctor?'

'I've got a bit of information you might find useful.'

'Oh yes?'

'I discovered that all the mothers of the Thirteen were treated early in their pregnancies by the same company, Malbone Health Services.'

'Treated for what?'

'Various early stage pregnancy worries. There's no pattern to that. The point is this, Malbone Health Services had a little mobile clinic that they sent down to the suburbo. It didn't stay long. They treated around twenty women according to their records and then left.'

'Odd,' Artema said.

'Obvious, really. They went down to the suburbo, did what they wanted to do, and left. I doubt they thought there'd be any monitoring of their activities because they did nothing to cover it up.'

'The name is vaguely familiar,' Artema said. 'But I can't think why. I have no connection to the health sector.'

'Maybe I can help with that too,' Doctor Leopold said, beaming out at him. 'Would it aid your memory if I told you the registered owner of Malbone Health Services is one Benedito Malbone?'

'Sancta Maria Patrino de Dio,' Artema swore. 'That bastard was my father's favourite student. Then he stole one of his books and vanished. He was never found, no matter how hard my father looked.'

'Exactly,' Leopold said. 'I thought that would be useful, huh?'

'It may well be, because that all happened twenty-five years ago. Which is when a certain Rushabarbo appeared in the suburbo.'

Eladio pricked up his ears at that.

'Is everything linked?'

'It's starting to look that way,' Artema said. 'Thank you, Doctor. If you learn anything more, please let me know immediately.'

Eladio didn't understand why Artema gave the phone back to him, but he was happy enough to keep it and stuck it in his trouser pocket.

'Why do you think they are linked?'

'Partly because of the timing, partly because Benedito had red hair, so the name seems appropriate,' Artema said.

'But also because of the book that was stolen. It was the complete dictionary of demonic icons. Because of Benedito, we now have an incomplete record of the icons. Which becomes relevant if I tell you there are a couple in the gang tags that I don't recognise.'

'So this Benedito Malbone is a demonologist?'

'An incomplete one, but yes, and good at it.'

Eladio nodded and contemplated the maze that was the Purple's territory. It looked like a wooden ship that had exploded and then put back together by a madman. He'd never actually seen a wooden ship, although he had gone through a phase of dreaming about being a pirate when he was a kid. It was a strange analogy to have popped into his head all the same.

Then again, he was so tired his thoughts were drifting in peculiar directions. It was as if he was on the verge of entering a dream. He shook his head to pull himself back to full wakefulness and tried to get his bearings. He wasn't familiar with this area, but he had a general idea of the direction he had to go.

'Are you alright?' Riviera said as she touched him lightly on the arm.

He blinked and looked up at her. She was a tall woman with short blonde hair that just peeped out from under the bowler hat. 'Just tired,' he muttered. He didn't really know what to make of her and her walrus moustachioed partner.

'Would you like me to fix that?'

'Can you?' Eladio asked and glanced across at Artema, who gave him a cryptic smile back.

'Sure,' Riviera said and touched her mace to Eladio's arm.

Golden warmth spread from his elbow in a wave across

his body and energy surged through him.

'Sancta Madonna, that's incredible. I feel like I've just woken from a deep sleep. But doesn't it tire you to do it?'

'It's like press ups, when you do the first few you reckon it's easy because you feel nothing. It's only when you reach the hundreds that you know you're making an effort.'

Eladio examined her obviously muscular body and nodded.

'I see. All the same, if this Rushabarbo is as powerful as Artema says, you'll need everything you have to throw at him.'

'Tactically speaking, having you awake and fully alert is an important component of this exercise. Therefore worth my effort. Besides, the mace gave you most of the energy. It has a store of its own.'

'It does? Magical energy?'

Riviera looked enquiringly at Artema, who gave a nod and she said, 'Kinetic energy. Magic is just—'

'Physics,' Eladio said. 'Yeah, Artema's told me that. So, are magic wands just energy storage devices?'

'Magic wands?' Riviera said and grinned at him. 'Have you been reading fairytales?'

'Not in a long time.'

'Well, we used to have wands. Hundreds of years ago when we didn't understand what magic was. The wands held kinetic energy. Only our ancestors didn't know about that. So they imbued ritual and mythology around it, and they thought the wand was special. Now we know what it is, and we know we can hold it in anything. That's why we beadles store energy in our maces.'

'And Artema stuck some of hers in a baton.'

'Exactly,' Artema said. 'And it looks like either Riviera

gave you one hell of a dose or you're more sensitive to the energy and absorbed more magic than an ordinary person would.'

'Oh,' Eladio said, aware that Artema thought it was his cells mopping up the magic. 'It felt great. I don't hurt any more.'

'Should I do the same for your friend?' Riviera asked, and waved her mace in Seraf's direction.

'No. I don't think that would be a good idea.'

'You don't?' Artema said. 'So that second explosion it was–'

'Yeah, it was Seraf. This time he only took out the ceiling in the orphanage and made a hole about three metres deep in the floor.'

'Less energy,' Artema murmured and stroked her chin thoughtfully.

'I think it will be safest to keep him... depleted,' Eladio said, and hoped he didn't just look like he was saying so for his own benefit.

'What exactly happened?'

'He was fine when I found him. No clothes, but fine otherwise and not glowing. Then he got worked up, and he started to glow. It wasn't the same as before. There were no cracks or anything like that, just his whole body lit up from inside and the next minute, bang.'

'And you were standing nearby?'

'He blew me off my feet. The thing is... aside from being sore, Luca and I were fine. The rest of the gang members who'd been sent to capture us were shredded.'

'Interesting,' Artema said. 'It sounds like you have some immunity to whatever Seraf is doing.'

'Yeah, but what is he doing?'

'Now that is the question,' Artema said in her annoyingly cryptic way.

Eladio's question sincerely bothered Artema. One, because she didn't like mysteries and two, because she did like Eladio. She wanted nothing untoward to happen to him. It also stunned her to discover what had happened to Benedito Malbone.

Benedito had been an excellent magisto. He'd graduated at the top of his class, which was more than Artema had managed. He'd then besieged her father with requests to study demonology as a postgrad.

Artema was five years younger than the man, but she'd never liked him. A lot of her dislike stemmed from the fact that her father thought more of his student than he did his daughter. That hurt.

Now she wondered whether she'd came across as her nephew did to her now. Not very interested. She was a young woman going through the motions when Benedito gave his studies his full attention.

He'd been single-minded, Artema recalled. A serious, red-haired young man. His face liberally sprinkled with freckles with long unkempt hair because he was too busy studying to do anything about it. His pale hazel eyes always looked Artema up and down without interest.

He had no sense of humour either. Artema couldn't recall a single time she'd seen Benedito even crack a smile. He was intense, and he wasn't interested in people.

Artema shuddered as she recalled the man, and a memory came back. It was more a sensation than anything visual, an uneasiness in Benedito's presence. Her father had it too, and she'd developed an aura over the years as well. It came from contact with demons.

The thing was... Benedito had it before he even started studying demonology. Then he'd stole the book and vanished. Immature as she'd been at the time, Artema had to rub it in and make her father feel worse about the situation. Benedito was gone, and the search for him yielded nothing.

Now she wished she'd been more grown up and thought about what that disappearance had meant. Down here in the suburbo it looked like Benedito had been busy. He'd carved out an empire for himself, and he'd got involved in human experimentation. An experiment that resulted in the deaths of around twenty women.

Now here she was rushing to Benedito's lair. It was a dramatic name for his house, but it felt appropriate. On top of it all, Artema didn't have enough information. She still had no grip on what was going on.

'Stop, wait, I need to think,' Artema said and came to a dead halt.

Riviera and Lupo stopped with her and, reassuringly, formed a protective guard. One watched ahead of them, the other watched her back.

'I thought you were in a hurry,' Eladio said as he turned back. 'Rushabarbo will know we're on our way. Even if we weren't, he'd be trying to hunt us down. He's determined to get me and Seraf and probably Luca as well.'

'But why?' Artema said.

'Because he made us?'

'Maybe, but then why is he only rounding you up now? Why not when you were children?'

'I don't know.'

Artema examined Luca. He was still carrying Seraf in his arms as if he weighed nothing at all.

'Do you think he's got the rest? The other nine?'

'Luca says he has six of them. Nanni went to the edge lands. It wouldn't be easy to find her again. A couple of others just vanished. But it seems like he got the rest. And he's got doctors looking at them too. Why do you think that is?'

'Doctors?' Artema said. 'Then my supposition is that he doesn't really understand the Thirteen. He had a cold and calculating personality. He'll be trying to work out if they're worth anything to him.'

'It makes even less sense that he tried to kill Seraf then. He's trying to capture me too. So why attack Seraf?'

'There's only one way we can find that out,' Artema said and nodded in Seraf's direction. 'I appreciate that he's dangerous, but Seraf may have answers to this mystery. At this point, we need something. Going against a magisto at any time is dangerous. Going against one we know next to nothing about is doubly so.'

'The thing is, if he explodes, Luca and I will be fine but the rest of you,' Eladio shook his head.

'I will keep him calm,' Artema said. 'Now, we need to wake him up.'

'I'll do it,' Vulpo said and tapped Seraf with his mace.

'Not too much,' Eladio said.

But it was done, and Seraf gasped in a huge lungful of air. He blinked and looked up at Luca.

'Where the devil did you come from?'

'You're awake,' Luca said, beaming down at him.

'Where are my clothes?' Seraf pushed himself out of Luca's arms and wrapped the blanket tighter about him, and his head jerked back on a loud sniff. 'This smells like the orphanage.'

'Yes, you were there,' Luca said, and he looked like a lost and confused child.

'How did I get to the orphanage? And bloody hell, you, Eladio?'

'Yeah,' Eladio said with a half wave. 'Luca and I got you out of the orphanage. Don't you remember?'

'The last thing I remember,' Seraf said, and his eyes narrowed in thought. 'The last thing I remember is being stabbed by a couple of Brotherhood soldiers.'

'Do you know why?' Artema asked.

Seraf spun around and said, 'You're here too? After I warned you to stay away?'

'I'm afraid I can't stay away. Your boss, the one trying to kill you,' Artema said and persisted despite the way Eladio was frowning at her, 'is a dangerous man. He's up to something that threatens us all. I therefore have no choice but to deal with him.'

'Well, good luck with that,' Seraf said. 'He's more likely to kill you. He's got guns covering every entrance to his house. You'll never get in. Especially not you.'

'What does that mean?'

'He really doesn't like you.'

'How do you know?'

'Because the moment he picked you up on the surveillance, he called me to his house. He was furious, and I've never seen him show any emotions before. He said, "Kill her and anyone else she's with, except the Thirteen."'

'When was that?'

'Late on Thursday.'

'He said nothing about meeting me?'

'He didn't, but I wanted to know what was going on. I could tell Rushabarbo sure as hell wouldn't tell me, so I sent Luca to fetch you. That was my mistake. I should have just killed you.'

'So you think he went after you because you didn't kill me?'

Seraf shrugged and said, 'Rushabarbo doesn't tolerate people who disobey him.'

'And you were plotting against him, I'll bet,' Eladio murmured.

'But I was being careful. I don't think he knows about that. At least, I didn't after the meeting.'

Eladio looked dubious. With good reason, Artema thought. Seraf might fancy himself as a leader, but he had some serious blind spots.

'So you went to see Rushabarbo at his house for the first time on Thursday.'

'How the hell do you know it was the first time?'

'I have my sources,' Artema said. 'And all he wanted to do was have a rant about me?'

'You never can tell with Rushabarbo,' Seraf said and pulled the blanket tighter about himself. 'I went all prepared to defend myself and instead he asks me about the Thirteen. Up till that moment I didn't even know that he knew about us.'

'What did he want to know?'

'He said he'd heard we all have special abilities. He wanted to know what they were. He was most interested to hear about Three.'

'I'll bet he was,' Artema said.

'He was also really interested in Eladio,' Seraf said with a nod in his direction. 'But I thought that was because Eladio was with you rather than because of his perfect memory.'

'Probably correct, if he'd picked the two of us up on surveillance.'

'I'll tell you something else. Since you're a demonologist, you'll like this. There's a rumour he has a demon captive, and it's true.'

'Is it?' Artema said, and this piece of information surprised her more than all the rest.

'Yeah, because when I first walked into his study, I heard this shriek and then a thump in the room next door. Then, all the way through our conversation, there was this muffled sound like somebody being tortured.

'It got so bad Rushabarbo suddenly jumps up and goes to the other room. He closed the door behind him, but it didn't close all the way. So I sneaked up and took a look. Blow me if I don't see this... this thing stapled to the wall with iron bars and a massive pentagram painted all around him. It's frothing at the mouth and swearing like I've never heard anything swear before.'

'Are you sure it was a demon?'

'Well, the iron bars pegged through it were glowing red hot. I don't know about you, but I've never heard of a person who could survive that. And it looked weird, not quite human.'

'Then what happened?'

'Rushabarbo told it to shut up. He said, "quiet Zochael."

And it said, "get the damned angel spawn away from me."

'And Rushabarbo comes back into the study and hustles me out of the house.'

Artema felt like she was getting too much information all at once, and none of it made any sense. She especially couldn't make out what part of this bizarre tale had been the source of her initial concerns about a demon incursion.

'Does Rushabarbo know what you saw?'

'I don't think so. I ran back to my chair when the boss turned away from the demon.'

'Did you see anything angelic?'

'Do you know,' Seraf said with a sly smile, 'I got the impression the demon was talking about me.'

'Is that so?'

'Yeah, and you don't look surprised by that. So now I wonder what you know.'

'That Rushabarbo was probably involved in an illegal experiment that altered the foetuses of several women. Those women all subsequently died of anaphylactic shock and their children turned up at the orphanage.'

'Sancta shit!' Seraf breathed. 'Did you know that, Eladio?'

'I just found out,' Eladio said.

'So you and me and the others have got angel genes?'

'Something like that.'

'Is that why I'm glowing?'

'I don't know,' Eladio said. 'Nobody does.'

'Not even Rushabarbo, I'm willing to bet,' Artema said.

'But what advantage does that get him then?' Seraf asked.

'I suspect Rushabarbo isn't sure about that either. Which may be why he left you at the orphanage.'

'He must have figured something out. Why else would he be rounding us up now?'

'Why indeed? Maybe because of his demon's reaction to you. But I suspect that is a new interest and not related to whatever else he's up to.'

'So you think something is going to happen? Something other than the Thirteen being rounded up?'

'I fear something much bigger than that, yes.'

'Sancta Madonna.' For the first time Seraf lost his, I'm not bothered by anything air, and looked genuinely shaken. 'But what?'

'I'm still trying to figure that out. I've just learned from the Purples that Rushabarbo fixed all the gang's borders and won't let them be changed,' Artema looked at Eladio as she spoke, telling him as much as Seraf. 'They gave me a map of the borders that my AI is analysing.'

'I don't see what use that would be,' Seraf said.

'I've been trying to find a pattern in the location of all the tags. Now I'm wondering whether it might not have more to do with the gang's borders.'

'Whether it does, or it doesn't, it has nothing to do with me,' Seraf said. 'If you and Eladio want to storm Rushabarbo's place, you go ahead. I'll wait and see who wins and I'm betting it won't be you.'

'I wouldn't take that bet,' Artema said. 'Besides, you'd be safer if you stick with me.'

'Let him go,' Eladio said.

Seraf grinned at him and said, 'Of course you don't want me to come along, do you?'

'You're too dangerous.'

'At least I know how to fight. You're like a girl, you avoid fights. I'll bet that's the real reason you didn't join the gang.'

'We don't have time for an argument,' Artema said. 'Seraf, Rushabarbo is after you and wants you dead, not to mention whatever else he's planning. But if you want to deal with him on your own, you go ahead.'

'Fine, then I'll be going,' Seraf said. 'Come on, Luca, this bunch are no use to us.'

'Right, boss.'

Luca gave Eladio a mournful look but followed Seraf.

'He's trouble,' Vulpo said as Seraf sauntered away. 'It would have been safer to keep him where you can see him.'

'No, it wouldn't,' Eladio said. 'He's unpredictable. He'll do whatever brings him benefit and to hell with the rest of us.'

'He could cause more trouble now.'

Eladio nodded and said, 'What are we doing anyway, Artema? This isn't something we should tackle on our own.'

'What would you have us do instead?' Artema said in a calm voice.

Eladio was looking as nervous as she'd ever seen him, and she wanted to calm the young man down.

'If this is as big and as dangerous as you say, then we should call in the polico.'

'You said they don't come down here.'

'They don't usually, but you're a blue blood. You could make them.'

Artema nearly laughed at Eladio's belief in what a blue blood could do as she said, 'And what should I tell them?'

'That a gang boss has kidnapped a whole group of people.'

'What would the polico usually do if, for instance, you told them that?'

'They'd tell me to tell the gangs. They enforce order down here. Only the gangs will never go to war against Rushabarbo. They've already shown that.'

'Eladio, you put too much faith in me. Even I couldn't get the polico to come down here. Not for a mere kidnapping. I also don't have sufficient evidence to get them to come down on what might or might not be a demon incursion. Besides which, they'd tell me that's my jurisdiction and they'd be right.'

'Would they? Seraf's a royal pain in the ass, but he's right about one thing, I'm no fighter.'

'Neither am I, dear boy. That's why we have Riviera and Vulpo.'

'Two people?'

'Two people who are as powerful as twenty.'

'Are they immune to bullets?'

'We can be,' Vulpo said.

'This is crazy,' Eladio said, looking from one person to the next. 'I don't even know why I'm here. This has less to do with me than it does with Seraf. I'm... I'm a barista. The most adventurous thing I've ever done is get a job in the mezaurbo. I don't go breaking into crime boss's homes or... or face down demons.'

'And despite all that, you're doing well for a first timer. You even found Seraf.'

'You'll go ahead even if I say it's suicidal, won't you?'

'I don't have a choice.'

Artema felt bad for Eladio and wondered whether she could do the next bit without him. The young man was right, it wasn't fair to expect him to come along. But he'd been very helpful so far, and Artema suspected he would be again.

'I can't force you to stay, Eladio, just as I didn't force Seraf to stay. But I believe we have a better chance of getting your friends out alive if you come with us.'

Eladio grimaced, and it looked like his decision was on a knife's edge and might go either way when he stiffened.

'Don't move,' he hissed.

'What is it?'

'The tags, they've all lit up really bright and there are lines of light going between them now.'

'Are any of us touched by the light?' Artema said and did a hasty revelation spell.

Beams of light now connected each tag to the other in a complex latticework.

'No, they aren't touching any of you,' Eladio said. 'But you take a step to either side and they will.'

'He can see that?' Riviera asked.

'He's special that way,' Artema said with a grin as she watched Eladio go up in Riviera and Vulpo's estimation.

'What do you think will happen if you touch them?' Eladio asked.

'It looks like it will trigger an alarm.'

'Like a motion detector? But that will be useless down here. There are hundreds of thousands of people walking around in the suburbo, blindly crossing these lines. Their alarm will go non stop.'

'Not if it's only set up to spot magistos,' Artema said.

That was the least of their worries. The tags lighting up could mean Rushabarbo was putting his plan into action. Whatever that plan may be.

Eladio sensed that Artema wasn't telling him everything and wondered whether he should be angry about that. It wasn't in his nature to be outraged, but he also didn't want to be disappointed by a woman he was coming to respect. This was despite the way she'd dragged him up, down and through the city. He decided he'd continue to follow her, no matter how suicidal. It felt better to have made the decision.

'What do we do now?'

'So you're coming with?'

'Yeah, somebody has to look out for the Thirteen.'

'Good man,' Artema said with a warm smile.

Foolish as it was, it made Eladio feel better about the whole venture.

'You need some way to get to Rushabarbo's without being seen. We need to avoid cameras and these beams.'

'I agree. Will you be able to guide us past the beams if I make us all invisible?'

'Can't you just use magic to see them?'

'I could, but the effect doesn't last long. I'd have to cast it over and over again, which would take time and be energy consuming.'

'Okay, you'll turn gold again, will you?'

'We will, except you, we'll need to be able to see you. However, you'll just look like another member of the public so it should be fine.'

'I'd do better if I had a hood to hide my face.'

'I can arrange that,' Artema said. With a wave of her hand, a hoodie appeared from thin air.

'You have a hoodie in your pocket universe?'

'I stashed it there in case I needed it on my next trip down. I didn't anticipate that the next trip would be so... abrupt.'

Eladio snorted, Artema and her understatements. He pulled the jacket on and flipped up the hood.

'Okay, follow me and duck when I duck.'

He stepped out of the Purple's territory, crossed the narrow lane that separated it from the Yellow Perils, ducked and then headed into a lane that was paved with a yellow substance.

'They actually paved their roads yellow?' Artema said.

She looked odd, like a badly made golden statue where none of the edges were well defined. Right now that golden statue was staring at him and it blinked.

'They have access to all the chemicals in the suburbo, so I guess they can do it. This area is known as Chemical City.'

'That would explain all the barrels around here too.'

'Yeah, it isn't a very healthy place to live.'

Eladio wasn't as familiar with this gang's territory as he was with others. He stayed out because it was a smelly district. They often built homes and businesses here from barrels that had held chemical waste. Looking around, he could see a rainbow of colours that ran down the sides of the buildings and tainted all the surfaces.

Still, there was no time to consider that now. He had to get to the colosseum area. Since everyone was invisible, the direct route was the best. He hoped he didn't look too odd and obvious as he ducked under each glowing beam he came across.

'I think this is the worst district I've seen down here so far,' Artema whispered.

Then she ducked under a beam Eladio was indicating by holding his arm out to show how high it was. It helped that the gang tags to either side were both visible. They acted as a guide for his invisible trio.

The beadles looked particularly odd with their hats on. At least they had developed a technique that meant they leaned their heads forward to ensure the hats didn't catch the beams. Meanwhile, all around them people went about their jobs, crossing the beams as they moved up and down the street.

Lots of the people here worked in chemical reprocessing. Steam from their factories, some of it tinted in unfamiliar colours, rose into the air and escaped through the gaps of the buildings.

'Watch out,' Eladio said as they ducked under a beam. 'That's a big puddle of God only knows what. You don't want to get that on you.'

They trooped around the pool. It was probably oil, but they would show up walking through that, and then leave oily footprints. Riviera took a hasty sidestep as a woman walked straight at her, and just missed being run into.

It was so bizarre that Eladio just stopped to stare. Maybe a quieter route would be better, but not as quick. So they'd stick to this main road unless it got too busy.

'What's that glow up ahead?' Artema whispered in his ear.

'That's daylight,' Eladio said with a grin.

'Down here? And it's greenish.'

'Yeah, well, it's the Forum Romanum and the Colosseum. It's surrounded by a massive glass tube to keep it safe. People from the mezaurbo and supraurbo fly down to it from above because it's the only thing at ground level that's still open to the sky.'

'How do people in the suburbo get in?' Riviera said.

'They don't,' Eladio said and set off back down the lane, heading towards the light.

'They didn't make an entrance for you?'

Riviera sounded surprised, although her expression was hard to read on her golden face.

'Why would they?' Eladio said with a shrug.

It was funny how the supras were so surprised by the things they were probably responsible for.

'It's your heritage too.'

'What use do we have for heritage? People around here

would just carry the stones away to make homes for themselves. Maybe that's why you lot glassed it off from us.'

'Not my lot,' Riviera said, and her voice sounded prickly even if her face didn't show it.

'So you aren't a blue blood?' Eladio said.

He wondered what people made of him, apparently talking to himself. Worse still, he was getting a disembodied, fierce whisper back. Hopefully, they just assumed he was talking to an overloud phone.

'No, I'm not a blue blood,' Riviera murmured. 'Did you think all magistos were blue bloods?'

'I was wondering.'

'Well, we aren't.'

'Is that why you're a beadle?'

'You think that's a hierarchy thing? No, Vulpo is a blue blood from a very ancient family. We became beadles because it suits us.'

'I see,' Eladio said and stopped.

From this point, the road dipped downwards. It connected at right angles to a wide road that circled around the most house-like looking set of homes to be found in the suburbo. Behind the buildings rose a massive glass tube that stretched up and away into the rest of the city.

'This is where the rich people of the suburbo live.'

'The rich people?' Artema said as she drew up beside Eladio.

'Some are suburbonites who've made their fortunes and decided to stay rather than buy their way into the mezaurbo. Others are like Rushabarbo who made their money from crime or need to stay hidden for some other reason.'

'And like the rich everywhere, they've taken the prime location for themselves.'

'Yeah,' Eladio said and pointed at a four story, very square building a little way down and to the right. 'I reckon that's Rushabarbo's house.'

'How do you know?'

'Take a look,' Eladio said, and did the gesture Artema always did to reveal magic.

To his surprise, a few golden sparks shimmered from his fingers, but nothing else happened. Artema apparently didn't notice. She made the same gesture, with a greater golden shimmer, and her eyes widened.

'Bono Dio, I don't think I've ever seen a house with so many demonic icons painted on it.'

'All invisible to the naked eye, right?' Eladio said.

'He must have painted them on in the same colour as the base paint.'

'And that works?'

'It does, but it needs to be renewed more regularly.'

'What do they all do?'

'Good question,' Vulpo said as he stepped up on the other side of Eladio.

'I have very little idea,' Artema said. 'I am familiar with some of the symbols, but not all of them. How they are arranged with each other also makes a–'

There was a strange whine and a thump and the lines between the gang icons flared. People all around them stopped to stare and shouted to one another about the strange light.

'Crap,' Artema said and waved her hands in an intricate pattern Eladio hadn't seen before. 'Protections up everybody. And for you, Eladio,' Artema said and wove a hasty pattern of lines around him so that he was encased in a cage of light.

'What is this?'

'Protection from whatever magic is at play. Look at the other people,' Artema said, and pointed at the inhabitants of Chemical City.

They were no longer looking in awe at the light or even talking to each other. They were all standing still and silent and staring straight ahead.

'What's going on?'

The people's strange behaviour and the low hum coming from the suddenly all too visible lines of light unsettled Eladio. So he nearly jumped sky high when the phone went off.

'Hello,' he shouted as he yanked it out of his pocket.

'Eladio?' Doctor Leopold said.

'Yes.'

'Can I have a word with Artema, please?'

'Leopold, we can't really talk now,' Artema said as she took the phone and dropped her invisibility.

'You'll have to. Your AI has just issued a red alert that got the whole Komitato here. Not that we have a clue what's going on besides the fact that it predicts a massive demon intervention or incursion from the suburbo. It's going to have dire outcomes for the entire city, maybe the world.'

'I was afraid of that. We're looking at thousands if not millions of activated demon icons down here. But I still don't have a clue what it's about. I'll have to confront Rushabarbo. We don't have the time to tiptoe around him working out what he's up to.'

'Your AI has something,' the doctor said, and the AI's face appeared on the screen.

'Master, the outlines of the gang's territory are ambiguous for icon recognition. At first assessment it appears to be a command-and-control icon,' the AI said, and a complex icon appeared on the screen.

'That sounds right,' Artema said as she glanced at the silent people around them.

'Secondary assessment indicates the possibility of a couple of other icons,' the AI continued. Two more icons appeared that looked similar but had a couple of extra hooks and lines added to the arrangement.

'What is the significance of that?'

'Unclear, neither icon is in my database. The second icon falls in the destruction category of icons. It's that possibility that pushed me to notify a code red situation.'

'Right, well see what else you come up with and keep me posted,' Artema said. 'Now we really have to go.'

'Before you do,' Doctor Leopold said as he popped back on the phone, 'You and Eladio better look at this video. I have no idea how it will help, but it's information you might be able to use.'

'What is it?'

'Archive footage from the Great Inter Plane War. Pay attention to the figure on the far right of the screen.'

Eladio wanted to see the footage but could understand Artema's impatience as he looked around at the eerily motionless people.

'Alright, play it,' Artema said.

The quality of the footage wasn't great, but Eladio could see why the doctor was keen that they watch it. The figure on the right was a magnificent being with tall bright white wings. That was secondary, because what he did was a revelation. As he stood on the battleground, demons approaching from every side, a white glowing orb formed around him. The moment the demons charged, the orb exploded and wiped out every living thing around him.

'The demons disintegrated into a red mist,' Eladio gasped. 'Seraf only shredded people, that angel obliterated them.'

'He obliterated demons. Maybe it's worse when used against them.'

'Or maybe Seraf doesn't do it to that extent. Did you notice something else?'

'What should I have seen?'

'That massive angel up front looks a lot like Luca in size and shape. And those black angels look a lot like Felicha, aside from the obsidian wings. And then, right at the back, too small to make out properly, are a group of angels who all have their eyes covered in what looks like bandages. Three can't see very well and does something similar with a scarf.'

'Interesting,' Artema said. 'But something to think about later. Although now we know how Seraf's exploding ability came about.'

'I guess so,' Eladio said. 'What do we do now?'

'Now,' Artema said and paused. Every bystander on the street had just turned to face them. 'Okay we, that's me, Riviera and Vulpo are going in via the front door to confront Rushabarbo. Eladio, see if there's another way in. You need to find the rest of the Thirteen and get them out. I'll cast an invisibility spell on you so you can sneak around. The spell works best in low contrast environments or if you're stationary. It will hold for about fifteen minutes so you'll have to work quickly.'

'Okay.'

Eladio wasn't thrilled to be separating, but he worried more about the Thirteen than Artema did, so it was only right he went for them.

'Here, take this,' Artema said as she reached into her pocket universe and handed Eladio her baton.

'Won't you need it?'

'I'm taking something else,' Artema said as she pulled out a staff with a golden ball attached to the tip encrusted with spikes.

'Nice,' Eladio said. 'An honest to god magisto's staff.'

He waited only long enough for Artema to cast her invisibility spell before he sloped off down the road, keeping to the shadows.

14

'Do you think he'll be alright?' Vulpo said, staring at the place where Eladio had been standing.

'I hope so,' Artema said. 'He's more resilient than I first gave him credit for. He also has a few advantages the rest of us don't have.'

A murmur from the people all around made the hairs stand at the back of her neck. Then, as one, they all took a step towards Artema and the beadles.

'Right, we don't have a choice,' Artema said as she made straight for Rushabarbo's door. 'It looks like they're coming for us. Get your protections up and be ready for his guns.'

On cue, a spray of bullets strafed the road at their feet and kept going as they approached. Vulpo and Riviera waved their maces in a combined protection spell so that the bullets ricocheted away from the clear air before them. Artema knew that there was the equivalent of a golden shield of light in front of them. They always practiced the spell that way as students. It was unnerving to not see it and only spot the sparks of the bullets bouncing off.

'It's hitting the civilians!' Riviera shouted.

Bullets bounced off their shields and more bullets sprayed straight from the guns and cut into the people following silently behind them. Those that were hit, fell without making a sound and lay immobile on the ground, their eyes still open and unblinking.

'Hell,' Artema said.

She cast a force field behind them that stopped the bullets. It also prevented the people from coming closer. It didn't stop their advance, though. They kept walking until they hit the field. They bumped against it, getting crushed as the people behind them got to the field and pushed to get through it.

'Enough of this!'

Artema aimed her most powerful blast of a concussive sound wave at the door. It hit with a solid bang. The door and wall around it caved inwards for a second, before it bounced back. At that moment, a potent defence icon flickered briefly on the door.

'The wall then.'

Artema focused the full force of her spell on the space beside the door. This time it cracked but held.

'Right, let's do this properly,' Artema muttered, and cast a disintegration spell aimed at the paint on the wall.

The spell hit the middle of the icon and peeled the paint away in a swirl that evaporated into the air.

'Now the rest.'

Artema took a deep breath and as she breathed out, she sent another concussive blast aimed squarely at the now paintless bit of wall. It shattered into a cascade of brick fragments that blasted into the house.

'In we go,' Artema said and ran for the hole.

'Behind me, Prof.,' Riviera said.

She bounded through the hole a second ahead of Artema, casting protection spells as she went. Artema leaped through the gap and stopped to get her bearings as Vulpo followed behind her.

The room was dim and filled with brick dust. Fragments

of brick crunched underfoot. A semicircle of gang members stood at the foot of an industrial-looking metal staircase, ominous in their distinctive black leather jackets.

'Charge,' the lead gang member shouted, and they rushed Artema.

'Oh no you don't,' Riviera said.

She swung her spell fuelled mace in an arc that flattened the soldiers in a wave. Artema hung back, assessing the situation while Vulpo joined Riviera with the long-range clobbering of the soldiers. Artema cast a revelation spell and discovered that the gang members were magically protected. A cage of green light emanated from their gang tags and surrounded their bodies.

So demon icons doing the protecting. It would last indefinitely, which was better than their own. They would have to act quickly if they were going to get through this horde. Since the gang were trying to block access to the stairs, she figured that was the route to get to Rushabarbo.

'Upstairs,' Artema said, and cast a spell to push the men away.

Magical defences worked well against things like mind control, but it did nothing against a good shove the gang members discovered as Artema pushed them aside. They had spirit, though, and fought to keep on their feet, swearing at the tops of their lungs.

A door upstairs swung open with such a loud bang that everybody stopped and looked up. A tall, powerfully built man looked down at the fighters. He had a liberally freckled face, short cropped hair and a bushy red beard.

'Benedito Malbone!'

The change in the man astonished Artema. He looked old, and none of his supraurbo polish remained. Now he looked as haggard as any other suburbo resident.

'Well, well, Artema Salonoy.' Rushabarbo leaned on the banister, his arms folded over each other as though he was just out for a chat. 'You turned out better than your father thought you would.'

His gang members looked surprised that he was talking. They were also unsure whether they should keep fighting or remain respectfully silent, so compromised by standing to attention.

'While you were a bitter disappointment to him,' Artema snapped, not deceived by his pretence at casualness. 'What would he think of you now? You're living up to every warning he ever gave an aspirant demonologist.'

'What's that supposed to mean?' Rushabarbo shouted as he snapped upright and his voice bounced around the rafters.

This was the Benedito Artema knew, uptight and arrogant.

'He warned you about the dangers of the demonic icons. He warned you to be careful, and what did you do instead? You stole his book and came down here to spray demonic icons all over the lowest levels of the suburbo like some demented dog marking his territory.'

Artema squeezed as much disdained into her voice as she could, because she knew it would enrage Benedito. Besides, it was exactly how she felt and it gave her satisfaction to say it to his face.

'A demented dog? A dog?' Rushabarbo shouted and slammed his hands on the railing, then gripped them till his knuckles went white. 'You have no idea what I am doing here.'

'No, I don't,' Artema said, forcing herself to sound cool

even if she didn't feel it. 'Do you?'

'You Salonoys are so arrogant,' Rushabarbo said leaning forward hissing out the words. 'You think you know everything. Well, you're wrong. I've been using demonic icons for decades and it hasn't affected me at all.'

'Well then, you must have been a psychopath from the start because looking at what you're doing to the people outside, I can't see a trace of human empathy in you.'

Rushabarbo's glanced at the people through the hole in his wall soundlessly crushing each other to death in their attempt to get at Artema.

'They are serving a greater purpose.'

'Really?' Artema said, dripping as much amused sarcasm as she could into the word, 'And what would that be?'

'I will build a better world for all of them.'

'Benedito, how can you be so stupid? Demons manipulate people with offers of power, only to betray them at the last minute. You're being used. Whatever your dream is, you will never see it come to fruition.'

'I am the one using a demon, not the other way around,' Benedito said, his fierce gaze boring into Artema. 'Zochael is my prisoner, and my slave.'

'That's what you think, you fool!' Artema shouted. 'But even with a demon's help you'll never take over the city, nobody has ever managed that.'

'There's always a first time,' Rushabarbo said with flat satisfaction.

'Do you hear yourself?' Artema said. 'Do you not see your delusion? That's the consequence of listening to demons.'

'You are not listening. I am the one in control. I will use this army of human waste down here to take over the rest of the city and you will stay by my side and see me do it,'

Rushabarbo snapped and cast a green fireball at Artema with one efficient wave of his hand.

Artema threw herself sideways. That demon icon powered spell would overwhelm her magical shield. She hit the ground, and the fire smacked into the floor next to her and hissed as sulphurous clouds filled her lungs. She rolled and landed too close to the feet of the gang's soldiers, who kicked her.

Riviera swung her mace and knocked them back. She grabbed Artema's jacket and hauled her to her feet. At the same time, Vulpo shot a percussive spell at Rushabarbo that rattled the stairs but appeared not to affect the man.

'Take them out,' Artema shouted, and cast a spell that turned the floor under the fighter's feet as smooth as ice.

Then she used a force field and a wind to push them towards the gap. Riviera augmented what she was doing and drove the howling gang members into a tight, angry huddle that was swept out through the hole in the wall.

Vulpo shot another blast at Rushabarbo, but it had no effect. He waved his hands in a complex pattern that brought a torrent of flaming rock down on their heads.

'Duck!' Artema shouted and ran for the gap under the stairs as Vulpo threw up a force field that only slowed the burning rocks. Then the gang came pouring back through the wall.

Riviera pushed them out again but shouted, 'We can't stay here. We need to get up the stairs.'

'We'll get obliterated by Rushabarbo if we try,' Artema said.

'What else do you suggest?' Vulpo said. 'There's an entire city waiting for us out there.'

'Alright, you deal with the gang, I'll sort out Rushabarbo.'

With that, Artema swung around the banister and ran up the stairs. She cast a malevolent red demonic icon of destruction at Rushabarbo that ripped at Artema's heart as it spun upwards.

Rushabarbo threw an icon back, and the two spells connected midway and exploded. The noise drummed through Artema. Fragments of wall splattered into her and stung her face, and the staircase collapsed in a metallic crash. Rushabarbo, arms and legs splayed wide, plummeted down on top of Artema.

Eladio headed for a narrow alleyway that separated Rushabarbo's house from his neighbour's, keeping to the shadows as much as possible. He'd just reached the entrance when the machine-guns went off and made him jump. He looked about anxiously for any guns aimed at the alleyway and spotted a couple. Fortunately, they sat immobile and apparently blind to him.

The alleyway glowed that peculiar green of light that had travelled through a very thick layer of glass. The translucent wall itself blocked off the end of the alleyway. Unlike in the rest of the suburbo, the alley was paved and spotlessly clean. Three gang members stood on the alert at a side door.

One man said, 'What do you think's happening?'

'I don't know and we're not moving. The boss told us to stay put, and that's what we'll do.'

The third gang member, a woman, grunted agreement.

That was a problem. Eladio stood still as the sound of bullets continued, and then the ground shook with a thud followed by the sound of shattering bricks. The gang members twitched, but stayed put.

Thanks to the noise, Eladio was confident they wouldn't hear his approach, but he stayed on the far side of the alleyway, hugging the wall of the neighbouring house. All was quiet there. They weren't even looking out through their window. Then again, maybe they'd also turned into eerily silent zombies.

A green cage of light surrounded the guards that Eladio guessed protected them from whatever spell was controlling the people. They also weren't budging from the solid-looking door. Knowing his luck, it was probably also locked.

How was he going to get through that? The insane hilarity of what he was up to suddenly struck him. He'd never so much as stolen food from a stall. Now he was trying to break into a house?

The noise of fighting inside intensified. It sounded like a full scale war. Then there was a moment of quiet where everyone leaned in the direction the noise had been coming from.

Was someone talking? Next there was more shouting, a loud thump that shook the building and an almighty crash of iron bars clattering to the ground.

'Oh shit!' the first gang member said and turned to his companions.

As one, they wrenched open the side door and charged inside.

Eladio leaped forward and caught the door just before it slammed shut. He stopped just inside in a dark dust filled corridor. That wasn't great. He'd leave a person shaped hole in the dust.

The gang members ran to the end of the corridor and pulled open the door at the far end. A wave of dust and the smell of blood and iron rolled towards him.

A door to his right swung open and bright white light shone out as a man in a white lab coat with a surgical mask over his mouth shouted, 'What the devil's going on out here?'

The man was ignored and decided it was safer to remain where he was. So he stepped back, pulling the door shut behind him. Eladio raced for the gap, bumped into the door as the doctor closed it and staggered into the room.

'What the hell?' the doctor muttered and looked back outside, trying to work out what he'd felt.

Eladio caught onto the side of an operating table to steady himself, stood as still as he could and held his breath. He prayed the spell would keep running too because he didn't know how long he'd been invisible and when it would fail.

He was in a laboratory. Aside from the table he was hanging onto, there were two rows of what he assumed were usually beds. But they had tilted each bed up so that the occupants, firmly secured with broad plastic straps, were in an almost upright position. The beds leaned back just so far that they were more leaning back than standing up. He'd found the Thirteen.

The doctor locked the door with a firm click and turned to the two women watching him.

'I'm sure whatever it is Rushabarbo can take care of it.'

Eladio hoped not. He noted that a green cage emanated from the gang tag embroidered onto their lab coat pockets and also protected the doctor and nurses. The Thirteen, or rather the six that had been captured weren't similarly protected.

Did this mean they were also now zombies? They hadn't spoken, but they had all turned to look at the door. Was that zombie behaviour?

If they were all under the influence of the demon icon, would he be able to get them out?

'You should let us go,' Three said. 'Before it's too late for you.'

'What?' the doctor said.

'I can see the future, and I've seen your fate. It isn't good if you don't release us.'

Thank god for Three, Eladio thought. She'd given him the sign he needed. The zombies weren't speaking, which meant his friends weren't zombies. As they also didn't have any magical defence about them, Eladio assumed they were immune. At least he hoped so, because that would mean he was immune too.

'Nobody asked you,' the doctor snapped as he walked up to Three.

'I was trying to give you and the nurses some help,' Three said. 'You can take it or leave it, but people have ignored my words at their peril.'

Eladio shuddered, she wasn't wrong, but then again she could be lying to the doctor. What she was definitely doing was distracting him and the nurses, who looked from the doctor to the door. Muffled sounds had returned to the corridor, which meant that whatever the explosion had done, it hadn't ended the battle.

Eladio slipped behind the beds and made his way to Felicha. She looked furious as she lay glaring at the doctor and nurses who'd all formed a cluster around Three and had picked up their tools. It looked like they were taking blood samples. Eladio didn't fancy their chances once he freed Felicha.

He put his mouth as close to her ear as possible and

whispered, 'It's me, Eladio. Don't react. I'm going to free you.'

Felicha gave a start and twisted her head to find him, then stared in confusion at the space. Eladio waved his hand in front of her face and she jerked her head backwards as the scowl on her face deepened. Eladio was so relieved to see her in her usual foul mood that it almost made him feel like everything would be alright as he set to unbuckling the restraints that held her arms pinned to her sides and to the bed.

He hoped she was patient enough to wait till he got her legs free as he listened to Three, who was regaling the doctor with a stomach churning view of his future. It included falling into a lake of fire. That didn't sound good, and it was so far-fetched that Eladio feared it could come true.

He got Felicha free and whispered, 'You take the doctor, I'll deal with the nurses.'

'Fine,' Felicha said in a strong clear voice and stepped away from the bed.

'Hey, how did you get free?' the doctor shouted and ran at Felicha.

More fool him, Eladio thought. He drew his baton, ran straight for a nurse, and hit the side of her head harder than he'd ever hit a living person in his life. She gasped and crumpled to the floor.

Felicha was on the doctor in a single bound and drove a left hook at his jaw and an uppercut to his stomach. He doubled over in a whoosh of escaping air and collapsed just as Eladio hit the second nurse. He felt ill as the baton connected with her skull and she also dropped.

'Eladio?' Felicha said.

'I'm here,' Eladio said as he bent over the body of the

nurse and felt for a pulse. He prayed he hadn't killed her.

'Here where?'

'Invisible. Artema's magic,' Eladio said, relieved the woman still had a pulse. 'Now, no more questions, let's get everyone out of here.'

'Yes, please,' Dimita said. 'I was sick of all the questions and blood tests. You don't know why they were doing it, do you?' She spoke to the air, off from Eladio's position.

'Because we're part angel, isn't that so?' Three said.

'It is,' Eladio said and hurried over to Three to untie her. 'When did you learn that?'

'Monday night. I saw... more later. Now you need to go to your friend Artema. She needs you.'

'Artema's tougher than me.'

'All the same. This isn't as simple as you think.'

'Simple!' Eladio said, an unbelieving laugh surprised out of him. 'I don't think it's simple.'

'Well, Artema needs your help anyway,' Three said as she stepped away from the bed, massaging her wrists to get the blood back into her hands.

'We aren't friends either,' Eladio said as he hurried across to Betto and started untying him. 'You're not going to help the gang, are you?' Eladio said.

'I'm not stupid,' Betto muttered. 'Rushabarbo didn't think twice before tying me and Piero up. I'll not go back to his gang.'

'Good, then you and him need to help the others escape, so I can find Artema.'

'You aren't even a fighter,' Betto said with an amused smile as he looked down at where he assumed Eladio was. 'What can you do?'

'I don't know yet.'

'He'll do fine,' Three said. 'As long as he has Dimita, Felicha and me with him.'

'Me?' Dimita said, pointing at herself, her eyes wide in nervous surprise.

'For a little while. They will only need you to do what you do best. You must ask him about us, the Thirteen, and where we came from,' Three said. 'The rest of you head for the river. The River Guardians aren't as far under Rushabarbo's control as the rest.'

'What do you mean?' Piero said, and he stamped his feet and waved his arms around the moment Felicha released him.

'There's a spell,' Eladio said. 'It's taken over the minds of everyone in the suburbo. It's coming from the gang tags. You'll see the lines of light connecting everything up when you go outside.'

'So we have to switch off the lights?' Betto asked.

'Sensible, Betto,' Three said. 'Tell the River Guardians to erase the tags. They will help you. Aim for the borders between the gangs for the best effect.'

The air shifted subtly around Eladio, and Betto blinked.

'Ah, I see,' he said.

Eladio held his hand out, and it looked normal again, not like it was encased in shiny gold plastic.

'That's the end of the invisibility spell.'

'At least I can see you now,' Felicha said and much to his surprise wrapped Eladio in a hug.

'We must go,' Three said. 'We don't have much time.'

'What about them?' Eladio asked, pointing at the doctor and his two nurses.

'What do you want to do about them?' Three said.

It took Eladio by surprise. As the youngest in the group,

he wasn't used to being asked for his opinion. 'Tie them to the beds. That should keep them out of the way.'

'We'll do that,' Betto said. 'You go.'

'Alright, but I'll need this,' Eladio said, and pulled the doctor's white coat off him, shrugged into it and headed out to the dust-filled corridor.

A drumming filled Artema's senses, throbbing through her, making it next to impossible to think as she was pulled out of the rubble by her arms. She wanted to resist but found she couldn't. An invisible weight bore down on her body, keeping her immobile. She tried to speak, but she couldn't make a sound. Her tongue was as trapped as the rest of her body.

The only advantage of the numbness and the drumming was that she couldn't feel any pain, or at least, she couldn't think about it. Her head lolled sideways and in that instance she saw Riviera and Vulpo also being pulled from the rubble by the gang.

Then a commanding voice said, 'Look at me.'

It cut through the drumming and filled her with an urgent desire to obey. She turned her head full into the dusty face of Rushabarbo.

'Now do you see my power?' Rushabarbo said but didn't wait for a reply.

Artema couldn't give him one, anyway. It seemed her magical defences had failed, and she was under the same demonic spell as the rest of the suburbonites. The gang members set her on her feet and she stood swaying back and forth. She wanted to look around and see whether Riviera and Vulpo were in the same position, but she couldn't.

Her gaze was fixed on Rushabarbo. The drumming made it imperative that she do everything the man ordered. She hated him for that and wondered whether everyone else under this spell felt the same. Were they all fuming at this bodily takeover? Or were they overwhelmed by the persistent drumbeat that rapped percussively in her head and threatened to rob her of the ability to think?

'Come,' Rushabarbo said, and with a wave of his hand the remnants of staircase rose into the air and rebuilt itself, and Rushabarbo walked up it as it came together.

It was fully rebuilt by the time he reached the top. Artema couldn't resist and climbed up after him.

Rushabarbo threw open a door to reveal a sumptuously decorated room, the furniture predominantly covered in a deep green velvet. The open windows cast a green light into the place. On the wall opposite, pegged like a trophy, was a hideously deformed demon surrounded by a glowing pentagram. The pegs glowed white hot and Artema could feel the heat clear across the room.

The demon was decaying. His skin hung from contorted bones that stood proud of the flesh and traced unfamiliar patterns. No human body fell apart like that.

Yet for all his decay he emanated a malevolence equal to any Artema had felt from a demon. His eyes were yellow, like someone suffering from jaundice, but piercing as he looked Artema over from top to bottom. Trapped as he was, he was still dangerous.

'My pet, Zochael,' Rushabarbo said and waved his hand in the creature's direction as he flopped down onto the sofa. 'You know, he thought you'd give me more difficulty than you did.'

Artema wished she could say something. She wanted to

ask Rushabarbo what madness had driven him to capture a demon. Her professional curiosity wondered how it was even possible. Instead she stood, unsteadily, just inside the room. Riviera was to her left, and Vulpo was on the right. She couldn't look back to see whether there were any gang members around, but suspected not.

'You, Artema, pour me a drink,' Rushabarbo said. 'There's whisky and tumblers in that cabinet.'

Artema wanted to tell him to go to hell. Instead, she walked to the cabinet, opened the beautifully carved and polished door, took out a bottle of whisky and poured out a double measure. She tried to resist, to slow her movements, but she was a puppet with no control over herself. The harder she tried to resist, the louder the drumming grew in her brain, blocking her ability to think.

She handed the drink to Rushabarbo, and then just stood, waiting for another order. Rushabarbo must have known how much it pained her because he grinned, took a sip of whisky and gazed at Artema over the top of his glass.

'This is only the beginning, you know,' he murmured. 'Today I have taken over the suburbo. Tomorrow my people will make for the elevators and the stairs with spray cans and buckets of paint, and they'll fill the mezaurbo with my tags. The moment they do, that section of the city will also belong to me.

'With them, I'll take over the supraurbo. Then I'll return in triumph to my family's ancestral home. I'll set the people to work in my new, orderly world, and everyone will pull together for my benefit. What do you think of that, Artema?'

To her surprise, she realised she could speak, or at least answer that question and she said, 'You're crazy. Did the demon tell you it would work?'

'Zochael told me nothing, except what was in the book of icons and I have put my knowledge to good use.'

Well, that answered that question, Artema thought, back to being unable to speak.

Because Artema was standing right in front of Rushabarbo, with the demon on the wall behind, she could see the creature. This demon was a puzzle. She found it impossible to believe that he could have been captured.

It didn't feel like a trapped being. That could just have been its demonic nature, but Artema wondered. Right now it looked more like a creature tensed in anticipation. For a second, its yellow eyes met Artema's. There was something, a tickle in her brain and the drumming practically fell silent.

'So what do I do with you now?' Rushabarbo said.

Artema's gaze was dragged unwillingly back to Rushabarbo, and the drumming returned at the same painful pitch. Which was worse? The mental captivity by Rushabarbo or the silence the demon could bring?

'My original intention was to kill you, but it occurs to me that to have a trio of tame magistos could be very handy. I'm sure a few of your brethren in the supraurbo will put up a fight. You, Artema, with your knowledge of demon icons, could be especially useful against them. As for the beadles, well!'

Artema wanted to scream in her rage. She dreaded what she could do with the demon icons if she had all inhibitions to use it removed. She dreaded what might happen to her if she did let rip with the icons. Both could mean the end of her.

'Tell me,' Rushabarbo said as he took another sip of whisky, 'How did you know about the Thirteen?'

'I didn't.'

'But you came down into the suburbo with one of them,' Rushabarbo said with a smile that implied he'd caught Artema out in a lie even though, under the influence of the spell, she found she couldn't lie.

'Ironically, all I was looking for was a suburbonite to act as my guide. Eladio was convenient because he worked in the mezaurbo.'

'You really knew nothing about him before that?'

'Only his name and his place of work,' Artema said, and wished she could withhold some information, anything that left her feeling in control, but she had nothing. 'Eladio told me about himself and the Thirteen later.'

Rushabarbo cast a glance back at the demon, and Artema wondered why. Maybe he wasn't as confident about his control as he liked to project.

'What do we do now?' Felicha whispered as they stood in the relative quiet of the corridor. It was a good question, and Eladio wished he had an answer. Clunking noises came from the door at the end. It sounded like large metal beams being dragged about. Then the laboratory door opened filling the space with its clinical white light and the rest of the Thirteen trooped out and headed for the side door that got them out of the house.

'Watch out for the guns,' Eladio said and headed deeper into the house. He pulled the lab coat on as he went. 'It's a cliche, but hopefully it will work,' he said to Dimita, Three and Felicha. 'I'll pretend to be the doctor and say I'm taking you to see Rushabarbo.'

'Do we want to confront him?' Felicha said, watching Three as she spoke. 'I mean, he's dangerous.'

'I don't see how else we can get Artema out of here.'

Eladio had long since stopped asking Three for advice. She gave it when she wished. Although there was one thing.

'I found Seraf.'

'And then you let him go,' Three said.

'He can't be trusted.'

'Seraf can be trusted to be Seraf, don't worry about him.'

'Huh,' Eladio grunted and put his ear to the door.

The lab coat felt odd on him. He didn't like the green cage it put up around him, protecting him from a mind control he didn't need protection from. Then again, it might protect him from more.

'It sounds like there's people there. So you three better look... zombie like. They hopefully don't know we're immune.'

'You've got a lot of hope riding on a lot of things,' Felicha said, but stepped in front of him and opened the door.

A group of gang members stopped their clearing up and looked at them. Bodies of more gang members and the rubble blown in from the hole in the wall lay at their feet. Beyond the hole, the street was filled with silent, stationary people. It terrified Eladio to see that. This was more of a disaster than the breach to the sewerage tanks.

'Where's Rushabarbo?' he snapped and hoped he sounded like a bossy doctor. 'He wants to see these–'

'He's up there,' a gang member said, pointing to the stairs, 'Top floor.'

'Fine, thank you,' Eladio said and looked up the tall dark staircase. His life had turned very peculiar. 'Come on,' he said, and poked Felicha with his baton.

She nearly turned back and thumped him, but controlled herself and started up the stairs when there was the sound of a couple of thuds outside. They looked as Luca emerged from the crowd, tossing people out of the way as if they were sides of beef. Seraf strolled in behind him, immaculately dressed in his gang clothes.

'Where's Rushabarbo?' he said as he stepped inside, ignoring Eladio.

'Seraf,' a gang member said, pointing vaguely upwards as he blinked in disbelief. 'We were told you were blown up.'

'Yeah, well, I was the one doing the exploding,' Seraf said and grinned at Eladio, the only one who would understand.

'What are you doing here?' Eladio said.

'I've come to have it out with the boss.'

'He's dangerous.'

'So you can't deal with him.'

Seraf pushed his way past Eladio and bounded up the stairs two at a time with Luca behind him.

'Wait, you'll put everyone in danger,' Eladio said, running after them.

'Wait for us,' Felicha shouted as she and Dimita followed them.

A shriek came from the room that was so loud Eladio dropped to his knees and covered his ears for fear he'd be deafened. Then he struggled back to his feet and ran towards the noise.

Seraf threw open the door and shouted, 'Hello, boss, didn't expect to see me, did you?'

'You forget I have an alarm,' Rushabarbo shouted pointing at the screaming demon who was writhing in agony on the wall pulling at the glowing metal pins and tearing his body open.

'Silence!' Rushabarbo yelled, and he cast a complex icon.

As its fiery red pattern widened out into the room, quiet

expanded with it. The demon still looked like it was screaming and it was twisting about so much it looked deformed, but they couldn't hear it.

'I am the master here,' Rushabarbo said, his voice clear and strong. 'I have the book,' he said and pulled a fat, leather-bound book out from behind the cushions of the sofa and waved it about. 'With it I have complete control.'

'Well, doesn't that make you special,' Dimita said, and she pushed past Luca, standing like a lump in the doorway, and approached Rushabarbo with all the appearance of one who was thrilled to be in his presence.

Eladio assumed it was a skill she'd gained entertaining men at her brothel. Some must have been hideous, but all were customers. Now she was putting it to good use for the mission Three had given her.

'Who the devil are you?' Rushabarbo said with less heat than before.

'I'm Dimita,' she said, her smile broadening as she lay a hand lovingly on Rushabarbo's shoulder.

That would be all it took, Eladio knew, and cast a warning glance at Seraf hoping he'd hold back a while.

'I heard you know all about the Thirteen.'

'Are you one of them?' Rushabarbo said, and he was completely under Dimita's own special spell now.

'I am, you naughty boy,' she said and leaned up close to whisper theatrically in his ear, 'what do you know about the Thirteen?'

'You're all part of an experiment my grandfather started,' Rushabarbo said, smiling adoringly at Dimita but also with a puzzled look on his face as if he couldn't understand what was going on.

'Grandad had an artefact. He got hold of the remnants of

an angel's hand and was convinced he could create a better human using it. He experimented with it for years without success.

'The experiment that created the Thirteen was his last before he died. All I knew about it until recently was that, unlike with previous experiments, the children survived. Since he died, though, I shut the project down and ditched the kids at an orphanage.'

'How fascinating,' Dimita said. 'But what reignited your interest in us then?'

'Zochel's reaction to Seraf when he came to visit. He really doesn't like anything to do with angels. Even grandpapa's decaying angel hand sends him into a tailspin. And it seems you lot are immune to my icons,' Rushabarbo said, and, with what looked like superhuman effort, he pushed Dimita away.

It impressed Eladio that he managed it. Dimita was impossible to resist by most people, especially men.

'You've been rumbled, Dimita,' Seraf said as he pulled her away and pushed her behind him. 'You won't find me so easy to deal with, Rushabarbo, you and your little book. I have the power to obliterate any book, and you along with it.'

'What are you talking about?'

'You don't know,' Seraf said, and his face creased into a grin. 'I explode, Rushabarbo. And when I do, I take out everything around me. You make me angry and you'll be sorry.'

'He's telling the truth,' Eladio said as his gaze flicked to Artema and the beadles who stood as motionless as the people outside, and were as vulnerable to Seraf.

Then he tilted his head to Dimita to tell her to leave. She

didn't need any further urging and bolted for the door.

'Look at him with a magic revelation,' Eladio said, turning back to Rushabarbo. 'He's already glowing. He could go off at any moment.'

'You tried to kill me,' Seraf said, stalking towards Rushabarbo. 'Now I'll make you pay.'

'You stupid bloody imbecile,' Rushabarbo said. 'Do you think I can't counter anything you might throw at me?'

The demon laughed, a high-pitched, crazed laugh that cut through everyone. Eladio used the opportunity to slip up behind Artema, closely followed by Felicha. He grabbed Artema by the wrist to drag her away.

As his hand tightened on the woman she gasped in air, turned to Eladio and said, 'What did you do?'

'Nothing,' Eladio said. 'I was just going to pull you away.'

'Are you immune?'

'I think so. Here, take this.'

Eladio shrugged out of the doctor's coat and hung it over Artema's shoulders.

'Oh no you don't,' Rushabarbo said and cast another icon at Artema, using the book much like a wand to trace the pattern.

'Hey, I'm talking to you!' Seraf shouted, lunged at Rushabarbo and punched him.

Artema intercepted the icon and nullified it as Rushabarbo crashed around from the punch and the book fell out of his hand and flew towards Eladio who caught it in midair and the pages fanned out in his hands.

'Give that back!'

Rushabarbo scrambled forward on hands and knees as Seraf leaped at him and wrapped his arms around the big man's waist, driving him to the floor.

The demon shrieked with laughter and with a hideous tearing sound pulled himself away from the wall, dragging the metal pins that came away in chunks obliterating the pentagram in places.

'Damn,' Artema cried and cast a protection spell over herself and the beadles before throwing the lab coat off her shoulders.

The beadles shook themselves out of their trance and turned to face the demon, casting spells that threw the creature back against the wall. Felicha grabbed a heavy looking brass lamp stand and held it ready like a club, protecting Eladio.

He hardly noticed. An icon had caught his eye as the leaves of the book flipped over and he opened the book again and hastily flicked through the pages, trying to find it.

'Don't,' Artema said, but Eladio wasn't sure it had been aimed at him, especially as Artema was heading straight at the demon, casting a spell as she went.

'Luca, don't just stand there,' Seraf yelled at the big man who was staring wide eyed at the chaos all around him. 'Help me!'

Rushabarbo threw Seraf off and cast a whirling icon, purple tinged with blue, straight at Seraf. Luca yanked him out of the way just in time and the icon tore into the big man's arm instead, spraying flesh and blood around the room.

Luca roared with pain, launched himself at Rushabarbo and head butted him. Rushabarbo's head snapped back, and he toppled over the sofa towards the demon.

'He's mine,' the demon hissed, grabbed the stunned man, cast an icon that released a torrent of flame at the wall with the windows and disintegrated them. The demon leaped out, dragging Rushabarbo along like a rag doll.

'Come on, Luca,' Seraf shouted and ran for the stairs, 'We can't let him get away now.'

'Hell,' Artema said as she ran to the edge of the hole the demon had made and looked down. 'He's vanished.'

'Yeah, but I think we've got a bigger problem.'

Eladio held up the book with his finger resting on an icon.

'What is it?'

'Remember this?' Eladio said and turned the book so Artema could see it properly.

The beadles gathered around too, examining the icon.

'Sancta Madonna, that's one of the other icons my AI thought the borders were tracing.'

'See what it's called?'

'Consumer of worlds,' Artema breathed as the full horror of the icon sank in.

'Yeah, that's not the same as a mind control icon, is it?' Eladio said, certain he wouldn't like Artema's answer.

'I fear not. Demons don't mess about with their descriptions. If they call it a consumer of worlds, that's what it will do.'

'So... we have to find the demon and stop it, right?'

'We have to disrupt the spell, and I can't think how that's done.'

Eladio examined the icon again and scanned his memory for the other options the AI had shown. 'There's a bit missing, maybe I'm wrong. Your AI showed us this icon, but that tiny dot was missing. The thing is... that bit could easily be added.'

'Where?' Artema said. 'Where would the demon have to go to add it?'

'Do you think he's going to do that?'

'Yeah,' Vulpo said. 'Or maybe the demon just took Rushabarbo to hell.'

'If I was a demon,' Artema said, 'That had been nailed to a wall for twenty-odd years I don't think I'd be satisfied with only that.'

'Three will know,' Felicha said.

'Where is she?' Eladio said, realising that she wasn't with them.

'I think she stayed downstairs.'

'Shit, she isn't safe there.'

Eladio dropped the book and ran for the door, followed by Felicha.

'Unless we neutralise this icon, nobody will be safe,' Artema said, picked the book up, tucked it inside her jacket and ran after them, the beadles in tow.

15

'I assume you got the others out,' Artema said as she followed after Eladio running down the stairs.

'Yeah, they're going to the River Guardians for help to wipe out some icons.'

'Good thinking,' Artema said, impressed that Eladio had even thought to do that.

'I don't know how useful it will be. They won't have had time to get there yet.'

'That is a problem,' Artema said as she reached the bottom of the stairs.

A young woman was sitting on the lowest step while all around her gang members stood silent and staring, their jackets on the ground.

'Three?' Eladio said.

'I suggested it was rather warm to be working with their jackets on,' Three said with a nod in the gang's direction.

'Ingenious,' Artema said with a chuckle. 'Although it also shows that the icon is still very much up and running and people are probably still under Rushabarbo's control.'

'So the demon hasn't pulled him into hell yet?' Riviera said.

'Unlikely, that would break the link to the spell caster,' Artema said. 'It also means that at any time these silent people could–'

The gang members turned as one and ran out of the

house via the hole Artema had made when she arrived.

'Rushabarbo's calling them?' Eladio said.

'I would if I was being dragged away by a demon.'

'So they're in danger.'

'Very much so.'

'Three, where should we go?' Eladio said.

Three stood up and said, 'The Black Brotherhood HQ and hurry.'

Eladio puffed out air and said, 'That's a long run.'

'And too slow. I doubt the demon ran all the way there,' Artema said, and looked about the floor amongst the rubble. 'Ah, I thought so,' she said, and with a wave, her staff clattered out of the dark and rose to meet her open hand.

The beadles did the same with their maces and Riviera said, 'Do you want to teleport?'

'I don't think we have a choice.'

'It's a tough spell.'

'Don't you think you should put on the gang's jackets?' Eladio said. 'It will protect you from the mind control.'

'By using a demon icon? Not a good idea,' Artema said. 'We will just have to keep refreshing our protection spell and if the worst comes to the worst, you, Felicha or Three can grab hold of us. It seems to be sufficient to break us out for long enough to cast our protection.'

'Right,' Eladio said. 'Then let's go.'

'Haven't you become all gung ho,' Artema said with a grin.

Then she began weaving a miniature wormhole that tunnelled itself through space. It was always a weird sight to see the hole form and then with a flash it connected with the other end.

'Not quite where I want it,' Artema said.

The opening was facing a very solid container wall. She waved her hand gently sideways, and the exit moved out into a lane. People were streaming past, running in silence towards the gang HQ gates. The silence was unnerving. Up ahead were the Black Brotherhood's gates, closed tight with not a gang member in sight.

'They're either in hiding or they've deserted the place. But the fact that everyone is running there shows that Rushabarbo is there and is calling for help.'

'Okay, well, we better get there before Seraf does,' Eladio said. 'And it won't take him long to figure out where all the people are headed.'

'Do you think he'll keep going after him?'

'Definitely,' Eladio said, and Three and Felicha nodded in agreement. 'He'll want to make sure he's the one on top at the end.'

'Maybe we should let him do that.'

'The thing is, if he explodes again he'll take all those people out, and who knows how far down he'll drop this time.'

'I got the impression he's figured it out.'

'He's a showoff. He'll let you believe the best of him no matter what the truth is.'

'I see,' Artema said as she stepped through the wormhole.

The unnerving sensation of being stretched into an incredibly thin rope before popping back into place with a snap threw her, as did arriving at a street that was rapidly filling with silent people. The first few had arrived at the gate and set to hammering at it.

'Wow!' Eladio said as he appeared with a pop from the wormhole, then turned to look back at Felicha and Three who were still in Rushabarbo's house. 'Come on, it's fine,' he said.

The rest stepped through, and Artema banished the wormhole. It took more effort than she wanted to show to have set it up, and it was best closed as quickly as possible.

'Can demons also do that?' Eladio asked.

'With more ease than we can. Which is probably why they keep popping up in our dimension.'

'So how do you defeat a demon?'

'By pinning them down with a force field and casting a dematerialisation spell.'

'You don't just send them back to hell?'

'No.'

'Because they'd come back?'

'All too easily. Centuries ago, we agreed that the best deterrent was to make sure no demon survived their trip to our plane.'

'Right.'

'That doesn't bother you?'

'Are you kidding?' Eladio said. 'I've seen Zochael and I've felt him. He's bad to the bone.'

'Yes he is,' Artema said and watched as a second wave of people crashed against the Black Brotherhood's mighty gates. 'Somebody will get crushed to death if we don't do something about this.'

'Leave that to us Prof.' Vulpo said.

He and Riviera aimed their maces at the door and let off a powerful percussive blast. It crashed into the gate with an almighty bang, and the doors cracked open where they met. It was all the silent mob needed as they shoved against the gates and widened the gap enough to flood in.

'If we go in that way we'll just get crushed,' Felicha said

pointing down the road where thousands were still running to the HQ. 'Look at them, there's no end in sight.'

'Then we have no choice but to go up,' Artema said, and wished it wasn't so. She was feeling the strain of this never ending pursuit.

'We'll do that,' Vulpo said. 'You focus on the demon.'

'Up?' Felicha said.

'Levitating,' Eladio said with a grin. 'It's okay, I promise. I've done it once before.'

'You're crazier than I thought,' Felicha said. 'But okay.'

'Right bunch up,' Riviera said. 'It works better if we're all close together.'

'I will remain here,' Three said.

'Okay,' Eladio said before Artema could ask her to change her mind.

She shrugged and accepted it. Eladio knew Three. If he accepted her pronouncements, Artema wouldn't argue, especially not now. The feel of the surrounding air had changed. They were running out of time.

'Quickly,' she said.

With a brief lifting movement the beadles got them levitated to just out of reach of anyone who might try to jump up and grab them. Then they drifted at speed through the opened gates.

'Sancta Maria, Patrino de Dio,' Artema gasped. Her surprise was justified.

Rushabarbo hung crucified on the far wall of the HQ, slightly higher than they were. His arms were bleeding profusely. Zochael rammed a stake through his hip as they arrived, so he hung lopsided.

'Do you like it?' Zochael hissed as he leaped across the compound and daubed an icon on the wall to Artema's right.

He used Rushabarbo's blood for the icon which was a potent spell component and it burned a malevolent bloody red and orange. The demon hadn't bothered to heal his body, or maybe he couldn't. It was possible to see right through his wounds, and his eyes were glowing a fiery yellow now.

'That fool thought he could force me to tell him the truth, but I planned my escape through him.'

'Artema,' Rushabarbo said, and his voice was faint. 'Don't let him do this.'

'Get lost!' the demon shrieked and threw a fiery icon at them.

'No,' Artema said, and put up a force field that stopped them from being incinerated.

But the spell knocked them clean across the quadrangle and into the far wall with a bang, a puff of yellow smoke and the stench of phosphorus.

The beadles dropped the levitation spell as they hit the wall and they slid down it for half a metre to the second-story balcony.

'Eladio, can you and Felicha can get up to Rushabarbo?' Artema asked.

'Yes,' Eladio said and headed for the stairs to the third floor.

'Good. We'll take care of the demon.'

Zochael leaped across the courtyard and landed, fly like, on the wall above the gates where he painted the same icon in blood. As he did, the icons all around them flared and a blood red light tinged with orange connected one to the other.

'Oh no you don't,' Artema said and cast an obliteration spell at the icon above their head.

It sucked at the energy she poured into it and only flickered for a second before the icon rebounded.

'Again!' Artema shouted, and the beadles joined her spell to dematerialise the icon.

This time it peeled away, and the lines between the rest snapped out of existence.

'Fool!' Zochael screamed, and leaped across to their wall.

His hands grew half metre long claws, and he swiped at Artema as he passed. Vulpo jumped between them and smashed the claws away with his mace.

'Now,' Artema said.

She aimed the most powerful force field she could at Zochael to pin him down. But he was a tougher demon than any she'd faced, and he appeared not to even notice the spell as he redrew his icon.

'I need more blood,' Zochael muttered, and in a single bound he leapt away and landed beside Rushabarbo.

Eladio and Felicha were halfway to him and stopped as the demon landed only metres from them. But it was the demon who screeched and jumped backwards away from them and landed on his back on the crowd below. They pushed at each other and grabbed at the demon to keep him down. Those that had got all the way across the courtyard to the far wall were now trying to scale it in their attempt to get to Rushabarbo.

Artema couldn't help but think it was ironic that he had millions of people under his control and yet he was pinned to the wall.

'Out of my way,' came a shout from below.

Seraf arrived, riding on Luca's shoulders. Luca was a good metre taller than all of them and waded through the people as if they weren't even there.

'Angel spawn!' Zochael shrieked.

He cast an icon that blew the people hanging onto him, back and leaped out of the crowd's grasping hands straight for Rushabarbo. He sank his fangs into Rushabarbo's neck and ripped his throat out. Blood fountained and he stuck his hand into it, leaped across to the wall above Artema and redrew his icon.

The lights dazzled into life, tracing out an inverse pentagram, and the ground below them shuddered.

'Bastard, he was mine,' Seraf shouted.

He stood up, balancing on Luca's shoulders, and leaped for the balcony.

The people all around gasped as they regained their autonomy. Then panic set in, and they ran, pushing and screaming to get away. Eladio and Felicha turned and ran full tilt back to Artema.

'Rushabarbo is dead,' Zochael hissed from his perch. 'But I'm not going back empty-handed,' he said, and launched himself at Artema.

Riviera and Vulpo leaped from either side to stop him, and Artema pointed her staff at the demon and put everything she had left into an obliteration spell.

It peeled a couple of layers off Zochael, who landed on top of Artema with a shriek. The most unbelievable stench she'd ever had to endure enveloped her and made her retch.

'Back off,' Vulpo said, and clobbered the demon with all his might across his head.

Zochael's head snapped sideways with a crack and then righted itself. He grinned as he sank his claws into Artema's shoulders and leaped over the balcony, taking Artema with him. They fell into an ever-expanding hole that widened to reveal a fiery landscape far, far below.

'Artema!'

Eladio ran, straining every sinew to get to the magisto. He stumbled and flew down the stairs, hit his head, rolled over, landed on his back and scrambled onto his feet as Zochael grabbed Artema and leaped.

Eladio threw himself into the air, aiming for the demon. He landed on his back and sank his fingers into the repulsive, soft, slippery skin.

'Eladio!' Felicha screamed.

Eladio hung on for dear life as Seraf launched himself at them and just made it to Zochael's legs. He wrapped his arms about them and also dug his fingers into the demon.

Zochael shrieked and thrashed about, trying to dislodge them both while still hanging onto Artema as they fell through the gap in the earth.

They were high, high up in a different place. Far below them, so far it was indistinct, was a shimmering red hot landscape, and they were falling, tumbling and twisting down to it. Above them the gap was growing ever wider and bits of earth were falling in after them.

'Seraf, blow him up!' Eladio screamed and hooked his hand into one of the holes in Zochael's side for a better grip.

'Get off me or I'll rip his throat out,' Zochael screeched.

'Do it, Seraf!' Eladio shouted and grabbed Zochael's throat as hard as he could with his other hand, to pull it away from Artema, and squeezed.

'Not so easy,' Seraf shouted over the roar of the hot wind buffeting them as they fell.

'You bloody useless imbecile. You make nothing better, you only destroy the things around you,' Eladio shouted, putting every ounce of his rage and frustration into his words.

Still hanging onto Zochael's throat, he tried to reach around the side of the demon. He had to get to Artema.

'Don't you try to guilt me!' Seraf shouted back.

'Well then fucking explode. We'll hit the ground and die so you may as well take the bastard with you.'

Eladio groped around and grabbed onto Artema's arm. He had no idea what he would do, he just needed to be holding onto Artema.

'I can't!' Seraf screamed.

'You're going to die!'

'It isn't that easy.'

'Why not? You've been blowing up with regular monotony lately,' Eladio shouted.

He squeezed the demon's throat harder as he felt him rear back and open his mouth to reveal rows of razor-sharp teeth and pulled the neck further back. He also shifted more to the side to get a better hold on Artema while the wind howled about them.

'I have to be in danger,' Seraf shouted.

'We've never been in more danger, you idiot!' Eladio yelled.

Zochael twisted around and bit Eladio in the arm as he simultaneously kicked hard at Seraf.

Seraf exploded. The world turned white. Eladio felt like he was in the centre of a bright white star hanging in an alien sky, radiating destruction. Zochael evaporated into a red mist, and Eladio fell through it and slammed into Artema. It put his body between the light and the woman and he prayed for all he was worth that it would be enough. For a moment they were suspended, shooting upwards on the blast as Seraf plummeted downwards and away from them.

'Seraf!' Eladio gasped.

'Home,' Artema mumbled through a swollen red and puffy face.

'Yeah, I don't think–'

'It's an icon, draw the icon, before it's too late.'

Eladio looked up. Either they had fallen further than he'd realised, or the hole above them was closing.

'Seraf–'

'The icon,' Artema whispered, her eyes closing.

Hot air whipped past Eladio as he closed his eyes and concentrated. He scanned his memory, flicking through the demonic book of icons for all he was worth, searching for anything that was home. And there it was, black and clear.

'Home,' he shouted and traced a half moon icon with a square to the side and a line drawn through the lot. 'Take me home!'

The icon burst to life, glowing silver and... was it his imagination or did they slow down.

'Home,' Eladio said more forcefully and drew the icon again. This time he tried to encompass Seraf, who was little more than a pale dot far below.

'Home!' he shouted.

They started to rise, and he reached for the gap. It was definitely closing.

'Home!' he roared as the dimensions ground together around him, closing each other off.

'Home!' he shrieked as they shot through the gap.

He tossed Artema out of the hole, dragged himself after and shot another icon downwards to the dot that was Seraf.

'Come on, you bastard,' he shouted down a black tunnel

that was rapidly closing. 'Riviera, Vulpo, keep it open, he's coming!'

'I'll do it,' Luca said and dropped into the gap, braced himself against the sides and strained every muscle till his face turned red.

'You can't, it's impossible,' Vulpo said as he wove a wormhole spell, aided by Riviera.

Luca grunted as he pushed against the closing dimensional walls and veins stood out across his neck and face.

'Come home!' Eladio shouted frantically to Seraf's form as he tumbled end over end towards them. 'Come on!' he yelled and cast the icon again, leaning into the hole with both arms outstretched.

Seraf rolled upwards and Eladio's fingertips brushed his skin. He put everything he had to lean forward and sink his fingers into the flesh. There was no time for anything else.

'I've got him! Luca, get out of there,' Eladio said and dragged Seraf out.

Felicha grabbed Luca by the scruff of his neck and pulled as the ground closed about him with a thud.

Eladio felt overwhelmingly dizzy. He staggered away, away from Seraf's naked body, and Artema lying bloody, pummelled nearly to death, on the ground. He looked down at his hand, badly burned up to his elbows. No wonder I feel so shit, he thought and passed out.

16

It was the pain that woke Eladio. He lay still for a moment, trying to work out what was wrong. He wasn't used to being ill, and he'd never felt worse in his life. Everything ached and his skin burned unendingly. He decided there was no point in dwelling on the pain and tried to distract himself with something else.

Maybe it would be a good idea to find out where he was. For all he knew, he was still in big trouble. He lay still and kept his breathing even, but widened his nostrils for a sniff. He got the soapy smell of clean linen. That was promising. He had a feeling hell didn't have beds or clean linen. These positive signs indicated it was safe to open his eyes. He found himself in a dim space with a ceiling he recognised.

'Good morning, idiot,' a very familiar voice said, and an equally familiar face leaned over him.

'Felicha,' Eladio said with a relieved sigh. 'I'm at your place.'

'For now, messing up my bed with all your wounds.'

'Sorry.'

'You'll be making up for it. Along with being so bloody stupid as to throw yourself into Hell.'

'Did... did Artema make it?'

'I assume so. Her people took her away at the double to a hospital.'

'And Seraf?'

'They took him too. He looked worse than you, really badly burned. Three said you had to stay.'

'Oh.'

'Now I know you aren't your usual self,' Felicha said and held a mug up for him to see. 'You always ask why.'

'Why then,' Eladio said, willing enough to play along.

Felicha's gruffness was just a front.

'She said we'd look after you, but that they could take Seraf.'

'What about Luca?'

'He went with. He was carrying Seraf actually.'

'When was that?'

'Two days ago. It's Friday morning. It might feel like you've been out for days, but you haven't, actually. Now drink this,' Felicha said and stuck a bendy straw in his mouth.

It hurt to raise his head, but he'd just realised that his mouth was bone dry and his throat was parched and sore. The water brought considerable relief, and he lay back feeling much better.

Felicha, unexpectedly, sat down on the edge of the bed beside him and said, 'Was it really a hole into Hell?'

'Yes.'

'So... Hell is actually below us?'

'No, it's another dimension. If the demon had done his spell in another direction, the space between our dimensions could have opened up above us, or even through a side wall.'

'It looked bad down there.'

'The worst.'

Eladio wasn't sure whether it was the place or the fact that they'd been plummeting to their deaths that most unsettled him. He did know it was a memory he'd happily excise.

'And you did magic to get everyone out.'

'After Seraf blew the demon to smithereens.'

'All the same, you did magic. Does that make you a magisto?'

'Don't be silly,' Eladio said. 'I used a demon icon. According to Artema, anyone can cast magic using an icon.'

'Oh,' Felicha said and held the straw out to him again. 'You mean, even I could do it?'

'Sure, but Artema said it's a dangerous thing to do.'

'Did it feel dangerous to you?'

'I was plummeting to my death, so I figured it was worth the risk. I was also so scared I wouldn't have noticed any other feeling of unease.'

'You're going to have to do it again then, to find out.'

'I don't think that will be a good idea,' Eladio said and realised he'd offended Felicha by dismissing her idea. 'How's the suburbo? Is everyone okay?'

'Pretty much,' Felicha said. 'Nobody really gets what happened. They all remember being trapped in their bodies, unable to control themselves and doing things they didn't understand. It seems Rushabarbo's control just got them to do stuff without them hearing a voice commanding them.'

'Did anyone die?'

'Some were shot or crushed to death at Rushabarbo's house. Others died at the Black Brotherhood's HQ which, incidentally, is being taken apart. People are so enraged they're ripping the place to pieces. Some people are missing and we don't know if they fell into, you know, Hell.'

'I hope not.'

'There was nothing you could have done to stop that. As it is, I nearly died of shock when you launched yourself after

Artema and the demon. I mean... an actual demon and actual Hell!'

'Yeah,' Eladio said.

'Never mind. Your buddies up top have taken all the credit for fixing the problem.'

'They know?'

'Of course they do. You can't look at the news these last few days without hearing about it.'

'I doubt it was Artema. If she's feeling anything like me, she's still in hospital.'

'Maybe. But her face is all over the news. Look.'

Felicha launched the news on her phone and held it out for Eladio to see. She was right; the headlines were huge, talking about what had happened in the suburbo.

'I see,' Eladio said, and hoped it would end the matter. He felt tired and not really up to this kind of chat.

Felicha picked up on that because she flicked the phone off.

'Dimita's place got burned to the ground by the Black Brotherhood when they came to take her away. Bellecannon told her your friend said she'd pay for the repairs. So I guess they'll have to wait till we find out whether she'll pull through before that happens. And Three stayed here overnight but went home yesterday. I got the impression she was staying to make sure you recovered.'

'Does she know her place was booby trapped?'

'She had it cleared out by the guys who put it in. You know what she's like; she knew their names and addresses, and she can be very persuasive. And Betto, Piero and Franchesca have been busy working with the River Guardians to remove all the tags. It annoyed them that everything went down before they even reached the river.

But they've got over themselves. Most of the suburbo's been out with buckets and scrubbing brushes to get rid of the tags.'

'That's good.'

'It is,' Felicha said. 'And you're still an idiot, also, for letting me ramble on when you're tired. Drink more water and then get some sleep. When you wake up again, I'll give you food so you can build up your strength.'

'Thank you.'

Felicha flashed him a huge grin and said, 'Look at me, I'm almost a natural at looking after sick people. Who'd have thought! Not that it's a free ride, mind you, once you're recovered you can pay me back by helping me get my shop sorted out again.'

'I will gladly do that,' Eladio said and closed his eyes.

He had no idea where the future would take him, but for now he wouldn't worry about it. He was just going to sleep and wallow in the oblivion that brought.

17

It was remarkable what modern science could achieve, especially when supplemented by magic, Artema thought, as she sat in the elevator and examined her hands. It was only a month since the fight with the demon, but she was fine. She didn't have a single scratch or scar. The doctors said she was completely healed, although she was convinced she had some new aches and pains that she'd not had before.

Considering that every bone in her body had been broken, it was an impressive recovery. She shuddered and pushed away the memory of what had happened. It was without a doubt the most terrifying experience of her life, and that was saying something.

She'd been convinced, as Zochael had grabbed her and launched into Hell, that her time was up. That Eladio had leaped in after her... Well, it was the single most heroic thing she'd ever seen. That the young man got all three of them out again was a miracle, and so she intended to tell him.

Artema had contacted Eladio as soon as she was sufficiently recovered. It disappointed her to discover that Eladio had simply resumed his old life and gone back to his job at the cafe. It was such an anticlimax after what had happened. She hoped she could change that for the better. But, knowing the young man, it would take some convincing. It was the reason she was heading down to speak to him in person.

She timed her arrival at the cafe for the end of Eladio's shift. As she walked along the upper promenade in the lightening dawn she looked about, enjoying the late summer sunshine. Aside from the newness of all the concrete around her and the shiny new shop fronts, you would never have guessed that an explosion had devastated the area. It impressed her that they repaired everything so quickly in this city. She hoped the same was true for the hole that had been blasted into the suburbo.

As Artema arrived at the cafe, she spotted Eladio stepping out of the shop. He paused in the soft yellow sunshine to yawn and followed it with a stretch. Then, blinking in the light, he looked around.

'Good morning,' Artema said, surprised by how nervous she felt.

'Artema!' Eladio said, and his face lit up with pleasure.

'So you really are just back at Doreen's.'

'For now. Doreen was so relieved to discover I didn't die in the explosion, she offered me my old job back. She even said she might promote me to night manager.'

'That sounds good,' Artema said, and got a knowing smile from Eladio. He already knew Artema didn't think it was good enough. 'I came to invite you to breakfast, or your dinner, if you like. Any place of your choosing.'

'Why?' Eladio said cautiously.

'To say thank you, and to make sure you are alright.'

Eladio obviously didn't believe that was all, but he gave an accepting nod, said, 'Okay,' and headed toward the elevators to the suburbo.

For a moment Artema wondered whether she would be catching the elevator all the way down for breakfast and didn't fancy the idea. It was a bit too soon to be going back down there.

Fortunately, Eladio turned into the cafe where they'd first discussed their collaboration and looked expectantly at her.

'You want to eat here?' Artema said. 'Not somewhere fancier?'

'This is fine,' Eladio said. 'Although you'll not find any floroy here.'

'I'll cope,' Artema said with a grin that turned into a nod to the waitress as she showed them to a table.

'Felicha said you took Seraf away with you. Is he alright?' Eladio said as he sat down opposite Artema.

'He has healed completely, much like you. But we are keeping him in a stasis field. The doctors are trying to understand his particular ah... condition. They felt it best to keep him unconcious while they work so as not to stress him.'

'He isn't aware of what's going on?'

'I fear he would explode if he was aware.'

'What about Luca?'

'The doctors are working with him too. They are trying to help his development or at least understand why it stalled. It's especially relevant as his genes show he should be of normal intelligence. To tell the truth, he seems perfectly happy just sitting beside Seraf, eating beef sandwiches and playing games on his phone.'

'Yeah, he has always been like that. It must be the angel bit of his cell making him big and stupid.'

'I can't help wondering why the angels would want anyone deliberately stupid. The current hypothesis is that there's a glitch, a disconnect between his human and angel bits that's caused it.'

Artema called up the menu on her new phone, watching Eladio closely as she did. He didn't look convinced by the explanation.

'We have a way to go before we properly understand what they did to you.'

Eladio nodded and Artema said, 'Order whatever you want, don't worry about the price.'

'Apple pie?' Eladio said.

'Sure, why not? But you must be hungrier than that.'

'Two slices of apple pie?' Eladio said with a hopeful grin.

'Go right ahead,' Artema said, pleased that Eladio didn't double check. When they'd first met, he would not have accepted this largess.

Eladio dug into his pocket and slid Artema's phone back to her.

'Here.'

'I've already replaced it. You keep it.'

'I've got the other phone you gave me and my jacket. Thanks for getting it back to me.'

'That was easy. I had my AI go through everything they recovered from the first blast scene. Your stuff was all still in your locker. Although the locker itself had been blown into the shop next door.'

'I also want to thank you for the payment. It meant a lot to me.'

'Did it mean you could get your old place back?'

Eladio shrugged.

'I haven't tried. I'm living with Felicha at the moment. She likes the extra rent and having me around to fix stuff.'

'Are you two in love?'

'No. I thought we were headed that way, but finding out we all have the same cells... like we're really related. It kind of put a damper on things.'

'Yes, I can see how it would.' Artema waited as the waitress laid out a substantial breakfast of scrambled eggs and smoked salmon for her and two sizeable slices of apple pie covered in soft serve ice-cream for a delighted Eladio. 'You look like all your Christmases have come at once.'

'This is much better than that,' Eladio said, and tucked into the pie with enthusiasm.

Artema wondered whether he'd been eating better of late. Considering the amount of money she'd sent him as his payment, prompted by the guilt of what she'd dragged Eladio into, he had the funds. But knowing Eladio, he was probably being as careful as always with his cash.

'Did the orphanage even celebrate Christmas?'

'They had a string of coloured lights draped over the staff's table and we all got a slice of synth-turkey.'

'Oh yes, that sounds very cheerful,' Artema said with a cynically raised eyebrow.

'It was okay.'

'Mmm,' Artema said and decided against yet another conversation where she discovered how dreadful life in the suburbo was. 'Tell me, are you going to the mayor's bash?'

Eladio paused, a forkful of apple pie halfway to his mouth, and said, 'What bash?'

'The big celebration to thank us for saving the city.'

'I know nothing about it,' Eladio said and went back to savouring his pie.

'Did you not get an invitation?'

'Why would I get an invitation?'

'But damn it all, I gave them your contact details, yours and Felicha's. I told them to send invitations via you for the rest of the Thirteen. Did none of you get it?'

Eladio put his fork down and grinned at Artema.

'They would never invite somebody from the suburbo, Artema. You surely know that by now. Have you not looked at any of the news about what happened? You and the beadles are the only ones mentioned.'

'You are joking!?'

'I didn't think you'd looked,' Eladio said with satisfaction as he went back to his pie. 'Felicha was sure you had engineered the whole thing.'

'I would never do that.'

'I know.'

'This is preposterous. I'll make sure they invite you and I'll correct all the news stories personally.'

'It doesn't matter.'

'Yes, Eladio, it does. It's shameful the way we treat suburbonites. I wanted you at the thanksgiving ball so people could see you're all perfectly normal, perfectly decent human beings. They have to stop treating everyone down there like third-class citizens, or worse. You know, I looked into that famine you mentioned back in the suburbo and it wasn't even reported in the supraurbo. In the mezaurbo it only resulted in a few inconvenient food shortages. There were complaints they ran out of asparagus, for goodness' sake. That just isn't right.'

'It isn't. But we can't change it,' Eladio said.

'Maybe you can if you have a blue blood behind you,' Artema said.

'You know there have been other charities who have tried. There's a whole lot of do-gooders of one sort or another in the suburbo. Some might even be blue bloods.'

'Maybe, but you're a role model. You are a fine example to the rest of the city of what a suburbanite can do.'

'I doubt I'm a good choice. One hint that I'm not totally human and your suburbanite role model will have a fatal flaw.'

Artema was about to deny it when she realised she couldn't.

'You have a point.'

'Besides, I want to move out. I want my next place to be in the mezaurbo.'

'You're still thinking of becoming a manager then?'

'I have properly investigated your idea of going to university. I've checked out all the universities and their fees and the living costs and I can't afford a single one, even with a full-time job.'

It gratified Artema that she had influenced Eladio that far. It gave her hope.

'What would you study if you could?'

'I'm not sure. I looked at all the well-paying jobs to work out the best course to take. But, they're all high status, so I don't think they'd hire me anyway, even if I got a great degree.'

'And if you weren't thinking about a job at the end of it? What if you had a guaranteed life of ease in your future and you could study anything you wanted to, anything at all? What would it be?'

'That's a pointless question.'

'No, it isn't. Some people study for the sheer pleasure of the subject. They don't necessarily have an end goal in mind, even if they don't come from wealthy families.'

Since Eladio looked singularly unconvinced, Artema said. 'Alright, let me ask the question like this. Now that you have your high school qualifications, what do you still work on improving? What educational things do you still do and read about?'

'Piano and maths,' Eladio said without hesitation, then paused and shook his head. 'I don't need to go to university to keep doing either of them.'

'But it might be a good idea if you wanted to get a job as a mathematician or a pianist, not so?'

'But I've told you, Artema, nobody would hire me as a mathematician.'

'I don't see why not.'

Eladio shook his head and Artema realised she'd hit a wall.

'Okay. I didn't come to give you a hard time. Given your background, lack of resources and care from the orphanage and working as a street sweeper, I can see that becoming a barista was a tremendous achievement. I can also understand that becoming a shop manager must have been inconceivable to you not so long ago. So I should be more understanding.'

Eladio nodded and pushed the remains of his apple pie around his plate, keeping his gaze down too.

'Actually, I wanted…' Artema paused, uncertain of how her suggestion would go down. She reached into her pocket universe and pulled out a cream-coloured folder heavily embossed in gold with the name and crest of the Eternal University of Magic and pushed it across the table to Eladio. 'There is another thing you could study that I've rather skirted around.'

'What's this?' Eladio asked, staring at the folder but not making a move to touch it.

'Remember how I told you that magic is mainly physics?'

'Yes.'

'Of course you do. And you know that physics and maths

are close, and that I also use a lot of statistics in my work.'

'Yes?'

'Then there are the icons.'

'What about them?' Eladio said and finally looked back up at Artema.

'You looked through the book of demonic icons.'

'I did.'

'And you remember them all, don't you?'

Eladio shrugged.

'Look, I know you do. I've seen your memory in action often enough to know it for a fact, and when we… when we were falling down to Hell, I told you to use the home icon. It was the longest of long shots. It was the only thing I could think of. And blow me if you didn't dredge it up from that remarkable mind of yours and, even more miraculously, cast the damn thing well enough to get us out.'

'You said demon icons power themselves.'

'They do, but you need a smidgen of talent to get them to work as well as it did for you.'

'Artema, the Eternal University, is the most expensive of all. It's a hundred thousand imps a year just for the fees.'

'So you looked.'

'I was curious,' Eladio muttered.

'There are other ways to get into a university,' Artema said and pushed the folder closer to Eladio. 'Look inside.'

Eladio picked the folder up, glanced at Artema and then down at the paper inside. His face scrunched up into a frown.

'What's a scholarship?'

'It's an award given to the most talented people. The brightest and the best have the fee waived. Sometimes they even have their living expenses paid for.'

'The Eternal University has scholarships?'

'They give out six a year.'

'To the brightest and the best,' Eladio said and turned to the second page of the file.

'Exactly.'

'That can't be me.'

'You score in the top quartile for intelligence and you got 99% for your matric. I would say that qualifies you.'

'There must be more, an entrance exam or interviews or something.'

'There is. There's an application form and three interviews over the course of three days. They quiz the candidates on their ability to hold a sensible conversation, solve problems creatively and otherwise demonstrate their intelligence.'

'I haven't done that.'

'No, you spent a week under gruelling field conditions with a criminally dangerous demonologist testing you relentlessly. I defy any other scholarship applicant to survive that.'

'It says here that you are funding this scholarship.'

'It's within my right and my ability to do so. Besides, I didn't want to rob the current six applicants of their place.'

'I can't, Artema, it's too much money.'

'My boy, you know money is no object for me.'

'A hundred thousand imps a year, Artema!'

'But one big saving. You'll have to live with me.'

'Why?'

'Like I just said, to keep costs down.'

'So money isn't entirely without meaning to you.'

'You got me. Actually, I want you to live with me so I can do for you what you did for me. I would have found it impossible to navigate the suburbo on my own. Allow me to be your guide in the supraurbo.'

Eladio started shaking his head so Artema said, 'Okay, I'll put this in terms you'll understand. Eladio, I owe you this.'

'What rubbish.'

'No. I failed against Zochael. He grabbed me, and I was on my way to Hell. I knew, without a shadow of doubt, that I was done for. Then, like a complete maniac, you threw yourself at him. You saved my life and I know how much that means. If giving somebody half a sandwich in the suburbo means they owe you, then saving a person's life means that too.'

'It wasn't a trade.'

'It would be the maddest trade in the world if that was your intention. I know you did it out of friendship. However, I can afford to repay you and what is more, I want to repay you. You are wasted down here looking after a coffee shop. And then there are still the icons.'

'Back to the icons?'

'You currently know more about demon icons than anyone else in the world. Do you realise that?'

'Yes.'

It was his refreshing honesty that Artema really liked about Eladio. It was also one of the reasons she wanted to mentor him.

'You should receive the training that will keep you safe from them.'

'I don't know.'

It was time to use her other trump card, Artema realised.

'What about your angel genes? Wouldn't you like to be involved in finding out all about it?'

'You'd let me do that?'

'I'd have to talk to Doctor Leopold. I'm sure he'd be thrilled to have you on the team.'

'Even when I have no scientific background?'

'That's something you can probably get up to speed with eerily quickly, if I'm any judge of the matter.'

Eladio looked more tempted by this offer than the rest. That disappointed Artema, but she supposed it was understandable. Eladio had been wondering about the differences in himself all his life, while the rest was all new to him.

'I won't push you to decide here and now. I just wanted to give you the proposal and my pitch. In my humble opinion, you should take it.'

Eladio snorted and said, 'You've never been humble.'

'Impudent boy,' Artema said, grinning back.

She reached into her pocket universe again and handed over a medicine case.

'That's all you need to make sure you don't suffer from altitude sickness should you decide to take up my offer. You've got the pass up to the supraurbo and a decent coat so you can come whenever you choose to and not look out of place. I might add that the official school year starts in mid-September, so I would aim for that.

'You also have my contact details on the phone, so I can pick you up from the elevator when you arrive. The choice of whether you do so is entirely up to you.'

'Artema... you've only known me for a week.'

'The longest bloody week of my life,' Artema said with a grin. 'Now, I've paid for the meal and I'll leave you to finish up. I hope I see you topside soon.'

With that, Artema left, feeling optimistic. At least Eladio

had listened, and it sounded like he'd been thinking about learning magic. Artema was confident she'd be seeing the young man again.

As she stepped out of the cafe into the bright morning sunshine, she looked back inside. Eladio had his head bowed over the scholarship paperwork. Yes, indeed, it was all looking very promising.

Write a review!

Enjoyed this book? You can make a huge difference Reviews are the most powerful tools in my arsenal when it comes to spreading the word about my work.

If you enjoyed this book, I would be very grateful if you could just spend a little time leaving a review (it can be as short as you like).

Thank you very much!

Offer

Get a free eBook – Sanctuary

Sign up for my no-spam newsletter that only goes out when there is a new book or freebie available.

You can sign up for Sanctuary, a medieval mystery romance at: www.marinapacheco.me

Sanctuary, a Medieval Mystery Romance

He needs shelter. She wants a way out. Will his brave move to protect risk both their hearts?

England, 1393 AD. Former child soldier Mal dreams of escaping his cruel existence. Barely surviving an ambush that killed a merciless sheriff and his henchmen, the injured young man seeks refuge at a nearby convent. But his plans to heal quietly before setting sail for a new life are interrupted when he sets eyes on a beautiful maid.

Pastry chef Anne Cook has her pick of men to marry. So when a despicable knight claims her as his bride, she begs the local baron to annul the forced engagement. But as the enraged suiter attempts a kidnapping, she's shocked when the secretive warehouse boy comes to her rescue.

Discovering an old foe led the deadly surprise attack, Mal fears he'll never be worthy of the pretty girl he's fallen for and he'll have to go on the run. But with treacherous schemes closing in on them both, Anne and her savior's only hope may be a desperate plan to stay together.

Will the besieged couple overcome dangerous enemies and fight their way to love?

Sanctuary is a sweet medieval mystery romance. If you like optimistic tales of redemption, heart-warming characters, and feel-good thrills, then you'll adore Marina Pacheco's historical tale.

Buy *Sanctuary* to find haven in another's arms today!

Books by Marina Pacheco

Historical Romance

Sanctuary – free ebook – He needs shelter. She wants a way out. Will his brave move to protect risk both their hearts? If you like optimistic tales of redemption, heart-warming characters, and feel-good thrills, then you'll adore this historical tale.

The Duke's Heart – His body may be weak, but his dreams know no bounds. Will she be the answer to his prayers? If you like unique leading men, strong and determined women, and slow-build relationships, then you'll adore this delightful courtship.

Duchess in Flight – She's on the run from a deadly enemy. He lives in the shadows of truth. When their lives merge, will their battle for survival lead to love? If you like reluctant heroes, strong women, and chances for redemption, then you'll adore this adventurous tale.

Medieval Historical Fiction

Life of Galen Series

Fraternity of Brothers – Life of Galen, Book 1 – Cast out for a crime committed against him, his future looks bleak. Until an unexpected visitor gives him hope for justice. If you like fighting for acceptance, finding absolution, and authentic depictions of the harsh Middle Ages, then you'll love this riveting novella.

Comfort of Home – Life of Galen, Book 2 – Proven innocent, he's returned from exile. Can he recover all that he lost? If you like captivating characters, chances for redemption, and uplifting quests, then you'll love this immersive tale.

Kindness of Strangers – Life of Galen, Book 3 – Trapped in a land plagued by vikings, can one small miracle be all they need to survive? If you like historical detail, human dilemmas, and a heartwarming story, then you'll love this absorbing tale.

The King's Hall– Life of Galen, Book 4 – As if being commissioned to create a book to turn back the Apocalypse isn't enough, intrigue and romance threaten to destroy everything he's come to rely upon. If you like stories about friendship overcoming the odds and intrigue at court, then you'll love this riveting novel.

Coming Soon

Restless Sea – Life of Galen, Book 5 End of September 2021
Friend of my Enemy – Life of Galen, Book 6
Road to Rome – Life of Galen, Book 7
Eternal City – Life of Galen, Book 8
Love and Loss – Life of Galen, Book 9
Return of the Wanderers – Life of Galen, Book 10

About the Author

Marina Pacheco is a travelling author who currently lives in Lisbon, after stints in London, Johannesburg and Bangkok. She is an introvert who writes feel-good novels that are perfect to curl up with on a rainy day. Her books often have a strong romantic element where good triumphs over evil and the girl gets the boy in the end.
Online home: https://marinapacheco.me
email: hi@marinapacheco.me

Acknowledgements

Although writing is a solitary exercise it is enhanced by the support and enthusiasm of friends, family and a team of professionals who have all encouraged me to keep going at various points in my life.

Special thanks to:
My writing group and fellow authors who are always ready to provide support, encouragement and helpful criticism.
My beta readers, who sent back great suggestions that improve the story.
My street team, who let the world know about my books.
My editor, Katharine D'Souza Editorial Services – http:// www.katharinedsouza.co.uk, who significantly improves on all my stories.

All I can say is thank you, and let's do it all again!